CW00816475

INFAMOUS LIKE US

BOOK 10 IN THE LIKE US SERIES

KRISTA & BECCA RITCHIE

CHARACTER LIST

Not all characters in this list will make an appearance in the book, but most will be mentioned. Ages represent the age of the character at chapter one of the book. Some characters will be older when they're introduced, depending on their birthday.

The Security Team

These are the bodyguards that protect the Hales, Cobalts, and Meadows.

KITSUWON SECURITIES INC.
SECURITY FORCE OMEGA

Akara Kitsuwon (boss) – 28

Thatcher Moretti (lead) – 30

Banks Moretti – 30

Farrow Hale – 30

Oscar Highland-Oliveira – 33

Quinn Oliveira – 23

Paul Donnelly – 28

Gabe Montgomery – 23

PRICE KEPLER'S TRIPLE SHIELD SERVICES
SECURITY FORCE EPSILON

Jon Sinclair (lead) – 40s

Greer Bell – 30s

…and more

SECURITY FORCE ALPHA

Price Kepler (lead) – 40s

Wylie Jones – 40s

Tony Ramella – 30

…and more

The Meadows

Ryke Meadows & Daisy Calloway

Sullivan – 22

Winona – 16

The Cobalts

Richard Connor Cobalt & Rose Calloway

Jane – 25

Charlie – 22

Beckett – 22

Eliot – 21

Tom – 20

Ben – 18

Audrey – 15

The Hales

Loren Hale & Lily Calloway

Maximoff – 25

Luna – 20

Xander – 17

Kinney – 15

The Abbeys

Garrison Abbey & Willow Hale

Vada – 16

A NOTE FROM THE AUTHORS

The Italian used in this book is an Italian-American language developed by Italian immigrants. It is an incomplete language and uses Italian, English, or both. Different Italians speak different dialects in certain areas, and what is used in the Like Us series is prominent on the East Coast. Words may vary in pronunciation and spelling in different communities. A glossary with pronunciations for Infamous Like Us is included at the end of the book.

Infamous Like Us is the tenth book in the Like Us Series. Even though the series changes POVs throughout, to understand events that took place in the previous novels, the series should be read in its order of publication.

Infamous Like Us should be read after *Fearless Like Us*.

LIKE US SERIES READING ORDER
1. Damaged Like Us
2. Lovers Like Us
3. Alphas Like Us
4. Tangled Like Us
5. Sinful Like Us
6. Headstrong Like Us
7. Charming Like Us
8. Wild Like Us
9. Fearless Like Us
10. Infamous Like Us
11. Misfits Like Us
12. Unlucky Like Us
13. Nobody Like Us

Celebrity Crush – January 20th

Sullivan Meadows Confirms Poly Relationship with Her Bodyguards!

The "American Royals" have been all over the news lately with the mysterious Royal Leaks, and no one has graced headlines more than Sullivan Minnie Meadows, daughter of renowned rock climber Ryke Meadows and Fizzle heiress Daisy Calloway. Sullivan Meadows has taken to Instagram to announce her relationship with bodyguards Akara Kitsuwon & Banks Moretti, and to add a cherry on top of the OMG, she also *just* bought Plan B (a recent leak).

If she's been sleeping with two men, then who's the baby daddy? How will she qualify for the Olympics if she's preggers? Subscribe to *Celebrity Crush* for all the updates as we track Sullivan Meadows' scandalous life.

Celebrity Crush – January 31st

Boyfriends of Sullivan Meadows Accosted by Fans at Aquatic Center

We've been hearing rumors that Sullivan Meadows has kept her head down and her eye on the prize in pursuit of the Summer Games. Looks like no bun is in the oven for this Olympian. But Sullivan Meadows' two boyfriends can't ignore the overwhelming reaction of dating a Meadows girl *at the same time.* Fans accosted Akara Kitsuwon & Banks Moretti while Sullivan was swimming laps in the Olympic-sized pool. The message on the posters was loud and clear:

Kitsulletti Sucks.
Kitsulletti Ruined Everything.

Ouch. That has to sting their egos. Will she ditch one boyfriend and make the other a real keeper? The fans are hoping *yes*.

Celebrity Crush – February 4th

Sullivan Meadows Celebrates 22nd Birthday with Boyfriends, Amid Polyamorous Controversy

Despite the backlash from fans who rooted for Sullivan Meadows to choose either Banks Moretti or Akara Kitsuwon, Sullivan is sticking to her guns and even doubling down. She appeared in public hand-in-hand with both boyfriends for her 22nd birthday celebration at...the Aquatic Center. She really has no quit in her. Swimming, even on her birthday!

Celebrity Crush – May 15th

Sullivan Meadows Set to Film Ziff Commercials for Upcoming Summer Games

Looks like Sullivan Meadows is banking on qualifying for the Olympics—she already has sports drink commercials lined up. What *Celebrity Crush* is wondering: will Sullivan Meadows *actually* talk to the press? Ever since her Instagram announcement back at the end of January, she's yet to respond to any messages from fans or questions posed by the media, including us! The audacity.

But really, will Sullivan Meadows *finally* speak up?

Celebrity Crush – June 10th
Sullivan Meadows Gives Press the Bird

Footage of Sullivan Meadows has gone viral! And no, it's not Sullivan Meadows leaving her competition in her wake during the 200m freestyle at Team Trials. Or the fact that Sullivan's hoping to compete in six events at the Olympics—she'll be defending her gold in four of those and appearing in two new events: relays! What's really rocking the world: a reporter from GBA Sports asked Sullivan Meadows how she feels about being the most beloved Olympian four years ago to becoming the most controversial.

Sullivan responded with a middle finger. There's her answer, folks! She doesn't care what any of us think.

Celebrity Crush – June 12th

Three Attendees in Audience Removed from Team Trials for Disturbance & Reckless Behavior

Have you seen this footage? Looks like Sullivan Meadows has more to worry about than swimming fast. Three attendees in the stadium stands shouted explicit messages for Sullivan to quit swimming. They began chanting "Sulli the Slut" until event security and Sullivan's personal security (identified as Paul Donnelly, Oscar Highland-Oliveira, and Thatcher Moretti), chased them down the bleachers. The attendees were feet from reaching Sullivan near a swim platform until her boyfriends apprehended them.

Celebrity Crush – June 23rd

Sullivan Meadows Appears Shaken after Dramatic Incident

Sadly, there is no video or camera footage this time, but sources close to *Celebrity Crush* tell us Sullivan Meadows went through a "dramatic incident" recently. As we continue to dive deeper, we're being met with legal roadblocks. What is Sullivan Meadows hiding? What happened? And why does she look so shaken in Philly after qualifying for all six events at the Team Trials?

All we know is she's on the road to the Summer Olympics with her two boyfriends and entire family. Expect more news surrounding the Hales, Meadows, and Cobalts in the coming weeks! We can hardly wait.

1

Sullivan Meadows

FIREWORKS BLAST OFF into the California night sky. I don't see colorful bursts of light, but the noise thunders around me and vibrates the ground. Even the bathroom stall rattles from the cacophony—a very real reminder that I shouldn't be squandering my time here on this fucking toilet.

Or as Banks calls it—a shitter.

My lips rise as soon as I think about one of my boyfriends. *Boyfriends.* Not such a bizarre fucking concept anymore. At least to me. I've lost a lot of faith that the world will *ever* understand. I told Akara that I bet they'd only approve if I died.

In my death, they'd accept my love of two men because I'd be gone and there'd be nothing left to criticize or hate. Or maybe they'd just keep on hating.

We're not letting anyone get to us, Akara reminded me. It's been our motto since we confirmed our relationship to the world.

We're not letting anyone get to us.

They won't break us apart.

They won't hurt us.

They won't win.

I'm fucking competitive, but I never imagined the harder race would be against anonymous faces and internet hatred than swimming an actual Olympic event.

They won't hurt us.

But fuck, does it hurt some days. Thick skin comes and goes like armor I'm renting from the Cobalt Empire, but Moffy says that the painful parts just make me human. Jane says Cobalts hurt too.

Beckett tells me not to worry—that *all* my family are here for me. And they are. Literally. Cousins, aunts, uncles, plus my mom, dad, and sister are in the packed stands somewhere outside this bathroom. Even Beckett, my notoriously busy best friend, has taken a couple weeks off ballet to cheer me on.

And here I am, holed up in a fucking toilet stall. Hoping my current mega-crisis will shrink to a mini-one. My pulse climbs, knees jostle. *Boom!*

I flinch.

Another firework bursts.

And then another.

It's just a firework.

It's just a fucking firework.

I blow out a measured breath and try to let my pulse decelerate. We arrived in Los Angeles over a week ago to frenzied crowds, aggressive paparazzi—more pushing and pulling—and I want to blame this fucking city for the extra mayhem, the extra stress, the invasive questions and blistering spotlight.

But it hasn't just been a week of fame I can't escape, can't circumvent, can't outwit, outplay, or outlast.

It's been six months.

Six months since I climbed into my childhood treehouse with my boyfriends. Six months since I announced to the world that I'm in a poly relationship with two bodyguards.

Six months since everything changed.

Sitting on the shut toilet lid, more worry crawls under my skin, but the source isn't from brash noises or impending danger.

Nerves swarm me as I stare hard at the slim white pregnancy test in my hand.

Boom!

I jerk my neck. *You're safe. You're fine, Sulli.* Fireworks are like a ticking clock, telling me I need to hurry. I need to *go*. Join the festivities.

Delight in all the hard work that brought me here.

The Summer Olympics.

Be with my boyfriends, who are no doubt a little fucking freaked out that I'm taking so long. But I can't leave until I have this one answer.

"Sulli, get your fucking shit together," I coach under my breath. My legs jostle more as I stare hard at the test.

I already pissed on the stick and recapped it.

Thirty-seconds through the 5-minute wait, and I swear I'm already sweating through this thick navy Ralph Lauren blazer.

"It's the Opening Ceremony to the fucking Olympics," I whisper. "And you're in a bathroom talking to yourself while you wait for..." I can't finish the words.

Not that I think someone will overhear. Akara and Banks searched the bathroom stalls before I even entered. All clear. Now my boyfriends stand guard outside the door, and my stomach is in knots.

I check my watch. "Three more minutes," I say to myself. Hearing my own voice calms me a bit more. Noise is a constant background whenever I'm in public, and I haven't been swimming in this much quiet during make-it-or-break-it, stress-induced situations in a while.

I could call Akara or Banks in here.

To wait with me. To be a shoulder to lean on. To comfort me. They both would. But here's the fucking thing: I haven't told them.

When I realized I missed my period recently, I didn't want to bring up the issue to Akara or Banks. We already had *one* scare months ago after the condom ripped. And fuck, we've been careful since that slip-up at the end of January. I took Plan B. I got my period.

Not pregnant.

Now it's the tail-end of July, and I'm in a worse situation. Too late for Plan B. A pregnancy test in hand.

The Olympics literally starting *now*.

Even buying a pregnancy test took Harry Potter levels of sorcery— exactly what Luna said to me when she slipped the pregnancy stick in my pocket like a badass James Bond.

Since Luna has experienced a pregnancy scare, I went to her for help. I thought about going to my mom, but I'm scared she'd tell Dad and he'll end up thinking worse of Banks and Akara. He's in my corner now, and he's also *slowly* building a good relationship with them.

Emphasis on fucking *slowly*.

I bet that'll all crumble like Humpty Dumpty if he believes they weren't careful with me. *Again.* Like the world, my dad also heard about me taking Plan B. We had a tense family dinner that ended with him cursing out my boyfriends for not wearing protection. To which they had to so awkwardly clarify that condoms *were* involved.

One just broke.

So I'm trying to avoid *that.* But *that* feels so minor and so inconsequential to the bigger picture. Which is the jarring fact that I could actually be pregnant right now.

I chew on the corner of my lip. Not realizing how hard I'm biting. The bitter, iron taste of blood reaches my tongue. Fuck. I wipe my mouth with the back of my hand.

I check the time again.

Luckily, the United States is last in the Parade of Nations as the host country this year. So I have some time.

"One more minute," I clock. My pulse quickens. Akara and Banks think I'm taking a shit. Fucking truly. I was lined up with the rest of the U.S. athletes when I pulled my boyfriends aside and whispered, "I have to take a nervous shit."

They were both super duper fucking concerned and whisked me to the nearest public bathroom. My heart literally swelled five-sizes too big during that single moment.

Now my heart is shriveling into a ball. I never wanted to be the kind of girlfriend who'd keep secrets from her boyfriends. Especially not ones this monumental and life-changing.

Telling them I could be pregnant has felt like info that'll be a blow to the head more than a warm, inviting hug.

So I didn't do it.

Not yet. I figure if it's negative, there's no point in causing them more stress. With all the publicity surrounding our relationship and my Olympic journey, they've been more on edge. More watchful. Observant. Danger feels like its creeping around the corner, a second away from breathing on my neck, but I'm here to compete.

I'm here to win gold.

I can take the test. See the negative results. End my own paranoia and return to total concentration. Total victory.

That's the goal.

I take a breath and glance up at the bathroom stall. Imagining Akara and Banks so close. My heart skips, and I open my mouth to call out for them.

But words catch in my throat.

My eyes burn.

I remember what Banks once told me. Way back after the cougar attack almost a year ago. He said, "The things you aren't ready to tell people, they're not really secrets. They're just vulnerable parts of you that need time to be shared."

This feels like one of those moments that's too vulnerable to share.

Too much to get out right now. I wipe at my scalding eyes, trying to subdue the bubbling emotion. I can already predict the headlines:

Sullivan Meadows Is Crying During Opening Ceremony!

Why is Sullivan Meadows Crying?

What's Wrong With Her?

Nothing.

Fucking nothing and then everything. I pinch my eyes and chew on the corner of my lip again. *Hey, hey, hey, stop, Sulli,* Banks would say quickly and clutch my face.

Some days, I've chewed my lips raw.

Some days, I've clung to Akara's arms like a petrified girl in a horror movie, and my biggest comfort is knowing and feeling that I have them.

Some days, I've cried into Banks' chest until I've fallen asleep.

No days have I said, *let's give up.* Their love is what keeps me upright on those terrible some days.

I just don't want today to be one of them.

The stadium is full.

The entire *world* is watching the Opening Ceremony.

These past six months might've been like living under the hottest spotlight, but these weeks at the Olympics will be like living under a microscope. There's no hiding.

Except, I guess, right now.

"Time," I whisper, staring at my wristwatch. Then I slowly remove the cap from the stick.

Two lines.

Pregnant.

Holy fucking shit.

2

Akara Kitsuwon

UNEASINESS MOUNTS the longer Sulli spends in the bathroom. I refix my comms earpiece, then glance to Banks, then to the mostly barren hallway. Footsteps clap, and with urgency, a camera guy and sports reporter walk briskly in the opposite direction. They cast glances back at us.

Lovely.

So very lovely.

They stop in place. Seeing us alone. Like loitering prey. Like we're more newsworthy than the Opening Ceremony of the actual *Olympics.*

Not exactly shocking.

Our faces have been all over entertainment news. Magazines paint Banks as the rugged Marine and me as the badass Muay Thai fighter—and yeah, people are still picking sides. It's beyond frustrating.

In a perfect world, they'd get over the "newsworthiness" of our poly relationship. In a perfect world, they'd accept that Sulli isn't going to choose one.

She's already made her decision.

And we've already made ours.

Together—the three of us—until the very end.

Banks grinds down on a toothpick. "Should we wave?"

"Nope." I stifle the urge to flip off the camera guy, who's seconds from approaching. "We're not playing nice with press."

Banks wears a crooked smile. "I'm loving this give-no-fucks Akara."

My lips almost rise. "We're not letting anyone get to us."

It's what I've been saying for months.

Banks smiles more. "Except for two nights ago, when we were a heartbeat from creating a fake Twitter account just to fight a troll. And a week before that, when I came close to decking a reporter. Then you restrained me, only to almost sucker-punch him."

I force myself not to roll my eyes. Honestly, last night, I still considered making fake accounts, which is supremely unprofessional and not a precedent I want to set for my men.

Still, I'm *considering*.

Just a little.

A lot, a little.

So yeah, Banks is right. I've been giving no fucks lately. And yet, still, some media and "fans" have crawled under my skin.

"We're not letting anyone get to us is a mantra that we're *trying* to follow," I whisper to him. "Not one that we're always following." I add firmly, "And they're not breaking us up."

Banks nods strongly. "Amen."

It's us against the world now. It has been for six months, and I've never been more assured of keeping course, no matter how dangerous it's been or how dangerous it'll become. I've never felt closer to Banks and Sulli.

"Akara Kitsuwon, right?!" the reporter with red lipstick and a blue blouse shouts down at us. Testing the waters to see if I'll engage.

I rotate my back to her. GTFO is practically written on my shoulder blades. The more the three of us reject the media, the more questions arise. But Banks and I have been bodyguards long enough to know that *anything* we give them can be twisted.

So we've left them with nothing.

The downside: Sulli is getting shit on for being a "bratty princess" after denying some Olympic press coverage.

For how hard she's worked, all the hours she's spent training, all the moments she's given up with family to put in the work—I hate seeing Sulli be pegged as something she's not. She didn't get a free ride to this year's Olympics.

She earned her spot.

"They're leaving," Banks says quietly to me, watching the reporter and camera guy exit. Fireworks boom in the distance, and our heads swivel to the bathroom.

I hope the noise isn't rattling our girlfriend.

"She's been in there a while, hasn't she?" I ask him.

"Around fifteen minutes." He eagle-eyes the bathroom door behind us. Shut to the public. Only because we're guarding the thing.

We share a look.

I call this one Boyfriend-to-Boyfriend, and no, Banks Moretti is technically not *my* boyfriend—but we're both hers, so this crap makes sense to me.

He slides a hand across his unshaven jaw. "Maybe the press is getting to her too."

"Or she's nervous about carrying the American flag with *her idol*." I put mocking emphasis on *her idol* like I'm a jealous toddler and not a twenty-eight-year-old entrepreneur-bodyguard-boyfriend.

Hey, at least I didn't gag.

Seriously, I'm never going to be a fan of Tobias Kingly. He has enough of those, one of which is Sulli.

"They should've just let her carry it," Banks retorts. "Fuckin' sports politics."

The national committee initially picked Sullivan as the flagbearer for Opening Ceremony, but the public outcry about Sulli being in an "indecent" relationship caused them to change their decision. So they also selected Tobias Kingly to appease everyone except me and Banks.

Sulli said she didn't care. Less eyes on her.

Banks cares.

I care.

We check the time again. Concern growing. I rock onto my heels, and with my back to the door, I rap my knuckles against the wood.

Banks calls out, "You doing alright, mermaid?" He raises his voice so she can hear.

"Fuck, sorry! I'll be out in a sec!"

Banks frowns to me. "She didn't say she's doing okay."

"Yeah, she's definitely nervous." It puts us on edge, and we're a couple seconds from just barging into the bathroom when comms crackle.

"France entered the stadium." Thatcher's stringent voice is in my ear.

"Finland looks dope," Donnelly says.

"They look like flight attendants," Oscar chimes in. "Brazil still beats everyone. Hands down, best looking country out there."

"Someone's biased," Farrow replies.

I click my mic. "I should only be hearing from Thatcher, guys." I pause. "But Finland does look like flight attendants."

Banks smiles beside me.

"Flying high," Donnelly adds.

I wait for Thatcher to include something. Anything. Maybe an *affirmative* that only him and I should be communicating. But comms go quiet.

I thought we'd be at a better place by now. But things are still tense. Awkward. Not where I want me and my friend to be. Let alone my lead.

"There's a country named Georgia?" Gabe Montgomery says on comms. "Oh shit, sorry didn't mean to put that through comms!"

Gabe is Gabe. Still new-ish. Green. Kind of an airhead. Hearing him makes me miss Quinn Oliveira's interjections through the radio. He's not even in Los Angeles. He's stuck back at Philly. Stuck rehabilitating his leg, which is taking longer than the expected six months. Stuck managing Studio 9—which I actually do appreciate.

Thank you, Quinn.

I lift my mic to my lips. "Thatcher?" He'll give us the cue to leave, so we won't miss out on rejoining Team USA. But maybe I also just want *more.* Like a firework that spells out, *we're still friends, man.*

"Germany."

Awesome.

Banks catches my disgruntled face. "Thatcher just feels like you've moved on." He lifts a shoulder. "I love my brother, but he's not that good at fixing what's broken. He stares at it for way too long."

I sigh. "Yeah, well, I feel like he's moved on to Farrow." Is this what's supposed to happen? We're just supposed to forget we were even friends? We're older now. The Moretti brothers turned thirty in June, and I'm twenty-eight.

I was *twenty* when I first met them. An eight-year friendship down the drain? Over what? My relationship with Sulli or my relationship with his brother?

Both?

I shift my weight and the sole of these ugly platform sneakers slip underneath me. Pain shoots in my ankle as I wobble. About to come down until Banks catches my fall.

"*Crap.*" I suck in a wince between my teeth. "*Fudge…nugget.*" Still can't curse unless I want a slug to the arm, but no f-bombs even explode in my brain. That's how long I've been tuned into a PG station.

Banks grips my shoulder while I try to put weight on my foot.

I grimace.

"That bad?" Banks asks, squatting down.

"Screw these *fudging* outfits." I want to kick off the platforms and light them on fire. But I can't. In order to walk in front of Sulli during the Parade of Nations, we had to agree to wear the same costumes as performers for the artistic portion of the ceremony. White nylon joggers, white tanks—we look like we could be members of The Backstreet Boys from the early 2000s.

These sneakers have a *four-inch* platform heel.

Banks is a second from laughing.

"It's not funny," I retort, trying not to smile.

His grin grows, toothpick still in his mouth. "I thought you'd have to catch me first."

"Yeah, me too."

He laughs, and the thing I love about Banks is how in bleak situations, I find myself laughing with him. My ankle might be screwed, but I'm not missing this moment with Sulli and Banks. I wouldn't. Not for a phone call. Not for a bum ankle.

Not for anything.

"Am I radioing Farrow to check it out?" Banks asks.

"No. It doesn't feel broken. Just take it off."

He nods. "Copy, Nine."

Banks has been calling me *Nine* more often these past months. Somewhere between the whole world assailing us with their unwanted opinions and the media hounding us, we've grown tighter. Not sure how that's possible. To become closer to someone who I already gave my heart to. But it happened.

I wince as he tugs my shoe off. While he's squatting, I grip his shoulder and put another hand on the back of his skull to keep balance.

And then footsteps sound.

Switzerland's bright red blazers and white pleated shorts enter the hallway. Two guys. Familiar faces. Swiss swimmers Vogel and Ackermann. They're quiet.

Not even chatting.

Unmistakably, they're zeroed in on me holding Banks while he's eyelevel with my dick. I don't remove my hands.

I'm glaring.

Banks is glaring.

They have to pass us, and as they do, they give us the look. The one that I've nicknamed Are You Two Fucking?

The only noise comes from the *pop pop* of fireworks. Like an emphasis on the awkward note this silent interaction has taken.

Cold frost from Banks and heat from me are enough to superglue their lips. Less than a minute later, they reach the end of the hall, round a corner, and disappear.

Tension winds between me and Banks.

"Doesn't look broken," Banks says. "But you know I only have an MG."

"Same here." We're both *making guesses*. With another sigh, I rotate my ankle, pain zipping up my leg. *Dang it.*

"Can you put any weight on it?"

I set my foot down and try to bear half my weight. I walk away from Banks. Sorry, I mean, *hobble*. I hobble from him and then turn back. "How does that look?"

He wipes his mouth, trying not to laugh. "Pretty ugly."

"Great."

As I return to him, he smacks my chest with the back of his hand. "Just hang onto me, Nine. I'll catch you."

"Trust falls with Banks Moretti were not on the Olympic itinerary." I gently put my foot back into the platform sneaker.

"Pencil it in under *let's check on our girlfriend*," he says, our attention shifting to the bathroom.

"One more sec! I'm just washing my hands!" Sulli shouts through the door. She must've heard us.

Silence falls, adding more tension between him and me.

People are confused about my relationship with Banks. They have questions. But most people are also too polite to ask them to our faces. So they bottle those questions, and in their restraint lies a single *look*.

Are You Two Fucking?

Everyone purges their questions and uncensored thoughts online enough for us to gauge this crap.

Banks adjusts his earpiece, then focuses on the spot where Vogel and Ackermann vanished.

Truthfully, one of my biggest fears in our relationship has been Banks shutting me out. His words back in Montana roll over me again and again. *"That's what we, Moretti boys, do. We bury the back-breaking, head-splitting shit and don't ever speak about it."*

What we've been through has been back-breaking, head-splitting shit.

I don't want him to bury me. Bury her. Bury *us*.

So every time I feel him slipping, I always make a point to press him to speak on it.

"What are you thinking, Banks?"

3

Banks Moretti

COWARDS.

Them, not us.

Part of me wishes they'd just say *it* to my face. Say what they're thinking. Say what people are spouting online.

Part of me is thankful they don't.

I have no good response queued up.

What's my next move then? To throw a knuckle-busting, blood-boiling, right hook and cause more harm than good? I have a tipping point like Akara, and I'm not looking to be set off.

Good grief, why am I even fucking aggravated?

I don't want to be defensive. I'm too confused to defend a thing right now. Except my love for Sulli. My love for him.

That, I understand.

I thump the back of my head to the wall. The bathroom door beside me. Sounds of fireworks grow faint, and if the pops frightened Sullivan, she'd call us inside, not push me or Akara away. Her nerves must be pre-ceremony jitters.

But she hates being alone, and I yearn to fill the void. I hope she's not feeling that emptiness right now—I hope that she really needed this alone time and that's why we're here and she's there.

I peel my concentration off the bathroom.

My mind travels back to Akara's question.

To Vogel and Ackermann. Swimmers on Team Switzerland.

To that look they gave us. It doesn't take fucking Scooby Doo to figure out what spun through their heads.

So I just tell my friend, "I can guess what they're thinking, but I wouldn't even know how to respond." I fix my eyes on Akara. "And I'm not my brother. I can find some verbal wisdom in a pile of shit. But I feel lost for fucking words."

Akara ends up smiling. "Only you'd say your wisdom originates from shit."

"You think it's born from someplace better?" I scan the empty hallway. "I'm a poor South Philly kid. Not a *pretty-faced* entrepreneur like you." I tap his cheek lightly.

His lips lift. "Hey, my pretty face has nothing to do with my wisdom." He pauses. "But mine definitely originates from higher places than shit."

I slug his shoulder for the swear word.

He doesn't flinch.

These days, if he curses it's usually on purpose, knowing knuckles-to-skin are coming.

I take the toothpick out of my mouth. "You like my shit-born wisdom."

"It has its moments." He glances at his phone, then pockets it. "Three out of five stars on average."

I point my toothpick at him. "You seeking out three-star advice all the damn time says more about you than me."

He lets out a laugh, the humor fading with the softening of his gaze. He pushes back his black hair, strands falling back into his eyes. "If the Swiss swimmers are just thinking—*are you two fucking?*—then we know the answer, Banks."

I raise my tense shoulders. "Yeah, we're not fucking each other. We're just fucking the same girl." I hate how crass I sound when what we're doing with Sulli is deeper than just a one-night fuck.

We're so committed to one another that it'd take a fuckin' tsunami to pull us apart at this point. Even then, Sulli is an Olympian. She'd find a way to swim back to us.

And I'd drown before I ever stopped trying to reach her and him.

Akara nods slowly. "Then they'd probably ask us, have you slept naked together?"

Yeah.

We have.

"Have our balls touched?" I say more bluntly.

He laughs at that one. "You know how many times I was spammed that comment last night on my Instagram?"

"Where'd you think I got it from?" I saw the trolls all over his photo of him, Sulli, and me at the Olympic Village. We both had our arms around her.

Akara shakes his head in thought. "The most annoying comment might be, *how can you be a man if you let another guy share your girl?*"

"Yeah. I fucking hate that one." I'm secure with myself. With my masculinity. But the personal jabs are grating on me.

I think back to me feeling defensive. Me not wanting to be.

But I know I will always defend *everything* that feels so goddamn personal to me. Akara and I have a lot of differences, but we're the same that way. I never imagined any opposition would get this close to the things that matter to me. My life, my loves, my people, my being— all of it is just sacred.

Quiet bathes the hallway and us as we contemplate the curiosity and accusations surrounding me and him. I think we knew it'd exist, but not to the level it's shot to. "For whatever it's worth," I cut into the silence, "you're all man to me, Nine."

His lips rise again. "Appreciate it, Banksy." He favors his right ankle and leans up against the wall beside me.

I squeeze his tattooed shoulder, then glance at the bathroom door with him.

"What's your least favorite question?" he asks.

"All of 'em."

"Cop out."

"Monaco," Thatcher announces over comms.

I know my fuckin' ABCs. If we're on countries that start with M, then Sulli is losing more time to rejoin Team USA. I consider banging on the door. But I don't want my girlfriend to jump out of her skin. Probably why Akara hesitates, too.

"We're at Monaco, mermaid!"

"I'll be out really fucking soon! I promise!"

"We're putting your poop-breaks on the clock, Sul," Akara teases. "You're being timed. Three more minutes."

We hear a faint *hardy-har-har.*

I slip my toothpick back in my mouth. Something I haven't told Akara or Sulli yet suddenly circles back to me. Every time the memory nears the front of my brain, I push it out of mind.

Unimportant.

Not now.

Later.

Maybe never.

Why drudge that shit up?

All the excuses fade to the background, and I suddenly confess, "My ma asked me if I'm bi."

Shock freezes his face. "Bisexual?"

"No, bilingual," I joke. "*Yes,* bisexual."

He jumps over my dry response. "Really? When? What'd you say?" He's eager for answers. Just like my mom was eager for one.

"Months ago," I admit, scratching my jaw.

I remember how my mom had been *over-the-moon* excited when I confirmed my relationship with Sulli back in Atlantic City. I didn't know how she'd react once she heard my relationship also includes Akara.

Turns out she's still excited. She loves Akara. But I think she's been more excited at the prospect of me being bi like her.

I take a longer beat. Quiet.

Akara is on pins and needles. "And?"

I don't answer right away.

He shoots me a look. "What's with the fracking cliffhanger?"

"It's not a cliffhanger." My mouth curves up. "It's a *fucking* pause."

"Are you really going to make me ask again?"

"I told my ma, *I don't know.*" I shake my head a couple times. "I don't know, Akara." Frustration I've felt and have been feeling starts to rumble to the surface again. "I don't fucking know what we are… and I thought I knew. I thought I was straight.…maybe I still am. *I don't know.*"

Before us, before this relationship, I had a clearer idea. And maybe I wouldn't care to define anything if people didn't constantly fucking ask.

On the internet.

From the press.

In person. (Thanks, Mom).

I breathe harder like I'm running up a fucking hill. "Do you know?" I gesture to him.

"No. I don't know either."

I expel a rougher breath. Wishing he had an answer, but maybe it's better that we're both fucking confused. Would I be upset if he said he had *no* attraction towards me?

Would I be upset if he did?

I don't know.

But at least we're at the same starting line.

Looking back, we haven't really dug deep into our sexualities. Too much has been going on. Sulli training. The media encroaching. Fan mail and hate mail piling up and taking half-a-day to sort through. For the most part, we've maintained a status quo for the past six months and haven't tried to leapfrog into new territory. We've just been preserving what we fought for. The three of us together. Our triad out in public.

I check the bathroom door. "Look, I don't care about being bi or queer or whatever-the-fuck, but I'm feeling aggravated having everyone tell me what I am before I figure it out."

Akara nods. "This uncertainty sucks." He lowers his voice to a whisper. "I wish I could tell them all, *having sex with the same girl doesn't mean we're gay or bi or not straight.* But it's not even the fracking answer they want."

I bite on the toothpick. "I guess there's only one way to figure out if we have *sexual* attraction. Nip this in the fucking bud." Though I know there's other forms of attraction like emotional and romantic attraction. But I think this is the one we're hung up on.

Akara smiles, one full of humor. "You asking to fuck me, Banks?"

"I was gonna start with a kiss." I put a hand to my chest. "Personally, I like to move slow, and I'm not sure you can take me, Kitsuwon."

He laughs.

Hell, we're both laughing. And then the sound fades, and we exchange a knowingness. That we both want answers.

"I'll kiss you," Akara tells me. "A real kiss this time though. Not any of that pecking-the-cheek bullcrap. That's the only way we'll know."

I remember during truth or dares we've kissed on the cheek. Never anything beyond that. I cock my head. "Or *I'll* kiss you."

"*Or* I'm kissing *you.*"

This isn't a hill I care to die on. "You are the logistics guy," I say just as the bathroom door swings open.

Our heads rotate to the twenty-two-year-old beauty. Aphrodite has nothing on her. Still and forever a smokeshow.

Sullivan Minnie Meadows—she's decked out in the Ralph Lauren Team USA outfit. Her dark-brown center-parted hair has grown longer in the past six months. Her traps are more pronounced. Her body leaner, shedding some muscle mass she gained from weightlifting during her retirement-phase.

Still, she can bench press me *and* Akara. She hasn't let us forget.

Seeing her usually does a fuckin' number on me. Like I'm in junior high with a lovelorn crush. But seeing her beet-red cheeks…and cagey glances right *now* does something else.

Alarm bells clang in my head. Kicking my ass towards her. "You alright, Sulli?" I shut the door behind her. Concern grips me to her uneasy expression.

Akara studies her in a sweep.

"Yeah?" She looks everywhere but at us and reties and unties her hair in a messy bun. "What were you guys talking about?"

"Later, string bean. We have places to be." Akara twirls a piece of *her* hair over his upper lip. The fake mustache is his effort to calm her nerves.

She stares at the fucking wall.

First try failed.

We watch her touch her cracked lips.

I dig into my pocket and pass Sulli a tube of vanilla Chapstick.

"Thanks..." She clears her throat, anxious. After one swipe, she pockets the Chapstick.

Akara hoists her wrist, checking the time from her watch. "We're late for your very important date, Lady Meadows. Hop to it." He smacks her ass forward.

Sulli would normally slug him. Or slap his ass back, but she rests her hands on her head, fingers threaded. I'm used to Sulli finding comfort in my eyes. In me.

But when she casts a glance to me, then to Akara, then back to me—her breathing hitches in a strange pattern. "No, not later. I actually need the fucking distraction before..." she trails off. "Just...what were you talking about? Kissing each other?"

I splay my arm over her broad shoulders. "Me kissing Akara."

"Me kissing *Banks*," Akara amends.

"He hopes."

She's not exactly shocked. She's asked us if we've ever wanted to "touch each other" during sex. Her exact words: *are you ever interested in going for each other's frank and beans?*

And we both just answered truthfully, *not really.*

If we did, I think we would've already. We enjoyed what we're doing. We still do, but now the questions are too big. Confusion is too strong.

Akara explains to her, "We were talking about sexual attraction earlier. We're not sure if it's there between me and him." He braces more weight on his uninjured ankle. "We've never really tested it or had a desire to. That's where the kiss comes in."

"Right. Yeah, fuck. You guys do what you gotta do. And...wait, fuck, I'm still a part of the equation in the end, right—"

"Of course you effing are," Akara cuts in.

"That's not changing," I assert.

She almost, almost smiles, but her hands finally fall off her head... and to her face. She's covering her face. My muscles tense. Stomach knotting.

"Sul?" Akara touches her wrist in comfort.

"I'm fine. I can do this," she mumbles in her palms. "I know I can fucking do this." Feels like she's speaking more to herself than to us.

"You can," I nod to Sulli. Though, she can't see me nod. "You're about to carry the flag for your country, and you're gonna look like a beautiful, un-fucking-stoppable woman out there."

She peers out between her fingers.

I hold her gaze. "Which is exactly what you are. And we're going to be cheering you on the whole way."

Sulli breathes in strongly. Her hands drop farther. Off her face and into my hand and into Akara's hand. I lace our fingers, and she flips our hands over, wrists up, all of us wearing braided bracelets. Blue. Red. Turquoise.

Her green eyes graze the black ink on my wrist, her wrist, and his wrist that spell out the same tattooed phrase.

Forward & Onward.

"I can fucking do this," Sulli says more confidently. Her grip tightens on our hands, turning my skin red. I'm not shaking hers away.

"We heard one country already dropped the flag," Akara lies. "They totally bombed out there. So you can't do worse than them, Sul."

I slip him a look.

He's lying. It's a half-baked lie, but I'd pretend I saw a pig flying across a rainbow if it meant eradicating Sulli's nerves. I'd also admit the lie. Eventually.

"Fuck, really?" Her eyes widen in surprise. "Which country?" She tries to peer around us, but the hallway is empty. She looks to me first.

So I say, "Canada. Guy just fumbled the thing. Fell on his face too."

"You're joking?"

"It happened," Akara professes. "Maple syrup memes are already all over the internet. No one's even talking about you."

She lets out a big breath. "Thank you, Canada. Taking one for the triad." She ends up letting her hair loose and free. The strands splay wild around her cheeks.

When her eyes rise to me, I dip my head a little. My hand slips against her squared jaw, and I steal a kiss that brushes my lips slowly against her lips. Something swells up in my chest as Sulli holds the kiss a beat longer. Deepening the moment.

And when I gently pull back, I see more anxiety in her eyes.

What's going on, Sulli?

I want to pull her into my arms. To let her bury herself into my body, into my soul. I even want to draw Akara closer. So she can feel the safety of two men, not just one.

She jumps at a *boom* of a firework, and Akara slips an arm around her hips. I touch her neck while she grabs onto my waistband and onto his pinky. Sulli blows out a breath, "I fucking *hate* fireworks. They can go blow up Satan's butthole. That's where you fucking belong!" she shouts at the ceiling.

"YEAH!" Akara yells upward.

"FUCK YEAH!" Sulli screams.

I laugh, and with an easiness, we're all headed to Team USA.

"Are you limping?" Sulli asks Akara.

"I'm fine. I'm cool. *I'm Kits.*" He tries to play off his sprained ankle as no big deal, but Sulli seems more concerned. His injury is a longer lasting distraction for her.

While we meet up with more athletes, I try to stay frosty. Which means shaking off the glimpse of anxiety I caught in her eyes. Sulli has a D- poker face. Encroaching on an *F.* But I'm not a fucking mind reader either.

And I can't press her on anything. I wouldn't. She's about to be broadcasted across the world. *Time and fucking place, Banks Roscoe Moretti.* This isn't it.

Likely, I could be worrying for nothing. I'm hawk-eyed, scrutinizing athlete to athlete to athlete. Trusting no one. Even if they're all on Team USA.

I knew going public with our relationship meant gambling my girlfriend's safety. And still, I made that gamble.

Out of sheer love for Sulli and Akara, I'd make that same gamble today. But there was a moment that put the fear of God in me.

Where I felt we'd lose her. Lawyers stopped tabloids from reporting the specifics of the incident, and we've all just tried to put the past behind us. At her parents' suggestion, Sulli's been seeing a therapist a couple times a month to help cope and move forward.

Akara always had the sense to imagine the worst of the worst, so he's not as hung up on the idea of almost *losing* Sulli. I never let myself truly believe *death* could be an outcome. Danger, we'd thwart, but no way in hell would she come that close to dying. No one would take her from me.

That was too much.

Fuck anyone else who tries again.

4

Banks Moretti

A NEEDLE BUZZES OVER my skin, piercing the flesh of my wrist with black ink. Donnelly has my arm propped on a rolling end table in our living room. I try to relax against the couch, but I'm sitting rigid. I couldn't care less if the ink blows out and I have another dumb fucking mistake on my body for life.

I'm still trying to shake-off the incident from two days ago. I can *feel* myself barely blinking. In a state of hypervigilance that keeps my mind humming. Breath is knotted. Brain alert.

Across from me, Akara watches from a chair, and every time our eyes catch, he's practically telling me, *breathe, Banks. She's safe.*

I want to sling back, *then why do you keep looking at her like she'll disappear?*

We're both dealing with this in our own way. Me, tensed like a fuckin' Tin Man, like I need to reload an extra gun and maybe unsheathe a few swords. Defend her to the bloody death.

Akara is more playful.

He's all "Lady Meadows" this and "string bean" that. Partly to take her mind off bad shit. Partly because he's holding tighter to Sulli. His bond with her. He even transferred himself off Luna Hale's detail and back onto Sulli's today.

She has two permanent bodyguards in her two boyfriends. But after the incident, I feel like she needs a battalion that we can't give her. Extra temporary guards have to be enough.

"Does it fucking hurt?" Sulli wonders, peering at Donnelly's skilled work. She's next to me on the couch.

"No. It barely stings." I'm so mentally checked out that the pain is dull. Numb. I try to focus. "Doesn't hurt as bad as my fucked tattoo I got at fourteen."

Donnelly doesn't look up. "The blown out one."

"That's the ugly bastard," I confirm.

"Been wondering what you got tattooed," Donnelly says, wiping off the ink. "My guess is script."

"Roman numerals." I watch him retrace the bold lettering on my wrist. No cursive. Legible. Clear. We all decided on the design when Donnelly showed us different sketches of the same phrase. I don't know why I tell him, but I just say, "It was the day my brother died."

Donnelly finally meets my eyes. "Sorry 'bout him, man. Shoulda known what happened before the leak, but I never paid much attention to that kinda news in South Philly." I love that he says South Philly like I do. *Sow Philly.*

"We were both kids, man." I lift my shoulder.

He pauses, and I realize I jerked my wrist.

Fuck, I try to keep my wrist stable for him. He continues tattooing, and I tell him, "My brother's death didn't make any kind of headline that a bunch of eyes woulda seen anyway. It was what it was."

Ugly.

Miserable.

A fuckin' grenade in my family.

Life moves on, though.

Forward & Onward. I stare at the words he's inking. Sulli places a hand on my knee, and I glance over at my beautiful girlfriend who recently qualified for the Olympics, who's headed for Training Camp in Hawaii in four days with Team USA. Who only stopped physically shaking this morning. Enough that she declared, "Let's get fucking tattoos. All of us. Together."

Without hesitation, Akara and I jumped on the plan.

So we ended up three-floors below the penthouse. In my apartment that I share with Akara, Donnelly, and Quinn.

With her hand on my knee and eyes on my eyes, Sulli's lips are rising. I notice that Akara is smiling more, too.

What?

What'd I do?

She gently elbows my side before lifting her knees to her chest. "You talked about Sky." Her voice is quiet. It's still strange to hear Sulli *whisper.* Like *really* whisper to a decibel that needs ear-straining. She's gotten better at lowering her voice in public. So I shouldn't be surprised she can do it in my apartment.

I patty-cake her words in my head.

You talked about Sky.

Yeah.

I'm getting better at that. Guess we're all improving at some things. Getting worse at others. 'Cause my fucking back is killing me from sitting this upright.

I might get Sulli to walk on my back before we go to bed. See if she can crack the kinks.

The more I feel how proud Akara and Sulli are of me, the more my muscles take a break from yanking taut. My shoulders loosen.

At least my head isn't pounding. Thank you, Farrow. I'm now the owner of a daith piercing. The silver hoop in my ear's inner cartilage has been a godsend. Migraines are infrequent enough that I wish I'd spoken to Farrow sooner. Gone to the doctor. I'm just glad I finally did.

Donnelly traces the letter *a.*

Sulli watches and tugs at a frayed ankle bracelet. "Should I get mine on the right or left?" She shows me her wrists.

"My vote is right. Match ours."

"You're getting yours on the right too, Kits?"

"I am." Akara tosses a purple gummy worm in his mouth.

Sulli opens her mouth from afar.

He wags a green gummy, then tosses that one in his mouth.

She gapes. "*Kits.*"

"What? You want one of these?" He wags a red one.

"What else am I fucking doing? Just eating air?"

I crack a smile. God, I love her. *You could've lost her.* I try to wipe that away.

"Here." Akara gears up to throw the red gummy. "Open wide, Sul."

She opens her mouth to catch again. My unholy mind pictures Sulli taking Akara's cock. "How am I doing, Banks? Good form?"

"You're no match for him."

Akara shoots me a half-hearted glare. "Hey, fudge you."

I almost laugh.

Donnelly smirks, inking the last little line.

Sulli's open mouth has closed to make way for a smile.

"You want the gummy worm or not, string bean?"

"Fuck yes," Sulli says competitively, "give me your worm, Kits."

He clearly adjusts forward like that sexual innuendo stroked him. But he twirls the red gummy. Fakes a throw. She sits off the cushion to catch before realizing he never threw the candy.

He eats the red one.

She chucks a couch pillow at him. "You fucking gummy worm tease."

He dodges the blow.

I can tell Donnelly has been tattooing for years—even if his current occupation is security. He lifts his needle as soon as the couch cushion undulates, then gets back to work like no time has passed.

Sulli chucks a second pillow.

Akara catches it, and his smile flickers in and out. Heavy with something. A feeling. I see the way he watches Sulli. Like he's engraining these little happy moments we're sharing.

Like he's safekeeping them in case things worsen. In case there's no light left—I don't know. In case of a next time?

There can't be a fucking next time.

This can't happen again.

Our gazes catch.

I slip him a look this time that says, *she's still here. She's not going anywhere, Akara.*

He exhales a breath, massaging his knuckles.

I thought Akara would go all G.I. Joe if danger crept in Sulli's sphere, but it looks like I was projecting. Because that's *me*.

I'm the Marine.

Literally.

Once Donnelly finishes my tattoo and cleans off the fresh ink, I roll out my stiff shoulders and let Akara take my seat. And then a knock sounds on our apartment door.

"I'll get it," I tell them. "It's probably Thatcher."

Sulli and Akara look unenthused at this prospect. My brother isn't winning any friendship awards with those two, but maybe he's come to his senses and he wants to make amends with Akara. Become BFFs again.

I want that for Akara.

But I also don't want him pining after my brother. If Thatcher is ready to move on, then I hope Akara feels like I can be enough of a friend.

"Should I leave?" Sulli asks.

"No," Akara and I say in unison.

Sulli picks at her anklet again. "I just don't have that good of a relationship with him. It's fucking awkward."

"It'll be alright," I try to assure. "He's just concerned. He'll be asking us the same thing everyone else is. *Are you okay? How are you feeling?* Easy shit to answer."

"Yeah, you're probably fucking right." Sulli rests her chin on her knee. On my way to the door, I hear her ask Akara, "Can you answer his questions for me? I don't feel like talking to Thatcher."

Gotta fix that.

Don't know how. My brother has been prickly. And since the incident, he's been a six-seven overly worried cactus. Maybe he's here to ask Akara for a longer security meeting about the clusterfuck.

Yesterday's meeting was cut short.

Akara cut it short. We wanted to be with Sulli. To console her. To hold her. Security logistics be fucking damned, she's all that mattered to us.

Of course, *professionally*, it wasn't smart. *Personally*, it was everything—there was no other option.

Akara Kitsuwon gave no fucks, and I could've kissed his fucking toes. I wanted out of that meeting so *fucking* badly, and he made it happen for us. I love that he understood she needed both of us and not just me.

Another knock raps the wood.

"Yeah, I'm coming!" I shout.

Akara and I haven't considered moving out of the apartment, but we do spend more time in Sulli's bedroom than in ours.

For one, it's bigger there.

For another, it has more personality. Ours is just a waypoint from here to there. Today, it's been a place with more privacy. Less cats and dogs. Less people to run into and ask, *how are you feeling?*

Can I get you anything?

If I want to feel that kind of overbearing concern, I'd rather just meet it with Sulli and Akara. Not with my brother. Not with his wife. Not with Farrow or Maximoff or Luna (not that Luna has badgered me—she's been her regular spunky self).

Another knock.

"Jesus, Thatcher." I peer into the peephole, and I go cold.

That's not my twin brother.

5

Banks Moretti

"WHO IS IT?" AKARA ASKS, studying me while Donnelly cleans his wrist for the tattoo.

My jaw hardens. Body crystalizes to some prehistoric stone that needs chiseled. "My dad." I take a short breath. "Don't get up. I'll deal with him."

"Seriously?" He's shocked.

Sulli is shocked.

Hell, *I'm* shocked that those words came out of my mouth. I would rather open the door to the devil himself than to my dad. But I refuse to be a fucking coward and pass this to Akara.

I'm done retreating and avoiding.

The last two days have reminded me that I'd sooner die on my feet than live on my knees. I won't live life ruled by fear of a father.

As I unlock the door, I realize I have no clue what he wants or what he's going to say. What's he even doing here? *He works for Akara.*

That's still true. My dad, Michael Moretti, trains the temp bodyguards.

I bet he just wants Akara.

Looks like he's getting his dispensable son instead.

I swing open the door, and instead of offering an invite into the apartment, I slip out into the hallway. And I shut the door behind me.

"Banks," my dad greets, brown eyes darting to the door I just closed.

"I didn't know you were stopping by," I say tightly.

He scratches the salt-and-pepper scruff on his jaw. He has a long face, olive skin, bushy brows, and thick hair—grayed enough that he's nicknamed "Silver Fox" by the temp bodyguards. He's in great shape. His black tee molds his muscles, and he carries himself like a Navy SEAL. No one is ever surprised when they learn he is one.

"I should've called," he realizes. "Or, I shouldn't have. Your brother said you probably wouldn't answer." He slips his hands in his jean pockets and lifts his shoulders up in a shrug. Something about his mannerisms remind me of *me*.

My eyes burn. Unblinking. "Thatcher is right." I have a few inches on my dad, but he makes himself feel taller somehow. "And it's not just you. I'm not really picking up the phone that much right now." *Not after the incident.*

"You haven't talked to your mom yet?" He's gotten rid of his South Philly accent. That irks me for some reason.

I run my tongue over my molars. "No, not yet. She's been calling, but…" I lift my shoulders. Fuck, I feel like I'm mimicking him.

He's mimicking me.

This is fucking stupid. I just want to turn around and go inside. "What are you doing here?" I ask, almost exasperated. "Akara's busy—"

"I'm not looking for Akara. I came to check on you."

My face twists, anger simmering at the surface. "*Why?*"

He gives me a look like it's obvious and I'm being dense. "You're my son."

I thread my arms over my taut chest. I'm gnawing on the words he just spoke like its decades old beef jerky. Tough. Grisly. *Inedible.* "No offense, but you haven't been much of a father to me."

I expect him to look away. Stare at the wall, the floor, the door. Anywhere but at me. Just like the night he said horrible, unforgivable things to my mom. To Thatcher. To me. Where he couldn't even look us in the eye at the end of it all.

But I watch now as he never tears away from my pain. He stares me dead-in-the-eye with a flicker of remorse. "I understand that."

"Do you?"

"I left you." He swallows hard. "A piece of me died with him… and I pray to God you'll never understand the pain of losing a child." He has to turn away to collect himself. I hear him sniff hard before he looks back. Eyes a little redder. "I lost all of you…and I can't get him back. But you're still here."

"I've *been* here," I growl.

"I know." Hurt flashes through his features. "I know."

I blow out a rough breath. Suppressing the urge to shake my head with these pent-up emotions that want out, but I force them in.

"I'm sorry," he professes.

"For what?"

"Everything." His voice nearly cracks. He swallows again, like a lump is in his throat.

A rock is in mine.

It can't be this easy. His apology. By the sunken lines on his face, maybe it isn't. *Why now?* I could fucking ask. But does it even matter why it's taken this long? We're Morettis. Digging up painful shit in the past has taken fuckin' eons. The Coyote would sooner catch the Road Runner. I'm lucky it's even happening at all.

He could've taken this to his grave.

I loosen my arms and rub the back of my neck. "So you're here to check on me?"

He senses my change in attitude. Easing more too. "Yeah."

I must want to switch subjects because I spit out, "You know I'm in a poly relationship with Akara and Sulli?"

Akara said he's stayed "strictly professional" with my dad. So they haven't surfaced this either.

"The world knows," he says. "Of course I know."

I bounce my head, reading his features. "You're fine with it?"

"It's your life." He lifts his shoulders again. "I have a close friend in California who's in an open triad. It's not unheard of to me."

"Ours is closed."

He nods. "If you aren't straight, you know I'd always support you."

Pressure to determine that answer weighs heavier. My dad always knew my mom was bi. Before they got together, she was dating Nicola in high school. It's not like I ever thought he'd have an issue with me being *not* straight.

I might still be straight.

"I know," is all I say.

An elevator *dings*. I whip my head down the hallway. Eyes pinpointed on the noise. No one exits. I scan the empty hallway, left and right, and then the elevator doors slide shut.

"Banks."

I almost jump.

My dad notices.

I rake a hand through my thick hair, curling the strands behind my left ear, then right. "What?"

"I know what happened to your girlfriend might not be easy to process, but you need to remember the good. You did *good*, son. There's nothing more you could've done."

I'm not Thatcher. I'm not my dad.

I'm not blaming myself for things out of my control.

I'm just looking for the extra ammunition and the target so this won't happen again. If that sets me on edge, so what? I'm on fuckin' edge.

"I get that, sir," I tell him, hating that I called him *sir*. I cringe at the taste in my mouth.

"She'll be fine tomorrow."

I can't help but glare. "You think she'll be *fine* tomorrow?" I know we're all trying to move past this, but who's *he* to say how fast it'll be?

"It could've been worse." He says it like this was a blip.

"It could've been fucking worse?" I'm almost shouting.

"At least she wasn't raped. At least she wasn't kidnapped, Banks."

"That shouldn't even be in fucking contention!" I yell, sick to my stomach even *thinking* about Sulli being raped or kidnapped. "The fact that we're applauding my girlfriend having the barrel of a gun pointed at her face is not okay."

"I'm not *applauding*," he snaps back. "But you take the win."

"It's not a win to me. I had to watch a man point a fucking *gun* at her." I grit the words out. "And I'm not a naïve twelve-year-old. I've been a bodyguard too long. I know it could happen again. But you're saying I should just be fuckin' *happy* she wasn't raped or kidnapped, so..." I extend my arms. "Whoopty-fucking-do."

"That's not what I meant," he says plainly, then sighs. "Sort of." He thinks again. "I just think you should be happy with the small gains because like you said, it could happen again. She's quickly becoming the *most* famous one in all the families. You and Akara are too. That's not something you can escape, so you can either embrace it or let it rule you. Because you can't fight it."

Breath heavy, I don't have long to think on his words.

The door opens.

Akara squeezes out in the hall, nailing a serious look on me. "She can hear you."

"Fuck," I curse, then glance at the other apartment doors. Hopefully they didn't hear shit.

"They signed NDAs," Akara reminds me.

I nod stiffly.

"Akara," my dad greets.

"Hey, Michael."

With one nod, I say a silent goodbye to my dad, and I slip into the apartment. Donnelly is disinfecting Sulli's skin for the tattoo.

Her green, green eyes land on me. She chews the corner of her lip.

"I'm sorry," I breathe, stomach knotted. "You're safe. We're not letting anything happen to you."

She nods. "Yeah, I fucking believe that. I do." Her eyes redden. "Can you sit beside me?"

Without pause, I'm at Sulli's side. I wrap my arm around her broad shoulders, and she leans into my chest. I kiss the spot beside her ear and whisper, "We'll get through this."

She exhales.

Soon Akara is back. He's seated at her feet. He teases his fingers under her anklet, distracting her from the buzz of the needle along her skin. "Next stop," Akara tells her, "to the Olympics."

Very strongly, Sullivan says, "Forward and onward."

6
Sullivan Meadows

I'M PREGNANT. I'm pregnant.

I'm fucking pregnant.

"It's happening. We're finally here!" Frankie Hansen squeals next to me and shakes my arm as we both wait with Team USA in the wings of the stadium. Her fair white skin contrasts the dark navy of her Ralph Lauren blazer, and she's totally put together. Ready for a network, worldwide *closeup*.

Frankie transformed from the Olympic hopeful that I briefly coached at Warwick University to my Olympic rival at Team Trials and now to my teammate in Los Angeles.

But fuck, really, we're *still* competing. She was only a couple seconds behind my 200m & 400m freestyle times, and yet, I can't deny how much I've grown to like Frankie.

Overzealous, upbeat, and untiring—she's my closest swim buddy here. Her platinum blonde hair and thick blonde eyebrows are the face of Nubell Cookie's Oaty Nut Bar. And as far as swimmers go, she's quickly become a face of the Summer Games alongside Olympic returnees Tobias Kingly, Christian Dean, and me.

Little does Frankie know at the moment, I've been in a daze since Akara and Banks left my side. They flank the wall and do their bodyguard business. Concentrated on security. Eyeing the perimeter. Eyeing me. My safety.

Out of instinct, I *almost* turn to them. I'm so used to my boyfriends being a place of solace. To calm my speeding pulse. To comfort me when the world feels like it's creeping in too snug. Too tight.

But I'm keeping a big chunky fucking secret from them. And the guilt is enough to plant my lying liar eyes elsewhere.

"It's so surreal," Frankie breathes in awe.

I'm pregnant. "Yeah, it really fucking is."

She grins at me, squeals again with the rattle of my arm, and I try to leech her excitement. *You made it here, Sulli.* My lungs swell, and I smile back at Frankie. Whether or not she can tell it's weak, I don't fucking care. I think she's too hypnotized by the majestic Olympic atmosphere. And to be frank, I want to be fucking hypnotized too.

I worked *so hard* to be here this year. Fucking determined, I practically ate, breathed, and slept *swimming.* The water could've been my bed. My roommates barely saw me in the penthouse. I was in and out like a wet ghost. Luna literally called me Sulli the Swim Specter for the past six months.

"We're all back here waiting for the United States to be called up," Christian Dean says to his internet fans, hoisting his cellphone and filming Team USA in the wings. "Say hi, guys!"

More than 600 athletes—from gymnasts to track stars, rowers, and javelin fucking throwers—cheer together as he pans the camera overhead.

I let out a little "woot woot" that feels honest. Last Olympics, I stayed true to myself, not engaging when I didn't want to engage—and I promised myself I'd do the same this time.

Christian Dean pushes through the throngs, hair cut short with a cool fade. I just call him Dean. He's black with dark-brown skin, a magnetic smile, killer backstroke, and A++ social media skills that seriously rival my cousin Jane's.

As the self-dubbed "hype man" on the team, he has over 5 million TikTok followers alone. The public has been eating up his behind-the-scenes videos leading to the Games.

"Meadows!" Dean points me out, coming over and wrapping an arm around my shoulder. The phone is still recording.

Oh fuck.

I have an awkward fucking smile at the selfie video.

"She's shy," Dean tells his viewers.

I actually laugh.

Because, yeah, four years ago, I kept to myself and avoided a lot of the press cameras. And four years ago, we were first-time Olympians together. Dean was my closest friend at the Games. We had the same coach at the club before qualifiers, and he didn't care that I didn't talk a lot or that when I did, it usually revolved around swimming.

Once I retired from the sport, we sort of fell out of touch.

My doing.

I never fucking trusted anyone enough to be their *real* friend. I couldn't tell them about my family. Couldn't talk about my life without fearing it'd wind up online. And so I pushed Dean away along with everyone else. Keeping them at a distance was fucking safe.

"Hey," I wave at his phone.

Dean squeezes me in a side-hug. "She's going to take gold for America. Watch out for this superstar."

I lightly slug his shoulder. "You're taking it home."

"*We're.*" He reminds his viewers, "Hundred-meter *mixed* relay with me, Meadows, Kingly, and Hansen. You better tune in to that one. It's gonna be *epic,* guys."

A stupid giddy smile plays at my lips.

I'm swimming with my fucking *idol.*

Tobias Kingly.

He's somewhere here.

"Kingly!" Dean pushes away from me and weaves through the throngs. I don't follow him. The closer we are to show time, the more the anticipation winds inside me, twisting my stomach.

I'm about to be on TV.

It could be way worse. The media finding out I'm pregnant—that is a petrifying scenario that I can't let come to fruition. God, all the questions they'd yell at me….

Who's the father, Sulli?

I don't know. One of two. Banks or Akara.

When'd you get pregnant, Sulli?

I can't be fucking sure. Maybe during Team Trials? Maybe in Hawaii at the Training Camp?

How far along are you?

I don't know. I don't fucking know!

With a sharp inhale, I glance at the wall. But instead of making eye-contact with my boyfriends, I find another familiar face.

I slip through the masses and approach him.

Backstage lanyard around his neck, he wears cargo khakis and a plain gray tee. His proud smile among his hardened, scruffy features transports me back to four years ago.

Eighteen.

Winning gold.

No, he's not my swim coach, but he's always been my biggest fan.

"Dad," I greet, and he instantly uncrosses his arms as I step in for a hug. He wraps his arms around me, and I hold tighter.

I'm pregnant, Dad.

I swallow the truth. I learned my lesson: don't drop a truth bomb on my dad. At least not in public. Maybe if we were back in the woods, I'd consider detonating this one and feeling the fucking moment again. Even against better judgment.

But above everything, it feels *wrong* to tell my dad before I tell my boyfriends.

He must feel that I'm nervous. When I draw back, he keeps his rough rock climber hands on my shoulders. "Fuck what anyone says or thinks. When you go out there, just be *you*. That's all that matters, champ."

Champ.

I smile.

I haven't heard my dad call me *champ* in a long time. He used to use the nickname whenever I needed a confidence boost for swimming.

And I definitely need one now. Just not for the reason he believes. Under normal circumstances, I'd be a little fucking intimidated that

I'm carrying my country's flag. It's a lot of responsibility. One that I'd probably hand over to Dean. He deserves it more.

Akara and Banks would quickly say, *no way* and *no way in hell*. They're so ready to lift me up as the world continues to call me undeserving. But the public is right, aren't they? I was chosen because I'm a famous face. Recognizable in the media.

Fuck what anyone says or thinks. When you go out there, just be you.

I intake a stronger breath. "Thanks, Dad. I guess I can't do worse than the Canadian flagbearer."

His brows harden in a tough furrow. "The what?"

"Canada," I say. "They fumbled the fucking flag. It's a whole meme and everything…" My voice tapers off at the dark confusion scrunching his face.

"I must've fucking missed that."

They lied.

My boyfriends fucking lied!

I find myself smiling. Maple syrup memes—God, I should've known! Kits is so corny. And it's kind of cute. How much they tried to rid my nerves.

I guess we all lied to each other, but theirs was an innocent white lie. Mine…not so much.

I look around. "Is Mom in the stands?"

"Yeah, she's with your aunts."

Mom is a big fan of mine too, but she worries about the pressure I put on myself when I strive for gold. Dad always told her I'd grow out of it like he did, but I never shook off my love and drive for competition.

Clearly, considering I came out of my retirement and shocked the world.

I notice Uncle Connor and Uncle Lo close by. They're talking quietly and scrutinizing the event's security and our own. My family has been overly concerned about my safety, and I've become used to seeing my aunts and uncles around. They try to draw attention off me whenever they can.

I appreciate it more than they know.

"Sullivan Meadows!" a woman shouts, waving me towards the front of the pack. She looks like an event coordinator, and the American flag is in her hand.

"Bye, Dad." I'm about to leave.

"I'm proud of you, Sulli." The emotion in his eyes tempts tears to rise in mine.

"*Dad*," I wipe the corners.

He laughs into a bigger, more profound smile like he's transported back to the past too. Like we've opened a time capsule together, and long ago, I was just the kid running through the woods next to him. Determined to keep stride. Dreaming of an Olympic moment.

And here I am, not once.

But twice.

In this second, I feel like his little kid. The one I fought so hard *not* to be in his eyes, and you know what? I don't fucking care.

I am his little girl.

I am a woman now.

I'm every fucking thing.

And yes, I'm pregnant.

You can fucking do this, Sulli.

My lungs reinflating with confidence and hope, I follow the sight of the flag. Then I brave a glance at my boyfriends. Mostly because I want to remember this moment with them.

I catch Banks' eyes first. His mouth begins to curve. The love in his gaze elevates me tenfold. He mouths, *I love you.*

I mouth back, *I love you more.*

He shakes his head like that's impossible.

And then Akara.

Kits—he smiles at me, one that lights up his eyes. One reminiscent of four years ago where he was my bodyguard and protected me during the Parade of Nations. Only this time, I'm older than eighteen. And he's looking at me like I'm beyond beautiful. Like I'm *his*.

He blows me a kiss.

I blow him a kiss back. Akara mimes catching it and palms the kiss onto Banks' cheek. Banks elbows his side before hawk-eyeing the crowds, and I don't realize I'm smiling like a lovesick puppy until I reach the event coordinator.

She's busy chitchatting with another official.

"That grin for me?"

I glance to my left.

Tobias fucking Kingly. Olive-skinned, crew-cut light brown hair, and oh-so-fucking confident at twenty-nine. An entire armpiece tattoo of a forest, eagle, and grizzly bear lies beneath his navy blazer. Not to mention, he *blew* his butterfly times out of the water at Team Trials.

There are stars in my eyes. "I, uh…"

He smiles more, laughing a little.

"I saw you set the new world record for the two-hundred-meter fly. It was fucking awesome."

"A definite highlight, huh?" He wags his brows. "Second year here, Meadows?"

I nod. We didn't talk much last Olympics. And even though we're in an event together, I've been too starstruck to really chat with Kingly.

"Wait until your third. The pressure only gets worse." With his hand, he blocks the sudden spotlight that glares down on the wing.

I squint.

"Change of plans!" It takes me a second to realize the event coordinator approaches me and Kingly, American flag in hand. "I've been told we're switching up flagbearers."

"Why?" Kingly frowns.

"You're still holding the flag," she explains. "Ms. Meadows, I'm sorry, you're out. It's just Kingly today."

My stomach does a weird nosedive. I'm guessing the national committee were pressured by the internet sentiment. I've seen the vitriol online. A lot of people think it's a disgrace that *I'm* carrying the flag. A girl who just openly declared she's in a polyamorous relationship. I said, *fuck no* to monogamy and somehow that's too fucking shameful?

Fuck that.

"Everyone already thinks I'm carrying it," I tell her. "It'll be a bigger fucking ordeal if you change flagbearers now."

"I just do what I'm told," she says, checking the time.

Banks and Akara are pushing ahead of me. To walk out in front of the U.S. athletes, and they almost pause by the coordinator, seeing the uncomfortable exchange.

I shake my head at them and motion them to keep going.

My boyfriends can't fix this, and I'd rather they just protect me from the possibility of hecklers. As they focus and go on ahead, I ask her, "Can't you call them? Tell them that."

"There's no time. It is what it is." She's anxious and juggling a clipboard, plus a comm system in her ear. "Okay, the United States of America, we're almost ready for you!" Team USA cheers in excitement. She hands the flagpole to Kingly. "Keep it upright. Don't let it touch the ground. And don't dip the flag to anyone."

Dean comes in, filming Kingly and the flag. "America refused to dip the flag to Hitler and the Nazi party during the Berlin Olympics. 1936. We haven't dipped the flag since."

Kingly laughs. "Thanks for the World History, Deano." They fist-bump.

Dean fist-bumps me. I don't have the fucking courage to announce *on camera* that I've been ousted from a flagbearer role.

I should be relieved. Eyes won't be all on me. But I'm not.

I hate that I feel *ashamed*.

Like I'm letting down my country. Like I'm letting down other people in poly relationships. Like I'm letting down my family, my boyfriends, everyone who loves me.

"Here we go!" Dean cheers. Unaware that Kingly isn't going to pass the flag to me.

Before I fade back into the masses and find Frankie, my swim idol briefly looks down at me.

And Kingly says, "Shit happens, kid."

7
Sullivan Meadows

@ollieoop7: knew Sullivan would get the shaft! Sucks to be her lol

@therealone20192: sulli the slut never deserved to carry the flag in the first place. Shes fucking gross

@callowaysfan_forever: The right call was made imo. Love the Meadows but Sulli joined the Olympics at last minute. Other athletes have given more to be there *shrugs*

@porcupine_dreamz: was she crying? I swear I saw her shed a tear haha

@vodkajuicer111: slutty sulli is a loser go get gangbanged bitch

FUCK YOU.

Fuck you.

And double fuck you.

Social media and Olympic commentators have been obsessing over the U.S. flagbearer drama, but even as I close out my socials, that chaos is background noise to a louder crisis.

Pregnant.

All night and morning after the Opening Ceremony, I keep tossing that big glaring word back and forth in my head. Like a ping-pong match in my brain. By the afternoon it doesn't land anywhere helpful.

Luna plops down on my single bed next to me, carrying a plastic baggie of multicolored gel pens. Neon-green glitter sparkles throughout her long, light brown hair, and I twist a glittery strand around my finger and begin braiding.

She opens the gel pen baggie.

We're not roommates in Los Angeles. She's been staying at a nearby hotel with our families, but she's visiting me at the Olympic Village after I texted her an SOS:

Need to fucking meet-up ASAP.

I included enough panicked emojis that she practically flew here at the first chance.

"Have you talked to Beckett?" she asks me.

"Not yet. You're the only one aware of this fucking pickle right now." Am I really calling my baby a disgusting *pickle*?

Ugh. I restrain the urge to bury my face in my bed pillow.

Luna glances cautiously at the door.

Locked.

Nobody here but us.

I lucked out receiving a highly coveted single room in the Olympic Village. Well, if you spell "luck" with the letters A.K.A.R.A.

My boyfriend went to bat for me, sighting *security* reasons. Even with the special treatment, my room isn't outfitted for a queen. I'm not Princess Sulli, as some trashy sports commentators try to paint me as.

Fuck them.

I have all the same fixtures as every other Olympic athlete, and I love the tiny bathroom, plain walls, itchy sheets, and ugly carpeted floor. Everything about my room screams *I made it to the Olympics.*

Dean has already documented the athletes' lodging conditions on social media, highlighting the single bed made from cardboard that'll be recycled after the Summer Games. Our beds also include fluffy comforters with the Olympic rings printed down the center and a sign that says, *Rigorous Activity Not Advised.*

Of course they meant no *jumping*, but my mind went to other things. Banks & Akara won't be banging me on the bed. Noted.

Whether or not they'll take me rough and hot and sweaty seems like such a silly, trivial thought now. I have more pressing issues. One I can't ignore for that long. Especially since Akara and Banks are rooming with me. They aren't down the hallway or lodging at a hotel.

They even slept here last night.

Partially because they're my boyfriends. *Mostly* because they're my bodyguards. Two cots are pushed against the wall. And I'm still grappling with *how* I should tell them.

Fuck, I'm still grappling with the reality that I am pregnant.

While I'm all submerged in my jumbled feelings, my boyfriends are currently in a security meeting with SFO. In their absence, a temp is guarding my bedroom door. The six qualifying events to advance to semifinals start tomorrow, and security is high-stressed about how to keep me safe while I compete.

I'm high-stressed for a completely different reason.

Luna speaks softly. "Have you taken the test yet?"

"Yeah." I let go of her braid. "It was positive."

She stops digging around in her bag of gel pens. "Whoa," she breathes out. Jaw dropping slowly. Eyes bugging.

"I know. Fucking whoa." I collapse back on the bed. It's surprisingly squishy for being made of cardboard.

"What if it's a false positive?" Luna theorizes. "It was only one test. I can go get you more."

"Oh hey, you don't have to do that again for me, Luna." I perch on my elbows. "It's too big of a risk if someone sees you with one. You'd be subjected to pregnancy rumors, and you shouldn't have to deal with that because of me."

"I didn't exactly go to the store myself." She uncaps a milky lilac pen. "I had help."

"You had help?" *Who?!* My heart races. "Fuck, please tell me you didn't tell Eliot and Tom—"

"No," she interjects fast. "I wouldn't do that to you, Sulli. I promise."

I ease a little. Luna is a kickass secret-keeper, so I remind myself to *trust*. I fucking trust Luna with all my heart, and I don't want to stop now.

"She thinks the test is for me. You're in the clear. And I can ask her to get another one."

"Who is she?" I finally ask.

"Frog. She's been cool. She won't snitch."

Oh fuck. I plant a hand over my face like I'm watching a train wreck. And I'm the one on the tracks. With Quinn still off-duty, Akara's been trying to find Luna a new 24/7 bodyguard. In the meantime, Frog has been one of Luna's temporary bodyguards.

She's Akara's *cousin*. A cousin that he said he never even talked to until a few months ago. She introduced herself to me with a handshake. *"I'm Kannika Kitsuwon. But everyone calls me Frog."*

She's only eighteen. Ten years younger than Kits.

And she's from New York. Since being born & raised in Philly is a prerequisite to be on the security team, Akara made an exception for Frog at his mom's request. She's not even here looking for a permanent bodyguard position.

It's a long story.

One that Akara hates repeating.

"Frog is also related to Akara," I say. "You aren't worried that she'll tell Kits that *you* asked for a pregnancy test?"

Luna shrugs. "She said she wouldn't. She hasn't given me a reason not to believe her yet, and I figure if she does tell your boyfriend, then we know Frog can't be trusted anymore."

That's smart. I think this over, two fingers to my lips. "Do you think Frog stole the pregnancy test?"

"I gave her money to buy it, but I guess it's possible." She sifts through more pens. "What'd Akara say she stole in New York?"

"CDs, I think." I frown more. "C fucking Ds. What do people even do with them anymore? I thought they were relics."

"CDs could be portals to other dimensions. Maybe she knows something we don't."

I want to say that I could use a bunch of CDs if that's the case. To escape my problems. But my stomach twists and knots into a stale pretzel. The Sulli who runs away is long gone.

Even the idea of moving backwards makes me recoil inside.

I glance at the inked script on my wrist.

Luna adds, "Tom likes CDs. He thinks they're vintage cool."

I snort.

Luna smiles, and for a split-second, I forget the elephant in the room.

I imagine Luna asking Frog for another test. "Won't she start questioning things? She might start believing you're actually pregnant, and then she could tell her cousin, who'd find out it's not you. Then we're both fucked!" I plop back down, staring at a stain on the ceiling. "It's too risky."

Luna lies back beside me.

I turn my head, our eyes meeting.

She says, "You're probably right. It's better if you tell Akara and Banks before anyone tells them. And we haven't known Frog for that long."

I nod and take a breath.

She sits up to grab the fallen lilac gel pen.

I watch her. "So let's just say the test is right and I am pregnant." *Let's roll with that fucking tornado.*

Luna grows quieter and stares harder at her gel pens.

I frown. "Luna?" I lift myself on my elbows again.

"I'm a horrible person."

"What?" I sit up fully now. Considering all that she's done for me, plus being here as support and audience to my panic and meltdown, I'd say she's a fucking superstar.

She colors in a planet tattoo on her thigh with the milky lilac pen. The galaxy fine-line tattoo peeks out from the hem of her jean shorts. Already half-colored with different types of marker. The more she draws, the more I see she's avoiding looking at me.

"Luna," I breathe. "You're *not* a horrible person. I don't believe that one fucking bit." Where is this even coming from?

"If you were in my head, you'd know how awful I am," she whispers softly. "My first thought should have been about *supporting* you."

But it wasn't? "You have been supporting me. You're here." My muscles pull taut, and I sit really fucking still. She's my roommate in Philly. She's one of the closest friends I currently have.

Guilt reddens her eyes. "I hate what I just thought."

I swallow a rock. "What were you thinking? And hey, this is a judgment-free fucking zone. You know me, I always put my foot in my mouth."

"I don't know why I brought it up." She's quiet again, looking tormented.

I nudge her hip. "The truth will set you fucking free." That's what her mom always says. I'm clearly doing an abysmal job following this where my boyfriends are concerned, but I don't point out my hypocrisy.

Luna lets out a long breath. "You really want to know?"

I probably should just let her bad thought perish. What if it changes our friendship? But I'd rather absolve Luna from whatever's plaguing her. That's what friends do, right? We dig through the nasty shit together.

So I say, "Lay it on me."

She tucks a piece of hair behind her ear. "I thought...*I'm so happy it didn't happen to me.*"

Oh.

"Luna..." I start but I don't know what else to say. I'm not great with words.

"It's just..." She stops drawing on her knee. Her amber eyes rest against my green. "The world thinks I'm going to walk the same path as my mom. Become a sex addict. Have a surprise baby. I guess...it could still happen, but now I'm not the first, so I was just...relieved."

She doesn't seem happy now. Just remorseful.

"It's okay," I breathe.

"It's not." Her head drops.

"Yeah, it fucking is." I elbow her until she raises her head. "You're allowed to feel whatever you want to feel, and you know, I'm glad you weren't first either if it's not something you want." She's gone through a lot of hell being bullied in high school. People might think she's an easy punching bag, but she's one of the most resilient people I know.

"Do you want to have the baby then?" Luna wonders.

"I think so." I pick at my ankle bracelet. "Plan B is different from an abortion…I don't think I can abort a baby, knowing how hard it was for my mom to get pregnant, to have *me*…" I trail off, going quiet. "No part of me really wants to."

Not even now.

At twenty-two.

With *two* boyfriends.

At the Summer Games.

I expel a heavy breath. "I just need to figure out how to tell Akara and Banks about it."

Who's the father? The thought plows into me. This might change everything all over again. I don't want one of them to feel lesser because I'm having the other's baby.

Jealousy hasn't been a big factor these days, and what if that monster rears its *fugly* head?

Luna offers a sparkly turquoise gel pen. "You could write them a letter."

Not a bad idea. While I take the pen, Luna lies on her belly and stretches to the floor, whisking a notebook from her backpack.

"Should I write *two* letters? One for each?" I ask. "Fuck, what if one letter sounds better than the other one and they compare—maybe I should just write *one* and address it to both. Ugh…" I rub my eyes, stress mounting.

Upright again, Luna places the notebook on my lap. "Don't overthink."

"That's my fucking problem. I literally *can't* stop overthinking."

Luna smiles. "Whenever I get in my head, I just tell myself—*do the opposite of what Moffy would do*. No thinking, just *go*."

"Really?"

"Uh-huh. And it's kind of…you know, put me in some interesting situations. Not all great. But at least I didn't stress about it."

We're both smiling.

She's right. I need to go with the path that has the least amount of stress. For starters, I'm pretty sure stress is bad for a baby.

"One letter," I say and flip open the notebook to a blank page. "I might give it to them the next time we cross paths." Which I hope is soon. Despite carrying this massive secret, I miss having my boyfriends around me. "Decision fucking made."

Telling them *before* trying to qualify for semifinals is probably not the best timing. But telling them *after* isn't great timing either.

A knock sounds on the door as I scribble out a few words.

"I've got it." Luna hops off the bed.

I glance down at my progress.

Dear Banks. Dear Kits.

I'm pregnant. And I'm keeping this little champ.

Champ. That word just came out of me like a second breath. I can practically hear my dad calling me *champ* for those confidence boosts. I stare at the letter for a long moment.

"It's better if you two just stay inside." Thatcher's voice rips me from my reverie.

What is he doing here?

Luna lets six-foot-seven Thatcher fucking Moretti inside. Stern, serious, and an awkward root among this messy tree that is my fucking life.

He was never cheering for my relationship with Banks *and* Akara. Now he says he supports us together, but it's obvious I'm not his favorite person. Being an untidy roommate doesn't help.

"What's going on?" I ask tensely.

Thatcher shuts and locks the door behind him. He's in full security mode. Black slacks. Black button-down. Mic wire running up to his ear.

"I'm here to grab your lunch orders," Thatcher says stiffly.

"It's that packed?" I told security I didn't want to go to the caf if it's above 90% capacity. Other athletes gawking and staring at me, I can take. But I've been bombarded with selfie requests since I showed up at the Olympic Village, and to maintain some level of focus, I'm trying to avoid that.

"It's peak lunchtime."

My ribs tighten. Hey, at least reporters and press aren't allowed in the Olympic Village. That's a small victory.

"What about the gym? I have to train later."

"We'll ensure the entrance to the gym is clear."

I exhale, then rest my chin on my knee. As Luna comes back over, I say, "You can go have lunch in the caf, if you want. I don't want to trap you here with me."

"You aren't trapping me." She sinks down on the bed. I must need the extra assurance because she elbows my side until I end up smiling and elbowing her back.

We both laugh a little.

Thatcher remains.

Putting an awkwardness in the air, and maybe it's me. Maybe *I'm* not making him feel more welcome. I want to rewrite our relationship, but all I can think is, *I wish Akara and Banks were here.*

"Where's Banks?" I ask, already knowing Kits can't miss an SFO meeting that he's running. But Banks can.

"Busy," Thatcher says curtly. "Akara sent me to help." He glances between Luna and me. "Lunch orders?"

"Surprise me," Luna sing-songs.

"Oh no, no surprise for me," I say quickly. "A chocolate protein smoothie is good."

He nods, and I swear he wavers for half a second. Then he turns to leave. My pulse races as Luna's words creep in.

No thinking, just go.

"Hey, Thatcher. Can I tell you something?"

He pauses at the door.

Luna bites the end of her gel pen, eyes wide.

If I really, *really* consider what the fuck I'm doing, maybe I'd realize that *no thinking, just go* is in the same vein as *feel the moment*. And feeling the moment hasn't always worked out in my total favor.

But then again, I think I wouldn't change anything.

For as hard as this year has been, for as many tears I've spilled and for as strongly as I've clung to my boyfriends, my heart hasn't been empty. It's been so awfully fucking full on this great and daring adventure. All with the men I love.

"Yeah?" Thatcher asks.

No thinking. Just go.

Feel the moment.

Come what may.

Forward.

Onward.

"I'm pregnant," I say.

His hand falls off the knob. His jaw tightens. "Say again?"

I think he heard me, so I don't bother. Instead, I offer some fucking details, since his *show no emotion* stance has accelerated my pulse. "I found out at the Opening Ceremony. Banks and Akara don't know."

"Who's the father?" Thatcher asks and immediately cringes when he says it.

For some reason, I don't even flinch. I always expected the question. And it's only a shock that Luna never asked.

"I don't know. And I don't know when I should tell them."

His brows rise. "You have to tell them *now*."

"Now?" I blanch.

"She hasn't finished her letter." Luna glares.

"Letter?" Thatcher frowns and shakes his head. "I don't care. You need to tell them today. If you're pregnant, your security is at even more risk."

It's like a bat to my gut. "Security," I whisper out the word like it's a curse. "Is that all you can fucking think about? Is that all I am to you? Your brother's client?"

Thatcher crosses his arms. "Sulli—"

"I'm his *girlfriend.*"

His jaw clenches even harder.

"Your wife is pregnant," I point out, hearing my voice rising, and I spring off the bed but stay at a fuming stance, throwing my arms out. "Shouldn't you be with her? Shouldn't you be worrying about *her* security in L.A.?!" *Not mine.*

Get out of my fucking life, Thatcher!

I'm boiling. But I'm not so petulant that I'd unleash *all* of this unbridled anger at him. Thatcher still means something to me. He's Banks' *twin.* He's Jane's husband.

I'm not trying to shred our awkward relationship apart, but I hate that he's trying to boss me around. Trying to dictate when I tell Banks and Akara the biggest news of my life. And I swear if he condemns my letter, I'm going to throw a gel pen at him.

Hurt flares through his stoic features.

I realize the softest pieces of Thatcher are where Jane resides.

"You can't even know how much I worry about Jane." His voice carries an aching strain of love. "She's five-months pregnant, and there's not a day that I haven't been..." He swallows hard, and shifts his harsh glare to the wall. He even pinches his eyes before he looks back to me. "What I'm feeling, my brother and Akara will feel a million times over for *you.* Your threat level right now is beyond anything—"

"I know," I cut in, frustrated. "I fucking know that!"

"Then tell them."

"I will!"

"Now."

I want to scream and strangle him.

Luna looks between us. Silence tenses the room in uncomfortable strains. No one budging from their stance.

"Sulli is competing in the *Olympics* tomorrow," Luna pipes in. "Shouldn't she have a choice when she tells her boyfriends about this?"

"Fucking thank you," I say the same time that Thatcher answers, "No."

I gape. "What?"

Has he lost his mind?

"It's a security issue," Thatcher says, but he shakes his head like he's conflicted too. His face screws up in some emotion. "I know it's also a personal issue. I don't want to take this choice away from you."

"Then don't. Trust me that I'll tell them."

"When?"

"Soon." Do I have to give him an exact timeline?

By the angst in his eyes, he needs one. Why did I think Thatcher would give me *advice* about when to tell his brother this news? Why did I think I was talking to someone who cares about me?

Hurt pools around me, and it's hard to swim out.

Thatcher must see the pain cross my face because he adds, "What about by tonight?"

"Tomorrow night."

He thinks, then nods resolutely. "Okay. By tomorrow night."

I appreciate him letting up a bit.

He looks me over for a second. "Can you even compete while you're pregnant?"

"Serena Williams," I say strongly. "The Australian Open. Kerri Walsh Jennings. The 2012 London Olympics. Kristie Moore, Sarah Brown. They all competed while pregnant," I tell Thatcher. I didn't even need to look up these names recently. When I was sixteen and had my eye on gold, I thought maybe one day I'd have a family. I wanted to know if I could still compete if I was pregnant. So many women already proved that it's possible.

"How far along were they?" Thatcher asks.

"Alysia Montaño," I say. "The 2014 U.S. track and field championships. She ran the 800 meter while eight-months pregnant." And I can't be more than five-weeks.

Thatcher nods a few times. "I don't doubt your skills for a second, Sulli."

"I know," I say. "You just doubt how I'm handling my relationship with your brother."

He doesn't say anything to that. He just goes back to the door. "A surprise lunch and a smoothie." With our lunch orders hanging in the air, he leaves.

Luna blows out a breath. "He's intense."

"Yeah," I agree. I go back to the notebook. "I'm sure everyone's going to think this baby news will distract me."

Luna smiles. "It won't." She doesn't phrase it like a question.

"Nope," I say. "Because when this baby grows up, I don't want them to *ever* think that they were the reason I didn't win gold. So there's only one solution." I take a determined breath. "Win."

8

Banks Moretti

"LET'S RUN IT AGAIN," Akara says to Omega.

No one groans or lets out a wave of complaints. All of us, especially me, realizes how important these next two weeks are. I have my head in my notes app.

Donnelly raises a hand. "Which one, boss?"

Akara snaps his finger to his palm. "All of them."

We've been running through about a million-and-one assbackwards, twizzle-fucked scenarios. The stadium pool is open to ticketed guests. The public.

Which means more bodies will be walking and frolicking around. Strangers. Reporters. Fans. Motherfuckers who *hate* these famous families. Who *hate* our clients.

Who *hate* Sulli.

Other athletes have been the only threat in the gated and highly secured Olympic Village. But soon, swim events will be more complicated and more dangerous.

Akara rests his elbows on the conference table. "Starting briefly, we'll go into the 'Core 6 are targeted' scenario."

Core 6 = the parents.

Donnelly scribbles notes in a small flip-up notepad. Reading glasses perched on his nose. My coffee has gone stale and cold, but I take a large gulp anyway and listen. Cold air blows into the tiny conference room. Chairs filled by Akara, Farrow, Oscar, Donnelly, and Gabe. Turkey wraps and deli sandwiches are spread out on the table for SFO.

The only person missing in action is my brother.

I cast a momentary glance at the door.

I thought about volunteering for Sulli's lunch-run. Just to see my girlfriend. But I shouldn't miss a briefing. I can't fuck up because my head isn't screwed on right and my priorities are jacked.

"...we're supposed to jump in wherever necessary," Oscar recounts the decision.

"Farrow?" Akara asks him to elaborate.

Farrow pops a bubblegum bubble with casualness. Guy has the demeanor of someone with their feet-kicked-on-a-table even without his boots touching the surface. "Security Force Alpha will be focused on the parents, but if they need help, we have to help. Simple as that."

"Banks?" Akara looks to me.

My brows pinch, a little disgruntled that he called on me after two Yale grads. I'm not a dumb fuck, but I'd rather stay quiet during this class.

He sees.

"Donnelly?" Akara asks, skipping over me.

I'd smile and kick my feet back, but Oscar lets out a choking noise. "What the hell, Kitsuwon? We aren't going to wait for Banks to answer?"

"He doesn't have one, guys."

"You become a mind reader or what?" Donnelly wonders, slipping the pen behind his ear.

"Eh, sounds more like special privileges," Farrow says.

Gabe scoots forward. "Where can I get those?"

The conference room falls dead at the unsaid answer: *you have to be dating Sulli.*

Awkward silence. We're all sitting in it. The Yale boys stare between me and Akara like we're in bed together.

And we are.

Literally. Figuratively.

Guilt roils up inside me. Akara isn't exactly losing respect with SFO, but his give-no-fucks attitude is drawing a strange line between us and them.

He tenses. "Guys—"

"I got it," I interject, not wanting him to dig a deeper hole. "We were talking about the parents." I try to backtrack. "If we have to leave behind our client, temps will shift onto them once we put in the call on comms."

Olympics have become "help the most threatened" kind of security.

There've been events where we've all had each other's backs. Everyone agreed this is the best tactic because it'll ensure a fortified barrier against a threat.

Akara switches scenarios. We rehash hecklers targeting the oldest five (Jane, Maximoff, Charlie, Beckett, Sullivan) to hecklers targeting Baby Ripley to fans encroaching our clients' space in the stadium. And after we fly through those, Akara announces another, "Pregnancy Emergency."

Farrow combs a hand through his bleach-white hair. "With Jane or Millie Kay?"

"Millie Kay. You start off."

He chews gum slowly. "She'll be around me and Maximoff. I don't see her leaving our side. It's not like she knows any of you fuckers that well, besides Thatcher."

I lift a shoulder. *True.*

Every time I've run into Millie Kay Miller at the penthouse, she's on her way out or in. Barely says a fuckin' word. Like she's intimidated or starstruck by half of us. What I know: she's twenty-four, born in Iowa, and currently the surrogate carrying Maximoff & Farrow's child.

Their baby is due one month after my brother's baby.

"In the case that Millie Kay needs medical assistance," Akara says, "there'll be a complete rotation in bodyguards to make sure she gets out of the stadium as fast as possible." I listen as Akara dives into details and then transitions into Jane's pregnancy.

Pregnant emergencies are something I hate we have to consider. Hell, I've prayed to about seven different saints to avoid *that* situation. But if one does come up, we have a plan.

The door opens.

Hello, Cinderella.

Thatcher enters with a chocolate smoothie and a Styrofoam to-go container. Look, I don't like when people compare us, and fuck me when I do it to myself. But *I'm* the one that loses everything.

I know my brother didn't lose his way to Sulli's room.

"What's up?" Akara asks him, zeroing in on the food. "Is Sulli okay?" He touches his mic, about to radio the temp guard, but Thatcher gives him a stiff, hearty nod.

So Akara slowly drops his hand.

For a blip of a second, Thatcher looks to me, and I swear something is torn up in his gaze. My best guess: my brother is having a fuckin' tug-of-war in his head.

I just hope it's not about me or Akara or Sulli.

"You miss us, Thatch?" Donnelly slips off his reading glasses.

"I'd bet five on *yes*," Oscar adds. "He made a pit stop just to say hi."

Farrow rolls his eyes. "He hasn't said anything yet."

"So you want to put five on *no*, Redford?"

I jump in, "Thatcher?" My frown deepens. *Is this about his wife?* "Is Janie okay?"

"Yeah." He nods, just as stiffly as before. One tensed breath later, he places the smoothie and to-go carton in front of me. "You take these to Sulli and Luna."

Confusion eats at me, but a strange urgency pushes me harder. I stand up, shoving my chair in, and whisper, "Why couldn't you do it?" *He said Sulli is fine.*

No.

He *nodded* to Akara.

Is that the same thing?

Unholy shit, my mind is whirling at five jarring speeds.

Wouldn't he think it'd be more important for me to be in this meeting? That's why he went to take their lunch orders in the first place. During the event, he'll be in the stands on Jane's detail and I'll be on the ground protecting the Olympian where more scenarios for failure exist.

He's cagey as fuck as he bends towards my ear. Whispering, he says, "You need to go talk to your girlfriend."

I cast a glance at Akara.

He mouths, *what is it?*

I shake my head, unsure, but I fist Thatcher's shirt and drag him over to the wall. Drag is a harsh word for what I do, considering his big, coordinated feet do a good job of following my movement.

"*Banks.*"

"Thatcher," I snap, drawing us further away from the Yale boys and Gabe and unfortunately Akara.

Get this right: I'm not about to rush out without Akara, my *metamour*—not when Thatcher's giving me absolute shit to go off of. I love my brother like something deep. And beneath his serious features, I can tell he's cut up over…

Over what?

"It can wait?" I ask him.

"No. It can't." He rakes a hand through his hair.

"What's going on?"

Thatcher would've used comms and radioed in an emergency. Christ, he would've *never* left my girlfriend if she were in trouble. He'd throw himself in front of a speeding train for Sulli. And I know that's been hard for her to believe—considering he's not warm and fuzzy—but he'd die for her without thought.

I know if I'm the six-seven teddy bear to Sulli, he's the fucking grizzly.

With our backs to the conference table, Thatcher growls out a frustrated noise. "I can't say."

"You can't say?" I scoff.

"Are you a fucking parrot?" he growls. "Yeah, I can't fucking say."

"Jeeesus." I hold up a hand, now confused *and* concerned.

He pinches his eyes and blows out a hot breath. "Just go talk to her," he says, voice rising just as Akara slides into our two-man huddle.

Akara whispers hotly, "I thought you said Sulli is fine?" He fits on a baseball cap backwards, waiting for my brother to speak. It takes him a second.

Thatcher rubs his face roughly. "Cutthemeetingshort." He slurs all of that together.

"What was that?" Akara asks, breathing harder in alarm.

"He said *cut the meeting short*," I translate.

"It's an emergency?" Akara asks tensely. "*Thatcher.*"

He's not speaking. Just shaking his head. "Forget it—"

"No," Akara and I say in unison.

The Yale boys are definitely staring. We all rotate a little more. Backs to them. Akara whispers, "Whatever strain there is between you and me"—he motions from his chest to Thatcher's—"it shouldn't get in the way of security. And it shouldn't be at the cost of anyone we *love*, man. If this were about Jane, I wouldn't be biting my tongue. Don't tell me we're *that* far gone, you and me."

Thatcher cranes his neck backwards. Staring painfully at the ceiling. "I already said too much. I shouldn't have said a thing." He groans into his hand. "I need to unfuck this."

"Unfuck it by telling us facts," I urge.

"I can't!"

"Yeah, you can!"

"She's pregnant!" he screams.

It physically jerks me back.

Akara has a hand over his mouth.

"*Fuck. Fuck.*" Thatcher touches his forehead like he's in deep shit.

I'm frozen cold. Barely processing.

Akara shifts his weight, then drops his hand. "You mean Jane—Jane's the pregnant one."

"I wasn't supposed to say anything," Thatcher says tightly, barely even looking at me or Akara. "Fucking Christ." He stares pained at the door.

So it is Sulli?

Sulli is pregnant.

I'm wide-eyed.

"No, *no*." Akara shakes his head with a slight laugh. "This doesn't make sense, man. Why would she tell you before me or Banks?"

"I don't fucking know, but I wish she didn't."

"Who's pregnant?" Gabe asks from the conference table.

"Lovely," Akara mutters under his breath. All of SFO heard Thatcher's outburst. Can't fault him. I pushed my brother there.

At least the Yale boys are shaking their head at Gabe to shut the fuck up. While they whisper to him, I exchange a severe look with Akara.

"We're going now?" I question. "Because I can't wait here knowing she could be…she's…" Why can't I say it? Why does it feel more unbelievable now than back when the condom ripped? Worse than anything is knowing she's been alone with this knowledge. For how long?

Part of me is happy that she told my brother.

Maybe she needed to confide in him.

God, I hope he wasn't a complete idiot and pushed her away or said something stupid.

"Yeah, you and I are leaving," Akara confirms, which eases me. To my brother, he says fast, "Take over. We were about to discuss the Fire Alarm Scenario." *Where some shitbag pulls the fire alarm.*

Like a bullet, I grab the to-go container and smoothie and bolt out of the conference room. Akara isn't on my ass. He's not leading the way.

He's at my side.

All this time we've been going over different Worst-Case scenarios.

We didn't think about this one.

Our girlfriend being pregnant.

Is it even a "worst case"? Am I that upset about it?

My emotions are hard to pick apart. Hard to pin down. What's *worse* to me right now, I have no idea how Sulli is coping with this news. And I have no idea what Akara is thinking. Is he in denial like when he flirted with Sulli and said he didn't? Has he been sling-shotted back into that ether, and will I have to pull him out?

9

Akara Kitsuwon

SULLIVAN MINNIE MEADOWS. The competitive, ever-endearing Meadows girl who I spent the majority of my career protecting. The girl who wishes she were a mermaid. The girl who eats donuts like a cliché cop in a sitcom. The girl who's hotter, inside and out, than every Disney princess combined (sorry not sorry, Ariel).

Sulli isn't just a babe.

She's *my* babe. *Our* babe, and now…she's pregnant.

When that *really* sinks in, my first thought crashes into me:

I'm not going anywhere.

No inkling or microscope piece of me is willing to self-eject. I physically can't give Sulli up. I physically can't give Banks up. I know what it feels like to leave, and I'd *never* walk into that pain again. So to hang on or to let go isn't even a question anymore.

I'm superglued to what I love. And I love them.

I just can't let a *dang* thing happen to what we've built together. What we fought to keep solid. It has to stay intact. No matter what we face.

Even a baby.

Pressure tries to bear on me. Because *I know* this could change our well-oiled, fortified dynamic into something more fragile. Vulnerable. At risk of a fatal blow.

I wish I could snap my fingers and magically appear beside Sulli. (Yeah, magic doesn't exist.) But the trek to her is like sprinting on nails, then *sitting* on nails.

Banks and I have climbed into a self-driving shuttle. No other people onboard. We pick seats in the middle. Doors slide shut, and the shuttle drives us away from the office building and to residential housing for athletes, coaches, and some security.

I check the time on my watch.

Screw this five-minute ride.

I'm impatient. Sue me.

Or don't—I'm definitely *squeezed* on cash and running up a credit card bill. Lawsuits aren't exactly in my budget plan this year.

Money.

Security.

Sulli's safety.

A baby.

Our *baby's* safety.

SFO.

The team.

More babies coming.

Baby Ripley.

Ugh, my brain is too full of responsibilities.

Banks places a hand on my jostling leg.

"Sorry," I sigh out, then shake my head, my phone clenched in a fist. "We should text her."

"And tell her what?" Banks asks. "Heard you were pregnant? Congrats? Heart emoji, thumbs-up emoji, hashtag proud dads?"

I almost laugh, but the sound catches against my dry throat. "I was thinking more along the lines of, *we heard you're pregnant. It's okay. We're on our way to you.* Something like that." I pause. "Plus, some heart emojis."

Banks cracks a fleeting smile. "Wouldn't it just be better to tell her face-to-face?"

"Probably." I try to lean back against the seat, but my shoulders are stiff. Body rigid like I'm a teenager again, about to be called into a ring for a Muay Thai fight. "How long do you think she's been dealing with this on her own?" I groan in realization. "She was nervous yesterday, *shit.*"

Banks barely slugs me for cursing. And he nods a couple times. "Her nerves weren't about carrying the flag."

I pry off my baseball cap, running a coarser hand through my black hair. "She felt like she couldn't tell us. Like we'd be upset or angry?"

"No," Banks shakes his head. "She was probably just scared. We have a lot goin' on with security. She's about to swim her fuckin' heart out on an Olympic stage, and this is a wrench in our plans to keep her safe and her goal to win gold."

I've always prided myself on *knowing* Sulli, on understanding what makes her tic and smile and frown, but sometimes I think Banks sees her in a completely different way than me. I like that he does because he helps put everything into clearer perspective.

"She's pregnant," I say that truth out loud. No cameras on the shuttle. No press. No driver. No other people. We're alone to really *process*.

Banks yanks at the collar of his white tee, the word *security* printed across in black letters. It's hot in the shuttle, and I reach up and fiddle with the vents. As cold air blows on us, he says, "It's not as clear-cut who the dad could be like last time."

I cringe. "*Last time.* How did this happen *again*?"

"When a dick goes inside a pussy—" He cuts himself off, laughing when I flash him a *shut up, Banks* look. "Careful what you ask for, Nine."

That makes me smile. Until I think about our dicks going inside Sulli. "We were careful," I say like it's known. "You ever remember a condom tearing again?"

"No, but it coulda been a small hole." He raises his shoulders. "She's not on birth control, man. Accidents happen."

I have a flashback of Ryke jumping down our throats for the *first* accident. I exhale a heavy breath. "Ryke is going to *fudging* murder us."

"Don't worry, I'll keep you safe."

How is Banks so dang chill about our girlfriend's father? "I need to keep *you* safe, Mr. We Already Touched Her, Sir."

I haven't forgotten Banks' death wish when he rubbed the salt in Ryke's wound and basically admitted to being *all over* Sulli.

Banks laughs a little and adjusts his earpiece as comms crackle. It's nice to hear him laugh. Especially since the incident. Hypervigilance and Banks can be an intense combo, but I know it's necessary at times.

I pass my phone from left hand to right.

Right to left.

Left to right. And I exhale slowly. "I always thought if Sulli and I had a baby, it'd be planned."

Banks smiles. "Welcome to the Accidental Pregnancy Club. Only perks of this membership are confusion and uncertainty about the possibility of being a father."

I try to relax. "I don't even want to revoke the membership. Not at the opportunity of sharing a child with her."

"I know the feeling."

It's not something either of us will pass up.

Comms go off in my ear. "Temp guards Keagan and Frog to SFO… is this thing on?" *Frog.* I pinch the bridge of my nose as I listen to her. "…uh, yeah, I guess it's working. Whatever. We're in the gym with Luna and Sulli. Peace out, motherfuckers."

Banks loses it. He laughs so hard, and I think his laughter is directed at my *why me?* face. Why did Frog have to come into my life? Why did I agree to make her a temp guard?

I grab my mic, about to respond, but it hits me. The gym is closest to the offices—where we just came from. "We're going the wrong fracking way."

"Fuck," Banks curses and barrels up to the front of the shuttle, to-go container and smoothie in hand. I follow suit. We hit the stop button and launch ourselves out.

Screw waiting for another shuttle. We *run.*

We run back to where we came from. Headed for Sulli.

10

Sullivan Meadows

THE OLYMPIC VILLAGE is outfitted with a three-story gym, equipped with the latest and greatest exercise equipment. Epic, for fucking sure. But it's not the gym of my dreams. That spot will always be claimed by Studio 9.

The third floor is the quietest. And I've secluded myself in a corner away from the other athletes. Fit with a weight bench, stair climber, and spin bike.

None of which are really being used at the moment.

Luna sits backwards on the bike. I'm idle on the stair climber, caging breath and watching Beckett and Maximoff on the weight bench.

They're reading the letter.

My letter that I wrote in gel pen. The one I plan to give to Banks and Akara later today. Or tomorrow, depending on unpredictable fucking factors. Like maybe I'll faint.

Maybe I'll lose the letter and get laryngitis.

Who knows?!

I'm not freaking out. I'm not freaking out. Obviously, I'm really, really freaking the fuck out. I chew the corner of my lip. When Moffy and Beckett showed up, I wanted to tell them the truth. I couldn't hold it in, and I figured this could be a test.

See if the letter is any fucking good.

"Are you going to say anything?" I ask Beckett, my best friend, and Moffy, who's the closest thing I have to a big brother.

"Oh wow!" Ripley says in his itty-bitty baby voice. His blue eyes grow big and astonished. He's climbed up beside Moffy and acts like he's reading the letter with his dad.

At a year and a half, he's the cutest fucking baby.

Will mine be that cute? Or will mine come out looking like a wrinkly old lady or dude?

"This is Auntie Sulli's letter, little guy. Be careful with it," Moffy tells his son as he tries to touch the paper.

Ripley gasps. "Awe Sow-wee?" His big blue eyes meet mine. He gasps again, then babbles. My heart swells. To Luna, he says, "Awe Loonee?"

Luna smiles.

"Yeah, it's mine, little dude," I tell him. "You want to bring it to me?"

Moffy lets Ripley hold the letter. The baby treats the paper like the Mona Lisa. Gingerly touching the edges before sliding off the weight bench.

Then he accidentally drops it. "Oh no! Oh no!" Ripley says, so cute that I catch Beckett, Luna, and Maximoff's smile. But my pulse is pounding not knowing what Beckett or Moffy think.

The baby squats, collects the letter, then rushes to me. "Awe Sow-wee."

"Thanks, Ripley."

He giggles, his smile dimpling his soft, fair cheeks with a rosy hue. He acts like he might want a hug, but he shuffles timidly back. Shy. Quickly, he races to his dad and climbs up on the weight bench. He hides behind Maximoff's arm.

Ripley will squish his stuffed animals and parents to fucking death, but with most everyone else, he likes his distance. Like he knows the world is cruel already.

Being a parent, dealing with the complexities of watching a tiny being grow up, trying to guide them into thoughtful, kind humans amid the ugly spotlight of the world—am I really ready for that?

I have to be.

Moffy lifts his gaze to me. Here it goes. His thoughts. His wisdom. "Are you okay?"

It nearly breaks me. His empathy. "Yeah...I think...I think so." *I hope so.* "I just need to tell Kits and Banks and then go from there."

Beckett lets out a long breath. "I think I'm in shock."

"Oh hey, that's where I've been," I tell him. "I get it."

He tries to give me an encouraging smile. "The letter is really good."

"Yeah?" I reread my brief words. "You think they'll like it?"

"They better," Moffy says toughly, protectively.

"Agreed," Beckett chimes in.

"Or else they'll have colossal hell to pay from this section of your fan club." Maximoff gestures to the three of them. "Avengers Assemble."

Luna flashes a Spock hand.

Beckett smiles a little more, but a sadness lies behind his yellow-green eyes that I didn't expect.

"What's wrong, Beckett?"

"I just didn't think it'd happen this fast. You, having a family like Jane and Moffy."

"Hey, you're not losing me," I remind him. "You can't. We're best friends for fucking ever. BFFFE's."

Luna looks a little downtrodden. More than I realized. Is she scared that I'll grow out of our friendship too?

Beckett just nods.

Having a baby won't catapult me out of Beckett and Luna's friendship circle, right? We'll all stay just as close? We can still eavesdrop on Maximoff and Jane when they're doing their couples thing at the penthouse, and we can stay up late eating s'mores and gummy worms.

Nothing will change between us.

Everything will change.

Am I making a mistake?

"SULLI!" Frankie shouts across the third floor.

Beckett and Maximoff turn their heads. We all see the platinum-blonde swimmer waving dramatically near the rowing machines.

Athletes start to gawk in my direction. Some even pull down their headphones.

Ugh fuck.

I want to shrink into myself or hide behind my bodyguard. But Kits and Banks aren't here, and I barely know my temp guard Keagan. Not well enough to use him as a human shield.

Frankie calls out to me, "Pump that iron, superstar!"

"Get it, girl!" I shout back our encouragements, but with less fucking enthusiasm and more *holy shit* tension in my face. Feels like *everyone* is staring. A Canadian athlete snaps photos of me and my cousins from his weight bench.

He captures Beckett's disgruntled face and black leather jacket coolness. I avoid staring into the lens of his camera phone.

Ignore.

Ignore.

I try to block it all out like Maximoff and Jane are always able to do. "That's Frankie," I tell them.

No one is shocked.

Not only have I talked about Frankie a ton, but she's been deemed the "biggest threat" to my chance at gold. Press won't shut up about it. But I'd rather them talk about that swim rivalry than the flagbearer drama.

Maximoff cracks a couple knuckles, then focuses back on me. "You want to tell Jane about you-know-what?"

Jane's absence at the gym is felt, but it's not like I disinvited her. She's been busy shopping for Olympic souvenirs with the girl squad today.

"Not particularly," I admit, feeling like shit though. I should want to embrace Jane. "I just don't want to be compared to Jane."

Beckett's eyes soften. "You won't be compared to my sister. At least not by me."

"She's pregnant, though, Beckett."

"Isn't that a bigger reason to see her?" Maximoff asks with furrowed brows. "Talk to her?"

"She was trying to have a baby, Moffy. And everyone was so *happy* for Jane. No one's going to be that happy for me—and I just…" I intake a breath. "I don't want to see a very pregnant Jane right now." I withhold my prickly feelings towards her husband. I wouldn't put that on Jane.

"We are happy for you, Sul," Moffy says strongly. "You can do this. You can do anything. You're a kickass human being, and I believe in you." He's said something similar when we were younger. When I thought I broke my ankle on a hike and he carried me through the desert.

Ever since I confirmed my relationship in the treehouse, Maximoff Hale has been the strongest force of nature against *anyone* who's against me, Akara, and Banks. He's vouched for us on a late-night talk show when they sprung a question on him.

He's advocated polyamorous relationships on his social media.

He's punched a heckler. (Farrow had to restrain him.)

He's condemned everyone who said I couldn't make it. Who said my love would fail. He has so much hope in my poly romance.

In me.

I see inside his tough green eyes that he is so unconditionally *happy* for me. Enough that he stands up, comes over, and wraps his arms around me.

I hold on tight. "I love you, Mof."

"I love you too, Sul."

Tears prick my eyes, and when we pull apart, I see two men barreling towards me like their feet are on fire. One beefcake.

One dreamboat.

One very anxious *me*. "Oh fuck." Here we go, part two. Letter in hand, I step off the stair climber.

They pause briefly at the cluster of temp guards, who remain out of earshot. Akara speaks to them for point-one seconds before keeping pace.

Their destination is me.

Partly, I'm fucking excited to see them. My lips tic into a smile, then flatline like my pulse. Fuck, am I even breathing?

You can do this.

You're a kickass human being.

"We'll be in the stands cheering you on, hot shot," Beckett says, suddenly right in front of me. "See you tomorrow." I'm on automatic, hugging him while my mind is on my boyfriends. He seems to notice and smiles when we pull back. "You won't choke." At first, I think he's referring to my swim events, but then he says, "They love you. You can't mess this up."

He knows I'm freaking about the pregnancy announcement.

"Thanks, Beckett." He squeezes my hand before he exits.

Maximoff picks up Ripley, and he gives me another side-hug. Baby Ripley buries his face into his dad's chest, hiding from me.

Let's just hope Banks and Akara don't have similar reactions.

In a flash, Moffy and Beckett are gone, and my boyfriends have arrived—and it suddenly dawns on me. They're delivering our food.

Where's Thatcher?

Why are they out of breath? Why do they look so fucking intense?

Questions swarm me, my pulse hiking up a million notches. "What are you guys doing here?" I sound accusatory. I cringe at myself, feeling dizzy with adrenaline. "I didn't mean it in a bad way—I'm glad you're here. Don't you guys have a VIFM to be at?"

Banks hands Luna the to-go container, then passes me the smoothie. Everything feels *tense*. Banks is searching my gaze, his muscles flexed. Kits is standing like I'm on the brink of a cliff and he's gripping my wrist for dear life.

"Yay food." Luna hops off the bike. She makes an uh-oh face like she's dismounted into a mess.

This mess is trademarked, certified Triad Turbulence.

Akara speaks. "The *very important fucking meeting* is not nearly as important as you, string bean." His inaccurate (but cute, I'll cop to it), nickname for me doesn't sound playful on his lips. He's too uptight.

"Kits?" My breathing is sporadic. "Banks?"

Don't tell me…?

Do they…?

"Sulli," Akara says with complete concern.

Banks' gaze drops to my belly.

"Oh my fucking God," I breathe. "He told you?!" I shout it.

I'm so stupid.

I cover my burning face with my hand as the gym goes dead silent. As heads turn. As athletes gawk again.

I feel my boyfriends' comforting arms on my shoulders. I feel them shielding me, and with my free hand, I grab onto a waist. Must be Akara, since my fingers brush his clip of keys.

With an angered breath, I uncover my face. "Thatcher *promised* he'd let me tell you." I lower my voice. "I need to go." I try to push away from them.

"Where are you going?" Akara asks fast.

"To kick him in the nuts!" I don't care that I yell it.

"You're gonna have to kick me in the nuts because I forced it out of him, mermaid." Banks looks remorseful. "Don't hate my brother, please."

I expel a pained breath. I don't want to hate him. Dizzy again, I turn to Luna. "Is this a dream?"

She sticks her finger in her mouth and then pops it out like she's checking the wind. "We seem to be in this universe."

"Fuuuuck," I exhale, trying to catch my breath. I look up at Banks. "I don't hate him, but your brother is a big dick." I blush. "Not because his dick is big—I've never seen it."

Fuck words. I hate them.

Banks has a shadow of a smile.

Akara laughs a little.

It eases the tension, and I explain, "Thatcher told me I had until tomorrow night to tell you before he'd open his big fucking mouth."

"That is a dick move," Banks agrees.

Akara nods. "Thatcher is dead to us."

Banks is in no mood for killing Thatcher jokes. "Says the guy who'd fall to his knees to be best friends with my brother again."

Akara makes a face. "I would *not* do that."

This is all fucking jumbled.

Luna eats a piece of sushi from the to-go container. "I'm supposed to meet up with Eliot and Tom. See ya tomorrow?"

"Yeah." I hug Luna before she goes.

"Bye, Luna," Akara says.

Banks nods goodbye, and Luna waves on her way out.

Akara scans the semi-public gym and the ogling athletes. "Let's go somewhere more private."

We end up in an aerobics room. Wooden floors, wall-to-wall mirrors, kettle bells, and ankle weights in baskets—I'm seated on a yoga ball. Bouncing slightly while my boyfriends tower above me.

Jeez, they're tall.

I don't really care to be the same height as them.

Tower over me. Protect me.

Please, always love me.

No matter where we go from here.

"You already know the truth, but I wrote this for both of you." I hand them the letter.

Akara takes it first, but they read together.

Very quiet. All I hear is my heavy breath.

"That's what Thatcher told you, right?" For a moment, I wonder if I'm totally off. What if I assumed wrong? "Right?"

Right?!

"Yeah," Akara answers, giving Banks the letter. And Banks carefully slips the paper into his back pocket while Akara tells me, "We knew you were pregnant, which is why we left the meeting."

The boss of SFO left his own meeting. My lips part in surprise. He could've just sent Banks, but he's here too. Something surges strongly inside my lungs.

To have them both so *fully*—that means everything to me.

"I wanted to keep the baby," I tell them before they can say a thing. My heart is lodged in my throat.

"Wanted?" Akara frowns.

"I think this might be a mistake."

11

Akara Kitsuwon

MISTAKE.

Mistake?

That word…

It crushes me, and I feel myself clawing at the letters.

Banks breathes as hard as I'm breathing. Like we're still racing after her. Like we're still chasing towards Sulli.

"It doesn't have to be a mistake," I say tightly, throat knotted.

She bounces a little on the yoga ball and stares at the floor-length mirror. I think she's studying her body. Maybe picturing her belly swollen and round. Or maybe that's just me.

Imagining.

Why is it so dang hot in here? I take off my baseball cap, shoving the thing in my back pocket.

Banks speaks, his voice deep and almost as raspy as hers. "I want what you want, Sulli—you know I do."

"I know, Banks." Her voice cracks a little. Before I chime in, she looks to me. "I know you do too, Kits."

I can barely nod. My neck is tensed. *I can't lose her. I can't lose the three of us.* I push back my hair a few times, but the black strands continue to fall into my eyelashes.

Need to cut my hair.

Such an unhelpful *fudging* thought.

"Why do you think it's one?" Banks asks. "A mistake?"

"There couldn't be a worse time, could there? I'm on *international* news swimming for Team USA. The world is watching me closer than ever." She springs off the yoga ball, then tucks her arms around her athletic frame.

I try to take a step forward.

She takes a step back, then rotates slightly away from us. Head hung. My pulse ascends. And a rock is in my ribcage.

"Sul—"

"Why do I feel fucking ashamed?" she asks, voice trembling.

"Because the world is dog crap. Because this wasn't planned. Because people will have nasty opinions, but at the end of the day, you need to remember something, Lady Meadows." I try to smile to bring one out of her.

She fights to lift her lips. "What?"

"Banks and I *love* you. Adore you. Would kneel at your feet and worship you." I actually drop to my knees at our girlfriend's feet.

Banks, with a shadow of a smile, follows suit.

Sulli chokes on a surprised sound, sniffing back emotion. "Stop." She smiles. "Get up."

We don't, but Banks lifts one knee and rests his elbow on his thigh. He catches his hand into hers. "What happened came from an act of love, planned or not—and fuck anyone who says it didn't."

Her chin quakes. "Fuck...I didn't realize..." She wipes her glassy eyes. "I really needed to hear that." As we pick ourselves up to our feet, Sulli questions, "You guys don't think it's bad timing?"

Banks raises his shoulder. "The Olympics aren't that long, mermaid. Two weeks and we'll be home."

"It's a blip," I agree.

"It's not a blip to me," Sulli mutters, staring at the floorboards of the aerobics room. Her green eyes glass again. "And fuck, maybe it's not just the bad timing, okay? Maybe it's more."

Banks frowns. "What do you mean?"

My eyes burn.

She looks between us, scared. Unsure. "Is it even fair to bring a baby into our world? I had a gun pointed at me not that long ago." Her voice breaks. "I don't want...what if that happens to them? What if our kid is scared to go outside like Xander? What if the world hates them before they have a chance to even be someone? What if they're bullied because we're in a poly relationship? What if they wished we made the decision to not have them at all?"

She's crying.

My heart is twisted in knots. Before she buries her face in her hands, Banks and I rush forward, and he slides an arm around her shoulders. I hug Sulli around her waist.

She clings to my shirt, his shirt. And her forehead touches Banks' chest. He rubs the back of her head, and while her tears slow, I exchange concern with him.

We should've expected Sulli to be questioning everything. But for some reason, we thought she'd be solidified on a decision.

"Hey, Sul," I breathe, "I wish I had the answers, but I just have what you and Banks have given me."

She catches her breath, then looks up. "And what's that, Kits?"

"Hope." My gaze stings. "You both believed our love could withstand the danger, the uncertainty, the change, any pain, and so why can't our kid withstand the same?" I lift her chin.

Banks thumbs away a tear on her cheek.

She thinks, her breath coming shallow.

"You grew up famous," Banks reminds her. "I'd say you turned out okay."

"But my parents weren't in an unconventional romance…" she trails off, contemplating her past. Her parents had an age gap. They dealt with rumors. Lies. Headlines. Paparazzi. Hecklers. And they still chose to have Sulli and Winona. "I don't want the media to dictate my life." Her voice shakes a little. "I fucking *don't*. We haven't let them yet."

I exhale a single breath.

We're reaching a better place.

Banks nods. "Amen to that."

Sulli lets go of our shirts. Hands on her head, winded. "What if I'm a bad mom? I'm not like Jane—"

"You don't have to be Janie to be a good mom," Banks assures. "Just like I know I don't have to be Thatcher to be a good dad." He cocks his head. "I just have to *not* be like my father."

I make a face. "And I have to figure out how to live up to mine." Impossible.

So very impossible.

I only had my dad for seventeen years, and in the eleven he's been gone, I've idolized him, memorialized him—to an apex I can never reach, no matter how high I ascend.

You'll be as good of a father, Nine.

I won't. I could never.

You will. Because you're mine. Hearing what he'd tell me—it breaks me. I turn my head.

"Kits?"

I pinch my watering eyes. "I'm fine."

Banks has a palm on my back.

Sulli holds my hand, and I don't know why now—but grief just punctures me. Legs nearly giving out, I squat down and bury my face in my palms.

"Shit," I choke out, and they don't slug me for the curse. "I'm sorry…"

Banks squeezes my shoulder. "What are you apologizing for, man?" He has crouched beside me. Sulli is knelt in front of me.

"We all shouldn't be on the ground." My voice is hoarse. "And I've brought us here." Pressure won't escape my chest.

"You miss your dad," Sulli says quietly. "You can be sad about it, Kits."

"It's been forever. I need to get over it." I press my eyes harder, wanting to *scream* the grief away.

"You know how many times I've wished that?" Banks tells me, and I drop my hand. Our gazes connecting with a depth that barrels into me. "I used to think memories of my brother were like shrapnel, and if I just extracted each one, the pain would be gone, but then he'd be gone. And no matter how much I hate Sky, I *loved* him, and

I realized I'd rather be in pain than lose any memory." He cups the back of my neck.

Now *I'm* crying. Crap.

Shit.

Sulli squeezes my hand.

I squeeze tighter.

"Fuck," I curse out loud, weight crushing my lungs. Banks is right. I could stop thinking about my dad. I could just push back his voice and forget what he'd tell me. What he'd caution me to do. And then maybe I'd stop encountering this seven-ton feeling.

But then I'd stop encountering him.

"What was he like as a dad?" Sulli wonders. "You don't have to answer if it's too fucking hard."

She's sweet to ask.

I think of him. I picture him slapping down the brim of my baseball cap, then lifting it up. I see his benevolent smile and his hand that opens to a Swedish Fish. "Playful. Thoughtful."

Feeling this pain, I'm compelled to just close off. Say goodbye. Be the best dad that I can be. Not one who'd bring Banks and Sulli to the floor with me. I feel selfish in my emotion. Especially while Sulli is pregnant.

Shit.

I rub at the tear streaks on my face. "I'm okay." I inhale. Exhale. Inhale.

"Positive?" Banks asks like he knows I need another second.

"Yeah." I'm already standing up.

He slips me a hard look with the shake of his head.

I slip him one back. "I'm fine."

"Alright."

Sulli and Banks are on their feet with me.

"We're a fucking mess," Sulli says, rubbing her nose on the bottom of her shirt.

"Hey, we're put-together," I say. "Stronger than ever. Resilient." And yeah, I'm not staring at my blotchy face in the mirror. I'd rather fling myself out of this reality and into the one *I* want to be true. "We can do this. The three of us."

Banks cracks a fleeting smile. "Give-no-fucks Akara is drunk on hope."

"Akara 2.0, baby." All I want is to keep the three of us together.

"*Baby*," Sulli sighs heavily, remembering the biggest issue at hand. "So what if it's not a mistake? To have the baby?"

I let out a breath. "Then you have the baby. We'll handle the security risks."

"No one can know while she's at the Olympics," Banks tells me. 100%.

Her pregnancy has to remain a secret. "Only her family and security know now, so it shouldn't be a prob—"

"Can we forget about security for like one fucking second?" Sulli interjects and kicks the yoga ball away. "Because this is so different than when I took Plan B."

Banks goes rigid.

I try to read his face as she says, "We don't know the dad, and what happens when one of you realizes you're not the biological father?"

My stomach somersaults. I'm terrified of a scenario where Banks isn't the dad. I *love* this triad. I love what we built here, and I know what it feels like to lose it.

We're all equals, but if the baby is mine and Sulli's—I don't want that to change how Banks feels towards us. Like he's on the outside of the picket fence and looking in through the window. I want him to stay.

But just like he couldn't make *me* stay. I can't make him.

"We're together as a family. All three of us," I tell Sulli and also Banks, in case he needs to hear. "It doesn't matter who the biological dad is."

"Yeah, I think Akara is right," Banks says. "Right now that doesn't matter as much as your health and the baby's health. We can deal with everything else when it comes." He nods to Sulli. "So what do you say? You wanna have this baby, mermaid?"

With a big inhale, Sulli looks from me to Banks. "If I think about what I want and not what scares me, I know the answer." And she proclaims, "I want to have this baby with both of you. And I want to be proud when we do."

We will be.

Banks and I express that sentiment, and we find ourselves hugging each other. Banks has his arms around us while somehow my arms are around them. Sulli tries to un-sandwich herself to hug us, but we've really melded her between our bodies.

"About the health stuff. I texted Farrow after I told Thatcher I was pregnant," she explains in our huddle. "He's going to take me to a women's clinic. Since tomorrow are qualifying heats to advance to semifinals, the appointment is the next morning after. In case you both want to be there."

"We'll be there," Banks says.

"On time and everything," I assure.

Farrow knew, I suddenly realize. He knew she was pregnant sometime during the security meeting. And he didn't let on.

How did Sulli even get the pregnancy test? Not a lot goes unnoticed between me and Banks, but that did.

Sulli tells us, "Farrow said he'd confirm the pregnancy and make sure everything is okay. It could be a false positive."

Could be. Am I happy? Sad?

I think we're all wading in a place of unrest. So the three of us make a pact not to get our hopes up one way or the other. The day after tomorrow, we'll have our answer.

GBANewYork.com – July 22nd

Sullivan Meadows Advances to Six Semifinals: 200m & 400m Freestyle & Individual Medley, plus 100m Medley Relay & Mixed Relay

Sullivan Meadows displayed total dominance in the freestyle tonight. She set a new Olympic record, a record she previously set, by finishing first in qualifiers with a time of 3:38:23 for 400m freestyle. Showcasing her overall skills, she also clenched heats for individual medley and will be swimming in both 200m and 400m IM semifinals. What really stood out was Meadows' teamwork, as she helped Team USA advance in both relays.

Tune in tomorrow night to see whether Meadows can keep her winning streak alive.

12

Sullivan Meadows

"I'M ROGER KNOLLS, your Olympic commentator. Women's semifinals for swimming are happening later tonight, Pacific Time here in Los Angeles." The fifty-something well-spoken GBA (Global Broadcasting Association) anchor has salt-and-pepper hair, horned-rimmed glasses, and a handful of notes, but he's seated on a white plush chair. Not behind a desk.

The camera pans outward to reveal a second "conversational" chair. Occupied by my childhood idol. Appearing dapper for press, a couple buttons are popped on his white button-down, and his armpiece tattoo peeks out of the rolled sleeves.

Kingly smiles at the camera. Charismatic. A fucking natural. A tiny twinge of jealousy rises. If I were that affable in front of a lens, maybe I'd agree to press segments too.

Roger continues, "Sitting down with me to take a look at the women's prospects for Team USA is none other than Tobias Kingly." He turns to Kingly. "Eight-time gold medalist and world record holder for the men's 400m butterfly and freestyle, and that's just a condensed list of your many accolades."

He laughs a little. "It took a lot of hard work, sacrifice, training. And I'm just hoping to do my best here in L.A., Roger, and hopefully that means a few more golds."

"We're hoping so too." They laugh lightly together.

"Uggh." Akara makes a disgusted face up at the TV, mounted in the corner of the clinic's exam room. "You can't tell me that's not a punchable face?" He's asking Banks.

"I'd punch him," Banks says like he's stating the fucking weather.

"No one's punching the greatest swimmer of our generation," I retort, not for the first time either. Our debate of his "punchable face" has been ongoing for months now. I am the lone Kingly defender.

Banks nods. "You're right, 'cause neither one of us is punching you."

It swells up in me for a second. He's calling me the greatest of our generation.

Akara smiles, noticing how Banks' compliment blows me backwards. "You're the current GOAT, Sul."

I shake my head. "I'm *your* GOAT." *The greatest of all time.* "To everyone else, Kingly is the greatest." Before Akara or Banks argues, I say, "Shhh, he's talking again."

They exchange a look like they're five-seconds from teasing me. So I'm un-fucking-surprised when Banks tells Akara, "It's a good fuckin' thing we're in a clinic. I think she has a disease."

"Kingly-itis," Akara quips. "The more she drools, the more fatal it's going to be."

I flip them off and then raise the volume on the remote.

They laugh, but the TV drowns the sound.

"…Frankie Hansen should easily do well in the 200m breaststroke semifinals tonight. She has an efficient technique that'll make her the one to look out for in the finals," Kingly explains. "And I could see her reaching first in her semifinal heats. She's competitive in breaststroke and freestyle."

"What about her teammate and competitor Sullivan Meadows?"

The remote is sweaty in my palm. Last Olympics, Kingly was never asked about me. I'd fucking *know* because I would've replayed the footage to death.

"Meadows is a powerhouse."

I touch my starstruck smile. My swim idol just called me a *powerhouse*. Put that on my tombstone. Bury me with the words.

"Get the paddles, we've lost her," Akara jokes to Banks.

"Shhh!" I swat the air, not tearing my eyes off the TV.

Kingly adds, "She's in six semifinal events, and she'll be swimming back-to-back tonight, so endurance will play a big factor in how well she does."

"What are her chances against Frankie?"

"Frankie is the underdog in their freestyle events," Kingly says. "But Meadows' greatest competitor isn't Frankie. It's herself."

"What do you mean by that?"

"Yeah," I say to the TV, sitting on the edge of my seat. Which happens to be an exam table with that super thin medical paper under my butt.

"She has to get her head in the game. I can't say whether she will or not when it comes time to compete."

"What?" I nearly yell, my jaw on the floor.

"What a prick," Banks says while gritting down on a toothpick.

Akara is glaring at the TV. No longer joking.

"Is there a reason why you think her head wouldn't be in the game?" Roger asks.

Kingly opens his hands like, *take your guess.* "Meadows' name is known to millions, and not just because she's a swimmer. If she's not careful, she'll let those distractions tank her chances here in Los Angeles."

"Who the fuck are you? To say that about me on global fucking TV? YOU ASSHOLE!" I resist the urge to chuck the remote at his 2D television face.

I suddenly *hate* Kingly.

I don't care if he's right. Do I have a lot of distractions here? *Fuck yes.* Am I known for being more than just a swimmer? *Fucking duh.* My parents are famous, and I was famous at birth. And now I'm on the cover of tabloid after tabloid with my boyfriends.

But Kingly—the swimmer I've revered for practically a decade— did *not* have to expose me like that on a global stage. He didn't have to cast doubt to the nation.

Akara comes over to take the remote. He pauses as Roger asks, "Could one of those distractions be her boyfriends?" He flips his notebook.

We all go eerily still.

Kingly clears his throat a little, waiting for Roger to continue.

"We've heard something happened recently at the Olympic Village. Athletes said they saw Sullivan Meadows and her boyfriends coming out of an aerobics room in the gym, and they looked visibly upset." He flips another page. "That, and I quote, 'Akara Kitsuwon had red, swollen eyes like he'd been crying.'"

My stomach plummets.

Akara looks murderous.

Banks slings his neck back and glares at the ceiling. "You gotta be fucking kidding me."

Kingly frowns. "I don't know anything about that. I wasn't there. I'm not going to speak on it."

I soften a little on Kingly. "Maybe you're not the biggest asshole."

"He's still an asshole," Akara says tensely, then eyes me and Banks. "We need to be more careful."

We rarely are. But this isn't about hiding our relationship anymore. To keep our baby safe, we have to keep my pregnancy secret. I already feel it putting a fire under my butt.

Banks nods strongly, and I nod too, only to hear Roger tell Kingly, "Thanks for your time this morning. We're rooting for you out there."

"Appreciate that, Roger." They shake hands, and the footage cuts to a 15-second ad.

Ziff Power
Official Protein Drink
of the
Summer Games

A bottle of Fizzle's chocolate shake with the *Ziff Power* label spins 360-degrees on a blue graphic. And then the ad cuts to a much longer commercial for the drink.

With me and my dad.

I instantly power off the TV. The CEO of Fizzle is my Uncle Stokes, and my other uncles joked how he hit nirvana when they landed the drink deal with the Olympics this year.

Fizzle products are everywhere.

I glance around the exam room. Akara and Banks have been standing, their arms crossed, mostly, and with the TV off, I have no distractions from our reality left.

Funny, isn't it?

That *swimming* is distracting me from the baby. Shouldn't it be the other way around?

"Athletes are gossiping," Banks tells Akara.

"They were always going to gossip," Akara says, staring at the blank TV. "We just didn't think they'd bring it to the press."

My lips downturn. "You don't think anyone in the clinic will start rumors?"

"No," Akara says more certainly, but I'm not sure how much is to appease me. "Everyone we ran into signed an NDA."

Most athletes have to sign them too, but that didn't stop them.

I try to stay positive. "Nothing has leaked yet."

Banks nods a few times, "Good signs."

I rest my eyes against his comforting, gentle gaze for a moment, and I breathe in three deep breaths.

We're okay.

We're fucking fine.

The world just knows Akara was crying. Not strange at all. He could've been upset about anything. No one is going to think I'm pregnant.

Because...I might not be.

I try to push away a surging emotion. But sorrow compounds for a moment, and I know now how badly I'm hoping this baby is real.

"What are you thinking, mermaid?" Banks still has his gaze on me. Mine is still on him.

"I know we said we wouldn't get our hopes up, but..." I take a beat, glancing between Banks and Akara. "I want a family of my own. I want to hold our little champ and teach him or her all the things my mom and dad taught me. I want to raise them with a fearlessness that I learned and grew into, and I want them to love their dads as much as I do."

Banks uncrosses his arms. "If we're confessing here, then I've been more afraid of the answer being *no*."

"Me too," Akara admits, passing his phone from hand to hand.

"Really?" I breathe.

Banks says, "I started thinking about *Blue Lagoon*."

This spring, he watched *Blue Lagoon* for the first time with me and Kits.

Emotional tears prick my eyes, just hearing him reference one of my favorite movies. Knowing he imagined it.

His voice is deep, husky. "And I kept picturing the three of us on our island with our kids. And I got happy." He swallows hard.

I wonder if Banks is happiest still envisioning us on an island. Because that's where we're all safest.

No kidnapping death threats.

Just happiness.

"I thought about *Blue Lagoon* too," Akara quips, full of shit.

Banks shoves his arm.

I snort.

They both laugh a little at the sound I make.

I smile some. And I blush, feeling fucking cute in their eyes and not like Sulli the Sasquatch...or I guess the new one, *Sulli the Slut*.

I throttle the thought away.

Be fucking gone.

"Seriously, though," Akara says to us.

"You seriously thought about *Blue Lagoon*?" I ask in surprise.

"No."

I throw the projectile in my hand, and I forget it's not a pillow but a hard *remote*. Akara catches the remote before it pelts his body.

I wince, "Sorry."

He points the remote at me. "Careful what your hands launch, powerhouse."

I grimace at *powerhouse*. "Don't even, Kits."

"What? I thought you liked it. You made googly eyes when he said that—"

"That was before he became a tiny fucking asshole."

"Earth to Sullivan, he's a *big* fucking asshole," Akara purposefully curses.

I look to Banks for an assist.

He holds up his hands. "I think he's just a regular fucking asshole."

I sigh, then ask Akara, "If not *Blue Lagoon*, then what were you thinking about?"

His features turn more serious this time. "How everything I've completely loved hasn't been safe or the easy decision. It's been the three of us taking the next step, and I don't want to move backwards. Forward. Onward. Always."

A strong sense of desire and want hangs in the air. Swimming around us. And suddenly, it feels like we have more to lose if I'm not pregnant.

I'M STILL SITTING ON THE EXAM TABLE AT THE clinic and staring at diagrams of vaginas. Luckily, I didn't have to do a full physical exam in a gown. I just peed in a cup and now I'm waiting for the lab results to return.

Akara and Banks both stand on either side of the bed. Really fucking supportive, despite this being a mega-surprise to us all.

One guy in the room is making this all *very* quiet and *very* awkward, and he happens to be my on-call doctor while I'm out in L.A. for the Olympics.

Farrow Redford Keene Hale.

Tattoos spindle down his arms and up his neck. He wears a black V-neck tucked into black jeans with a belt. With a pierced lip, hoop in his nose, and barbells on his eyebrow, nothing about Farrow screams *doctor*, yet I trust him more than anyone else walking the clinic floors.

"I'm sensing a lot of fucking tension," I announce. I don't believe this will make things better, but I would like very much to at least end the silence.

Farrow leans against the wall, his back touching a *Wash Your Hands* poster with the proper way to wash ones' hands. (Didn't know people needed a poster for that.) Farrow careens his head to me. "Do you want me to leave?"

"No," I say. "You can stay." He's waiting for the lab reports too, and this clinic was kind enough to allow Dr. Hale access to the facilities for the night. He said there was a lot of paperwork involved. Knowing Farrow (I do live with him), he probably is avoiding the small talk and chit-chat with other doctors and nurses outside those doors.

"There's no tension, Sul," Akara tells me.

"Just a little tension," Banks corrects.

"No tension," Akara rebuts.

Farrow raises his eyebrows. "I don't want to know."

"See he doesn't want to know," Akara tells Banks.

Banks makes a noise under his breath that sounds like a cross between a scoff and a groan.

Now *I'd* like to know what's going on. "Is this about the cinnamon roll?" I wonder. *Cinnamon roll* is our code name for the "bun in the oven" because if I do have a bun in the oven, I'm hoping it's the sweet kind. My fucking favorite.

"No," Banks says. "It's about Farrow being best friends with my brother."

Farrow's brows shoot to the moon. "What?"

"Yeah, what?" I frown.

"You stole Thatcher from Akara," Banks says plainly.

Farrow holds up both hands. "I did not do that." He turns to Akara. "You can have him back." He cringes as soon as he says it, like maybe he doesn't mean it.

"I'm not worried about your friendship with Thatcher," Akara shoots Banks a look like *shut up.*

Friendships.

I don't understand the non-family kind of friends as much as Akara and Banks. Being on the outside of their friendship drama is where I like to be. Far, *far* away from the bullseye. Observing is more fun anyway.

Farrow's cellphone beeps. Without hospital scrubs or a white coat, he looks more like my roommate than my physician. It makes this a little less nerve-racking. His eyes lift to me. "I'll be right back with your lab work." He leaves the room.

"Moment of truth." I loosen my grip in their hands to wipe my sweaty palms on my jeans. I thought we'd have to wait at least fifteen minutes.

Maybe thirty-seconds later, a knock sounds on the door.

We all go quiet.

13

Banks Moretti

SHE'S PREGNANT.

Farrow makes the announcement, and I could double-back into a million different earth-shattering, soul-swelling feelings. Elation. Fear. Pride. Insecurity.

Motherfucking insecurities.

I bunt those aside, and I embrace what matters the most. *Sulli. Akara.* Our triad. Our future together. A baby.

A fucking *baby.*

I begin to smile.

(Look, Mom, I got a girl pregnant.) Maybe. Could be Akara's baby. The humor inside my head deflates like a whoopie cushion fart.

Sulli's grip in my hand only tightens with the news. "I'm pregnant? You're fucking sure?"

"I'm sure," Farrow says easily. "By the information you gave me, you're about 4-weeks along. I'm going to grab an ultrasound and confirm the fetal heartbeat." He smiles at her. "Congratulations."

An overwhelmed smile plays at her lips.

I could toss Farrow the keys to heaven's gates if I had them. For not casting doubt or shame on Sulli. But instead, he elevates the happiness in the room.

I bend down and kiss her cheek. She clutches my bicep, keeping my head near her head. "You're not going anywhere?" She's scared, which is a gut-punch, a soul-punch, a dick-kick. And everything in my being wants to soothe Sulli.

"I'm not going anywhere." I promise like I always have. Akara is the one who has left before, but I understand needing extra reassurance from me too. One of her greatest fears is being left behind, and a baby is complicating the fucking system we have in place. "I'm always beside you. Or in front of you. Or behind you. Depending on where I need to be."

"Where I tell him to go," Akara smiles.

My mouth curves up. "Can't get enough of ordering my ass around."

"Can't get enough of you."

I love you too, Nine. I don't say the words because she's asking him, "You're not leaving, Kits, right?"

"Never." Akara kisses the top of her head. "I'm always on the other side of you." He's implying that I exist next to Sulli too.

That gets to me. How strongly Akara has been holding onto not just Sulli…but onto me.

Sulli soaks up our happiness. "We're fucking doing this. We're having a baby."

"Our fudging baby," Akara teases.

Sulli grins. "Our little fudgsicle."

We all laugh. Mother of God, I'm so in love with Sulli. And I know I'm rooted to her, but sometimes being *this* deeply in love feels like jumping into a bottomless crater. Where I'm falling for eternity.

Where I'm reaching out for the other two sets of hands as they fall with me.

"Congratulations to you, Kitsuwon," Farrow tells Akara, and cold blows over me—thinking Farrow knows something we don't. *Can't be fucking right.* No one took our DNA. "And to you, Banks."

I almost had a heart attack. I exhale a tensed breath. Knowing Farrow only took a half-second to mention me too, but Christ, that felt longer.

Akara is eagle-eyeing the fuck out of me. I want to tell him *I'm fine* if the kid is his biological kid. I'll be a great uncle. I've been preparing for uncle-hood more than fatherhood. But I can't stomach saying the words in front of Farrow. Just so he'll run off and possibly tell Thatcher.

Love my brother to the ends of the fucking earth, but I don't want him to be overprotective of me when it comes to Akara. He doesn't need to take sides or come to my defense. I'm not in a lose-lose competition with Akara Kitsuwon anymore. We haven't been since Yellowstone, and that feels like eons ago.

"Thanks, Farrow," I say first.

Akara tries to nod in gratitude, but he's still trying to read my face.

Sulli focuses on Farrow. "I didn't think anyone would congratulate us."

His smile stretches. "See, that's where you're wrong, Meadows." He lifts his brows. "Many more than just me will be happy to hear you're having a baby."

"Like who?"

"You'll see."

I think that gives Sulli more hope. It definitely gives me some. I was preparing to combat some jackass reactions, and I wouldn't be surprised if Akara and I still have to shut up Alpha and Epsilon. Price's men.

"Do you have any questions?" Farrow asks.

"Um…should I be doing anything…avoiding anything? Prenatal vitamins…or…" She touches her temple. "Okay, none of that probably made sense. I feel like my brain is Alphabet Soup right now."

"It's okay," Farrow says with ease. "I have a list. We'll go over it together." He glances to me and Akara. "I can also get a paternity test, if that's something you'd both like."

"No," I say just as Akara says, "We don't want one."

We discussed this last night. Briefly.

No paternity test.

Sulli was on board. Whatever makes this easier for us.

Akara explains to Farrow, "We'll learn who the biological dad is at birth, but it won't change anything."

Farrow nods like he understands completely. And then his attention reroutes to Sulli. "A gown is on the counter over there. You can change into it, and I'll be back in ten. Sound good?"

She nods. "Yeah, sounds good."

With a casual stride, Farrow leaves, the door shutting with a solid *thud* behind him.

Akara spins onto me. "Are you having second thoughts?"

"No way in hell."

"You're upset?"

"No," I refute, a little angrily. "I'm fine, Akara."

Sulli hops off the table to grab the gown.

We watch her for a half-a-second before Akara asks me, "When the condom broke, did you ever imagine the three of us that far into the future? What it'd look like with a baby?"

"Not really," I admit. "She took Plan B." I cast my gaze over to Sulli. She's watching us while she returns to the exam table, setting down the gown. I exhale a heavy breath. "Did you gear up for that scenario? Where the baby was mine?"

Akara shakes his head slowly. "No, I wasn't even picturing what a baby between you two would look like."

"Cute, clear as day." I motion from my face to her face. I'm not an ugly motherfucker. And she's such a fucking beauty.

Sulli smiles.

Akara's lips rise. "Yeah, they'd be adorable. Not as adorable as mine though."

Sulli snorts, but she stays smiling.

"Can't argue with that," I say. Akara is a good-looking guy. He's way more photogenic than me. He pops on tabloid covers, and I'm six-seven. It's hard to steal the show when you're standing next to a giant.

Seriousness draws Akara's lips back down. "Are you ready for the possibility that the baby is mine?"

"Yeah." *I want to be ready.* Isn't that enough?

He sighs like I'm full of shit.

"I'd be a great uncle to the kid."

"You aren't going to be some fun uncle to our kid," Akara says strongly, eyes flashing hot.

"You want me to be a mean uncle?"

"I don't want you to be an uncle at all!" Akara shouts like I'm not seeing the picture.

I rake a hand through my hair. Sulli tensely pulls off her shirt, and Akara and I are distracted at the push-up bra lifting her breasts.

Fuck me sideways. Heat gathers and drives south seeing Sulli bite the corner of her lip and study our desire. *Yeah, we have the eternal hots for you, mermaid.*

"Oh hey, um...don't mind me, fuck." She smiles, a little giddy. "Just um, fucking proceed. Work out what you need to work out."

I try to ignore my rising hard-on.

Akara pushes back his black hair. Glancing from her breasts to me, to her breasts, then to me.

"Eyes up here," I tell him.

"A little hard."

"I know the feeling."

He smiles into a short laugh. "Banks." Seriousness is back. Great. "You're going to be a dad. An equal. Just like I'll be a dad to your kid. They probably shouldn't even call us uncles since we're their parent too."

I like that idea. I love it, really. "You'll be a great dad to my kid," I tell him, "but you really want me to be one to yours?"

"Why wouldn't I?"

"I have a shit role model, Nine."

"I don't care."

I do. What if I'm better as the fun uncle? Even if that's not what I want to be.

His phone buzzes.

"Shoot." He digs harshly into his pocket.

While he does, Sulli shimmies out of her jeans. She hands the clothes to me, and I fold them on the exam table. We're both glancing back at Akara.

"He seems distressed," Sulli says softly to me.

"It's not good," I agree.

Akara lets out an aggravated, pained noise. "It's Quinn. He just texted, *Gabe said he's moving into the apartment. That's wrong, right?* What am I supposed to tell him?"

"The truth," I say. "That Gabe is taking our room, and we're moving in with Sulli."

"He thinks he's being replaced by Gabe…I hate that he thinks that." Akara wants to assuage Quinn's feelings.

Omega has gone through a lot of shifts, but for a while, it used to be the Yale boys and then me, Thatcher, and Akara, with Quinn in the middle. The two groups treating him like a little brother.

Now that he's been out with a broken leg, Gabe has filled the middle-man spot and he's the same age as Quinn. Twenty-three. On paper, maybe it'd be easy to think Gabe is Quinn.

But I'd choose Quinn every time. Hands down. No falter.

"Tell Quinn that we miss him," Sulli says.

"Tell him Gabe doesn't know what Animal Planet is," I chime in.

Akara gives me a *what the fuck?* look.

"He's not the sharpest tool, man."

"No, I know that. But he didn't know what *Animal Planet* is?"

"He thought it was a part of our galaxy. Next to fuckin' Jupiter. A planet named *Animal.*"

Sulli bursts into laughter.

Akara smiles. "You're fracking with me."

"I'm dead-ass." I can't even remember how the conversation started. Every time I talk to the guy, my IQ begins to melt away. I'm not looking for some Einstein or a mental math conversation that'd send me to the moon. But there've been times where Gabe has made me question my own intelligence. Like, am I the idiot here or is his head really that full of air?

Akara starts to text. Midway through, he pauses. "Dang it, he's calling me."

"Take it," Sulli suggests. "He probably needs the pep talk."

"I'll be back." Akara puts a phone to his ear. "Quinn…" His voice trails off as the door closes behind him.

Quiet falls in the room. While Sulli slips her arms through the gown, I'm behind her and tying the strings at her bare back. My knuckles graze her soft skin as I make a knot.

Her breathing sounds slow and easy. "Thanks." She turns her head a little. Looking up at me over her shoulder, Sulli only has love in her eyes. "I agree with Kits, just so you know. I think you'd be a good parent to his biological kid, just like he'd be a good one to yours."

"I want to believe that too, just so *you* know." I finish tying her gown. She hops up on the exam table, and I climb up beside Sulli. Tall, the two of us—both of our feet touch the floor. "My dad is nothing like yours. He made terrible choices when it came to his family."

"So then you have a fucking road map of what *not* to do. Which paths to not go down. That counts for something, Banks."

I rest a hand on her thigh. She collects my hand in hers, lacing our fingers. With my other, I dig out a pack of cigarettes. Still in plastic. Unopened.

I quit smoking again.

Back in the spring.

Why I carry around these fucking cigarettes—I have no idea. Because I know I can? Because they're a crutch in case shit goes to hell? Because I know it's a mistake that I'm destined to repeat?

Am I just like my father then?

I push that away. I can't fathom *abandoning* anyone the way that he just up and left me. Let alone a child.

I'm not like him.

I try to remember that.

"Maybe it does count for something," I tell her, then I skim her calm breathing. "You're okay?"

"Yeah, it's sinking in." She leans into my side, and I wrap an arm around her. "Can I have those?" she asks, eyeing the cigarettes.

"Please. Take 'em."

She grabs the cigarettes. "I'm trashing these when we leave."

"Fine by me." I think for a second, and I don't realize I'm staring at the cigarettes until she says, "Are the cravings that bad?"

I shake my head. "Not right now, anyway. I was just thinking…" I let out a soft laugh. "Life is a strange ride, and I don't think I *really* hopped on until I started yearning for something more than a cigarette. Not until I started longing for you and Akara…and now a baby."

Sulli hangs onto my gaze. I'm staring deeply into her, remembering our first kiss in the motel. Remembering the first time we met. Remembering every single piece in between.

"Sometimes," I breathe, "I wonder how much of a ghost I was before. Just background. Floating through people's lives. Helping them. Being there for them. No other purpose but that."

"Is that what you're afraid of?" Sulli wonders. "Being background again?"

It fists me—that possibility. My eyes burn. "I know there's no way you or Akara would treat me like that. But I'd be a liar if I said it didn't scare me." Before she speaks, I add quickly, "I will *love* this kid no matter who the biological dad is, and I'm not going anywhere." I promise again. "I'm not. And don't *yearn* for a kid with my genes because it'd make me feel better. I'm stronger than that."

She breaks into a smile. "I know you are, Banks. But I'm here, you know, if you ever need to talk again?"

I hug her close. She lifts her chin, and I slide a hand along her squared jaw. As our lips near, I whisper, "Thank you."

"I feel like I should thank you."

"For what?"

"For falling in love with me."

"You don't need to thank me for loving you, mermaid. My love for you isn't a gift that can be given and taken away. It's just eternally there, and it's yours to do with what you want."

She kisses me.

I breathe in the kiss, pulling her closer. My pulse beats strongly as emotion builds under her fingers. She grips my hair with desperate desire, and my hand encases her jaw in the longing I spoke on. Our tongues meld in natural, soulful strokes, her lips swelling beneath mine. And I wish I could say it lasted minutes—but comms go off in my ear.

"…Roosters…" Crackle. "Roosters…I repeat, the…" Static.

"Banks?" Sulli draws back as my hand flies to my ear.

I wince at the comms interference. But finally, the sound is more audible. "…the Roosters are here." What the fuck are they doing in Los Angeles? At the Olympics?

Akara slips inside, chest rising and falling in months' long fury. "Did you hear?" he asks me.

"Yeah." I'm burning up.

"What's going on?" Sulli questions. "Is anyone going to fucking tell me?"

I look to Akara. It's his call. This is security.

He makes a choice. And he announces, "The Rochesters are here."

14

Sullivan Meadows

5 MONTHS BEFORE THE OLYMPICS

FEBRUARY

I GRIP A BASEBALL bat in a furious fist.

Venom seeps in my bloodstream like I'm fueled by an invisible chorus, pounding drums in my heart and screaming harmonies in my head.

Go. Go. Go.

My feet strike pavement. Rage carrying me ahead.

Fuck him.

Fuck him.

Fuck him!

Outside of anyone who's ever messed with my sister, I've never wanted to cause someone pain in my entire life. Not like this. But if someone deserves it, it's my ex-boyfriend.

Will Rochester has returned home from a vacation in Maui. Fucking *Maui*. He jetted off to an island after dropping bomb after bomb on me and my family with The Royal Leaks. And he's not licking his wounds. No he's fucking sunbathing!

On Instagram, he's posted photos of himself tanning on a yacht, drinking fruity cocktails out of a coconut, and jet-skiing along the Pacific. I'm tired of wishing he'd slam his jet-ski into a rock.

For one, he's no longer in Hawaii.

He's back in Philly.

And he didn't reject my DM when I asked to "meet up" outside his family's house.

One month has passed since we discovered the Rochesters were the mole behind The Royal Leaks, and in that month, my anger has not been put to rest. I've cradled it like a newborn baby. Nourished it. Let it blossom into something angrier than before. For this moment.

On behalf of my *entire* family, I'm going to confront him.

"Hey, let's think about this," Akara says, keeping the same lengthy stride as me and Banks. We trek heatedly down a suburban street. The Rochesters live a few streets over in the same gated neighborhood as my parents.

A quick flyby to my childhood home to retrieve a bat, and now we're on foot to the real destination.

"I've had a month to think about it, Kits," I tell him. "Fuck him and his stupid chiseled jaw and his bland personality and his deceitful fucking butthole!"

"He showed you his butthole?" Akara banters with mock rage.

I growl, in no mood to try to laugh or be cheered up or swayed from this path.

Akara looks to Banks. "Back me up here, man."

"You heard our girl," Banks says. "Fuck him."

Akara grimaces, "Not you, too."

I cut in, "I've made my decision, Kits. Someone has to talk to my ex, and that person *has* to be me."

"Right on," Banks says, eyes pinned ahead like he's focused on a target. Ever since I laid down the plan, Banks has been one-hundred-percent ready to confront Will.

Akara, on the other hand, has been more cautious. He hop-steps in front of us and walks backwards to speak face-to-face. "You need a baseball bat just to talk?"

"It's for intimidation." Will doesn't need to think he can push me around.

Akara spreads open his arms. "Aren't you a lover, not a fighter?"

That's what I'm always telling him. He's been my fighter, my defender. They both have. And when push comes to shove, they'd use the bat. I wouldn't.

"Then you hold the bat." I toss him the baseball bat.

He has top-notch reflexes, but Akara lets the bat thump against his firm chest and clatter to the fucking pavement.

"Seriously?!" I shout.

"No bat."

"We're taking the bat!"

Banks picks up the bat.

"Thank you," I say loudly, still heated.

Akara glares at Banks. "Drop the effing bat."

I interject, "Stop ordering my boyfriend around, *Kits*."

"He's *my* man, *Sul*. It's my job to order him."

"Keep the bat," I tell Banks. "Don't let your boss make you do something you don't want to fucking do."

Banks has a shadow of a grin.

Akara almost smiles. He ends up laughing. "I can't believe this is fudging happening right now."

Banks states plainly, "I'm not hopping into your fight, so you two work out that shit." He casually braces the bat on his shoulder.

"Just stop for a second," Akara holds up his hands, and before I barrel into him, I slow to a halt. Banks beside me. A mansion looms beside us, but the three-story white brick and column structure doesn't belong to the Rochesters. "Just maybe, Sul, we don't go in guns blazing like three cowboys."

Banks says, "There's no better way."

"I agree with Banks. Cowboy-up, Kits."

With two fingers threading through his black hair in exasperation, Akara exhales a knotted breath. "*Fuck*."

I slug his shoulder.

He knew it was coming and barely reacts. After one second, he nods tightly. "Fine. Okay. I'm always going to have your backs. But let it be known that this is a *bad* call, and I'm only making it because I love you two way too much, apparently."

"It's known," I nod. "Crystal fucking clear. If this turns to shit, you can blame me."

Banks shakes his head. "That's not how it goes, mermaid."

Akara tells me, "I'm in charge. Screw ups are on me."

I scrunch my face. "No, it's not. We're all equal in our triad."

"This is a *security* issue. We're not equals." He demonstrates with his hands. "I am here." He mimes a rung ladder, raising his hand high. "Banks is here." He puts him in the middle. "You are here." He puts me at the fucking bottom.

I'd be more insulted if this were a swimming issue and he ranked me last. They're highly trained and skilled in security work. I'm not, and I can't pretend that I'm the boss of a field that I know nothing about. *That* is insulting to them.

I'm going to feel like utter fucking shit if this plan goes haywire. But I'm not ready to say goodbye and cower. I know this is what'll make me feel better in the end.

I nod in understanding. "Justice needs to be served."

"Okay, Bat Girl," Akara teases.

"I gave my bat to Banks, thank you very fucking much."

"Actually, you gave it to me—"

Banks interjects, "Let's go before you two give me a migraine."

Even though he's joking, that kicks us into action and ends our bickering. No way do I want Banks to encounter a migraine. He hasn't had a severe one since the daith piercing and his doctor's visit.

Walking forward, Akara returns to my side. I'm surprised when he slinks a muscular arm over my shoulder. He feels like armor.

Building me up for battle. Containing my smile through my anger proves impossible. I have two boyfriends ready to stoke the fire that blazes under my soles.

And I even appreciate Akara's concern and caution. He cares enough to voice doubt. And loves us enough to stick with us.

We keep our stride.

Cold in February, I should be shivering under my fleece-lined jean jacket, but anger and adrenaline heat me inside-out. Akara already joked that I look straight out of *Stranger Things* with my jacket, striped tee, and bell-bottoms, and that I'm not the character Eleven. I can't hurt Will with my mind.

I fucking wish. It'd save us a lot of time.

Passing two more houses, we finally reach a stone mansion. Sun shines on skeletal cherry blossom trees that landscape the massive home. The lawn rolls forever, and a long and twisty driveway leads to the curb and an ornate stone mailbox.

My pace slows considerably.

What in the ever-loving…fuck? A black Escalade is parked next to the mailbox.

No, no, *no.* My pulse beats oddly. Frantically. The SUV is the same model and make as some vehicles in security firms.

"Did the Rochesters hire security?" I ask.

A worse thought: they hired Triple Shield.

My stomach sours. Why would Price Kepler, my mom's bodyguard since her early twenties, do something as heinous as working for the clear enemy?

I don't believe he would.

Price might be a stick-in-the-mud, but he's protected my family for most of *his* life. He wouldn't betray us.

Banks chews down on a toothpick. "I don't know." He lowers the bat and strengthens his grip on the handle.

Akara is drilling a hole into the Escalade, and then the SUV doors swing open.

I hold my breath.

I recognize the driver. Slicked-back golden hair, short dark-blond beard, and a broad, brawny build. Aunt Lily and Aunt Willow used to have hot takes on Wylie being a forty-something Thor lookalike or a Viking on the History Channel.

It ended with Uncle Lo calling him Walmart Thor. Wylie Jones is my dad's 24/7 bodyguard. He's protected him for what feels like forever.

And maybe my aunts are right. Wylie has always appeared as threatening and commanding as a lightning wielding god.

His right-hand protégé hops out of the passenger seat.

Greer.

My former bodyguard and currently my little sister's. He shaved since last I saw him. His copper-beard now just red stubble.

Both Navy vets, Wylie was the one who recommended Greer for the security job post-military. Akara told me it's why Greer was instantly put onto a Meadows detail when he was hired. Greer didn't have to "fight" for the position. In fact, Wylie and Greer have only ever been bodyguards to my family members.

They're Team Meadows to the dying end.

So seeing them here, like this—like they're guarding the Rochester's mansion, is fucking *weird*.

As we keep trekking forward, Wylie and Greer take a few steps to meet us in the middle of the quiet neighborhood street.

"What's going on?" Akara asks first.

"Why are you here?" I pipe in.

Banks stays quiet, eyes pinging from Wylie to Greer.

"We were driving through the neighborhood," Wylie explains to everyone, but he's looking at me. "We noticed you carrying that bat and heading down the street." He studies the bat now in Banks' possession. "So we circled around and came here in case my suspicions were right." He crosses his arms, but his stance is causal. Calm. "I was hoping to be wrong here, Sulli."

My heart thumps like I was caught vandalizing a neighbor's yard with toilet paper. But I haven't done anything wrong. I hate that he's making me feel like I fucking have.

"*You* are wrong." Akara sticks up for me immediately. "It's not your place to be here, Wylie."

Wylie cuts Akara a severe look.

Bodyguard dynamics within the security teams are like complex pieces in a strategic board game. Like playing a game of Catan against Charlie—my brain pounds trying to figure it all out.

What I know: Wylie, Greer, and Price (the Meadows bodyguards on Triple Shield) are not happy with Akara and Banks crossing lines and dating me. And now they all have to work together.

Maybe they're also pissed that my bodyguards *almost* got me pregnant. But shark week came. Plan B worked. So I'm on the road to the Olympics now.

"It's my place," Wylie says. "Members of the family have instructed Price to keep other members of the family *away* from the Rochesters. They don't want drama in the neighborhood. Not while the kids still live here."

The kids are the teenagers.

My little sister. The girl squad. Xander and Ben.

I'm stuck on *members of the family*. What the fuck does that mean? Who's instructing Price and Triple Shield to protect the Rochesters? And which *members of the family* do they think will go after the Rochesters?

Me, fucking obviously.

I'm in that second category.

I burn beneath my jacket. "I'm here to talk to my ex-boyfriend. I'm allowed to do that."

"Respectfully, I think you should back up, sir," Banks says, voice deep.

Greer mutters something under his breath, but I think I hear *crayon-eater*.

Banks must hear because his eyes cut to Greer and frost.

Wylie rests a palm on Greer's chest. Keeping him stationary, even when Greer hasn't taken a step forward. Wylie says to Banks, "If you want to give me respect, you'll turn around and walk your asses back the other way."

"It's not happening," Akara says. Words resolute. They lift me up. He wasn't fully on board with this plan, but he's always been fully on board with protecting me.

Wylie looks grave. "I understand the need to engage with the people who created The Royal Leaks. We're all mad about it—"

"But it didn't fucking affect you," I snap at Wylie. "That asshole and his family hurt *mine*. You can't expect me to just walk away."

"I do expect that," Wylie says sternly. "Because I stood right here with your dad, and he had to make that choice too."

What…?

My dad?

I rock back, blown off-kilter for a moment. "He tried to confront the Rochesters?"

Wylie nods. "Your mom, Aunt Lily, and Uncle Connor have instructed Price to make sure that Triple Shield keeps the peace. They're handling the Rochesters the legal route. It's just going to take time."

My mom.

Aunt Lily.

Uncle Connor.

My head spins.

I don't have *time* for legal recourse, which could take years. I need to talk to Will *now*.

My eyes snap to the Rochester's mansion. *My dad walked away.*

Why is it so hard for me to do the same?

Hot-tempered breaths inflate and deflate my lungs in uneven patterns. My resolve begins to weaken the longer I think about my family. About creating a bigger mess in search of revenge.

Akara rotates to me, whispering, "We're with you, Sul. Whatever you decide."

I take the bat from Banks. Mostly to lean my weight on the bat like a cane, my body feeling heavy and fixed in place. "What do you think?" I ask Banks, but before he can answer, before I have time to make a decision—it's made for me.

Will Rochester—my-ex-boyfriend—struts down the driveway with an urgent pace. He's alone. Eyes pinned to me and wind whipping at his dishwater-blond hair and J.Crew button-down.

I'm caught off guard. Standing in the street with not just my boyfriends but two more bodyguards. To Will, this must look shady as fuck. Showing up with *four* bodyguards for a meeting that I requested.

I straighten up, the bat slack in my hand.

Closer my ex is to us, the more confusion and anger twists his face. He hikes across the lawn to reach our spot by the curb. "What's this?" Will asks. No greeting. Just an angry wave towards Wylie, Greer, Akara, and Banks.

I'm burning up. "I didn't know if I could fucking trust you…"

"We're just talking, right?" Will sees the bat and his eyes bug. "Jesus…you're crazy. Just like my brother warned me about you and your family."

Akara snaps, "Hey—"

Banks takes a threatening step forward.

Wylie and Greer stay back, but their hatred, their fury, and lethal glares on Will are unmistakable. They might not like Akara and Banks right now, but they all have a common enemy.

Will looks between us. "Fuck this." His eyes land on me. "Fuck you, Sulli."

"Don't," Akara warns, seething.

Banks is boiling, his hand balled in a fist.

Will sees, then slips me a hurt look. "Unbelievable." He just storms back up his driveway.

I can tell my boyfriends are biting their tongues until they bleed. Banks paces away a few steps, fuming. If they weren't on-duty, if they weren't in front of Triple Shield—I wonder how different this would've gone.

My anger is replaced by shame. For feeling bad for *Will.* He caused so much hurt. He stole my sanity and my privacy for *months.* So then why did he just make me feel like an epic pile of shit. Why did I lose my voice? I hate myself in this moment.

I hate having to choose to shut up and walk away.

I hate that I couldn't even *speak* and tell him how I really feel. I hate that I had the chance, and I didn't take it.

He'll probably block my texts, my calls, and block me on social media. I doubt I'll ever get another chance again.

15

Banks Moretti

NOW

Date: July 23rd
Subject: the Rochester situation
From: pricekepler@tripleshield.com
To: akarakitsuwon@kitsuwonsecurities.com
FW: banksmoretti@kitsuwonsecurities.com,
pauldonnelly@kitsuwonsecurities.com,
thatchermoretti@kitsuwonsecurities.com, *and others.*

Akara:
Do not engage with the Rochesters.
*Tell your men to not engage. Since Omega has personal relationships with their clients, it'd be good to also tell your men to advise their clients to **not engage** tonight and for the rest of the Olympics.*

Best,
Price

* forwarding Price's email to all of you. He has a point, even if none of us like it. – Akara

BACKS TO A WALL, Akara casts a quick glance to me as I pocket my phone. "You read it?"

I nod stiffly. "He's emailing you now?"

"Yep."

I catch his disgruntled features before I scan the "ready room" with him, where swimmers are mentally preparing for their upcoming semifinal heats. Sulli among them, and I rest my gaze on our girlfriend for longer than I should.

She stretches on a mat. Bulky headphones blocking out chatter from coaches and other athletes. She's in the zone, and Jesus Christ, for her sake, I need to be in *mine*.

Hypervigilant and ultra-sharp. But I know the real threats are in the stadium where ticketed attendees pack the stands.

She's safer here.

Stay frosty.

Don't let your guards down.

I study her surroundings while Akara whispers, "Price and I basically have no personal relationship at this point. He can't even *text* me an effing *hello*. It's like he's putting me on probation for getting with Sulli."

"He's always taken the stance of *we're not here to be friends with clients, we're here to protect them*," I mention under my breath. "He was never gonna love anyone dating a client. Let alone a Meadows girl." I scrutinize the entrances and exits. "I don't think it helped that Price heard she took Plan B. He might stop emailing you and revert to snail mail once he finds out she's actually…"

Pregnant.

I don't need to say the word. And I wouldn't. We might be out of earshot from most people but we're still in public.

Akara rolls his eyes at that idea. "He's so petty."

"Passive aggressive."

"Both."

I nod.

Akara rests the back of his head against the wall. He focuses in on movement at our four o'clock. Just an Australian swimmer jumping and loosening their shoulders and arms.

Akara lifts his mic to his lips. "Akara to SFO, don't forget to read the email I forwarded." He drops his hand, then says to me, "I hate that we can't do a fracking thing about the Rochesters."

I welcome Akara's dialogue, since it's making me less paranoid about a threat targeting Sulli. I glance at him. "Yeah, but for as much as I'd give my left nut to put the Rochesters in their place, I wouldn't make a move tonight."

Olympic semifinals for swimming. Where Sulli is competing back-to-back six times over.

I'm not screwing my girlfriend's chances at gold.

So I'm glad Triple Shield and Kitsuwon Securities agreed to passive perimeters tonight.

Disengage.

Let the Rochesters rot in the fucking stadium stands.

We've all been guessing why they're here. To rub in the fact that they took personal aims at the Meadows, Hales, and Cobalts, tanked their stocks, and walked away without a single slap on the wrist? To show how invincible and untouchable they are?

Hell, maybe they just want to watch the Olympics.

Whatever the case, I don't have eyes on them.

Neither does Akara. Not while we're in a back room.

He whispers, "Same."

We both know revenge at the cost of Sulli's goal is a no-brainer. Revenge is taking a motherfucking backseat.

"Hey, I'll be a sec." Akara rests a hand on my shoulder. I just now realize someone is calling him. "Keep an eye on our girl, Banksy." With haste, he exits the ready room, phone to his ear.

I'm hawk-eying every person. If a toe moves, I plan on seeing it. Two camera crews from GBA News are stationed in a corner. Thank God they're not allowed to interview anyone and pester Sulli. They're capturing B-Roll of the Olympians.

At least that's what Jack Highland-Oliveira told me when I said it was horseshit those distracting lens probers were back here.

With Akara gone, I blink a few times and my mind races in bad directions and my breath heavies.

What kind of father will I be?

Never thought I'd have a question rage-fucking in my head as much as that one. But it's been loud. Like a teenager blaring their metal music at 3 a.m., that question is gonna keep me up at night. It's stayed with me all day.

Every time I try to shove it away, it creeps back in. There's no real answer. I have no downright clue what being a dad looks like for me. Can't conceptualize it, so now I'm tormented with thinking about it.

Focusing on my job—bodyguard to my beautiful girlfriend—is another *welcome* distraction to my own thoughts. And so I zero in on Sulli.

She's moved to a bench. Sitting cross-legged, she still listens to music, her concentration face as cute as a pack of puppies. Her forehead wrinkles as she thinks harder.

Alright, definitely cuter than puppies.

My mouth curves upward.

Her 200m IM heat is first, and I've been giving Sulli a wide berth of space. Anything she needs. And so I almost keel over in fucking shock when she raises her head, locks eyes with me, and waves me closer. To her.

Kid you not, I glance over my shoulder like a royal dumbass, looking at the wall, like she called over some other bastard.

Sulli smiles, noticing what I just did.

I almost laugh at myself. She doesn't have to call me twice. I move my ass and reach her bench. "How you holding up?"

"I can't stop...*thinking* about everything except what I need to be thinking about," Sulli admits in one stressed breath. She sees me towering. "Can you take a seat for a sec?"

I sit down, adjusting my radio and then resting my forearms on my thighs. "I'm not distracting you?"

"My thoughts are a bigger distraction." She yanks the headphones to her neck. "I just need to be here. In the present moment. And not stuck up in my head."

"Yeah," I say deeply, "I understand that. I've been trying to get my mind right too." Our eyes search one another with a vigor that digs to the depth of my core. And I hate needing to break that connection and scan her surroundings. But I do. And I say, "Let's stay in the moment together, mermaid."

Sulli exhales another anxious breath, then scoots closer to me. "Usually listening to *All Saints* is enough." She completely removes her headphones. "But it's just making me think of the…cinnamon roll."

I take her headphones. "You need a different song?"

She shakes her head. "I like hearing you, Banks."

That reaches a soft part of me. And I must wear some type of smile because her eyes drift along my lips like she's tracing the movement.

After placing the headphones behind me, I collect her hands in mine. Something overcomes me—love, stupidity, brilliance, *passion* for her—whatever the affliction I'm drowning inside, I find myself *singing*.

I can't really sing.

But here I am, belting softly, slowly, and off-key to Sulli. The lyrics to "Song to the Siren" by Tim Buckley come out scratchy, rough, but quietly enough that I know no one can really hear but her.

She clutches onto my knees. Her eyes nearly glassing, and I hold her cheek as the music pours out of me. We sway a little.

Cameras on us. Athletes watching.

I couldn't care less.

Watch.

Sulli looks at me the way I'd think Juliet would look at Romeo. Like our stars crossed in some fabled tale, and here we are.

"Swim to me," I whisper, my voice breaking. "Oh my heart." I change up the lyrics now and sing, "You're gonna smoke your competition. Yes you are."

Sulli laughs into a heartfelt smile. "…wow." She breathes a strong breath. "I've never heard that song before."

"It's an oldie, mixed in with Banks Roscoe Moretti original lyrics." I almost tell her why I thought of the song, but that might not help get her mind right.

Sulli has this overwhelmed smile now. "Fuck, that was the most *10 Things I Hate About You* romantic moment of my life."

I end up smiling too. "Never seen that movie."

"Heath Ledger sings to Julia Stiles…pretty fucking dramatically and in the best, cutest way. But this…this was better."

"That was the first time I've ever sung to a girl."

"Really fucking really?"

"Really fucking really." I skim her up and down. "I guess I won't make it the last time."

"As long as it's to me."

"Only to you, mermaid. And maybe Akara."

"Definitely Akara." She rotates a little. "Speaking of the asshole."

"Ha ha," Akara says dryly, a smile cresting as he approaches. He waves the phone. "Your dad called, Banks."

I try not to tense. *She's safe here.* "What about?"

"We were just going over positions of the temps before the heats. Everything looks good."

Sulli relaxes.

I nod a couple times. Trusting that everyone will do their jobs tonight. But I'm keeping my head on a swivel.

Sulli makes more room on the bench. "Take a seat, Kits."

Akara lowers down on the other side of our girlfriend, phone still in his hand. And then Sulli's swim coach nears. "Can I have a minute with Sullivan?"

She answers first, "Yeah, sure." Sulli stands and shuffles away, slipping us a pleading look that says, *don't go anywhere.*

Despite Akara leaving for some phone calls, he's stuck around her detail a lot more ever since the gun incident. I love when he's with us, so no way in hell am I complaining about the change.

We watch the coach give her tips.

"What were you guys talking about?" Akara wonders.

Sudden guilt creeps in. We've been sharing a close-to-equal amount of time with Sulli lately. Christ, usually we're all three together. Somehow I've managed to have multiple moments alone with Sulli. More than he's experienced recently. And I feel fucking bad.

"She was trying to get her mind right and block out intrusive thoughts," I explain. "So I sang to her." Why the hell am I nervous to tell him this?

Akara makes a face at me. Half amused, half confusion. "You can't sing."

"I didn't say it was any good."

Akara laughs. "What song?"

"'Song to the Siren.' Tim Buckley."

He contemplates this, maybe thinking about the lyrics, and his lips slowly rise.

"You know it?" I wonder.

"Yeah." He smiles more. "That's a good one." He lets out a laugh at another thought.

"What?"

"You don't give yourself enough credit, man." He catches my gaze. "You claim you know nothing about relationships and romance, but you've *consistently* swept Sulli off her feet since we've been together. You're good at this whole romance thing."

He's full of it. "You fling a piece of her own hair at her and she bursts like a shooting comet. Once in a blue moon, I have some bastardly charm."

"You are so *fudging* wrong, Banks. You know how impossible it is not to love you?" He focuses back on Sulli. "Now, me, on the other hand—it takes work to love me." He acts like it's a joke. But I can tell he thinks there's truth beneath the words.

"Please," I say under my breath. "It took less than five-minutes for the two of us to become friends, Nine. That's not work." Akara has always been an easy ally. To a lot of people. But he's vulnerable with very few. "You know Sulli has loved you for years."

Akara breathes this in as he scans the ready room. "Sometimes I worry that Sulli thinks our back-and-forth is too innocent, too... playful—but that's just always what we've done."

Is he saying what I think he's saying? "You think *I'm* better at being romantic than you?"

"Yeah," he says seriously. Looking insecure. Akara fuckin' Kitsuwon—the confident flirt is insecure about being *romantic*. Something he does *effortlessly* with Sulli on a daily, hourly basis. When he doesn't even fucking realize he's doing it!

I can't help it.

I laugh.

He shoots me a glare. "Sorry I shared."

"I'm not." I catch his gaze before I have to scan our surroundings. "Akara, you literally took her on a sleigh ride at the Winter Fest."

His brows scrunch in agonized thought. "That was planned. Being romantic shouldn't be *strategic* like some op for security. It should be spontaneous and unprompted. My dad was so much better at that than I am..."

My gaze softens. "Now you're not giving yourself enough credit." I fix the wire to my mic. "She loves how you are with her, but something tells me I'm not the one you need to hear that from." I squeeze his shoulder and stand up as Sulli approaches.

Akara rises with me, especially as Sulli seems perturbed. He asks, "What's wrong, Sul?"

"I fucking forgot my lucky bracelet." From Team Trials to now, she kissed a braided turquoise bracelet before swimming. "I think I left it with my dad. He didn't answer my text." She frowns more. "It's fine. I don't need it."

"I can go get it," I offer.

"No, fuck, don't worry about it. There's no time."

"I can try." The smart thing to do would be to radio Ryke's bodyguard. But Lord knows I'm not looking to chat with *Wylie*. He might even be a shitbag and ignore me over something like my girlfriend's bracelet.

"Radio Wylie," Akara tells me.

Fuck.

Begrudgingly, I follow orders. "Banks to Wylie, Sulli is missing her lucky bracelet. Is it with her dad?"

Silence.

I try again.

More silence.

Akara mutters, "Petty pricks."

"I'd lump Greer in the Petty Pricks Pack."

"Price as President."

Sulli rocks on her feet, nervous. She's not even listening to our banter.

"I'm going," I tell him.

"Okay, be quick."

"Stay frosty." I adjust my earpiece. Truth: I know the chances of retrieving the bracelet before her first heat is low, but leaving now means I'm giving Akara some alone-time with our girlfriend.

He deserves that, too.

16

Banks Moretti

CHLORINE, THE FAMILIAR scent is more powerful among the domed stadium. The air stickier, more humid, and I have my back turned to the Olympic pool, the center spectacle, as I'm stuck on the bottom stairs. Mission: Acquire Sulli's bracelet. Status: Waiting behind a line of people as they try to take their seats in the stands.

I need to go *up*.

The famous ones are gathered in a middle section that I'm trying to reach. Alpha, Omega, and Epsilon are seated in the rows behind their clients, and they seem quiet, observant. The Yale boys aren't even cracking jokes. Donnelly, Oscar, and Farrow are all surveying the packed audience.

Our temp guards are stationed at the bottom and top of the stands along with event security. And by *event security*, I'm talking military.

The United States has spent millions on Olympic security for the Summer Games. I've seen Army National Guard manning screening devices and flashing mirrors under parked cars, checking for IEDs. Special Forces have been tasked as bodyguards for dignitaries and athletes and work quietly among private security like us. And there are *tons* of private security here. Being in L.A., other high-profile celebrities fill the stands and have brought along their own personal bodyguards.

Before the Olympics, Kitsuwon Securities and Triple Shield went through two-weeks of drills to physically prepare for worst case scenarios.

Like kidnappings.

At least she wasn't raped. At least she wasn't kidnapped, Banks.

I grind my teeth. My dad's words haunt my ass, and I want them out of my fucking head like a gravedigger wants a fucking shovel. I'd dig them out if I could.

I look around.

I see security posted everywhere.

"All good things, Banks," I mutter to myself.

Still, my pulse pitches. Eyes dart at the tiniest finger twitch of a teenage girl ahead of me. She's fiddling with her purse, tugging at the zipper.

Thatcher—I just sense my brother watching me. Sure enough, he's eagle-eyeing my hypervigilant stance, and I want to tell him what he always tells me: *Watch your AO. I'm not the objective.*

His concern is a lot.

Too much.

I shift my gaze.

In front of him, Janie is passing turquoise pompoms down the row to her siblings and cousins. Ripley, on Maximoff's lap, reaches for a pompom tassel. Sulli's sixteen-year-old sister Winona proudly hoists the letter *S*. The rest of the girl squad, plus Ben Cobalt and Xander Hale, hold the other letters that spell out *Sulli!*

Xander has the exclamation mark.

In front of them, camera operators for *We Are Calloway* film some of the famous ones for the docuseries. Eighteen-year-old Jesse Highland directs his lens at Jane and my brother. From what Jack said, his little brother Jesse was hired to help film the Olympics for *We Are Calloway*. After this summer, he's attending the University of Pennsylvania and following in Jack's footsteps.

And Jack—I don't see him.

Akara said something about Jack being stationed with press near the pool. He must want footage of Sulli in the water, but he won't be following Sulli around day-in, day-out. She rejected the idea of "a day in the life" footage so she could concentrate on competing.

God has some kind of sense of humor, seeing as how *We Are Calloway* has to be a nothing burger of a distraction to Sulli compared to the pregnancy whopper.

I wait to ascend the stairs. A small thump starts beating against my temple. The beginnings of a thunder-fucking migraine, I'm sure. I'm not cured, but at least they're infrequent. At least it's not going to put my ass on the floor anymore.

I climb a stair.

Then I come to a halt. Mother of fuckin' God. I knew this would take a hot second, but I didn't think it'd be a hot half hour.

Closer to where I stand, around the first few rows, I feel more eyes on me.

And that's when I see the Rochesters. Wyatt, Will, Wesley, Winnifred, and their parents. Blue-blooded, affluent WASPs, dressed in black designer suits and dresses like they're East Coast socialites— which they are. Wesley Rochester, Will's younger brother, has a snide smirk aimed at me that I'd love to wipe off.

He whispers to Will, who's avoiding my cold, lethal glare.

In the back of my head, I hear Will Rochester saying, *fuck you, Sulli*, from months ago, and I almost see red.

"Thatcher to Banks, don't engage." My brother is on comms and in my ear. "Stand down."

I tear my glare off them.

Get her bracelet.

In and out.

"Whoa." A nearby voice triggers my focus. My head jerks to my ten o'clock.

Seated next to the stairs, a college-aged girl with a blonde high-bun is pointing her phone at me. She's recording or snapping photos. "Which one are you?"

Before I became famous, I'd answer honestly. Nicely, actually.

But my patience has short-circuited. It's not her fault. Not really.

"The tall one," I say.

Her nose crinkles. "No, I mean, are you Thatcher Moretti or Banks Moretti?"

My stomach churns. *Ignore.* But hell, I don't want anything I do to come back to my brother. "Banks," I tell her.

She gasps. "Are you nervous about Sullivan Meadows swimming today?"

I used to think it was funny how fans use their full names. *Sullivan Meadows. Maximoff Hale. Jane Cobalt.* Christ, no one even calls her *Jane Moretti.*

Marriage.

I shove the word away fast, my heartbeat spiking.

My narrowed gaze meets her phone's camera. I didn't sign up for some random girl's insta-story. So I rotate my body and close off to the girl. Muscles stiff. *Come on.* One stair up.

Another.

I put more and more distance between her and me. But the further I climb, the more eyes pin to me. The stares slide a cold chill down my spine.

Six-seven.

Can't hide.

"Hey." A familiar, sharp-edged voice cuts into the crowd. "Can you guys make some room? Jesus, this isn't a midnight Avengers release. We all don't need to be dead-stopping on the staircase."

Loren Hale.

"Fucking move," Ryke Meadows adds.

Like the crowd has been zapped by an electric current, everyone picks up their pace. Ryke and Loren are standing at the edge of their row. Both glare at the crowds, not giving a shit what it means for their public image.

I wear a slight smile. Feeling a kinship on that front. Akara would be the first to say that it's been freeing. Having no more fucks to give.

Once I'm close enough, Ryke nods down to me. "You alright, Banks?"

"Yes, sir." I take a tight breath. Hating that I said *sir* after he went at me for the whole *yes, sir* thing a while back. But this doesn't seem to bother him.

He just reminds me, "You don't need to call me *sir.*"

"Yeah." I nod to him again. "You have Sulli's brace—"

Before I finish, he's cursing and reaching into his pocket. "I fucking forgot. Fucking fuck."

Lo laughs. "Anymore fucks and they'll be kicking us out. There are *children* here."

Ryke growls into a groan, "I'm trying."

Families do pack the stands, but I've tried not to notice.

What kind of father will I be?

There it is.

That question again.

It freezes me over for a second. My dad bombed hard at fatherhood. He left my mom, my brother, and me without a second thought. When shit hit the fan and he lost one son, he decided to lose us all. I can't—for a moment—believe I have that in me. To leave my kid. To *abandon* them.

But I am my father's son.

I have his DNA.

I have some parts of him that I don't even understand. All my life it'd been so easy to not lay roots. And if I don't ground myself to anything, then I can't be accused of abandoning it. I'm terrified of being like him.

Of having some inherited *thing* that I can't excise away.

And part of me thinks maybe all this time—not jumping into a serious relationship—that was my dad in me all along. He never remarried after my mom, and as far as I know, he's never had anything serious since.

I'm different now, I assure myself.

I have Sulli.

I have Akara.

I'm different than him.

Stay frosty.

I blink back those thoughts. Coming to focus on the space around me. I'm stuck in the middle of the staircase waiting for Ryke to find Sulli's bracelet.

"Fuck, shit, fuck." He curses under his breath, emptying out every pocket in his jeans.

Loren stares at his brother like he's out of his mind. "*Children,*" Loren whisper-hisses in a reminder. "Sensitive ears. Sensitive souls. Those little things."

I'm gonna have one of those little things.

I rake a tensed hand across my unshaven jaw. Good grief, Ryke has no clue his daughter is pregnant. And I'm standing in front of my girlfriend's dad cradling this massive secret.

"Sorry, Banks." He eyes me for a split-second while he keeps digging in his ass pockets.

I knocked up your daughter, Ryke.

Not sure though. Could be Akara's since we probably both fucked her that night. Surprise.

You're gonna be a grandpa.

I might be brazen enough to say shit I shouldn't say to Ryke, but no way am I telling him that. I'd never announce Sulli's pregnancy without Sulli. That's a shitbag move. And I'm a lot of things, but I'm not a shitbag.

I watch his search continue. "No problem."

A bracelet is the least of our fuckin' worries. The throbbing in my temple increases, and I squint from the bright fluorescent lights. Fuck. I reach into my pocket and pull out some pain meds. Quickly, I pop a couple. No water, but I make do.

"Fucking *A*," Ryke curses.

"Bro," Lo warns.

"I know. I know," Ryke growls at Lo and then looks to me. "I don't think I have it." As soon as he says those words, guilt and worry stretches across his face. "I must've left it in my jacket back at the hotel."

"Can we call someone to pick it up?" Lo asks him, trying to problem solve for his brother.

I catch movement at the pool. "I don't think there's time."

Swimmers emerge from the ready room. Crowds burst into applause, excited for the heats to start. Sulli's sister and cousins spring up, cheering and waving pompoms and signs. Janie whistles loudly with her Aunt Daisy.

Noises echo throughout the stadium.

It pricks my ears. I'm barely blinking.

Canvassing the audience with a narrowed gaze until I land back on the pool.

Swimmers swing their arms back and forth and slowly approach the starting blocks. Everyone loitering on the stairs are rushing to their seats.

Everyone but me.

I want back down to the pool.

Near the ready room exit, I spot Akara standing stoically at a colorful wall—blues, pinks, and yellows blend together and *Los Angeles Olympics* with the year are printed in big white letters behind him. Press bleachers are only a few meters to his three o'clock, and large lenses are aimed at the water and ten lanes. But only eight swimmers will fill the lanes.

Officials cup their hands behind their backs and are scattered around the pool, tasked to judge the competitors.

I subconsciously touch my lanyard and badge that says *security*.

The fact that I can watch my girlfriend compete from the poolside is a blessing and a gift only granted to her closest bodyguards. And I'm not trying to completely waste this perk tonight.

But if I were a better boyfriend, I'd have the bracelet for her to kiss—for at least *one* heat. Knowing I'm about to reach her empty-handed is a gut-punch.

Sulli is shaking out her arms. Swim cap on, she wears a Team USA knee-length, bodyskin swimsuit. She said she doesn't care about the bracelet, but Sulli is superstitious—and I'm praying this won't fuck her concentration.

"It's alright." Loren's words hang in the air, and for a dumb moment, I think they're meant for me. His hand is on Ryke's shoulder, comforting his brother. "She's going to win without an ugly bracelet."

Ryke shoots him a look. "Daisy made it for her."

"Still stand by what I said." Lo flashes a dry smile.

I need to be with Akara. "Thanks for your help," I tell Ryke quickly. Before he can say anything, I rush down the stairs. Skipping a few.

"Slut!" some prick yells.

I immediately stop dead.

Awkward chatter melds with the normal commotion, and I see Connor and Lo restraining Ryke from barreling down the stairs towards a lower row.

Where is this prick?

"Sullivan's a SLUT!"

Found him. He has his hands cupped around his mouth. A shit-eating grin. He can't be older than sixteen, seventeen. His friends snicker, but the people around him drill nastier looks.

Comms crackle in my ear. "Price to Banks…ignore hecklers. Keep moving."

I don't work for Price.

But we're all supposed to work together at the Summer Games. *Teamwork.* It might as well be the fire burning the Olympic torch, and I'd be an idiot to snuff it out.

I keep moving.

"Sluuuuut!"

I grit my teeth. He's not loud enough to disturb the swimmers, but people shift uncomfortably in his section of the stands.

"She takes two dicks up the butt! Sluuut—"

"Hey!"

I whip my head back and upward. Ryke isn't the first one to yell.

It was Sulli's sister.

Winona Meadows hurries out of her row. Faster than Ryke can stop her. "Nona!" he warns. Greer shifts quickly out of his row. Attempting to keep pace with Winona.

Ryke is right behind Greer.

Like a bullet, Winona whizzes fast into the stairs between the sections. I'm further down. Watching as she descends and barrels towards this teenager. "You think you're so cool?! You think you're so *funny*?!"

He's laughing.

I see hell in slow-motion. The girl—the girl with the high-bun who was recording me—she *sticks* her foot into the aisle. No other bodyguard has this vantage but me.

"WINONA!" I yell at the top of my lungs. Thinking she'll stop.

She'll slow.

She doesn't.

She's a fucking Meadows.

I race up the steep, *concrete* stairs just as Winona's foot catches on the girl's ankle. She falls forward. Face-first towards the hard cement lip of the stair.

My muscles scream as I run faster. Harder, and I drop, pounding my knees against concrete to catch Winona under the arms, before her face smashes into cement.

"Oh my God!"

Shrieking.

"Is she okay?!"

People are on their feet. People are crowding the aisle. Crowding us.

I have Winona tucked against me. Her head digging against my abs in an awkward position. But I hesitate to move her right away. She takes shallow, shocked breaths. "Banks?"

"You didn't hit your head," I tell her.

"Is she okay?" people ask me repeatedly. "Don't move her," someone else says.

"She's fine. Can you give her some space?" I jerk my head, signaling the good Samaritans to take a seat.

Winona breathes more uneven, realizing how close she came to eating the stairs. She could've broken her nose, knocked out her teeth, somersaulted until she was concussed, cracked her head wide open.

"Your legs alright? Think you can move?"

"I…" She shifts her head up. "Yeah—"

"Winona!" Ryke has reached his daughter. So has Daisy and their bodyguards. I feel the heat of Wylie, Greer, and Price, and despite me being Winona's sister's boyfriend—Price has the fucking nerve to whisper to me, "We have this, Banks."

I'm glaring every which way. But I don't leave.

I help Winona to her feet. And my knees sear and roar in pain. She's fisting my shirt like I'm the railing.

"You could've killed her, you troll!" Kinney is yelling at the girl who tripped Winona. Lo and Lily are speaking fast to their daughter, and Vada is being talked into staying seated by her parents.

Audrey is pointing at the tripper and speaking to her mom. Ben is in a heated argument with his dad. And the only one who's left unrestrained isn't even famous.

"Feel good about that viral video?" Jesse Highland, the shaggy-haired surfer boy, has entered the stairs. Camera at his side, he shouts down to the tripper. "Delete it."

She huffs, looking uncertain. "I don't have to do anything you say."

"*Jesse*," another camera operator snaps. "Get back here. *Now.*"

He doesn't move.

The camera operator whisper-sneers, "Do you want to lose your job?"

Winona watches as Jesse considers this. "It's okay, Jesse." She lets go of my shirt, and with quaking arms, she clasps her mom's hand.

Jesse reluctantly backs away, and when I turn to the pool, my pulse skips.

Swimmers are already on their blocks. But they're watching the stands. Watching us.

Sulli saw her sister free-fall and almost face-plant.

Hell, millions of TV viewers probably saw the drama, but I'm more concerned about Sulli's focus. Her goals.

Goggles over her eyes, I know she's staring at me.

And I tug my ear twice.

She intakes a big breath.

We came up with signals during the Olympics—the three of us—knowing there'd be moments where we couldn't talk.

In fucking hindsight, we should've made up a signal for *everything's okay*.

But I default to the ear-tug.

Which simply means, *I love you*.

Her earlobe peeks from her swim cap. And she does a quick tug.

Now I breathe stronger, and with sore knees, I try not to limp as I resume my course to the pool. To Akara. He's forcing himself not to shift a muscle and come to my fuckin' rescue. I almost smile. Arms crossed, he's gripping the hell out of his biceps.

Officials instruct ten swimmers to recommence the heat. They assume the starting position. Arms arched over the knees and about to grasp the front edge of the platform.

"Take your mark," the starter commands, causing the stadium to fall hushed.

I reach the last few rows.

Expecting a *beep* next.

Instead, there's a *splash*.

Everyone gasps.

My heart lurches to my throat at the sight of a false start.

17

Akara Kitsuwon

THE FALSE START IS BRUTAL, and I'm wincing.

I should pad-lock any reactions until Sulli's heat is over. Be totally cool and emotionless like Price is hoping the head of Kitsuwon Securities will be. Like press isn't expecting me to be. They're waiting to spin a camera on my face so they can tether together a dramatic storyline between me and Banks and Sulli.

Before, I might've glared and thought, *I'm giving you nothing to work with. Go find another camera whore.*

Now—*now*, I don't care. Make me a *fudging* camera whore. Make me whatever you want—because all that really matters is the girl in the pool, the guy on his way to me, and my men.

Everyone else can suck a sour pickle.

Anna Laurent, the eighteen-year-old French swimmer who dove into the water before the *beep*, starts bawling. Hands to her face, she treads water, shaking and crying like her life has ended. I wince more.

That could've been Sulli.

Thank fudge it wasn't.

We're all seriously pushing our luck today. Winona was a single second from slamming face-first into concrete stairs. I'm still on edge from seeing her go down into Banks, and I bet Sulli isn't one-hundred percent ready to compete after watching her sister fall.

Banks caught her. The three of us—we've experienced unexplainable moments, like currents in time placing us in perfect symmetry with each other, and something put Banks *there* today. Sulli's love for her sister. His love for Sulli. Maybe even his love for me—because I know he left to give me alone-time with our girlfriend.

The fact that he was there—that's what saved Winona. He wasn't supposed to be on those stairs. He wasn't supposed to go retrieve a missing bracelet. And he wasn't supposed to be on his way back to me. Ready to turn and catch her fall.

I can drum it *all* up to luck or coincidence, but I won't.

I can't.

The spiritual pieces of me know it's more.

But yeah, I'm sure there's a morsel of luck wedged in there too. Let's hope that hasn't all run out.

"Horrifying false start for France," a sports commentator speaks quietly into his headset. He's the closest to me from the press bleachers. "Swimmers are waiting for a reset as the referee and officials decide over Laurent's chances to return. To remind viewers at home, officials enforce all rules and decisions of FINA, and there *is* a no false-start rule. This is likely the end of the road for Laurent."

Laurent climbs out of the pool, hand encased over her mouth. Eyes squeezed shut, she drops into a squat and sobs into her arm. Olympic dreams crushed.

Don't let that be Sulli.

I should have empathy for the French swimmer, but instead, I'm just afraid for my girlfriend. Four years ago, I remember the same nerves racing through me—because this powerful thing I feel for Sulli—it's always existed.

It lived and breathed back then.

But I wouldn't show the fear or how I could've crouched down and bit my nails to the bed. Now I feel the worry flood my face, and I let it.

"Officials are telling swimmers to remain on the block. They're going to resume the heat, as Laurent has just been disqualified."

Sulli turns her head, her goggled eyes pointed in my direction. I smile and mouth, *six.* She only has six girls left to beat in her heat. It's a good thing.

Better Anna Laurent goes down than Sullivan Meadows.

My girlfriend shares the same kill or be killed mentality when it comes to competing. She looks more readied, determination in her stance and as she swings her arms and bends, waiting to grip the starting platform. One more glance to me.

I tug on my ear.

Her lips rise.

Four years ago, I wasn't dating Sulli. I hadn't kissed her yet. I hadn't slept with her. I hadn't seen her bare and wanting and craving. I hadn't seen her cry over more than swimming. I hadn't learned how to quell her deepest fears. I hadn't held her with another man. I hadn't heard her say she's in love with me and she's pregnant. I hadn't told her just how much she means to me.

Four years ago was light-years different than today, but then, some things really are the same.

These feelings.

They overpower me. My chest rises, and I can't take my eyes off Sulli. Not as she's seconds from diving into the water.

"Take your mark," the starter commands.

Beep.

All seven swimmers are in the pool. Their arms propel over their heads in the butterfly stroke. I cage oxygen like I'm under the water with her.

Come on, Sul.

Come on, Sul.

"Come on, Sul," I mutter under my breath.

"Meadows is in the lead," the commentator narrates. "She's the only swimmer for the United States to qualify for women's 200m IM. After butterfly, they'll be changing to backstroke, but breaststroke is crucial here. It is all legs, and Meadows doesn't want to gas out."

Sulli reaches the end of the pool first.

I inhale slightly.

"Great turn for Meadows—and Meadows at the first fifty. In front of Australia and Japan, close behind. Backstroke is strong as Meadows leads the pack."

I smile at his words, and I hear the sounds of the stadium. Cheers echoing off the dome and the splash of water and the stadium announcer speaking through a booming mic as swimmers reach one end of the fifty-meter pool and turn. This is the music Sulli has missed and loved and *loves*.

"Meadows quickly comes into the breaststroke leg—she makes the turn and kicks. Oh no."

My face plummets.

Sulli's goggles are slipping off her face.

"Meadows is losing her goggles. Her goggles are now beneath her nose and completely off her eyes. She is maintaining pace, but not for long—Australia and Japan are gaining speed."

No, no, *no*.

I bite my tongue so I don't shout. I'm not in the stands. I can't yell from poolside, but *shit*, I want to shout at Sulli to keep going. She has this. She's okay.

She's okay.

"Meadows is clearly trying her hardest, but the goggles are wrapped around her mouth and she's struggling to spit them out or free them. This is painful to watch."

I'm cringing.

I'm wincing.

I have a hand to my forehead. Where's Banks? I want to look around for him, but I can't shift my attention off Sulli. She needs me rooting for her, and I wish I could clap her on. But the best I have is muttering quietly, "You have this, Sul. You can do this, Sul. Come on. *Come on.*"

"Meadows is falling far behind—oh, bad turn from Meadows. The goggles are clearly affecting her technique and pace as she goes into freestyle, her best stroke."

I smear my hand down to my mouth. Still as a statute, I just wait for the last fifty meters.

"Australia in one. Japan in two…and can Meadows do it, can she advance to the finals? Meadows comes in fifth, but will that be enough?"

Sulli yanks off her goggles and whips her head to the aquatic scoreboard. There are only two heats for the 200m IM. The first has already gone. She's a part of the second heat, and among those two groups, the fastest eight will see the finals.

So she's fifth in her heat, but she's definitely not fifth overall.

I quickly look for Sulli's name and where she's fallen in the ranking. Come on. Please, let her make the finals. Please.

Nine.

The number *nine*.

My number.

Me.

Next to her name.

I blink hard, my heart shattering.

Sulli.

If I could, I'd do anything to erase that number and type in *eight*. Preferably number *one*, but right now, I just want her to have a chance at the finals. Last Olympics, she easily breezed into them.

She never got out this early.

"By less than three-tenths of a second, Meadows has finished in 9th place. Disappointment from the stands. Remember, Meadows is the only U.S. swimmer in this event, and she's representing the host country this year."

Okay, he's grating on me now. I shoot the commentator a glare.

He's unaware, fixed on his tiny TV monitor, and he couldn't hear me if I said a thing. Not with his microphone headset on.

"If you've seen those clips today, her family is here watching. Meadows hangs her head for a second. She's yet to leave the water. At poolside, her boyfriend Akara Kitsuwon watches in horror."

Awesome.

Just awesome.

I don't change my face. And I'm *not* horrified. I'm concerned. There's a difference.

"Her second boyfriend is approaching Kitsuwon." *He's not second to me or to her.*

I see Banks before the sports commentator announces his arrival. He chews on a toothpick, his brows bunched in worry, and he keeps glancing back at Sulli.

"Not good," I whisper.

"I saw." He speaks really deeply, huskily, almost inaudibly. "Shot to the heart."

"Right through." My nose flares. "She has five more heats. It's not over. She just needs more confidence."

"And a new pair of fucking goggles."

"She'll probably double-cap to secure them better." I massage my knuckles, then pause. Is Banks limping? "Are you limping?"

He tenses. "Busted my knees pretty bad."

"Go ice it."

"Nine—"

"That's an order."

"Go talk to her. She needs one of us."

"She needs both of us," I correct.

Banks cracks a waning smile. "One is all she's getting right now." He puts a hand on my shoulder, and I can feel him bracing his weight on me. He must've really tweaked his knees.

"I don't like this feeling," I tell him before we separate.

He nods. "Yeah, I know."

It's the feeling of choosing one over the other in a given moment. Sulli over Banks. Banks over Sulli. We all need each other, we all want each other, but there are times where we have to choose whose needs come first.

And right now, I head for Sulli.

18

Sullivan Meadows

"THE FUCKING GOGGLES," is all I keep saying, is all I keep feeling. *Those fucking goggles.* What a stupid mistake that cost me a medal.

It is tearing and clawing at my insides.

"Hey, screw the goggles, strong bean." Akara is squatting at my lane.

"You mean *string bean*?"

"*Strong* bean. The mightiest of beans. The one that's built from giant beanstalks that not even guys named Jack can climb."

I laugh.

Kits has the ability to make me laugh when sadness mounts to un-fucking-bearable heights. Tears gather in my eyes, more easily than normal.

"Hey," Akara whispers, seeing my eyes glass.

"They're not sad tears, Kits. I'm just…" *Fucking emotional.* Hormonal, I guess.

He looks like he wants to hug me.

I'd love a hug from my boyfriend.

But I'm submerged in the water. The next event is in thirty-minutes. Women's 400m freestyle, and my heat is first, so I'm gripping onto the pool's edge with one hand and chugging a Ziff Power chocolate protein shake with the other.

I've already double-capped and secured my goggles. I won't be making the same mistake twice. No fucking way.

And at least Banks is okay. He's icing his knees, Akara said. My sister is okay.

"You're going to advance to the finals for the other five heats," Akara assures. "Easily. Like last Olympics."

Like last Olympics.

Where I didn't have boyfriends.

I had never been kissed.

I ignored even the *thought* of romance. If, for a second, I thought Akara was hot on the sidelines, I said, *who the fuck cares? Swimming is my first and only love. Swimming is all that matters.*

Now, it's not all that matters to me.

I've felt their lips against mine. I've felt their strong arms around my waist. I've felt their hands dripping down my body. I've felt their desire and their lust and their love, and I've wanted for more—I've wanted for them.

I have them.

"Sulli?" Akara can see me drowning in my thoughts.

"What if I was only great four years ago because I loved nothing else but swimming?" I ask in a quiet, raspy voice, a lump swelling in my throat. "What if I've split myself into too many pieces and I've given this sport the smallest one?"

"I don't believe that at all." Akara stares deeply into me. "There are so many athletes who could give up *everything* and never be where you are. You're here because you were born to swim. And you, more than anyone, should know you can love more than one thing without severing that love into pieces."

I let that wash over me, and his words lift me and my spirits.

I am filled with more love than four years ago. That should propel me further, not hold me back.

"Thanks, Kits." I'm about to put the rim of the protein drink to my mouth. But Akara stretches closer—and he kisses me.

I smile against his kissable lips.

He deepens the kiss with sensual sweetness that hums throughout my limbs. I could practically float into his arms.

TV cameras are definitely rolling, and chatter spreads like threads of gossip across the pool and to the stands. But like the kiss with Banks from the clinic, I wish this could last longer.

Akara has to pull back. He's smiling like me, but he hesitates a little. Almost nervous, I think. "Is that going to distract you, Sul?"

"Just the opposite." I swig the protein shake. "It's going to motivate me." I'm done trying to block everything out. Done trying to forget I'm pregnant. Done trying to be the Sullivan Minnie Meadows from four years ago.

I'm a new fucking woman. I have two boyfriends who I want to kiss at the end of the race. Who I want to swim towards. The song that Banks sang to me fills my head.

Swim to me.

Swim to Banks.

Swim to Akara.

Swim to our baby.

Swim to them.

19

Akara Kitsuwon

WE ARE CALLOWAY 4EVER – Facebook Page
For fans of the Hales, Cobalts, & Meadows – we discuss the docuseries & current events following our fav families!
42m like this page

Posted 1hr ago:
BREAKING NEWS
Sullivan loses the 200m IM after a tragic goggle malfunction, but she advances to finals in 5 other events!

15.7k likes - 600 shares - 2.4k comments:

Cynthia Bird: Knew she'd kill it tonight! The goggle thing was such a fluke accident.

Talia Rey: She's totally going to beat that Hansen girl. There's no way Sullivan won't take 5 golds home.

Sav Lionel: Anyone think she seemed off? Like I know Akara & Banks are hawt (I'd prob drown just seeing them) but that can't be healthy having them RIGHT THERE while she's swimming

Hiromi Toda: @Sav Lionel Akara kissed her, then she killed the 400m freestyle. Doubt they're screwing up her chances

Agatha Thompson: @Sav Lionel she shouldn't be with two men. That's the problem. It's disgusting.

Talia Rey: @Agatha Thompson if this was Reddit, I'd be downvoting the hell out of you.

Agatha Thompson: @Talia Rey this isn't Reddit, it's Facebook.

Karter P: @Sav Lionel if she doesnt get a gold this yr we know its there fault. They shouldve just stayed home

Hiromi Toda: @Karter P they're her bodyguards they can't stay home

Karter P: @Hiromi Toda u really believe that? SFO is super fake. There all def dating whoever they claim there protecting

Mary Westermoore: Can we PLEASE have a post-thread about Banks saving Winona Meadows from a fall? EPIC!

"WHAT'S FUCKING WRONG with people?" Banks grumbles hotly under his breath, sounding a little pained and a lot pissed.

Showered and shirtless, we're both in sweatpants and sitting on the same rickety cot. Our shoulders to the wall of Sulli's room in the Olympic Village—we're doing a quick social media check to end our long night.

Just what I completely adore.

Reading about "SFO is fake" conspiracies and how my relationship is "disgusting" to people who have no room to judge. Break out the confetti and let it rain on *Agatha*. She's so righteous. So smart.

So very stupendous.

Love her.

I scroll down through the comments and try to focus on the positives. Quietly, I tell Banks, "Same old shit, different day."

He makes a gruff, heated noise, and I peel my attention off the Facebook page, my phone cupped in my hand.

Banks is searing holes into his own cellphone. His jaw muscle tics. Nose flares. I feel his entire body contract and flex beside me.

If this is affecting Banks that badly, then maybe I should pull him off social media checks. Give the task solely to the tech team. Shoot, *I've* considered letting this part of the job go, but I can be a control freak. And I like understanding the temperature of the public perception without running to Jack Highland-Oliveira.

"I'm gonna kill him," Banks grumbles, so lowly that I almost miss the words.

He can't be on a fan page like me.

"What are you reading?" I lean over to see, the cot creaking.

He shows me Twitter with the trending hashtag #SullivanMeadows.

@lowandbehold23: hope that slut chokes on pool water #SullivanMeadows

@CoolBeanz_haha: We're all rooting for you #SullivanMeadows!!!!! Don't fuck it up!!!!!

@tee2hee: im gonna rape that slut after she loses to Australia #SullivanMeadows

@calloways-thots1: #SullivanMeadows is with the hottest guys. I don't make the rules #facts #LAOlympics

@RykeMeadowwsNumber1Stan: @calloways-thots1 in what world? Ryke is wayyyy hotter than Banks and Akara

@calloways-thots1: @RykeMeadowwsNumber1Stan ew Ryke is old

@RykeMeadowwsNumber1Stan: @calloways-thots1 ur old!
U smell like aged gouda

I wish I could laugh at the absurd gouda tweet. But I fixate on the tweet that I'm positive is grating on Banks.

@tee2hee: im gonna rape that slut after she loses to Australia #SullivanMeadows

I go still. Fire starts brewing in my chest that I need to extinguish. Only one of us should be amped at once. At most *two*, and preferably, it'll be her and him and I won't be fueled off impassioned feelings that exist inside me, churning. Stirring.

Burning.

"Those aren't people, Banks," I whisper strongly. "They're anonymous trolls hiding behind their screens and keyboards, and they spout off empty threats that are meant to incite." Banks knows I can pop off, but we can't pop off on the internet.

It's a bad call.

Banks is stewing and still glaring at the rape tweet.

"*Banks.*" I reach for the phone.

He jerks it away. "For every single rape threat, there's a dozen more death threats, and I know—I fucking *know* it's messy and dumb to respond. But not telling these guys they're sick in the head is fuckin' killing me, Akara."

I want to tell him to stick to fan pages. It's safer. Good mixed in with some bad. Tech team can handle hashtags. They have the software, so they'll do a better job anyway.

But the words sit like tar in the back of my throat.

I can't release them.

Banks is saying everything that I feel deep-down. He's craving to do what I wish I could do. But I'm the *boss* of this security firm. I have to consider the reputation of Kitsuwon Securities. About the example I set for my bodyguards.

Part of me envies Banks. That he can be so carefree with his emotions. Part of me hates that I have the power to stop him, and I should. It'd be smart.

It might even be the right call.

Listen to your heart, Nine.

I stiffen, not sure if I should be listening to *my dad* in my head anymore.

"I made Donnelly suspend his Twitter account for fighting with Farrow-haters," I remind him.

Banks still looks amped. "You're always saying that."

"Because we've been here before." This isn't the first time that Banks has considered replying to hatred and me talking him down. He'll eventually concede to just posting positive things about Sulli on his own Instagram.

"I can't get over it," Banks admits, a rough hand running through his hair. "I just keep picturing them getting away with my worst fucking nightmare."

"They won't," I say with heat, my chest on fire. "You know we'd scorch the ground before anyone hurts her. And these sick pricks aren't coming out of the computer, Banks. It's faraway."

"It feels close."

"Yeah," I breathe tightly. I can say it'll never happen, but that doesn't mean it doesn't hurt to see and know someone out in the world is *thinking* these vile things about the person we love.

Banks holds my gaze in a vice. "It's *Sulli.*"

The way he says her name, I feel that desperate love seep deeper into my bloodstream.

It's Sulli.

I think about the past. "I've been here before with Farrow," I tell Banks. "He was obsessing over that Instagram account with murder photos of Maximoff. He was convinced it was a real threat, and it seemed like one-in-a-million at the time." I take a tensed breath. "Even when we found out the threat was real, I told Farrow to stop looking at the account. He was too close to it."

Banks rests his eyes on mine. "You're going to tell me to stop looking at social media?"

"I should." I pause. "I should ban you from Twitter. Make you delete your accounts."

Banks studies me. "But you're not?"

"No, I'm not."

"Why?"

"Because it's Sulli." I inhale a bigger breath, "And you're Banks. And even if it makes me a bad boss, I'd rather be free with you than hold us both back."

He cracks a shadow of a smile. "I guess my brother was right."

"What do you mean?"

"He said I've always been your exception."

I let out a laugh. Yeah.

Banks Moretti is my favorite, and I'm done trying to hide that or underscore what he means to me. I've been done, and it's too dang obvious to conceal anyway. Maybe it always has been. "If the Yale boys give you more crap for the special privileges, just tell them to come argue with me."

Banks bends a knee as he sits higher up the wall. He winces slightly. "It's never bothered me. They can pout about it."

Under his sweatpants, his kneecaps are black-and-blue from the fall tonight. Before I draw attention to the injury, he clicks into the rape tweet.

"Wait."

He pauses.

"Way to go, Viktor!" someone shouts in the hallway. Chatter ignites with some cheering. Frat house commotion, but we're not on fraternity row. Just the Olympic Village. Late-night noises are constant in the thin-walled residential building for athletes.

Sulli hasn't minded skipping out on the big social part of the Olympics. She didn't join these celebrations four years ago. Too focused.

Too determined.

When the chatter dies down, I tell Banks, "You send one tweet under your account, it'll be reposted on every single tabloid and become headlines. Then we're going to have more eyes on Sulli than before."

Banks frowns. "So we're not responding?"

"No, we are. Just not as ourselves."

His mouth curves upward. "We're making a fake account?"

"A *fan* account."

He actually grins. "Right on, right on." He signs out and starts to create a new account. We discuss the username for a few minutes before picking @Love4Sullivan.

"Profile pic should be water. Like a pool," I tell him.

He finds one off the internet. Uploads. "Got it. First tweet?"

"Take it away." I'm giving Banks the reins.

"You sure?"

"Yeah." He needs this. Whether it'll help him or us—I don't know. That's the thing about mistakes, I usually don't know I make them until it's too late.

Leaning into Banks, I watch him type out a reply tweet.

@Love4Sullivan: @tee2hee you're really going to threaten to rape a girl? What's fucking wrong with you??

That's more restrained than I thought. "I'm shocked you didn't call *teehee* names."

"I want to know *why* he's thinking this sick, unconscionable, unholy fucking thing." Banks leans back. "Then I'm going to call him names."

"You really think he'll reply?"

He shrugs, then sticks his hand in a box. He shovels cereal in his mouth.

I zero in on the box. "What are you eating?"

"Cereal. Want some?"

I reach over his chest and snatch the box. Granola O's. Tobias Kingly's face is on the fracking box, staring smugly at me. "Really?"

"I was hungry," Banks protests.

I chuck the cereal. And the box skids across the floorboards.

Banks cocks his head to me. "We aren't supposed to be the petty ones."

"His cardboard face can go eat the floor." I remind Banks, "He put doubt in Sulli's head."

Banks nods strongly. "Until he calls Sulli what she is—the *greatest*—he's been dead to me, too. I just don't let him dictate what I'm eating."

"Love you a whale-y ton too, Nona-Frog." Sulli emerges from the bathroom in nothing but a towel. I drink in her long legs, athletic frame, and her cute, messy bun. In a hot second, I start imagining my hand slipping between the crease of the towel.

Skimming her inner-thigh. My fingertips grazing closer and closer towards her heat. I want so deep inside Sulli.

"He responded to us," Banks whispers to me, but not quietly enough. Sulli can hear, and I feel her zeroing in on us as I urgently read his phone.

@tee2hee: @Love4Sullivan you can rape her too

I'm glaring.

Banks is fuming. He's typing back quickly.

"Okay, yeah…bye." Sulli hangs up. "What's going on, guys?"

We both look up like we've been caught plotting murder.

20
Sullivan Meadows

"SECURITY STUFF, SUL," Akara answers me. But his tensed features make me believe it's *more*. They're hovering over Banks' phone like they're in an after-school clique and I'm the loser asking the cool kids to befriend me.

That's not what this is.

I'm not being left out.

They're my boyfriends, for fuck's sake.

Right?

The rational parts of my brain are biting back at my insecurities.

"Security stuff?" I repeat. "Not boyfriend stuff?"

"Well…" Akara scrunches his face.

Banks softens his gaze on me, his head dipped a little. "Partly boyfriend stuff."

"A quarter," Akara amends.

Banks clearly thinks otherwise. He slips Akara a hard look like he's wrong.

Akara shoots a look back like *I'm not wrong, man.*

And I'm fucking proud of myself for being able to discern their silent glances. Only people a part of the *clique* would understand the *clique*, right? Therefore, I'm in the inner-fucking-circle.

Math isn't my strong suit, but fuck it, I'm liking my math.

"A quarter, half—whatever it is, are you going to tell me what's up?" I leave wet footprints as I pass my single-bed and approach them. Muscles aching and sore from swimming tonight.

They're sitting on the cot like a couch against the wall, and Akara shoves Banks' hand, clearly telling him to put the phone away.

"Kits?" Hurt stabs me.

He winces. "It's nothing, Sul."

"It's not nothing. You're acting like it's *something*."

Banks keeps his phone in hand, glaring at the screen, and with a heavy breath, Banks tells me, "It's not anything good." His face is hardened, moodier, nose flaring.

Banks is mad? He avoids my eyes a little bit. I've seen him overprotective. Aggravated. Angry, even, but I'd say Akara is feistier than him.

What could've struck a nerve with Banks?

"Is it the viral video of Dean and Kingly?"

"What video?" Banks asks.

Not the video then.

"Just…something annoying." I expel a breath. "Dean recorded himself and Kingly jumping on a bed to see how many jumps it'd take to break. Luna said they're being called the 'best Olympic bromance' or something like that. Which A. is totally false, because the best platonic bromance at the Olympics is you two."

Fucking duh.

As soon as I say *platonic*, they seem off—and realization kicks me back. "Fuck, sorry. I forgot…*fuck*. You two haven't kissed yet, or maybe you have and I wasn't there—"

"We haven't," Akara cuts me off, thankfully.

I breathe. "Right, okay."

"I mean, we could still be platonic," he explains. "No sexual attraction."

"We haven't tested it," Banks adds, an awkwardness in the air. I think mostly due to the uncertainty.

"Cool." *Cool?* God, I suck at conversational segues. I wipe a driblet of shower water off my brow. "Um, and you know B.—my second point—if I made a funny video jumping on the bed, I'd be called 'disrespectful' and probably scolded by national media. Whereas, Kingly is being praised."

"It's not fair," Banks agrees. "They're gonna hold him to a different standard because he's a guy."

I realize that Banks and Akara hold Kingly to a normal standard. Probably more normal than anyone watching on TV or anyone here. Even me. I've elevated him to extreme, untouchable *godly* levels because...because I did revere him.

Part of me wishes I still could, in the same rose-colored way.

As Banks returns to his phone, my mind reels back onto their hidden agenda.

I wince at a thought. "Oh fuck, is the internet still obsessing over the goggle thing?"

Banks shakes his head.

I can tell I'm really off. "The flagbearer drama?"

Another head shake.

"No one leaked anything about the cinnamon roll, did they?" I panic for less than a second. Seeing Banks with a heartier head-shake.

"Sul," Akara cringes like I'm stepping into a five-car pile-up. "Can you stop guessing?"

"Is it that bad?"

Their silence is a big fucking *yes*.

"Cum, fuck," I mutter, and I eye the phone, how Banks is typing. Confusion amasses higher than even curiosity, and I just want to climb this confusion like it's the mountain keeping me from winning.

Maybe if I grab the phone...?

Hair sopping wet in a messy bun, I regrip my towel snug around my chest.

Akara stares right at my boobs.

I instantly smile.

His breath shallows. He licks his kissable lips. He runs a hand through his black hair, and even as he shifts his gaze off my boobs, they return and drip down the length of my body.

He thinks I'm hot.

I feel sexy beneath his desire, and I can't help but remember last Olympics. At eighteen, all hope that Akara found me attractive began depleting. Like sand in an hourglass, I watched the likelihood of us ever kissing or having passionate, wild sex or falling in World Series kind of love flit away.

But now, I think it was always supposed to be this path, this way. Akara and Banks with me.

Grab the phone. I haven't forgotten.

I come so close that my knees knock into Akara's knees. I tower above him. The flap of towel draws his carnal gaze towards my bare thighs. "Can I get a hint?" I kick his feet apart.

"It's social media."

Un-fucking-surprising.

With his legs spread, I take a seat between them. Resting my back against his chest, I feel his muscles warm and flex in arousal.

I start to ache for hardness inside me. Throbbing for Akara and Banks. But I concentrate. "Another hint?" My voice sounds raspier.

Banks turns his head. He freezes. I look right at Banks as he looks at me, and I part my sore legs so they spread open against Akara's. The towel hides my pussy, but the temptation is all over their roaming gazes.

I bottle their reaction like liquid arousal, and the fumes intoxicate the air. Intoxicate me. I melt back against Akara.

His hands glide down my thighs along the towel. Tantalizing, *tormenting.* I quiver, needing his skin on my skin, but his fingertips stop at the fabric's edge. "Kits."

"Are you trying to seduce us?" he whispers against my hair.

"Maybe."

"I'm better at this game, Lady Meadows."

God, Akara is hot, and I don't doubt he is better at seduction. He's had more practice, and he oozes sex appeal. "I said *maybe* it's my goal." And that's when I reach for the phone.

"Fuck," Banks curses as I capture his cell.

I flip over the screen and see a username and a word that overturns my stomach. And then Banks steals the phone away. He looks concerned. I think…I think I saw the bad thing, but I push that word to the side.

"Love4Sullivan?" I question. "Someone loves me out there."

"A lot of people love you," Banks says sweetly.

"I know I have some fans still, but it's not like four years ago. A lot more people were rooting for me to succeed than to fail."

I wonder how many girls ripped posters of me off their walls when my life didn't turn out *exactly* how they envisioned for me. It stings, knowing I disappointed people, but it hurts more thinking of life without Banks and Akara. And I won't apologize for loving them.

"Banks and I are @Love4Sullivan," Akara suddenly confesses.

"What?"

"We made a fan account on social media."

My jaw drops, and I turn a little so I can see his face behind me. "I thought you can't do that. Like…it's against security policy or something?"

"He's the boss," Banks reminds me.

A sexy smile inches up Akara's lips.

I flush, and I glance back at Banks, who suddenly stands off the cot. Fuck, he's tall. *Duh, Sulli.* But I'm so entranced at how Banks commands a room with quiet confidence. He's not arrogant or showboating. He's rough on the outside from a hard youth but soft and sweet on the inside.

I knock my knees together as I pulse. "So what are you guys posting then?"

They go quiet.

My spirits pop. "You can't tell me?"

Banks grimaces, not liking when I'm down. "We're responding to some shit."

"Some shit…" I shake my head, but I almost lose my thought as Akara takes a hand off my thigh and massages my trap.

Oh fuck, that feels…*glorious.* I let out a soft noise, and he uses both hands to knead the tender muscle around my neck.

Eyes almost shutting, I force them open to ask, "Are you sure that's a good idea? Responding to negativity?" I'm mostly looking at Banks since Akara is giving me a sensual, toe-tingling massage.

Banks tosses his phone on his duffel bag. "It wasn't our only idea."

That doesn't make me feel better.

We're all freshly new to being devastatingly famous where me sneezing outside a Wawa could make a headline. But I've been under a spotlight a lot longer than them. "I think ignoring negative stuff on social media is better than fueling the flames."

"It's an anonymous account," Akara clarifies. "No one is going to attack us or you for responding."

"That's not what I'm concerned about, Kits. I've learned that even *peeking* at that stuff is bad for the soul. It's toxic and I don't want either of you to harbor hatred in your heart because of hateful people."

"We won't," Banks assures. "Look, it's done for now." He raises his hands to show the phone is gone.

"For now?"

"I can't promise I won't use the account again," Banks says seriously. "I just need to vent, Sulli. This isn't easy for me." Something raw in his eyes says the answer they've been withholding. I think I saw the word... when I glanced at the phone...I just didn't want to fully accept it.

Rape.

A rape threat.

They'll protect me. I'm safe. The thought quells some anxiety, but I've been fucking terrified of being kidnapped and worse ever since I overheard Michael Moretti, Banks' dad, say it's in the realm of possibilities.

I think about how Banks just needs an outlet to vent.

Maybe it'll be cathartic for him. Maybe it'll hurt him. I don't know. I don't fucking know, so who am I to tell him to stop? Akara is clearly okaying this too.

"Okay," I breathe. "I think I get it." I relax further into Akara's stroking and kneading hands, and I watch Banks consider going to the bathroom.

Stay.

Don't leave.

Touch me.

He's about to cross the room, and I break apart my thighs. Sliding them flush against Akara's spread legs again. The towel falls slightly open, and Banks has a clear view of my pussy. I already feel soaked for my boyfriends.

Akara and Banks exchange a wordless, hungered look, and then Banks stalks towards me while Akara presses his lips to the edge of my jaw, then trails burning, feather-light kisses to my earlobe. Shivers ripple down my body.

"Kits," I rasp.

I crave force between my legs, the fullness. I crave their caring, loving, starved hands, the knowledge that I'm theirs to protect and adore in every stroke, in every grip, in every kiss and glance.

Akara's breath warms the nape of my neck. His palms glide slowly along the towel at my thighs. I try to move his hands further between my legs, and he grips harder to the towel. He whispers sexily in the pit of my ear, "Not yet, Sulli." God, his voice is another feather-light kiss, another caressing hand, another thread of love wound around my eagerness and longing.

The soreness from swimming is beginning to dissolve into melting desire.

Banks slowly kneels between my legs. "Banks—your knees."

"They're fine." He hides any pain. While I'm leaning back against Akara, I keep my eyes on Banks. He clutches my calf, massaging the kinks.

"Oh God…yes, fuck." My lips part, and a whimper comes out the second Banks slips his other hand beneath the towel. *Oh my God.* I'm being massaged to blissful paradise by two men who I trust and love, and I could throw myself at them and say, *take me.*

But they already have me completely.

Akara and Banks knead and toy, intensifying a primal, sexual craving inside me. I pulsate, needing. Wanting. Their bodies. In me. Against me.

On top of me.

All over me.

Banks rubs my clit, and I squirm against Kits, who makes a breathy, deep noise against my ear. He hardens against my ass, and I dig backward, aching for friction.

"Sulli," he warns.

I want him.

I want them.

They grow a little rougher and urgent. Akara opens the towel further, exposing my boobs and perked nipples. He flicks his thumb over one and then leans over, sucking the other. My toes curl.

Oh fuck me.

I shudder and grab hold of his thigh and Banks' bicep. I'm falling into these feelings, and I'd happily drown with them.

Banks stops massaging my bundle of nerves, and then he dips his head between my legs. "Banks," I rasp and choke on a sharp breath. He kisses my heat, his skilled tongue swirling and sucking—and the sensitivity lights my entire body on fucking fire.

Holy...fuck.

I arch my back. "I can't...I need..." *More.*

Akara kisses my collarbone, then my neck. "You need my cock?"

Fuck me please. I gasp at Akara's words and Banks' tongue. I almost rock into Banks' face, but Akara clutches my legs, keeping them wide open. Keeping me stretched and throbbing.

I lean further back into Akara. Letting him hold me while Banks eats me out, and I dizzy, eyes rolling in carnal ecstasy.

He unties my bun, damp hair cascading wildly on my shoulders. Akara brushes my hair to one side, his fingertips sending shockwaves to my toes.

"You need his cock?" Akara breathes against my ear.

Fuck me please, I think again. *Slip inside me all at once, at the same time.* Closing in on a climax, I don't want to come yet. I want to feel the fullness. I want to be closer than close to my boyfriends. Deeper than deep.

Both of them inside me.

"...can we?" I gasp out.

"Can we what?" Akara whispers.

"I'm pregnant," I say like it's an unknown fact.

Banks peers up from my pussy. They both go still. Stopping all movement and assessing me. I flush, a different kind of heat bathing me. I feel young.

I feel inexperienced. But why should I? It's not like they've knocked up another girl before. As far as I'm aware, I'm their first.

Banks eyes my abdomen, and Akara's fingers graze the soft skin below my belly button.

I'm not far enough along to show, but I've brought a glaring spotlight to the cinnamon roll in the oven. A new sort of intimacy strings between the three of us that didn't exist before. Tethering us.

But the vulnerability causes a mild case of panic.

How much is really going to change? Will they want to touch me?

"Will you guys still want to have sex?" I ask, trying to snuff out the alarm. "Even if I'm pregnant?"

Unable to see Akara behind me, I wonder what expression they exchange. Amusement? Banks is smiling a little, and Akara's hands affectionately sweep my belly.

My pulse calms.

Very huskily, Banks says, "Yeah, mermaid. We still want to make love to you. All night. All day."

I smile, then peek up at Akara.

He smiles down at me. "Just not roughly." He takes a short beat. "And we'll probably all hate this, but I don't think we should DP while you're pregnant." *DP. Double Penetration.*

Banks nods, agreeing, and his eyes drift back to my abdomen.

Disappointment punctures my smile. We've already worked up to the moment where Akara and Banks are inside me, together, and I've fantasized about returning to that peak of intimacy. To say that I enjoyed DP would be a big fucking understatement, and hearing that it'll be put on a backburner for nine-months is a letdown. "What if we're really fucking careful?"

"I don't wanna test it," Banks tells me.

"We're not doing anything that could hurt you or the baby," Akara adds.

"Cumbuckets," I mutter.

"She's sad," Akara says in a teasing voice to Banks.

He wears a shadow of a smile. "She wants our cocks." He speaks directly to me, and Akara cups my heat.

A strange, whiney cry comes out of me. "Fuck," I breathe, voice higher-pitched. I just want them. I thrust against Akara's hand.

Banks is watching and rubs himself while he's on his knees.

"Come…in me," I beg. "Banks." He's so hard.

"I need inside her," Banks says gruffly, passionately—standing up. They move blisteringly fast. Dizzying. He picks me off Akara, his hands careful but rough, and Akara rises to his feet and goes to the single bed, leading Banks.

I'm suddenly lying on my back. My head meets a pillow. Legs spread open. Banks strips. Akara strips, and I eat up their hardened lengths, standing at attention.

"I guess you don't need condoms…" I swear their cocks twitch as soon as I speak.

"You feel badly at all, you tell us," Akara says like an order.

"I will," I promise.

Banks' rock-hard build hovers over my frame, my thighs around him, and he clutches my cheek, kissing me strongly before slipping slowly—so, so slowly—inside me. My eyes roll again.

A pleasured noise catches in my throat.

"Fuck," he grunts, thrusting. Our gazes connect in deep desire before I turn my head. Akara is crouching near my flushed face, and he clasps my hands. I watch in rapt attention. Tenderly, he spools nylon rope around my wrists, tying them together above my head. All the while, my body rocks in the hypnotizing rhythm of Banks' thrusts.

Akara is watching Banks make love to me.

A moan breaches my lips. Akara kisses the sound away, and Banks groans out my name with emotion and heat. I'm lit alive like a million Olympic torches blazing through me.

Before I come, they switch places. Taking turns inside me, I lose sense of time to these entrapped, harmonious feelings. To their groans and grunts and whispers of *I love you* and *Sulli*. And I cry against the passion that fucking swells and erupts between us—*don't end.*

Never end.

I love and hate when I reach the quaking peak.

Hot and sweaty and relaxed after the come-down, Akara and Banks lean against the headboard—which is really just the fucking wall—and I lie naked across their laps. I rest a lot of my upper body against Banks' firm chest while Akara is massaging my hamstrings.

I replay the sex we had. Did their arms graze? *Maybe.* Did they touch each other? *I don't think so.* Their biceps meld now, sitting closer than close on the single bed, and they've always been comfortable sharing intimate space.

"Did you guys kiss?" I wonder if I missed something.

The look they share says, *no.*

"Do you want to?"

Banks lifts a shoulder to Akara.

"Now?" Akara asks him, and I see their eyes drop to each other's lips.

21

Akara Kitsuwon

THIS IS HAPPENING NOW.

Okay.

Okay.

My pulse ratchets up in anticipation of the *great* unknown. Land that I've never crossed, but for a while, Banks and I have been eyeing the turf in the horizon. Wondering when we should reach the shore.

"Only if you fucking want to," Sulli adds quickly. "I'm not trying to pressure you guys or anything."

"You aren't, Sul." Honestly, her naked body across our laps is sending signals to my dick more than the idea of kissing Banks.

But the curiosity is too heightened to keep ignoring. We both want answers.

Banks tries to smile to me. "No pressure, Nine."

I almost laugh. "Yeah, the only pressure we feel is from the entire world." I tilt my head to our girlfriend. "Not from you, string bean."

"Okay, good." She exhales. "Not about you feeling pressured at all. But you know."

"Do we know?" I tease.

She sits up further and lightly slugs my arm.

I make a wounded face. "I didn't curse, Lady Meadows."

"That was just extra for the asshole."

Banks laughs.

I smile hearing him and seeing her.

"Are you guys sure about this?" Sulli slides off our laps. After wrapping up in a blanket, she faces us. "I just don't want things to change in a bad way between you two."

Change.

That word makes home in my soul.

Not all change is bad, which is why I know Sulli added that word. Some change can be good. And I think we're all built for it either way.

"I'm sure," I say, confident.

Banks already slides his hand on the back of my neck. "I'm ready." He cracks a "cowboy-up" smile. "Ready for your lips, Kitsuwon."

I try hard not to laugh. "We have to be serious about this, man."

He bounces his head. "I'm serious." His voice carries a deeper tone. "I'm kissing you—"

Before he can finish, I grab the back of his head, and *I'm* the one to close the distance between our lips. It's an odd feeling. Not bad.

Just different.

Feeling his stubble as our lips meld together. His hand is larger than Sulli's, and I don't mind the strong, masculine grip on the back of my neck. I've felt it there before. I still can't tell if I'm completely turned on—so I deepen the kiss.

He reciprocates. His hand falling to my bare thigh.

His breath comes in heavier like mine, like we're fighting for clarification. For an answer. From someone somewhere to wipe the fog and make clear what we mean to each other. Emotion starts barreling through me and I grip at his bicep. His fingers dig into the flesh of my neck. My thigh.

Our kiss is angrier.

I can feel and taste his desperation and frustration. It matches mine.

We claw at each other, and I push him back into the wall. He takes the force but hangs onto me like a life raft. But I'm drowning too.

When our lips break apart, I struggle to catch my breath. His chest rises and falls in unsteady rhythms, and we both cling harder to each other. Banks buries his head in my shoulder. I rest my forehead atop his head. We stay like this for what feels like an eternity. Trying to breathe.

There's nothing sexual about what just happened.

I'm not aroused. And I can *feel* that he's not either.

I'm just spent.

"Nine," Banks whispers. "You okay?"

"I think so." I swallow hard. "You?"

"Yeah, I'm alright."

"I still love you, you know."

"I love you too." Banks sniffs. "I wish it were simpler than this."

"I know." I kiss the top of his head. It'd be easier to just tell everyone we fuck the same girl and we fuck each other. It's harder for people to understand that I'm straight (at least, this label is the one that feels right to me), but I still love a man. And is this kiss even a good enough test for our sexualities? I don't know. Probably not. It's just one part of the equation—the sexual part.

Sexual attraction. Romantic attraction. Emotional attraction. Are those things that can even be so easily defined? Who has those answers anyway? And maybe it's not about fitting into a certain label. Maybe it's just being comfortable with what I believe I am.

We both break apart to look at Sulli.

She has her knuckles to her lips. Her eyes are glassed, breath a little uneven.

"Why are you crying, string bean?" I ask, even though no tears are really escaping. She looks *near* tears. "Don't you know it's bad for the bean sprout?"

She makes a noise and crinkles her nose. "Did you just call our baby a *bean sprout?*" She launches a pillow at me. I catch it easily.

Banks laughs. "I like it."

"Thank you," I say to him, just as Sulli kicks his ankle.

I grab hold of her foot and yank. Her back thumps against the bed. "Wait—Kits." She props herself on her elbows. "I just want to know… you're both okay, right?"

I love Sulli so dang much. "We're not the ones crying."

"I'm *not* crying."

"And so what if she was?" Banks tells me, and I'm happy about the interjection. I don't want Sulli to think she can't cry.

"Switching allegiances so quickly, Banksy," I banter to him.

He wears a crooked grin.

Sulli sits up fully, questions in her eyes. "So you two aren't attracted to each other then?"

Banks looks to me. "We're both limp, if that's what you're asking."

"Is that how you determine sexual attraction?" Sulli wonders.

"Don't know." Banks shrugs.

"I don't either, but it's as good as we have," I say.

"Yeah, and if the goal is to get my blood pumping, I'm not dying to kiss you again."

"Same." Kissing Banks is like being in a hurricane. It's not something that turns me on, but it rotates my world.

I climb off the bed, but as I grab my clothes, we all share a look that says, *stay close*. The cot feels a thousand miles away, and without speaking, we just move. Throwing pillows and blankets on the floor. In minutes, we all cuddle up together.

Sulli curls against my chest while I hold her back against me, and she buries her face into Banks' warm body. We should go to sleep. The lights are off, and the commotion in the hallway dies down as athletes gear up for tomorrow.

But Sulli glances from me to Banks, back to me. She has to crane her neck to meet my gaze, and her eyes say, *I don't want this to end.* This moment.

Us.

Together.

I don't either. I could spend eternity in the solace of this room with Banks and Sulli. It's always felt safer. Just us three.

It's going to be four.

That thought nearly tosses me into another dimension. My expression falters.

"What is it, Kits?" Sulli breathes.

I shake my head. I don't want her to think I have doubts about having a kid with her. I have none. It's just...a change. A *big* change. As soon as we find our footing with a new change, we're being pushed harder into another.

We don't live on land. The three of us.

We're made for the unsteady waters. Balancing upon the waves as they crash underfoot.

22

Sullivan Meadows

400M INDIVIDUAL MEDLEY is underway.

My first of five finals.

Arms propel over my head with strength and purpose in the butterfly. The first stroke in IM. Breath is locked in my lungs as I push stronger, faster, harder. *Don't overdo the first 50 meters.* I can't gas out, but every fucking second counts.

The splash of water, the thump of blood pumping through my heart, and my narrowed focus drowns out the noisy crowds. I am a windmill powering the Earth.

I am a fucking torpedo blasting through the ocean.

Nothing can stop me…but me.

Don't lose focus.

Don't fuck up.

I'm in the zone as I touch the wall and make the turn. Gliding through the water like this is my permanent residence.

Once I tap the wall at 100 meters, I turn into the backstroke.

I can feel myself capture the lead. Pulling out in front of the seven other swimmers, but Gabriela Moreno from Spain is closing in on my left. She hugs my lane. Her hands plunge into the pool, and I sense the splash of water around my torso.

She's way too fucking close.

Focus.

Remembering my breathing and technique. All the hours I pumped into training matter *now*. Not yesterday.

Now.

My feet hit the wall in a flawless turn.

Swim to the finish.

Swim to them.

After backstroke and breaststroke, I change to a front crawl for freestyle. My fastest stroke. The one I'm most comfortable in. The final two lengths are here. Muscles and lungs shrieking, I swim. 100 meters of pure adrenaline. Of pure power. Of pure heart.

Gogogogo. No time to think. No time for hesitation. Stop for nothing.

The final two lengths are here.

I just plow ahead.

Gold.

I want gold.

For him or her.

My baby.

Our baby.

I slice through the water, giving *everything* I have. Every ounce of oxygen and grit and fucking fortitude. I don't stop. I hit the wall again and kick off once more. *Final length.*

50 meters left.

My pulse beats hard in my ears. My goggles feel tight, and I take a hearty breath before continuing my stroke. I'm loose and relaxed with no drag, and I'm cutting into the water with ultimate speed. My legs burn from kicking, and instinctively, I know I'm closing in on the wall.

This is it.

Under the water, I press the wall for a final time. Once I pop up, air feels thin as I struggle for breath, but I immediately spin in the pool to check the scoreboard.

The results are unmistakable. *What the fuck?*

I tear off my goggles to see better.

My name lands underneath Sienna Jones from Australia. Where... where did she even come from? She wasn't even near me in qualifiers.

I reread the times.

The 2nd next to my name.

It's like a punch to the gut.

I lost gold by two-tenths of a second.

Two fucking *tenths*. I blink a few times. Water droplets drip off my eyelashes and blur my vision. I can't hide my disappointment, and I struggle to care that the world is seeing every muscle twitch on my face right now. Press is probably zoomed up hyper-close.

It's hard to breathe. Inhaling is labored from everything I gave that race. I wince at that time.

I did *everything* right. It felt like a *great* swim. The time is one of my best, but not *the* best I've ever had. And that makes all the difference.

I rack my brain for someplace that I fucked up, but I thought I had it. And that realization is worse than anything. I could blame not qualifying for the 200m IM on a goggle malfunction, but I have no excuses for this 400m IM.

Silver might seem like a great placement, but the world believes I should be sweeping golds. I thought I had it in me too.

Fuck.

Pulling myself out of the pool, I avoid the gazes and just keep checking the scoreboard. Trying to recover breath, I inhale a lungful of oxygen.

I only want to see two people. Akara and Banks are somewhere poolside, and I force back tears. Later, I might cry against their chests and snot up their shirts.

Fuck, I'd really like a hug right now.

As I yank off my swim cap and grab a towel, my lungs expand and contract painfully. Emotion hurts my recovery for breath, and I pad along the pool tiles towards the exit when, suddenly, a reporter in a black pantsuit shoves a microphone in my face.

I barrel to a stop.

Oh fuck.

I rest my hands on my hips, too winded to find an out. I'm trapped in front of a camera lens.

Her badge says *GBA News*. "Sullivan, how does it feel winning silver?"

"Fuck…" My breath is heavy. My head is spinning. "Fucking… awful." I look around for my boyfriends. I see them approaching. My pulse skips like its attempting to calm. I imagine racing into their arms. Where I'd much rather be.

Her eyes are widened orbs.

"…What?" I pant, confused. *Was I too honest?*

"We're live," she whispers to me.

Oh…

I dropped two f-bombs on live television. I heat from head-to-toe. I fucked up the 400m IM finals. Now I'm fucking this up. Is there anything else? God, I don't want to be here. I wipe my face with my towel, my hair sticking up in a million directions.

Sickness rises to my mouth. My chest tightens the longer I stand here.

"What do you think caused you to fall behind Australia?" the reporter asks me.

I open my mouth and then close it. I don't have an answer. I don't really know what went wrong.

Her brows rise. "Do you think it's because you have new distractions in your life?"

"No," I say sharply, still out of breath. "I don't…fucking think… that."

She sours at my curse again.

"Excuse me." I walk past the reporter, quickly leaving the impromptu interview. Before I even make two steps, a hand rests on my shoulder. Akara sidles next to me in a quick beat. Banks somehow slips out front.

It's easier to intake air. Easier to move.

I keep pace with my boyfriends. In total bodyguard mode, they block my view from passersby and more press, but I still catch a few wandering eyes. Pity. Disappointment. Disdain. Those sentiments flash through me on our trek to the rec room for cool downs, and once inside, I instantly veer towards a TV.

Only a few other people are in here. Coaches, I think. My boyfriends flank my sides, and for as much as I want to embrace them—for as much as I want a fucking hug and shoulder to cry on—I need to watch this first.

"Sulli," Akara says softly.

"I just need to see what went wrong." My voice is tight, shaky. I watch the replay of my swim and listen to the commentors.

"...no one saw this coming. Heartbreaking for Meadows...it was hers to lose, and she lost it."

It hurts to breathe.

Tears blur my focus of the TV, of seeing my freestyle overpower everyone but Sienna Jones.

"She was unable to defend her gold, and it's possible her showing at the last Summer Games can't be duplicated. Because one thing is for sure, this is not what we expected for Meadows. She has four more events, so we'll see if she can bring home a gold. Tune in..."

I tune *out*.

I'm crying, and I turn into Banks' chest. He brings me closer, cupping my head with comforting, loving affection. He hugs me, and his heartbeat tries to slow mine.

Akara rubs my back in soothing circles as he whispers, "Don't listen to them, Sul. They're just trying to create drama for ratings. It's what they do. Okay? You swam your hardest. I saw it. Banks saw it. Everyone *fudging* saw it."

I choke on a breath. *It wasn't enough, Kits.*

"You did fuckin' amazing, mermaid," Banks tells me. "Silver is *amazing*."

I swallow bile. "...it's not what I came here for." I lift my head out of his shirt and try to wipe the snot marks.

Banks captures my hands, not letting me waste energy cleaning his shirt. Concern is all over his face. I must look as torn up as I feel. Fuck, I *feel* like a mess. I rub my splotchy cheek, and I hug Akara.

He hugs me back.

After a couple comforting beats, I pull away, but they stand close, not letting me wallow alone. *Good,* I think tearfully. *I really, really don't want to be alone right now.*

Akara's brown eyes carry understanding from years ago. Maybe he once feared he'd have to see this. But last Olympics, he never did. Because I didn't lose back then.

"I'm washed up?" I ask them.

Banks shakes his head like that's impossible.

Akara gives me a firm look. "You're way too talented to be washed up at *twenty-two.*"

I failed though. "It just wasn't good enough," I swipe at my eyes.

"It was good enough," Akara refutes like he's cementing that statement into his own heart.

"Someone was just better," I say the words that feel like a thousand knives in my body. Sienna Jones swam better and faster than me.

Maybe there was nothing I could've done differently.

Maybe this was just mine to lose.

Mine to win silver.

Hers to win gold.

But what if I never win another gold—what if I keep racing for second or third or no podium placement at all?

I'll go from one of the greatest swimmers of my generation to one of the greatest failures. And I'm scared I'm going to regret coming here at all. Tarnishing my legacy by becoming a one-hit wonder, a has-been.

Banks and Akara watch me plop dazedly onto the rec couch. A coordinator calls into the room, "Five minutes till medal ceremony." She's looking at me.

After every final, they award the medals.

Soon, I'll be holding silver.

I nod to her, then she disappears.

When my boyfriends sit beside me, I do a sweep of the room. Realizing we're alone now, I exhale a big breath. Pain still bears on my chest. "I never thought it'd hurt this much." I lean into both of them. Their arms are around me. Holding me.

I bury my head in my hands.

They're quiet, until Akara says, "I know you're hard on yourself. But coming in second shouldn't kill you this bad, Sul. What's going on?"

My chin quakes. "I…" I shake my head.

Banks rubs his hand along my thigh. "We need to go ham on the @Love4Sullivan account? Talk about how good you look in silver? 'Cause I'll do it now." He pulls out his phone. "Hell, I'll post on my main account."

Akara jokes, "Hashtag Silver Is Cuter Than Gold."

I snort into a half-hearted laugh. I smile at Kits and Banks. Their humor lifts me a little higher, and I sit up straighter, gathering my resolve. "I wanted gold for our baby." Hurt pierces me just thinking about how much I failed. "I never wanted her or him to think I failed because I'm pregnant with them. And then the reporter asked if I've had any distractions. I can't be certain this whole pregnancy news *wasn't* a distraction." I wince and hold onto my knees at my chest, like I'm breaking apart. "A week ago, I was swimming a faster time for the 400 IM than what I swam today. And I hate that. I hate how much I choked. Not just for myself but for our kid."

Banks frowns. "I think you're too hard on yourself, Sulli. You don't need to prove anything to anyone. Least of all a baby that's not here yet."

"It's too much pressure," Akara adds.

Tears rise. "I don't know how to release it."

"Just breathe, Sul," Akara whispers against my ear.

Banks places a sweet, soft kiss against my cheek. I like how he caresses my face, holds my jaw and wipes the last of my tears. I like how Akara's thumb rubs circles around my hip. Easing me. I'm not even sure I deserve this.

Their comfort, their love and support.

The reporter intimated that they were my distractions. That Akara and Banks were the ones that tilted my focus and caused me to lose. I wish I could shield any hatred directed their way, but I don't know how.

I don't want the world to hate them or be disappointed in me because of them.

I have four more chances to win gold. And it's not their fault if I fail.

It's only mine.

23

Banks Moretti

THREE IN THE MORNING at the muggy Aquatic Center, and I'm wondering if I should pull the mermaid out of the pool. She's been in there for *hours*. Longer than usual. And that was after her total ass kicking during "dry land" training this afternoon.

When Sulli announced that she'd be coming out of retirement and returning to the Olympics, Akara warned me about her strict training regimen. I thought I geared myself up for it—but the reality is different. I nearly doubled over in shock when Sulli told me she was skipping her sister's sixteenth birthday tonight to train instead.

I overheard their FaceTime call this morning. "It's the Olympics. I get it, Sulli-Bear," Winona said. "I'll have other birthdays."

Sulli forced a smile and nodded. Maybe she hoped her sister would beg her to miss out on training, but most of her family shower her with support and understanding. It's almost like they know what she *has* to do, and they're trying to make it easier on her.

But hell, I see it affecting her in some way.

I watched her all day. Quieter. More focused than usual as she dove into the pool tonight. Now she's staying in the water late, and I wonder if it's to make her sacrifice worth it.

My phone beeps.

Here. Open door. – Akara

The smell of chlorine permeates around me. I grew used to it as a floater on Maximoff's detail. Back when he taught little kids how to swim at this Aquatic Center.

Sulli would be on the rooftop pool at the penthouse if it were regulation size. But she rents out the Aquatic Center pool most nights.

Akara stands outside in the dark, illuminated by the streetlamps and lingering camera flashes from paparazzi. He carries a bag of takeout. My stomach grumbles seeing him through the glass doors. I unlock them.

"I love you," I tell him like he was sent from heaven.

He lets out a laugh, his smile rising as he slips inside while I brace the door open. He keeps an eye on the paparazzi. "You don't even know what it is."

"Only thing I care about is if it's edible."

One foot through the door and he says, "Well, according to Greer, you eat crayons."

Fuck. He heard that?

His expression is full of pent-up annoyance.

I lock the door behind him. "That was a month ago, Akara. How long have you been stewing on that?"

He takes a tight breath. "For a month. I didn't get it until I looked it up." He shoots me a look. "You're not dumb enough to eat crayons."

He's pretty serious about it. Like he wants to make sure Greer didn't get to me. I'm not sensitive enough to let that insult sink too deep, but I appreciate Akara's concern.

"I know that. Greer knows that. He was just grabbing at the low hanging fruit." I steal the takeout bag from his hand. "Are we going to have problems with them?"

Akara stares at the ceiling. Scratch that—*glares* at the ceiling. "Probably."

"Which one?"

"All three."

I groan. "Mother of Christ. Price, Wylie, and Greer. Throw me off a bridge."

"Don't say that," Akara says.

"Lightly push me."

He gives me a harder look. "I love you, Banks, but I'm not pushing you off anything higher than the ground, even if you beg."

I laugh a little and pull out a container and pass the bag back. And then an icy chill trickles and snakes down my spine as a stomach-turning, pulse-skipping memory washes over me.

"Banks?" Akara studies me. "Hey, you okay?"

"Yeah." I try to shake off the eerie discomfort that I unearthed. "Why wouldn't I be?"

"All the color drained out of your face." Akara thinks back. "Is it something I said?"

"Something I said," I mumble, hoping my appetite returns. 'Cause right now, I feel like upchucking in the nearest shitter. Quick glance to Sulli—still swimming—I focus on the container.

Akara racks his brain, confused and concerned. "From literally the first time we've met, you've been making jokes about drowning and jumping off cliffs and crap, so what's going on?"

"Gotta cope somehow with the big brother who got himself killed in a quarry," I say light-heartedly, but the weight of my statement sinks heavily on me and Akara.

Realization rocks him. "It's about Skylar?"

"Yeah. Isn't it always?" I hear my bitterness, but I force myself not to shut down. I'm done burying Skylar. Talking about him, even in frustration or anger, has helped me understand these emotions and the casket of pain. It's been heavy, carrying that around.

Opening it hurts more, in a different way. But I'm starting to not mind the pain.

"I just remembered something I'd forgotten for a long time…I guess something I tried to forget." The memory still ices over my blood. How do I say this? I pop the lid to…*Stromboli*, and I nearly smile. God, I love Akara. Two beats later, I finally tell him, "I'm not sure it was an accident."

"Skylar's death?"

I nod tensely.

"You think someone killed him?"

"No. I've always been afraid he did it…" A rock enters my throat. My vision clouds with emotion. Eyes burning, I lower my gaze. "He did it himself." I've never said that out loud. Never voiced my fear or gave power to the thought.

But here I am.

Eighteen years later.

"Wasn't it ruled as an accident?" Akara asks softly.

"Everyone thinks he couldn't see the water level in the dark and didn't know it was that shallow."

"But you don't think that?"

I have no words.

Akara rests a comforting hand on my strained shoulder. "Hey, it's okay. Maybe you're just looking back in hindsight after protecting Xander and going through his…" He trails off, seeing me shake my head.

"I always thought protecting someone like Xander was my second-shot at doing for him what my family couldn't do for Sky. What *I* couldn't do for my brother."

Akara frowns. "So you've always thought Skylar killed himself that night?"

I want to tell him *yeah*. I want to tell him why. But my throat is swollen. Choked, I just nod once.

"It's not your fault, you know? Whatever happened to Skylar—you were *twelve*, Banks. You were a kid."

"I know that," I say tightly and quietly. "But God, was I an idiot."

"You're not," Akara snaps.

Even though he has half the story, I listen to his words and let them wash over me. Gratitude in my eyes, I nod to him.

Akara keeps a strong arm across my shoulders. Even it if means reaching up some to reach my height. At the sound of splashing, our heads turn. Attention veering on the mermaid.

Sulli pulls herself out of the water. Not even a glimpse our way, she returns to the block. Her dedication is impressive. And terrifying as hell.

"Should we call it?" I ask Akara.

Concern pulls at his brows. He holds his breath as she jumps back into the pool. "Shit," he curses.

I lightly tap his shoulder.

He barely flinches. Just checks his watch. "She has to stop on her own time."

"She's a cute prune," I say into a bite of cheese and pepperoni. "But I don't like seeing her pushing herself like this."

"You'll get used to it," Akara breathes.

"I don't want to." Another thought knocks into me. Nearly blows me back. "What if she loses?"

"What?" Akara frowns.

"What if she loses, Akara?" I ask again. "Like *no* gold."

He goes stone-cold.

"It'd be bad?" I ask, my gut sinking. The Stromboli not sitting right. She just skipped out on her sister's sweet sixteen. She's missed birthdays. She's missed family charity events. She's missed *everything* since she started training. I need this to be worth it for her sake.

Akara runs a hand through his black hair, pulling at the strands a little. "Yeah, it'd be bad. Really fracking bad." We exchange a graver look.

I'm praying that's not gonna be her reality.

GBANewYork.com – July 26th

Akara Kitsuwon & Banks Moretti React to the 400m IM Upset, Sullivan Meadows Taking Silver

Standing poolside, bodyguards to Sullivan Meadows show clear concern and devastation as Meadows places second in the 400m IM and fails at defending her gold. A now infamous photo has circulated tabloid and sports covers since the crushing upset last night. In the picture, Akara Kitsuwon is crouching with steepled fingers to his agonized face, and Banks Moretti remains standing in an utter state of shock—one hand on his head and another hand on Kitsuwon's shoulder.

More videos are trending of their instant reaction to the loss, as Moretti and Kitsuwon are not just bodyguards but *boyfriends* to Sullivan Meadows. The confirmation of their polyamorous relationship back in late January has been a hot button topic all year long. Tomorrow night, Meadows will return to the water to defend yet another gold. This time, in the 200m freestyle event against teammate and rival Frankie Hansen.

24

Akara Kitsuwon

I HATE WATCHING THIS.

Banks white-knuckles the back of my shirt, standing a breath behind me and watching over my shoulder. Sulli swims like she was born in the water, but I can't stand how close Frankie Hansen trails her in the 200m free.

"Fuckfuckfuck," Banks curses, still clutching my tee. His jaw tics as he clenches his teeth. Breathing hard through his nose.

Press bleachers are packed to our right, and half the cameras are now on *us*. We've graced every major news and sports cover for simply caring about our girlfriend. Knowing she'd be hurt taking home her first silver. Knowing she'd consider second place a defeat like the world keeps spinning it.

It's not.

She *medaled* at the Olympics. How many will ever get to say that? Banks is right when he read the magazines this morning and said, "Fuck everyone to hell and back who keeps acting like she's not an Olympic phenomenon."

Still, we want this win for Sulli.

So I'm wincing as Frankie closes in on Sulli's lead. "*Shit*," I curse out loud. Banks doesn't even bother slugging me.

"Meadows at the turn," the sports commentator says nearest me. "Hansen gaining at the final fifty, and at poolside, the boyfriends of Meadows are holding their breaths with the rest of the world."

Yeah we are.

And we could morph into statutes. We're experienced at that. Give them next to nothing to work with out of spite and duty to our jobs, but ultimately, Banks and I decided we'd rather be written in the history books as caring about our girlfriend than standing emotionless as bodyguards.

I love that I'm not poolside alone. I love that Banks is experiencing the on-the-edge anticipation of Sulli swimming for gold up close and with me.

I catch his shoulder, excitement surging as Sulli pulls out further. "She has this."

"Come on, mermaid," he whispers.

Everyone in the stands are on their feet. Roaring and cheering.

"The final stretch," the commentator announces. "Hansen is closing in! Look at her speed!"

No.

No.

Banks is clutching my bicep. His fingers digging into my flesh while mine dig into his shoulder. *No, no, no.*

She's can't lose another one.

She can't.

It's going to kill her.

It's going to kill me.

"Hansen and Meadows! They're neck and neck now! Final twenty!"

Cheers and screams and horns blast off in the stands. I imagine her family are among the supporters with just as much lively fervor. I wish I could jump up and down with support, but I can't move. Like if I make a single *twitch*, she'll falter and lose focus.

"She's going to do it," Banks says in a last-ditch hope.

I blink, and it's over.

It's over.

"Hansen takes gold!" the commentator yells in surprise. "Holy cow! Meadows takes silver for the second time in Los Angeles. Another upset. Two silvers for Meadows at the Olympics. Zero golds."

"Fuck." Banks buries his head in my shoulder as he releases his grip. "Mother of *fuck…*" He growls into my trap, and I rest a hand on his neck.

"Shit," I breathe out, chest tight.

We let go of each other and watch Frankie. Seeing the scoreboard, her hand flies to her lips and she immediately breaks down in uncontained, overwhelmed tears.

The Olympic commentators barely focus on Frankie. One near me says, "Everyone is wondering how Meadows will take this loss. Two nights ago, she was not happy about silver in the 400m IM—wait, it looks like she's ducking under the ropes."

Sure enough, Sulli swims under the lane ropes, crossing two lanes to reach Frankie. I watch our girlfriend put her arms around the young swimmer and give her a hug. Frankie cries harder, happy tears.

My muscles tighten, emotion surging. I know how hard this is for Sulli.

Banks has a softened expression, his lips slowly lifting. Sometimes I see how much Banks admires Sulli, and I think, *shit, how long did I know he liked her? How long did I keep them apart?*

It's too late to change the past, but I also tend to believe this is how we were supposed to come to be. Us three.

"Meadows embraces Hansen and Hansen embraces Meadows— this is the Olympic spirit right here, people. Teammates supporting teammates."

Sulli whispers something in Frankie's ear. Frankie laughs into a big smile and they both exit the pool together.

Banks fixes his earpiece. "She's Oscar Mike." *On the move.*

"Yep." We switch into a focused stance. The two of us head towards Sulli as she collects a towel and peels off her swim cap. We're able to cut in front of reporters. Blocking press from cornering Sulli like last time.

Sulli catches her breath and slips us a look of *thanks.*

Banks touches the small of her back. "You killed it out there, mermaid."

"And you nearly sent Banksy into cardiac arrest," I add with a rising smile. I twirl a piece of her wet hair around my finger. She leans more into me.

"And Akara looked like Medusa eye-fucked him."

I glare like he's way off.

He cracks a grin.

Sulli laughs a short laugh, still unable to recover her breath. It's good. I don't want to bombard her with twenty questions right after her swim.

On our way out of the pool, we hear a reporter saying loudly, "It looks like Sullivan Meadows whispered to you out there."

We all look behind us. Frankie stands nearby in front of a GBA News camera.

"What did she tell you after your win?"

Frankie, equally winded, takes large breaths. "She said…I deserve… it. And thanks…for the good…competition."

Sulli stares at her feet, but she's smiling softly. Lost in her head somewhere.

"Ready to go?" I ask.

She nods.

I lead her to the rec room where we wait before the medal ceremony. It feels a little like déjà vu. Another silver. Another second place finish. But she's not as broken up about this one.

"You alright, Sulli?" Banks finally asks when we find a quiet private corner on some yoga mats.

Sulli keeps her towel around her shoulders. "I think so…" She tries hard not to cry. "I am happy for Frankie. I meant all that stuff I said." She goes quiet for a second and then just whispers, "I don't really want to talk about it though…if that's okay?"

I nod strongly. "Yeah, Sul."

Banks gives her hand a squeeze. She interlaces her fingers with his fingers, then she picks up my hand with her free one.

I can tell she's kicking herself over the loss, and it doesn't take Banks, the Sulli Whisperer, to see that she's not going to climb over the defeat that easily. But I'm not pushy.

When a coordinator gives Sulli the "five minutes to ceremony" call, we all stand up and Sulli tugs on a Team USA jacket over her arms.

Static suddenly scratches my eardrums. Someone must be pushing the wrong button on comms.

I pinch the bridge of my nose. *Please, don't be Frog.*

Just as I think it, her bubbly voice comes over muffled. "Don't any of you temps know how to use deodorant? Or is BO like some sort of weird intimidation tactic?"

Banks laughs lightly at the sheer look of horror on my face. Sulli frowns, and he dips his head and quietly catches her up to speed while I click my mic.

"Akara to Frog, turn your comms off."

"Shit, sorry, Nine."

I cringe again.

"But seriously," she adds, "can you tell your temps how to use some anti-perspirant?"

Banks and Sulli laugh softly. He's unspooled his mic so she can listen.

I take a steadying breath as I reply to my cousin, "I'll take it under consideration."

"My nostrils thank you."

Letting out a long sigh, I stare up at the ceiling. Did I make the wrong choice by letting her join the team? *She's just a temp.* My brain is trying to defend the decision, but it's hard to produce any real evidence. She's here because of nepotism. Because she's family.

Let's just hope it wasn't a mistake.

25

Akara Kitsuwon

BLOOD DRIPS ON MY P&L sheets for Studio 9. "It's still bleeding," I tell Banks, checking his nose. "Stuff that back in, and call Farrow."

He shoves tissue back up his nostrils. "It'll stop in another hour. I'm not running to Farrow for a nosebleed." Purple bruises already shadow his eyes, but I can see he's more concerned about Sulli, who hugs her knees to her chest.

She's shaking.

Shit.

Nighttime on the penthouse roof—I wish I could say Sulli is just cold. The crisp wind blows around us, but she's curled up in a fuzzy blanket on a pool lounge chair and stares faraway.

"Hey, string bean." I leave Banks and my bloodied P&L sheets. "We're supposed to be roasting marshmallows *not* traveling into La La Land." I rip open the marshmallow bag and chuck one at her face.

It pings off her forehead. Her green eyes finally rise to me. Still haunted. "...what...what happened back there? It went by so fast...I can't..." She shivers and winces.

Banks takes a seat on her lounge chair, and she lets him hold her. I explain, "We were leaving the Aquatic Center. The end."

Heat returns to her eyes. "That's not the fucking end."

Yeah, but at least you're here with me, string bean. It hurts seeing her replay these chaotic events over and over, and I'll do anything to keep them from torturing her. Even coming home and declaring "marshmallow roasting time" like we're all kids at summer camp.

I snap a finger to my palm. "Everyone knows you're at the Aquatic Center all day, Sul, so we weren't surprised the paparazzi were there. We had Farrow and Thatcher with us." I've had SFO help us most times Sulli leaves for the night, and I shift myself off Luna's detail to be present too.

"But there were so many more cameras than usual. They seemed more fucking aggressive..." She stares off again.

Banks holds her tighter and slips me a concerned, pained look.

How many hands touched her?

How many cameras stared her down?

How many flashes caught her eye and disoriented our girlfriend?

I can't think this. He's thinking this, and *one* of us needs to not feel sick every time paparazzi descend like vultures. And that has to be me. I'm in charge.

"Banks got hurt," she chokes out, upset. She looks at him. "You got hurt."

"I'm fine," he says strongly and nasally. "Barely hurts."

I swallow hard. "The Olympics are getting closer. We're all in the news more than we were in January. Paparazzi are just overly eager right now, which is why Banks took an elbow to the nose."

Outside the Aquatic Center, I made a path for Sulli and Banks. He had our girlfriend's back flush against his chest. He held her arms and practically moved her feet for her. Lifting her up foot by foot. She was frozen. In shock at the sheer amount of cameras and paparazzi and yelling and flashes in the night.

I could faintly hear Sulli saying repeatedly, "I can't see."

I can't see.

I jogged around to the driver's side of Sulli's Jeep. Shouting at everyone to get back. *Get back.*

Banks pushed Sulli into Booger. He shut the door. I was already inside the Jeep, and I had poor visual of everything beyond the cameras. The flashing.

According to Thatcher's report, Banks spun around, went to grab a water bottle that Sulli unknowingly dropped, and he took an elbow to the nose.

Blood splashed against the window of her door, and Sulli screamed like she'd been eviscerated. That sound still slices me open. For a second, I thought Banks had been shot.

I swallow another rock. "I'll have more men help us when you leave the Aquatic Center, Sul. It'll get better."

It has to.

How many times can she go through total mayhem before she's wrecked completely?

How many times can I see Banks and Sulli hurt?

What about you, Nine?

I'm perfect. I'm standing.

Literally, I'm on my feet, and I fit a marshmallow on a stick. Passing the thing to Sulli, she leans over the fancy gas firepit. Flames lick glossy stones, and glass forms a tabletop around the heat. She scoots and sits more against Banks, right between his legs while his arms stay around her waist, and I take a seat on her left, the lounge chair creaking underneath me.

We're quiet for a long beat. Watching the flames. Piercing more marshmallows on more sticks.

"I lost my virginity to Will Rochester," Sulli suddenly says.

Blood drains out of my head. "What?" She…she had sex with Will? That means…when we had sex. It wasn't her first?

Banks has gone motionless, his arms unmoving around Sulli. "That doesn't make sense." His gaze flits to me, and I bet I'm thinking what he's thinking.

She bled her first time with me. When the three of us were in the bathtub together.

I popped her cherry. Unless…did I hurt her? *I was careful. Banks and I were careful.*

Did I hurt Sulli?

I feel sick.

Why wouldn't she tell us about Will? Why would she lie?

"April Fools'," Sulli says fast.

"*Fuck,*" I curse out, and she lightly slugs my arm. I capture breath into my lungs as shock wears off. "That wasn't funny."

Sulli tries to laugh. "I got you both, though."

It is April 1st.

Banks ends up laughing deeply. "Yeah, you got us good. Akara almost shit himself."

"Why are you laughing?" I ask him. "You almost crapped yourself too."

He laughs more, his features brightening in the firelight. The vibrant noise from his lips makes me laugh, and then Sulli shares in our laughter too.

When the sound fades, a levity still remains between us.

"The triad survives another day," Sulli says softly but with a little more hope as she roasts her marshmallow.

Beneath his bruises, Banks starts to smile. "We're not the easy kind to drag down." His smile vanishes as quickly as it appeared. "They'll have to kill us."

I shoot him a look, but he's not exactly wrong.

"No one is fucking dying," Sulli says adamantly. "That better be an April Fools' joke."

"April Fools'," Banks banters, "we're already dead."

I let out a laugh. "Wouldn't that be a plot twist? We're fighting to stay alive, but we've already kicked the bucket."

Banks tilts his head. "My heaven does include you two."

Sulli isn't finding humor in our death jokes. She stares haunted at the flames.

"Hey." I nudge her arm. "Sul?"

"Don't die protecting me," she whispers. "You promise?" She stares from me to Banks, back to me. "Promise, Kits?"

I can't.

I hate that I can't hook pinkies with Sulli and be playful about a promise I'd love to keep. "I promise we'll try not to die."

Sulli looks heartbroken. "What if that's not good enough?"

"What if that's all I have, Sul?" My pulse is in my throat.

She rotates her marshmallow in the fire. "I understand...I just wish you two weren't put in these situations because of me—"

"Not because of you," Banks interjects. "We chose this."

"It's for you," I whisper.

"Don't die for me," she chokes out.

Banks and I share a smile, and he's the one who says, "I couldn't think of a better person to die for."

"Lady Meadows," I finish.

She snorts into a small, rising smile and her marshmallow catches on fire. She lets it solidly char.

Banks breaks apart chocolate squares, then sees the flames. "You're gonna need to blow that one, mermaid."

My lips rise. "I've heard that before."

Sulli elbows me softly. "Because you're usually the one saying it, Kits." She ends up resting her head on my bicep. I kiss her lips.

She kisses gently back and concentrates on her marshmallow. I think she's finally letting go of tonight's mayhem.

Good.

Really good.

I exhale a breath.

"Cumbuckets," Sulli mutters after she blows off a flaming marshmallow. It's charred. Unrecognizable.

"Told ya," Banks says and hands her the marshmallow bag.

"I like it crispy, though." Sulli appraises the singe, then grabs another stick with a fresh marshmallow. "The challenge is getting the *perfect* crispiness without it being a fucking hockey puck of ash." Her face goes into full-determination mode. "I'll get it this time."

I smile. It's nice seeing Sulli focused on something other than swimming or our rising popularity. These days, that's not often. For any of us, really.

My phone rings.

I groan.

"Who is it?" Sulli asks.

I don't even have to look. "My mom. She's been calling all day."

Sulli frowns deeply. "You've ignored her calls?"

"I've been on-duty all day." Luna was in class at Penn, and I couldn't dip out of the lecture to answer my mom's call. I realize though, that I've been at the penthouse for at least an hour…maybe two.

And I've been *off-duty* in that time.

Not to sound like a dick, I add, "I texted her that I was busy."

Banks licks chocolate off his thumb, then nods to me. "Answer it."

Truth is that I'm not looking forward to what she has to say. It's been months since we've had a real conversation. And that talk wasn't productive or helpful. We went in circles. Mostly with her blaming me for not telling her about my relationship sooner. *"I didn't want to learn from the TV, Nine."*

It was my fault.

My fault for thinking she wouldn't care about my love life. She's the one who left when I was nineteen. She wrote herself out of my story. Thinking those words sends a bitterness through me that I don't like.

My phone rings out.

Banks and Sulli continue to stare at me like I'm making the wrong choice. Maybe I am.

"Fine," I sigh. "I'll be a sec." I stand off the lounge chair we share, and I leave the warmth of the fire. The warmth of them. And I pace over to the cold iron patio table. Constellations twinkle overhead, a clear night, and I wonder if my mom is staring at the same stars in New York.

Not that far away, but she couldn't feel further from me.

As soon as I call back, she answers on the first ring. "Nine," she says in relief. "I've been trying to reach you all day."

I wince. "I was working, Mom." I wince harder. "I'm sorry."

"You always work too hard." She has a slight New York accent.

I slouch onto a cold patio chair. Across the pool, Banks and Sulli pretend not to watch, but in the firelight, I see their eyes clearly on me.

I breathe easier.

Comforted by the love of my girlfriend and metamour.

Resting my arms on my knees, I clutch the phone tight to my ear. I know she didn't call to remind me of my work ethic. "Is everything okay?" I ask, feeling guilty this wasn't the first thing out of my mouth. "How are you feeling?" *No brain aneurysms.*

If she had another one, I would've known about it. I'd *hope* she'd tell me.

Just like you told her about your relationship, Nine.

Guilt compounds heavier.

"I feel good." She doesn't elaborate. Doesn't want me to worry, I think. "I have to ask you something serious."

My head spins at that last word. *Serious.* Nothing has been too serious between us since my dad died. She's made sure our relationship is all sunshine and butterflies.

Immediately, I rise from the chair and head towards the brick ledge that overlooks Philly. Wind sweeps me in a big gust. Closer to the edge of the roof, I can breathe better. "What is it?" I ask.

"Do you remember your cousin Frog?"

"Frog?" I scrunch my face.

"It's a nickname."

"I figured that." Everyone calls my mom *Mint.* Apparently my grandma had a craving for mint ice cream while she was pregnant with my mom, and most Thai nicknames are given at birth. I never knew my grandma before she passed in her early fifties.

Never knew any of my cousins, so why is my mom asking me about Frog?

"And no," I say, "I don't remember Frog."

"Kannika Kitsuwon?"

"No. Where would've I met her?"

"She was at the funeral."

I frown more. *My dad's funeral.* One of the most vivid memories I have, but also one of the biggest blurs. I can barely remember a quarter of the family I met that day.

"She was only seven at the time," my mom adds.

Seven?

Mental math…that'd make Frog *nineteen* now. I assume she's been in Queens with the rest of the family.

"Okay…?" *Where is this going, Mom?* She's slowly leading me somewhere, and I have a feeling she knows I won't like the destination.

"She's Uncle Prin's daughter."

Uncle Prin.

Our dads were brothers. "She's Uncle Prin's daughter?" I repeat.

"Yes. After the divorce, she moved to Buffalo to live with her mom."

Her parents divorced? The way my mom says it, it sounds like I should know this already. Like it's ancient history.

My mind whirls. Before I was even born, my dad moved away from New York for his job. I lived my life in Philly because that's where my dad wanted me to grow up. He talked about his brother Prin sometimes, but I didn't see them much, and I always thought that's what my dad wanted.

My mom continues on, "Frog was having a rough time in Buffalo. Getting into all kinds of trouble, so I invited her to Queens to stay with some family here. But…this place isn't good for her, Nine. She needs a fresh start. Structure. I think *you* can give her that."

Me?

I close my eyes. "Mom."

"Just listen," she pleads like she knows what I'm going to say. "Uncle Prin will send her down with money for rent and food just to get started before she can get on her own feet. All she needs is a job and family."

I'm family.

But I don't even know her.

"She's nineteen?"

"Eighteen."

Effing hell.

"I don't have work for her," I say the truth. "My gym is fully staffed."

"What about security?"

"Security?" I say in shock. "Mom. What skills does Frog have to work in security?" I realize I'm judging harshly. I really don't know anything about my cousin. Quickly, I ask, "Is she a Muay Thai fighter like you?"

"Well...no," she says. "But I can train her for a month before sending her down. Maybe she can be a backup bodyguard."

I pinch the bridge of my nose. "We don't have backup bodyguards, Mom."

"There has to be a position she can fill," my mom says, almost breathless. Desperation is clear in her voice. "She's *family*, Nine."

I don't understand why this matters so much.

I'm quiet.

She fills the silence with a short sigh. "I haven't asked you for anything over the years. Have I?"

"No."

My heart clenches. *I wish you did.* Maybe then it would have felt like she cared.

She's asking now, Nine. I hear my dad's voice in my head.

Shit.

I stare out at the city lights. "This isn't an April Fools' joke?"

"No," she almost laughs. "It's definitely not a joke."

Okay.

I take a breath. "Temp bodyguards mostly just stand around and control crowds. There's some desk work involved sometimes. Going through mail." I can practically feel my mom's excitement on the other end. "It might work. But it'll be a probationary thing. And I'll probably need you to train her for a month before she gets out here. Teach her some basic defense moves. Thank you for offering that." Because there's absolutely no way Frog will pass Michael Moretti's temp training.

I'm going to have to get Oscar Oliveira to train my cousin for the temp job instead.

A job she's not qualified for.

"Thank you, Nine," my mom breathes.

I just nod, but she can't see. My throat swells. I don't know what I'm jumping into. I don't even ask what "trouble" Frog got into in New York.

All I know is that I'm doing this.

There's no turning back now.

Welcome to Philly, Frog.

After I hang up, I walk back to the fire, back to them, and I say, "You won't believe this."

26

Sullivan Meadows

"YOU WON SILVER IN the 200m free yesterday. Losing to your teammate Frankie Hansen. How are you feeling after those results?" the news reporter asks politely.

Normally, I'd refuse the interview but the higher-ups on the U.S. Olympic Committee practically begged me to at least give GBA News *five* solid minutes. GBA promised not to drudge up my personal life and keep the topics strictly about swimming.

So far so good.

I'm outside in a pop-up studio, located on a hotel rooftop in L.A. The sky is clear. Sun is beaming, but nothing is hotter and brighter than the interview lights bearing down on me and the reporter. Sweat has built up under my pits, and I try not to shift in the uncomfortable seat, which resembles a director's chair.

On a small table between our chairs, a few magazines are stacked up. The top one is a popular sports magazine. My face on the cover. Both fingers to my lips as I stare up at the scoreboard during Team Trials. The headline: *Meadows Advances to the Olympics.* People always refer to that look as my iconic concentration face, but I usually can't even fucking remember doing it until it's in print or online somewhere.

I tear my eyes off the magazine to look at the reporter.

"I'm really proud of Frankie." I tuck a piece of hair behind my ear, the strand smelling like chlorine since I came to this hotel directly from the pool. "She swam great, and she deserved the win."

I'm a blender of emotions, swirling together. Pride for her. Disappointment for me. Too mixed to pick apart. My stomach tosses and turns.

The reporter crosses her leg on the opposing chair. I'm not sure I gave her the answer she was looking for, and I notice how she scrutinizes my jacket—a red windbreaker.

I'm not wearing Team USA merch.

I'm wearing Akara's windbreaker, sleeves bunched up to my elbows. Usually, I *never* wear red. Not since we confirmed our relationship publicly. It draws too much attention—paparazzi can spot me in the masses too fast, but I saw the jacket lying on Akara's duffel in my room. And I just slipped it on before we left.

Like a layer of confidence.

To remind myself, *I can be public.* I can give an interview like the other athletes. I'm here.

But the longer she studies the jacket, I wonder if she's going to ask who it belongs to. I sit on pins and needles and finally breathe when she glances at her notes and changes to a different question.

"You'll be swimming with Tobias Kingly later tonight in the Mixed Relay. Twitter is *buzzing* with anticipation about that final. Are you nervous at all?"

Kingly.

I never imagined competing with my childhood idol, and even though I've seen an assholish side of him this year, I'm still looking forward to that event.

Even if I'm scared as fuck to let him down. Let myself down. With the way these Summer Games have been going, I'm probably looking at another silver. It's hard to be happy about that result. Especially when the other swimmers on the relay team are relying on my time.

I choose my words carefully, so I don't drop an f-bomb. "I'm a little nervous."

I *suck* at lying, so I don't even try.

"But," I continue, "I'm more excited to get into the water and compete again." *To prove I'm not a second-place finisher.* I have to prove it to myself and to my baby.

My baby.

Please don't ask questions about the cinnamon roll. Not that the reporter has *anything* to go on. We've been very cautious and very secretive about my pregnancy so far. But we haven't had to shelter the news for that long yet.

Plus, Akara, Banks, and I have a track record for being fucking awful at keeping secrets. Someone usually finds out. I just don't want that "someone" to be the media, or worse, the world.

I risk a glance to my right. Crew for GBA News are gathered around camera equipment, and next to them, my boyfriends look dapper in white button-downs and black slacks. Earpieces in, they're 100% on-duty and stand stoic and on guard, waiting for my interview to end.

Akara whispers something to Banks, while Banks nods subtly to me like *you're doing great, mermaid.* I take a bigger breath.

And then Akara winks in my direction.

I try not to burst into a smile.

"Last Olympics, you had *no* nerves," the reporter reminds me. "And I quote, 'I'm too focused to let those feelings in'."

Damn.

She had a quote from my eighteen-year-old self at the ready just to fling at my face.

Total seriousness in her perfectly penciled brows, she asks, "What's changed from then to now?"

I know she's baiting me.

I'm not fucking dumb. She wants me to broach the topic of my boyfriends so that it becomes free game to bring my relationship into this interview.

I hate thinking it, but my first thought is: *What would Charlie do?*

He's run circles around my head before, and if anyone can help me navigate an interview where I'm being cornered, it'd probably be my cousin.

"The biggest change…" I say, building up the anticipation.

She leans forward in her chair.

I smile softly. "…is probably being in a relay with Tobias Kingly." It's not a lie.

She sinks backward, a little disappointed by the less than salacious truth. But I'm not done. I'm about to admit something that'll be super embarrassing, but it'll at least pry the attention off my poly relationship and give her what she wants—*entertainment*. "I never told the press this. But I used to have a poster of Kingly in my bedroom."

Her face lights up. "Is that so?"

I'd bet Akara is internally groaning.

"I really wanted to be as great as him." My heart hurts saying these words out loud because a part of me doesn't feel as if I've earned that title yet, and with my lack of golds this year, I might not ever be that great.

The reporter nods. "He is one of a kind."

Then what am I?

I just nod stiffly.

"We polled the audience to see which question they wanted answered most." She glances down at her notes, and my stomach does a little nosedive. "The most popular topic is body hair regime." *Fuck me.* I keep a composed face. "Do you wax or shave or do full laser hair removal like other swimmers?"

It's a common question, I guess. I'm sure Kingly has had to answer it before.

"I like to shave my arms and legs to reduce drag."

It's a pain in the butt, but I don't want to permanently laser my hair off completely. I feel more like myself when I have hair on my arms and when it comes back prickly on my legs sometimes. Waxing is a fucking waste. You have to wait for the hair to grow to a certain length just to wax again, and in that time, there's too much drag, and I'd rather just fucking shave.

The reporter smiles. "Taking notes from Kingly, I see." She gives me a wink.

So Kingly did answer this question—and apparently, he shaves his arms and legs too. I restrain from looking at the crew because I know Akara is eyerolling the fuck out of this segment. I press my lips together to stop from laughing.

She changes topics to the Ziff Power commercial I did with my dad and then the interview ends. Easy enough. I actually thank her at the end. It was more painless than I thought it'd be, even if I feel a little raw. The most important information wasn't spilled today, and that's the best success.

Operation Keep the Bean Sprout a Secret is still very much in effect.

Akara and Banks lead me down the rooftop stairs to a carpeted hallway. An assistant with a tray of coffee rushes past us, delivering beverages to crew and hosts on the roof. The further we walk along the twisting hall, we pass posters of old Hollywood classics like *Casablanca* and *The Philadelphia Story*.

Press has been staying at this 5-star hotel just outside the Olympic Village. Coming here is a little more unnerving, but hopefully this interview was good enough to appease the higher-ups for the rest of the Olympics.

Banks braces a door open that leads into another hall.

"Fucking jeez, are we in the *Labyrinth*?"

"Not unless Akara is David Bowie," Banks jokes.

I laugh. "Maybe we should shake Kits down. See if he's still Kits."

Banks smiles down at me. "You just want to fondle his ass."

"So what if I do? I like his ass."

"She likes your ass," Banks says to Akara.

"I knew it," Akara says to him, like I professed my undying *love*.

Their teasing is flushing me head to toe. And I just really love their friendship, and fuck, I'm glad it's fully intact.

"After you," Banks tells me, and I realize I haven't stepped through the doorway.

I go into the next hall first, but I can tell they checked for threats. No one is out in front of me. So I walk a little ahead until they lead again. They go left.

How they've memorized this maze of a hotel, I'll never understand. Banks casts a glance back. "You aced that interview."

"Fuck, really?" I'm not the best at interviews. Never have been. Even from the FanCon tour days, I've seemed to either stumble and fuck up or be too quiet.

Banks nods.

Akara shakes his head.

I gape.

Akara says, "Could've used a little less Kingly."

I almost snort.

Of course he'd say that. I want to tell him how bringing up Kingly was a total diversion, something my cousin Charlie would have concocted. Like a powerhouse chess move. I don't say anything though, mostly because Charlie is a sore subject.

Banks resents him for blackmailing me in Yellowstone.

Akara dislikes him because he says he can't trust him. He thinks Charlie will always hurt people he loves. He's done it too many times now.

I'm trying to forgive Charlie for being an ass. The more Akara and Banks hate him, the more I find myself coming to his defense. Like the *hate* is just too fucking strong towards my family member, and he needs another person in his corner.

The fucking irony is that Charlie would probably kick me out of his corner and want to stand alone.

By the time we reach a *long* stretch of hallway, elevators in view at the end, my stomach grumbles.

"Hungry?" Banks asks.

"Yeah, we should definitely head to the fucking caf after this…" I trail off, noticing four broad-built men slip behind us into the hallway, which has been mostly desolate since we left the roof.

No notebooks or "reporter" vibes—they look like they stepped out of a King of the Ring pay-per-view that I've watched with Banks.

It's nothing. I try to shrug off their presence. I bet they're just security for anchors. These are big-time news reporters after all.

Akara slides a hand to the small of my back. He pushes me forward towards the elevator. Banks steps behind me too.

It's nothing. "No boob coverage?" I joke.

"In a sec," Akara says lightly as we keep walking.

My pulse hikes because that *second* quickly becomes a minute. I want to make a joke about double-ass coverage, but I can't surface the words.

We reach the elevators.

"What do you feel like eating today?" Akara asks, casual enough. I can't detect any hint of worry in his voice.

Banks punches the button beside the closed elevator doors. His hand feels heavier on my shoulder.

"Um…if I could say a donut, I would," I reply. "Fuck, I'm going to have the biggest baddest donut when we get back home." Home meaning *Philly.*

After the Olympics.

"We'll have a couple with you, mermaid," Banks tells me, his voice a little stilted.

He's less good at acting casual. Or maybe I can just tell that he's more tensed than I can tell with Akara. Are they that concerned about the four men behind us? I brave a glance.

The men linger for the elevator. They aren't in suits or button-downs. Just plain tees and jeans. No lanyards. No badges.

Banks sidesteps and blocks my view before the men can catch me staring. They wait for the elevator too, but this is probably the only elevator on this floor.

Beep.

The elevator light blinks. Metal doors slide open. I'm leading the pack, the first one to step inside. Akara follows me, but Banks remains out in the hall. My heartbeat spikes. What's going on? He's turned around and saying something softly to the four men.

"Kits," I breathe, raw concern latching my voice. "Tell Banks to get in here. Tell him."

Akara presses P1 on the panel of buttons. He turns to me, and our eyes lock for a fraction of a second but what feels like centuries.

"We'll meet you down there," he whispers.

"*Kits.*" I hear my sheer terror. And I almost reach for his hand, but I stop myself. My breath halts. No.

We can go.

The three of us.

We can leave together.

This isn't happening.

They're fine.

"I love you, Sul." He slips out of the elevator. My throat dries and I pin myself to this spot. *Do what he says. Do what he says. Don't make their jobs harder.*

Pulse racing, I convince myself those four guys are just there to talk to Akara and Banks. I convince myself that they're waiting to catch an elevator ride to the lobby, and my bodyguards just don't want them to share the same small space as me.

I convince myself of all these things.

The elevator doors begin to slide closed, and in an instant, my illusion ruptures.

All four men charge the elevator.

The last thing I see is Banks holding back the assault, and Akara buckling forward.

27
Banks Moretti

THEY WANT IN THE elevator—they want Sulli—and I'm a brick wall they're never sledge-hammering through. 1 to 4, I'm expecting a knockout battle considering they outweigh me. The Fucker, the Bastard, the Shitbag, and the Prick.

I'm prepared for hell as the four of them crash forward, and with a scream inside my lungs—*you're not reaching Sulli*—I deck the Fucker and physically restrain the Shitbag and Prick with hand thrusts and a fist to the gut.

The fourth guy, the Bastard—I'm not taking care of him.

Because Akara is.

I just notice my metamour at my side. *He's not with Sulli. Sulli is safe in the elevator. Give her enough time to escape.* The three thoughts torpedo through my head.

2 to 4. It's still an unfair fight anyway I toss it, but with my size and our combined skill, I like our odds a lot more.

That's until I see Akara caving inward and blood pooling between his closed fingers.

I lose it.

Red with rage, I throw the strongest elbow to the Prick's windpipe. He chokes and buckles at the knees. Hacking up a lung.

2 to 3.

I'm already tearing through two men to reach the Bastard that hurt Akara.

"Get back!" I yell.

Right as I reach the Bastard, he kicks Akara in the ribs, and then I thrash an uppercut to his jaw. He grunts and stumbles with a *thunk* into the wall. A bloodied knife clatters out of his hand.

I go to grab the weapon.

And from behind me, a bicep suddenly hooks around my throat.

Fuck.

He tries dragging me backwards. I try to turn out and throw the Fucker over my head. He's too heavy. Just as strong, and I struggle to breathe. Mic yanks out of my ear—didn't have time to call backup to meet Sulli.

She's safe in the elevator.

Give her more time to escape.

Hyper-focused to my strained breath, to the noises of grunting and thrashing—I see another man, the Shitbag, rushing to the elevator.

No.

The doors are already slid shut, and the numbers tic down to parking. Before he reaches the button, Akara—with a hand to a wound—cuts off his path and slams his forehead into the Shitbag's nose. *Crack.*

Blood pours.

2 to 2.

I'm choking for air, and I jam my elbow at the Fucker's ribs, then hook his leg with my foot and sweep him. He lands on his back, taking me down. He's close enough that I can smell the rotted garlic on his breath.

As I roll out, he grabs a hallway vase and smashes the glass against my head.

Pain explodes around my temple and eye, but I whirl on him and land a blow to his cheekbone. His eye. His head. Over and over, until the lights go out. Part of my instinct—to stand up and unholster my gun—I fight away. Pulling out my Glock has to be a last resort.

Pulse pounding, I shift off the unconscious Fucker.

Near the elevator, the Shitbag is groaning and clutching his broken nose. "Fuuuuck." He's still out for the count.

But the Prick wheezes from the much earlier windpipe blow and struggles to his feet.

The Bastard also remains. He's already recovered from my uppercut—for how long, I don't know. *The knife.* The knife is gone. Disappeared off the floor.

Akara is wrestling the Bastard, and I start to sprint to Akara's aid when the Prick charges for the stairwell door.

Fuck.

Fuck.

Backtracking fast, I shove him, ram a fist in his face, and at the same time, he nails my ribcage with all his weight. I lose breath.

I cough.

We're on the floor.

We're on the floor? Mother of...he's kicking. I'm gripping. I pin my forearm to his neck. He flails, and all I'm thinking is, *Akara, Akara, Akara, Akara.* The Bastard he's fighting is armed. I think he might have the knife.

In one swift move, I unholster my gun in a tight grip and point the barrel right between the Prick's eyes.

He goes slack beneath me.

"You try to take my gun like this is a fuckin' action movie, and I'll blow your brains out." I think about knocking him unconscious.

Just as I make a move, Akara calls out in a wince, "Wait."

I barely shift my gaze off the Prick.

The man that Akara has been wrestling—he's now facedown on the carpet. A knife is deep in his back. My pulse hammers in my ears.

He's...not dead. I see him twitch and moan in pain.

Pressure eases off my chest just as Akara speaks.

"Who sent you?" Akara bends down to the Prick pinned under my weight.

I let up on his throat so he can reply.

Fear bleeds through his eyes. He's not armed like his friend. "Who didn't?" the guy says, a tremor to his voice. "You know how many people are betting on her not medaling? Low odds pay high."

Sickness slams into me, and then I slam my fist into his face.

He coughs up blood.

Akara shoots me a look. *What?* I did what he probably wished he could do. I glance at Akara's waist. Blood soaks his white button-down. He still has a hand pressed against the knife wound. Urgently, I tear off my own shirt and toss it to him.

"Tell whoever is paying you," Akara says, wadding up the fabric against his waist, "that if they send someone else to try and hurt her, I'll be coming for them next. Do you *fucking* hear me?"

He squeaks out, "It was just supposed to be a broken arm or a leg! We weren't going to kill her."

"Tell that to the fucker with the knife," Akara hisses in anger.

He mumbles something to me like, "Can you stop pointing that at me?"

You were going to hurt my pregnant girlfriend. You're lucky all I'm doing is pointing a gun at you right now. I'm not having a full-blown conversation with this prick.

I knock him out and stand off him.

"Sulli," I tell Akara.

And like a godsend, security for GBA News that'd been on the rooftop suddenly appear at the other end of the hallway. Akara is so quick to order them to call the cops. To detain the four men that are left, and they listen fast. And we're not waiting around for reporters to show.

We're not waiting around for police.

We have to go.

We have to catch up to Sulli. We have to meet her down in the parking garage before the elevator drops. Are there more men in the lobby?

In the parking deck?

Are they waiting for her?

We're both running to the stairwell.

"Hey, *hey*," I shout at Akara as we race down the first flight. "You need to *walk*, Nine. You're losing too much blood."

My wadded-up shirt is bright red.

"Better yet, sit down. I'll be back for you with Sulli."

Akara shakes his head. "No."

I stop him. Literally, I stop right in fucking front of him. He walks into my chest and we both almost tumble down the stairs, but I grip the railing.

He glares and tries to push forward. "Banks, we don't have time for this!"

"Yeah, we don't!" I shout back, veins popping in adrenaline, and I hold his arms. "You're not helping me or her if you're on the fucking ground, so sit down. Don't make me fight you."

Pain crests his face. He's afraid for Sulli. He wants to shield Sulli. He wants to pull her into his arms. I know this because it's thumping against my soul like an extra heartbeat.

"I don't tell you to do much, Akara. I'm telling you now; I need your ass on this stair. *Please.*"

I can't lose him.

The white button-down is saturating with blood fast. And he needs to sit and put more pressure on the wound.

Slowly, Akara sinks down on the stair.

"We'll be back for you," I promise.

"Get her out of here," Akara chokes. "Don't come back."

I have no time to argue. I just nod.

And I run. I run down ten more flights of stairs. Akara made the call to leave Sulli in the elevator—to help me. To be there for me.

And I'm leaving him to help her.

To be there for her.

Knowing he's bleeding out while she's alone and missing is ripping me straight in half. If I could be two places at once, I'd give my right side to him and my left to her—but I can't.

I had to choose.

I can't feel my feet by the time I reach the parking garage. I race to the elevators and I punch a button. The doors whoosh open like it just landed here. Empty.

The elevator is empty.

Panic and alarm blast off as I whirl around and around in circles. Looking for her. No sign of any red windbreaker. No cascade of dark hair.

No Sulli.

Fuckfuckfuck.

Someone got to her?

Someone grabbed her?

Someone took her?

The elevator could have stopped on a different level. That was a risk Akara must've been willing to take because the clear threats were the four men in front of us.

He should've chosen her. He should've left me out there alone.

I would've gone down four on one.

I would've been stabbed to hell and back.

She'd be safe. That's all that fucking matters. Screw the rest. I whirl around.

And around.

Shit. Fuck. Shit.

I run a hand through my hair and jog halfway up the row of Teslas. I'm tempted to call out her name, but I don't want to draw attention. A trendy fedora-wearing couple walk hand-in-hand through the parking garage. The sound of a beeping car lock goes off.

I pull out my phone.

"Banks?"

I spin around.

Seeing the candy-apple red windbreaker, long legs—Sulli slips out from behind a large blue garbage can where she'd been hiding, and I run to my girlfriend with all my might. She holds her arms around herself, her eyes bloodshot.

"Thank God," I breathe and pull her into my arms, holding her tight.

She shudders and clings against me in more than just post-shock. "Your face…" *I must be bleeding.* Panic lights her eyes. "Akara—where's Kits?" Her voice spikes. "Is he…?"

"We have to go." I grab her hand, and with a racing pulse, we move out.

28
Akara Kitsuwon

I CAN'T DO NOTHING. Just sitting here. Weakly and with searing heat along my waist, I use comms and alert SFO of the detained threat. Thatcher and Oscar are on their way. Just in case we need more backup.

I call in the assault to the authorities. Just in case GBA's security didn't listen to me. They're not my men. They're not even Triple Shield. I honestly have no fudging clue *who* they are or what they're trained to do. They could be three floors up struggling to restrain the men we knocked out.

Somehow, I get out the words. Our location. The assailants. The danger. All over again.

It's already been called in, I'm told.

When I hang up the phone, I'm not even thinking about the hours I'm going to have to spend detailing what happened to the cops. Or the paperwork my own firm is going to have on their hands.

I'm just thinking about her.

I imagine Banks pulling her to safety. I imagine his arms around her while she tucks herself to his chest, and it's the only solace I have in this damn stairwell.

It's the only peace I want to die inside.

Lightheaded, I rest my temple against the wall. And then I think, *do I have enough strength in me to move?* If I stand up on my own, will I pass out?

I want to try, but as soon as I bend my knees, stars dot my vision, and I almost black-out.

I stop.

I breathe.

And just when I'm about to succumb to the fact that I might die alone and forgotten—I hear footsteps. Ascending towards me.

"Kits!" she shouts.

Tears prick my eyes. Angry, happy tears—and as soon as she races into view and I see she's okay, I glare at Banks, "I said *get her out.*"

"I couldn't leave you."

I have no reply because for once, I'm glad he didn't listen to me.

He grabs my forearm and heaves me to my feet. Sulli pulls my other arm over her broad shoulders. They brace my weight.

And help me move.

Celebrity Crush – July 28th
Sullivan Meadows' Bodyguard & Boyfriend, Akara Kitsuwon, Stabbed Protecting the Olympic Swimmer

We've just received news that Akara Kitsuwon & Banks Moretti were in an altercation with four unidentified men in the Haverford Hotel in L.A. The police were called to the scene after the incident, and all four men have been arrested. Sources say that the assailants were looking to stop Sullivan Meadows from competing in her upcoming Olympic events by attacking the swimmer. With a leg break? A stab wound? *Celebrity Crush* can't verify their complete intentions, but boy, does this sound familiar. Echoes of the 1994 incident with ice skater Tonya Harding and Nancy Kerrigan, anyone? (**See article:** *Ice Skater Nancy Kerrigan Attacked!)* Luckily, Sullivan Meadows' bodyguards were there to protect her! While our Olympic star walked away unscathed, the same can't be said for her boyfriends. Sources say that Akara Kitsuwon was stabbed, and Banks Moretti has minor injuries from the fight.

No word on whether Akara Kitsuwon was hospitalized.

Subscribe to *Celebrity Crush* to keep updated on his whereabouts.

29

Akara Kitsuwon

I DIDN'T GO TO the hospital.

Despite Sulli and Banks' pleas, I've parked myself in Farrow's hotel suite. The place where the Hales, Meadows, and Cobalts are staying was only a couple blocks from the attack. What Banks called "a resort not a fucking hotel" after seeing the pool's water slide and grotto swim-up bar our first day in California.

I'd rather be here than stoking more headlines about being effing *stabbed*.

But mostly, this is way faster than waiting in the ER. We're outside the Olympic Village right now, and Sulli needs to be in the stadium and prepping for the Mixed Relay in less than two hours.

Factor in L.A. traffic, and we don't have time to waste.

She's been refusing to go with Banks until she's 100% positive I'm not going to take a turn for the worse.

"I'm not leaving," Sulli declares again, probably off the intensity of my gaze.

"Imagining you losing a medal tonight because of me hurts worse than being stabbed in the *fudging* abdomen."

"And you *bleeding out* while I'm in a pool trying to win a trinket will haunt me for fucking life."

"An Olympic medal isn't a trinket."

"You mean so much more to me, Kits," she combats. "So stop telling me to go."

I've never wanted to be the reason Sulli has failed, anymore than she's wanted to be the reason I need to sell Studio 9. But I love her, and I'm listening to her pleas.

Just to make our lives more interesting—and awkward—the suite is packed.

SFO is here, and they're hearing me argue with Sul. I'm honestly surprised Oscar hasn't broken out a Snickers bar and popcorn yet.

Banks has his arms around Sulli while she hovers near me at the suite's dining table. First-aid gauze and antiseptic spread out. I'm shirtless, slouched on a dining chair with a water bottle in a limp hand.

Farrow is seated close. "He's not going to bleed out, Meadows." Wearing surgical gloves, he meticulously uses forceps and suture thread to stitch my wound. "The blade didn't hit any arteries or nerves or organs. No infection, from what I can tell." His eyes flit up to mine. "You're a lucky fucker. Again."

Again.

It takes me a solid second to realize he's referring to the cougar attack from last fall.

I shift a little in the chair. Stifling a wince, and I focus on Banks.

He has butterfly tape over a gash in his eyebrow. Farrow said he'd stitch him after me. But except for the cut and a couple busted ribs, Banks is okay.

He's okay.

She's okay.

Everyone knows I'm not okay, but like the cougar attack, I don't give a crap about the severity of the injury—as long as I'm able to stand up and walk over to Sulli.

Banks and Sulli's concern crashes into me like giant waves only to recede and crash again. It becomes hard to look at them. Especially when I know they'd rather take me to a hospital.

Bloody gauze fills a trash bin beside our feet. Pain blooms in my side, but I've already tossed a couple of Vicodin, and the piercing heat has started to subside to a dull throb. I thanked Maximoff for the water.

Now Farrow just needs to hurry. The faster I'm done, the faster Sulli can compete.

I smile to try to lighten the mood. "Hey, it was skill. Not luck."

The suite is still tensed.

Like they can all see through me.

Sitting stiffly on the cream couch, Oscar and Donnelly have been whispering and glancing in constant worry.

Quinn isn't here. He's back in Philly running Studio 9.

Gabe hides in the bathroom with the door cracked open, feeling woozy from the sight of all the blood.

Thatcher stands stoically by the closed curtains of a floor-length window. The terrace is locked, but he peeks out of the curtains every so often, then peeks at me.

Silence hangs heavy after my poor shot at levity.

Fantastic.

I'm not used to having people care this deeply about my well-being. I'm more used to worrying about the team than being someone to worry about. And honestly, I'm not the only guy who's uncomfortable with this attention.

Most of us would rather fling the concern onto our clients or our friends.

Shoot, Banks *barely* talks about his injuries. He'll say, "I'm good to go" when he's flat on his aching back.

Farrow grimaces if you ask him if he's okay more than twice. (Unless you're his husband.)

Donnelly will bury himself in his shirt before you ever see him upset.

Oscar has a "serious face" that supersedes *hurt*.

Thatcher is Thatcher.

And Quinn will snap, "I'm fine!" until you lay off.

Does this profession just attract this type of person? Or are we all here because we've needed each other?

I think I've always needed Omega, as much as they've needed me.

"Every couple of hours, I'll need to check on this," Farrow says strictly. "No avoiding me like last time, Akara."

"Yeah," I agree.

Anything to get out of here faster.

Thatcher remains quiet at the window. His silence is louder than anyone talking. He asked me if I was alright and that's been the extent of our conversation. But he keeps peeking over.

I know he cares about me.

I know he realizes that I risked Sulli's life for a moment, just to protect his brother. And if I screwed up—if that'd been the bad call...

I can't think about it.

It's an alternate history, and I remind myself that I'm a good bodyguard, a great leader. Because I know which calls to make in those split-second moments. If I didn't, I could've lost Banks tonight.

Donnelly raises a hand. "Anyone else feeling like the boss is playing favorites with the boss?"

I shoot him a look.

His hand slowly lowers. "Nevermind. I said nothing."

Oscar finally pops the tab of a Pringles can. "No, bro, you were definitely making a good point. Why does Kitsuwon get a free pass from the hospital? I barely stub my big toe and he makes me go."

He's exaggerating.

"I'm fine," I groan for what feels like the hundredth time. "I don't need the hospital, guys."

Farrow raises his brows and gives me a look I've seen him give his husband a million times. The one that says, *you're being a stubborn ass.* At least, that's how I read it.

Speaking of his husband, Maximoff has his arms crossed like he's ready for twenty knife-wielding linebackers to burst through the door. Baby Ripley has been flipping through a picture book on the floor. Babbling to himself.

But Farrow follows my gaze to Maximoff. "Relax, wolf scout. The world is not burning down."

Maximoff uncrosses his arms and cracks his knuckles. "Four guys attacked Sulli and you don't think the world is burning?"

"They didn't attack me, Mof," Sulli pipes in. "They attacked Akara and Banks."

"They were after *you*, Sul."

Maximoff isn't wrong. Banks and I weren't the targets, and the only reason we ended up in the middle of the fight is because it's our job to protect her. And we did this time.

"Hey, we avoided the worst," I tell him.

Maximoff scrunches his face. "You've been *stabbed*, man. How is this not a bad thing?" He spins around the suite, searching for one of my men to back him up. "Am I living in the Twilight Zone?"

Farrow's smile stretches wide. "Once a famous one. Always a famous one."

Oscar laughs.

Donnelly smirks. "Stamp."

Maximoff actually flushes, but his frustration and anger rotates onto his husband quickly. He opens his mouth, but Farrow beats him, "We're bodyguards, wolf scout." He snaps off his gloves. "All of us are willing—shit, we're anticipating—to get hurt on the job for any one of you."

"I get that," Maximoff says strongly, "but things are getting so god-damn dangerous. Sulli has already had a gun pulled on her this year."

Air vacuums out of the suite.

Banks hugs Sulli tighter, and she holds onto his arms like she's falling off a cliff.

Thinking about the gun incident is another stab to the abdomen. Seeing Sulli go into shock is about *fifty* more stabs. I'm about to stand.

Farrow catches my wrist, silently saying, *not yet, Kitsuwon.*

Shit.

"Sorry, Sul," Maximoff says, seeing my girlfriend's reaction.

She's wide-eyed. "It's alright, Mof. I just don't like remembering."

"We're more prepared," I remind Maximoff and so Sulli remembers this too.

He nods a few times. "I just really don't want to see anyone else get hurt." He rakes a hand through his thick hair. "And I know it's impossible to ask."

Oscar nods, "Either we get hurt or our clients get hurt."

Donnelly softens his smile. "If we succeed, we're the ones getting hurt."

"Every time," Farrow finishes.

Sulli winces. "I'm with Mof—this sucks."

Oscar tosses a Pringle in his mouth. "And that's why you don't date your bodyguards."

"*Oscar,*" I snap.

Farrow rolls his eyes at his friend.

Banks whispers to Sulli.

Donnelly is suspiciously quiet. He gets up. To check the window.

"What?" Oscar says innocently. "I'm not saying she can't hang, Kitsuwon. If she couldn't handle the heat, she would've already left the bodyguard kitchen."

"No, you're just saying she's dumb to date a bodyguard."

"Technically, she's dating two," Farrow says matter-of-factly.

"Not helping," I tell him.

His lips rise.

The Yale boys are killing me.

"*Or,*" Oscar says, "I'm saying you all are some stupid motherfuckers to date your clients, and my intelligent ass had enough sense to date outside the family."

Donnelly slow-claps from the window.

Thatcher surprisingly joins in with Farrow.

"Thank you. Thank you." Oscar stands and mockingly bows.

Banks throws out, "Guess that makes Donnelly as smart as you. Seeing as how he's never been with a famous one."

The room goes quiet.

A pin could drop.

Everyone is on edge.

And I realize fast that *everyone* here knows what's going on. With what happened in the past between Donnelly and I'm guessing Luna. Except me. Except Banks. Did they hook up? Did they go on a date?

Are they still together?

Secretly?

Donnelly is staring out the window. Pretending to observe the mayhem outside. "Anyone want an ice cream?" he says like nothing is amiss.

Banks lifts a shoulder to me like *you wanna press on?*

No.

No, I don't.

Not now. Not while we're here. Not while I have a gash in my abdomen and Sulli is two hours away from missing a competition of a lifetime.

"I'll pass on the Rocky Road," I tell Donnelly tightly.

"Mint chocolate chip?"

"On all ice cream."

"Sure thing, boss."

Ripley shuts his storybook, and everyone's attention suddenly diverts to the baby. He picks up the book. Unsteady on his feet, he stumbles over to Sulli.

She freezes like she's unsure what to do.

Sulli is pregnant. I didn't forget. I doubt the rest of SFO did, but the fact is highlighted ten times over. *Sulli is pregnant.* With my baby or Banks' baby, and now a baby is teetering over to her.

Sulli. A baby. Sulli and a baby. These things start rolling around in my head like Bingo balls.

"Hey, Rip," Sulli greets with an easy smile.

Ripley sets the book at her feet, then races back to his dad. Tightly, he hugs and clings to Maximoff's calf.

"He's just shy," Maximoff says to his cousin. "It's not you."

"Oh hey, yeah, I get it," Sulli says with a withering smile. Something's eating at her.

Banks leans into her ear. I jerk towards them like I'm about to leave this chair. Time to go be with my people.

Farrow grips my leg. Keeping me here again.

"Come on."

"I'm not done." He rummages around in his med kit. Maybe a bandage. Gauze. I don't know. But I'd really like this to be over. He quickens his pace.

Ripley peels away from Maximoff. We all watch as he races over to Farrow. "Papa, Papa! Look." He picks up the book he'd set down. He shows off the cover of a red convertible.

Farrow smiles, sifting quickly through his med kit. "Is that a car, little man?"

Ripley tries to make a *vroom* noise.

Baby still needs a bodyguard. *Babies*—they're having another one. Sulli is also pregnant. Jane is pregnant. It's messy.

So very messy.

"Is Akara's phone going off?" Sulli asks Banks.

Yep, it's vibrating in his hand. He stole my phone earlier. And he's the only one I'd even let thieve my phone...besides Sulli.

Banks checks the cell. "Quinn texted."

"Little bro is missing all the action." Oscar crunches on a Pringle. "He probably has that FOMEFT right now."

Sulli perks up a little at her phrase being used by someone else. Someone other than her family. I smile, happy to see her spirits brighten.

Banks reads my phone. "*Wishing you a speedy recovery, Akara. I know how shitty it feels to be on the sidelines.*"

Sidelines.

I didn't tell anyone I was benching myself, but I guess it's easy to assume. Still, I feel the heat of all the eyes on me. Questioning. I wonder who will ask first.

Then a door from the bathroom creaks open slightly. Gabe sticks his head out. "You're taking yourself off-duty, Akara?"

Oscar speaks up next. "Yeah, Kitsuwon. You off-duty?" I swear he only chimes in so I don't dodge the question.

I avoid Sulli and Banks' eyes. It'd be hypocritical of me to remain on-duty with fresh stitches on my abdomen when I'd *never* allow my men to do the same.

"I'm thinking about it," I end up saying. Silence. Tension. All of the above start to fill the room again.

Guess I'm a hypocrite.

And I have zero fucks left to give.

I'd rather help protect Sulli and SFO during an event that poses countless dangers. Even if I said, *I won't get involved,* I'd find myself sticking my neck out for them. And anyway, Banks is with me.

I'm not alone.

30

Akara Kitsuwon

BODY SLICK WITH SWEAT, I quickly yank on sweatpants to my waist. Urgency grinds my muscles, and I have trouble avoiding their gazes. Both Sulli and Banks watch me from the iron-framed bed, sheets twisted up around their naked bodies. Tons of pillows litter the floor of Sulli's penthouse bedroom, and I'm careful not to trip on the cupcake-shaped one.

Or the one that looks like a dick in the dark.

Curtains shroud the morning light, but I'm almost certain that's the eggplant emoji pillow.

"Just text him that you'll check in later," Banks says, toothpick between his lips. He's rubbing Sulli's perked nipple, and she's grazing her foot against his hamstring, while her fingers circle his abs and ascend to his dog tags. But her green doe-eyes are on *me*.

I try to focus on anything but them.

"Can't." I bend down to the pile of clothes, hunting for my shirt in the mess. Looks like a hurricane plowed through her bedroom. "I brushed Quinn off last week."

"It's not up to you whether he can come back to security," Banks complains. "He needs to stop badgering you. You want me to tell him?"

"No."

"'Cause I don't mind being the bad guy."

"I love you, but no."

He cracks a crooked smile. Banks is on good terms with just about everyone in SFO, and if Quinn wants to be disgruntled with someone, it should be me.

I abandon the clothes pile and head to the dresser. "And it actually is up to me whether he can return." *I'm the boss.*

Sulli interjects, "But I thought Farrow didn't clear him yet?" She's been more in-the-know about security drama since Banks and I prattle on about work around her.

"He hasn't. But Quinn knows I can overturn that." So the youngest Oliveira brother keeps calling me to check out his progress. I don't know what I'm walking into—a boxing demonstration? But I do owe him some of my time since he's been managing Studio 9.

"Don't nail and bail, Nine," Banks rephrases.

"I'm not nailing and bailing," I refute.

"Smashing and bashing," Sulli banters.

"No bashing."

"Hit it and quit it," Banks adds.

"No quitting, Banksy."

"You're pouncing and bouncing, and you can't change my mind, Kits," she says.

I almost smile.

No, I *am* smiling.

Banks takes out his toothpick. "At least cuddle her for ten minutes."

I stand over the dresser and let out a long sigh. *I want that.*

"Let him go," Sulli says to Banks. "If he wants to pounce and bounce, he can pounce and bounce. We'll cuddle-fuck later."

Slowly, I rotate to face them again and lean back against the wood dresser. I zero in on Sulli. "I sense a heavy dose of reverse psychology coming from this corner of the bed." I wave my hands toward her.

She splays a hand over her heart. "I'm a shit liar-manipulator."

"Just great at sexual innuendos and April Fools' jokes," I tease.

She breaks into a laugh.

Hearing her laugh just adds another ache, a want, to be closer.

"What do you think, Banks?" Sulli asks him.

"That he can cuddle-fuck you later if he wants and you want." He shifts his hand down between her legs.

She writhes a little at the touch and nearly turns into him for more. For deeper.

My muscles tighten and blood rushes south at the sight of her lips parting. His fingers disappear inside Sulli, and her eyes lock on me. Unmoving. Everything we do together sends my arousal over the edge. And the longer we're together, the more we all know how to rope each other in.

At the beginning of every morning and at the end of every night, they're my joy. The origin of my happiness. Stress is harder to fall into when they're here.

She twitches in pleasure. Her eyes are still glued to mine.

Banks glances between me and Sulli, amusement brewing across his face. "Nine?"

"Ten minutes," I say with a rasped voice. Swiftly, I step out of my sweatpants and crawl back into bed beside Sulli. She turns on her side, facing Banks. He pumps his fingers inside her, and I cocoon myself against her back. She lets out a trembling breath.

I skim my hand over the curve of her round ass, and I touch the silicone of a plug. Breath against her ear, I whisper, "This feel okay? You want me to take it out?" We've been fucking all morning, and this might be the longest she's had it in. A few weeks ago, we all agreed to start practicing and prepping for the day we try double penetration.

"Not yet," she says softly. "I think I can go longer."

"Listen to your body, Lady Meadows. Not to your fortitude."

She smiles back at me. "I will, Kits. I promise."

I scoot closer, her ass tucked against me, and I hold Sulli stronger against my athletic body while Banks gets her off. A pleasured sigh parts her lips. She rocks her hips against him. Her ass against me. Until we pin her so strongly with our builds that she can't move.

She mumbles against his chest, "This feels so fucking good."

Yeah, I *love* being this close too. The three of us. Intimate and uninhibited. Everything feels easier when we shut the world out, but in the same breath, these moments feel like a battery charge. Like we're all powering each other up to face what's outside.

Today, I face Quinn.

"SHUT THE FRIDGE," I MUTTER TO MYSELF IN shock.

College-aged twenty-somethings in leggings and muscle shirts—all women—snake around the block, the long, twisting line leading into *Studio 9*. They hold water bottles filled with water and fresh fruit.

I'm more used to fans of the Hales, Meadows, Cobalts loitering outside my gym. Waiting to spot a famous face or a famous Omega bodyguard.

Crowds of people who actually want to work out?

New.

Tipping my red baseball cap down, I slink to the front of the line.

"Hey, you can't cut," a girl with pink hair and boxer braids whines.

I ignore her, pushing my way inside. Surprise obliterates every nerve-ending. The gym is crammed. Not with the typical Muay Thai fighter or muscled gym rat ready to hit the boxing bags. It's packed with more women, who I'd probably peg as yogis. Way more likely to frequent a Center City yoga studio.

But they're here.

Looking over a few heads, I spot Quinn at the front desk. Four, I repeat *four* women are bent over the desk chatting with him. All in the same legging, muscle-shirt attire. Lots of colorful sports bras.

Instantly, a flash of Sulli and her baggy workout clothes fills my head, and I end up smiling. She'd look like a babe in anything, but I like that she's never changed.

Especially not for me.

After I take a breath, I raise a hand and shout, "Quinn!"

The room deadens quiet like I just shouted *Who farted?!*

Quinn's face brightens immediately, and he pushes out of his chair. "Akara!"

"Ohmygod, it's Akara Kitsuwon!" someone near the lockers shouts. Phones are whipped out. I jab my thumb toward the back room.

"Office," I tell Quinn.

He's still grinning as he nods. "I'll be there in a sec!"

Leaving the women, I enter the sanctuary of the Studio 9 office. A boardroom table lying barren and unused. No papers. No coffee stains. The whiteboard is wiped clean.

Blowing out a breath, I sink down into a leather chair. Have I neglected the gym so much that I don't even know what's happening here? Sure, I keep up with the P&L's to ensure we're not in the red—and I've seen we're doing better than usual—but besides that I've left most of the daily operations and decisions up to Quinn.

I rub my face. *This is good. More gym memberships are good.* Then why do I feel so strange?

The office door slowly opens, and Quinn slips inside. He's no longer on crutches, but he occasionally wears a boot on his leg during the day. Right now, it's off.

He shuts the door. "Thanks for coming."

"I'm sorry it took so long. Everything has been busy with the security firm." And it's not like I don't see Quinn. We live together. And yeah, I'm around less because I crash at Sulli's, but it's not like I'm actively ignoring him.

"No worries, bro." Anticipation lines his brow, and I eye the scar underneath his eye. Quinn can appear intimidating, but once you know him, he has more soft layers under the brittle, tough ones. It's almost hard to believe he beat the crap out of people in a ring.

Before he can change the subject, I point towards the door. "What was that all about?"

He follows my finger. "What do you mean?"

I laugh. "Quinn, I haven't seen that many women in my gym...well, ever."

"Ohhhh right." Quinn opens his hands. "I don't know. I guess word got around that I was managing the place. I think Nessa might have Tweeted it."

Nessa Nolan.

His girlfriend.

The one he met on the ski slopes when he crashed into a tree. Luna calls it a sweet "meet cute" but I just remember how attached Nessa seems to be to social media. I'm worried that part of Nessa will inevitably put a strain on Quinn. But hey, she did something good I guess, if she helped promote the gym.

"So they're just here for *the young stud?*" I find that a little hard to believe. Sure, Quinn is considered the best-looking guy on the team, but he can't pull that many people here.

"I'm also doing Ladies Night. Free classes on Wednesdays. It's bringing in a lot of new memberships."

That'll do it.

I guess I never thought to do something like that. Mainly because the gym had always been geared to pro-fighters over fitness buffs. *Change isn't bad.*

I know that, and it doesn't feel like it is. The new, maybe better course for my gym isn't what's sinking my stomach.

"Smart," I tell him.

He takes a seat at the board table beside me. "What can I say, I'm good at my job." His smile falters. "But I'm ready to come back to the team. My leg's *way* better, bro. I can even do some kicks on the bag. I'll show you." He hops up as fast as he sat down, then jabs his thumb to the door.

I shake my head. "The person you'll need to impress isn't me. I'm defaulting to Farrow's advice on that one."

Quinn's face falls. "Akara, my brother is in his ear. Farrow will *never* clear me unless I'm the bionic man. Okay, he wants me to be 150%."

"Then you should be 150%."

His expression sours further. "Dammit." He leans his ass on the table, staring at the floor.

I wince. "It's not forever."

"Yeah…yeah, whatever," Quinn mumbles. "Have fun with New Quinn."

"Gabe isn't—" I don't get out the words. He storms out of the office.

I let out a frustrated breath, and then it hits me. Why I'm feeling sick to my stomach. Quinn. He's *good* at managing Studio 9. *Great, actually.* He might even be a better gym manager than a bodyguard. That thought twists me up because I shouldn't want to keep him here in a position he clearly doesn't love. It benefits me more, but it hurts him.

For the first time in forever, I don't have to worry about Studio 9. I don't have to mull over ways to sell my gym. But at what cost?

31

Sullivan Meadows

NOW

@CelebrityCrushOfficial: our sources say Sullivan Meadows is pulling out of the Mixed Relay.

@apprehensive-spoon321: So Sullivan Meadows isn't gonna compete??? God that SUCKS for Kingly. She's robbing him of another gold. Wut a selfish bitch

@queenrose_xoxo: @apprehensive-spoon321 omg her boyfriend just got stabbed! Stop blaming Sullivan for everything! #KitsullettiKicksass

@PuhLease22: Sullivan has choked the entire Olympics. Just quit cheering for her. She's not that good of a swimmer

@ItssBetty: lol anyone who likes Sullivan Meadows is a clown

@TigerBangarang: does anyone ship Sullivan & Kingly? Just me???

I bang my cellphone to my forehead, hating most of these fucking tweets. And *fuck* Celebrity Crush for the misinformation. I haven't pulled out of the Mixed Relay.

I'm just stuck in traffic.

Minutes tick by, and to be frank, I *only* went on Twitter in search of a certain username, who tweeted at random death threats and trolls.

@Love4Sullivan: @porkipine3 the negativity is too much. Would you say that to Sullivan's face?

@Love4Sullivan: @KyleSoccerAce Sullivan Meadows deserves love. Why are you so hateful, Kyle?

I might be stalking my boyfriends' fan account.

Seeing them defend me online makes me feel better about the possibility of letting down the world. I'm reminded that *they* matter. They're in my corner.

They are real.

They are right here in the fucking car with me.

The trolls online—I won't ever meet the majority of them. They're not my life. They're not what matters.

But I can't lie—one of the tweets cuts into my thick-ish skin.

"What's that face, Sul?" Akara asks from the passenger seat of our rental car. A fancy SUV with black leather seats and dark tinted windows. Banks mans the wheel, and he's been grumbling Italian curses the past half hour while battling L.A. traffic.

In the backseat, I read from my phone. "*Lol anyone who likes Sullivan Meadows is a clown.*" I get that celebrities get called *clowns* all the time, but that fucking hurt for some reason.

"Give me a red nose," Akara says. "Orange hair."

I start to smile. "Stop."

"Face paint. Those big clown shoes."

My heart and lungs swell. Crushing on my dreamboat so fucking hard.

"And I'll give them to Banks."

My smile is punctured. "*Kits.*" I'd kick the back of his chair if he wasn't injured.

He laughs, then cradles an arm around his abdomen and winces.

I wince. "Don't fucking laugh."

"Don't make me laugh."

Banks mumbles, "You fuckin' stunad." His voice rises. "Ah, come on! Get the fuck outta here." He slams on the horn along with the rest of L.A.

Akara tries to draw my attention off the madness outside. Paparazzi vans are hugging close to us. I slouch further in my seat as he talks. "Banks, you a clown for Sulli?"

Banks cools down at that question. "If just *liking* Sulli makes me a clown, then pack me up and ship me to the circus. 'Cause I'm the biggest fucking clown in town."

My heart *flutters*. I bite the corner of my lip, smiling.

"See," Akara says to me. "Banks needs the clown shoes."

"And you don't?"

"Don't I look better in Vans?" he teases.

I humph. "You're such a—"

"Asshole," he finishes.

"I was going to say *clown*."

He laughs, then groans. "Sulli."

"Sorry," I cringe.

Akara goes eerily quiet for a second.

"Does it hurt that bad?" I'm about to unbuckle and squeeze between the middle console.

He must predict my next move because he says, "Don't unsnap your seatbelt. I'm fine—really." He tries to smile at me. And I have a weird feeling his quietness wasn't from his stab wound. He seems nervous. "You know, I am a clown for you too, right?"

"Yeah?" I frown. "I know you're just joking about it." He doesn't need to be like Banks. Just like Banks doesn't need to be like Akara. I need them to be themselves. Just as they fucking are, because they've always loved me just as I fucking am.

The strange tension breaks when Akara sticks his tongue out at me. I stick mine out at him.

We're both smiling.

Until I catch sight of the clock on the dashboard. Until Akara spins back and helps Banks navigate around an aggressive sedan.

Fuck, we're cutting this close.

Banks is trying his hardest to get us there on time.

I close out of Twitter. Seeing my boyfriends defend me = good. Staring at all the hate = really fucking bad. I know not to be swept up into the mess, but I really wish more people asked how Akara is doing. If he's okay.

He's just as important as me. And he's *way* more important than gold. Remembering the medal on the line today is a reminder of three names.

Kingly.

Frankie.

Dean.

My teammates. They're not just usernames and profile pictures. They're real too, and if I can't make the relay, they'll feel the brunt-force impact of my decision. *I needed to ensure Kits was okay.*

I had to.

If we don't reach the pool, then I can't be upset with anyone. Not even myself. This is what had to happen, and I wouldn't do anything differently.

But a part of me will feel the sting knowing I hurt someone's Olympic dreams. I'm not even sure *I* would forgive myself if our positions were reversed. I've never been much of a forgiving person, but God, I'm trying to be better at forgiveness. Every day, I'm trying.

Kingly has full right to hate me or spit in my face. (Okay, maybe not spit in my face—I wouldn't even do that.) But if he wants to yell, I'll let him fucking yell.

My boyfriends might not let him.

Fuck.

This is going to end badly, isn't it? I cringe all the way to the stadium, imagining a train wreck as the minutes deplete faster and faster.

"SORRY, SORRY! FUCK!" I SHOUT, RACING INTO the ready room. "I'm here!" Swim cap on, bodyskin swimsuit on, I'm prepared to compete.

My pulse jackhammers as every athlete and official turn and stare at my loud entrance. Did I make it? Am I too late?

"Sulli!" Frankie races to me, flinging her arms around my broad shoulders. "Ahhh! I'm so freaking happy to see you. You made it." She rattles my shoulders.

All my nerves jostle with the movement. "I made it?" Shock globes my eyes. "You're fucking sure?"

"Yep." She grins. "It starts in five."

"Oh thank fuck." I touch my speeding heart.

"The torpedo is here!" Dean announces, hoisting his phone up so I fill the frame with him. Is he on Instagram Live?

I can't tell which social media Dean is using, but I see my relieved smile staring back at me. Glad to even be present for Dean's viral videos. "I'm fucking here." I give a thumbs-up. "And Dean is the torpedo."

"Now she's being kind. I'm the otter." He mimes doing a backstroke with one hand.

I laugh, my pulse beginning to slow.

Some people are silent in the ready room as they try to maintain total focus. That's definitely not Dean. He tends to psyche out his competition with his carefree energy.

"See you soon," Dean winks at his phone. "Peace out." He shuts off the video, then flings an arm around my shoulders. "We've got this, Meadows. Don't worry about today."

He means the stabbing.

My boyfriend was attacked literally *hours* ago.

Dean is careful to dodge those words. Probably knowing not to psyche *me* out. I'm his teammate in the relay. Not his competition.

I try to exhale. "Thanks, Dean." I swing my arms and shake them out while Dean gives me a second alone. *Where's Kingly?* I didn't want to search for him or act like I care, but fuck, it's impossible not to wonder what he thinks or if he's angry.

Finally, I spot Kingly on the bench. Headphones on his ears, he swings his arms like me. Keeping to himself like my usual routine.

We're not the same.

Or are we?

I'd be just as fucking pissed at someone showing up late.

Maybe he thinks I don't care *enough* about the sport. Like I'm not dedicated. Not sacrificing everything, including my boyfriend.

To deserve any good in my life, I have to bleed every drop of love and light—I don't believe it. I don't believe that I'm only *great* because I am solely swimming.

I think I'm *great* because I am more.

They've been saying that all along. Akara and Banks.

My boyfriends.

I glance over at them. They're taking their post at the wall. Akara leans a little into Banks. He looks casual, not like he's propping himself up from the pain in his abdomen.

I try not to wince.

But I'm fucking wincing. The mental image of Akara—bloody on the stairwell—floods my brain. I've made a lot of sacrifices to be here, and I realize those around me have made sacrifices too. Akara and Banks are constantly putting themselves at more risk in order for me to achieve a dream.

"Meadows."

I jump, "Fuck."

"Didn't mean to scare you, kid." Kingly is standing a foot from me, headphones around his neck. "You prepared to go out there?"

I swing my arms more. "Yeah. Are you?"

He cocks his head a little. "Look, no one will blame you if your head's not fully *here* right now." Is he consoling me? Is this how Kingly consoles?

Because he fucking sucks at it.

"Your boyfriend was stabbed," he says point-blank.

I stew. "Thanks for the fucking reminder."

He lets out a breath, then lowers his voice so no one else can hear. "I'm not going to lie to you. I am worried. You've been underperforming these past few days, and we all want first place. I *need* this gold to set records."

Records.

Most Olympic golds for men's swimming. Kingly is sitting close to Phelps' number one title, which barely anyone has ever encroached on until now.

My childhood self is practically screaming at me not to ruin this for him.

But I'm not a *kid* anymore with some silly idol crush.

I have goals too and records *I* want to set. If I do my best in the pool, it won't be for Kingly. I assure myself that.

"My head is *here*. If we lose, it won't be because of me."

He looks unconvinced, and I don't care to try to convince him. He'll see soon enough, anyway. Dean bounces over with outstretched arms. "The King." He weaves his arm over Kingly's shoulder.

Kingly's uptight, focused demeanor melts into something softer. He slips Dean a grin. "I hate when you call me that, Deano."

"And I love when you call me Deano." He whispers something in Kingly's ear, and they laugh together. Bromance in full force, I guess.

Before I feel on the outs of a clique, we're given a two-minute countdown. I peel away from them, surprised when Frankie approaches my side.

"How you holding up?" Frankie wonders.

I shrug, words caught in my throat. I've been asked that question by my parents, my aunts and uncles and cousins, by texts from my coach and other teammates. I'm just tired of answering *I'm fine* when the person everyone should be asking is standing ten feet behind me.

She sips a Ziff Power. "I think I'm way more nervous for the relay than for any individual event. It's…a lot, you know?" Her worry meets my eyes.

And I get it.

Boy, do I fucking get it. "Yeah. Just know that I'd never blame you or Dean or Kingly if something went wrong." Four years ago, I might've. But four years ago, I didn't even *try* to do relays.

I didn't want to rely on anyone but me.

I didn't trust anyone enough.

"I wouldn't blame you either," Frankie assures. "We're all in this together."

She hugs me, and I hug back just as strongly, telling her, "You're a fucking pro in the water, Frankie. Just keep doing what you've been doing."

She lights up when we break apart. "Thanks, Sulli."

"Swimmers for the Mixed Relay!" a coordinator calls out.

It's time.

Before I leave for the pool deck, I cast a quick glance at my boyfriends.

Akara smiles. He stubbornly wanted to be here for this.

It means something to me. His presence has a calming factor. Like a reminder of *before*. Four years ago. When I did succeed.

Banks' shadow of a smile plays at his lips, and I hang onto the comfort inside his gaze. "Swim your heart out, mermaid."

"Go kick ass," Akara cheers.

I will.

I can.

And I go.

A REFEREE BLOWS INTO A WHISTLE, SIGNALING swimmers to enter the pool. Backstroke starts in the water, not on a starting block.

Dean hops in the pool with the other seven swimmers and readies himself. America versus Japan, Spain, Great Britain, Italy, China, Australia, and Canada. We didn't come first in our semifinal heat. Great Britain beat us and is super competitive in this relay. Everyone at home is watching and hoping.

"Take your mark."

If we don't win for our country…*don't think about it, Sulli.* Pressure packs tight, and I swing my arms out again.

Beep.

Dean propels backwards, arms in perfect stroke.

"You have this, Deano," Kingly mutters over and over and fucking *over.* More than I've ever heard him mutter Dean's name. Frankie is closest to the starting block, already crouched and ready to dive. She's up next, and I'm last, standing behind Kingly's muscled back.

Crowds roar and cheer.

The noises fuel me. Adrenaline amped, blood pumping.

We all try to stay focused.

I peek out at the lane.

Dean is ahead, but not by much. Great Britain is only *fingers* away. My teammate reaches the first fifty. Makes a smooth fucking turn. As he swims back to the starting block, the breaststroke swimmers prepare for the exchange.

He touches the wall.

Frankie dives into the pool. Her head breaches the water for the breaststroke, and Dean climbs out of the pool, sopping wet. Kingly briefly touches his arm in a *good job*—but for the most part, we're all focused on the event.

Against better fucking judgement, my eyes flit to the stands.

I can make out more signs than faces.

KINGLY FOR GOLD!
THE KING GOAT

And then…

SULLIVAN MEADOWS IS MY IDOL!
SWIM, SULLI, SWIM!
KITSULLETTI KICKSASS

That last one makes me smile the most. I expected more *Kitsulletti Ruined Everything* signs, and I don't try to search for the hate.

I just breathe in the love I see.

The cheers I hear.

We can do this.

When I see Frankie reach the first fifty, my stomach nosedives. We've lost our lead. Great Britain makes the turn before us.

"It's okay. It's okay," Dean says, clapping behind me. "We can make it up. You've both got this." He squeezes my shoulder. Kingly is already on the block.

Oh fuck.

We're *really* behind.

Like *third* place behind, and Frankie touches the wall, huffing and puffing. Kingly dives into the water—the stadium erupts like God fell from heaven. Frankie pulls herself out of the pool, looking crushed. Cheeks beet-red.

"It's okay," I whisper before I need to take the block. Dean gives her a consoling hug.

I prepare myself for the exchange.

And I have the greatest view of Kingly in the water. Possibly the best view of a lifetime. Staring down our lane, Kingly swims the butterfly with power and precision. Like the greatest before him, he is a phenom. A marvel.

A soon-to-be legend.

He barrels ahead of Australia. And he shortens the distance between us and Great Britain. But he doesn't completely close the gap. Their swimmer for fly is still too far out in front.

I can already hear the commentor in my head.

It's all coming down to Meadows. Can she pull it off?

Kingly swims towards me. And the first time we practiced relay, I nearly *fainted* seeing him touch the wall at my feet. Now, now I know he's just like me.

He's just human.

Never meet your idols, they say.

They always let you down.

I know I've let little girls down. I know I haven't been what people expected, but maybe Kingly did more for me by being human. He's not a god.

He's not untouchable.

And the pinnacle he's reached—I can reach it too.

Kingly's hand meets the wall, and I dive into water. Coolness all around me, I kick and sink my arms into the surface in my favorite stroke. I'm unthinking.

Just swimming.

Just power and fuel and happiness.

Fuck, I *love* this sport.

I love the way my breath burns in my lungs. I love the way my muscles stretch and sear with power. I take a breath, then return my face to water.

I love the way I glide.

The way I soar.

Like every race, I hold nothing back. I expel everything in the tank. And when I crash a hand into the wall, I pop my head up to voracious roars. Kingly is bellowing in a cheer, and Dean is jumping, his hands on his head. I splash my hand in the water, my lungs full of light.

Gold.

"SULLI!" Frankie cheers as I climb out with them and yank off my goggles. We all stare at the scoreboard like it might erase. Like this might just be a big fucking dream.

It is.

It's our dreams coming true.

"You did it!" Frankie screeches, crying.

I'm tearing up too. "We did it!" I shout, panting breath.

And then Kingly hugs my shoulders, his breath still coming out in heavy waves too, and he tells me, "You're a great swimmer, Meadows."

I smile and let out a laugh. For the longest time, I fantasized about hearing Kingly praise me, but the funny thing is, I don't need to hear those words from him.

The ones that should've always mattered most—the ones that I know from now on will *always* lift me higher than high—are from them.

I turn and find Akara and Banks on the pool deck. They're clapping with love and pride in their eyes, and through a glassy, tearful gaze, I burst into a greater smile.

This isn't the end.

I have more to prove to myself here.

Individual gold.

But at least I know one thing, I'll never take their admiration for granted. To be loved is an awfully wonderful thing.

32

Banks Moretti

GOLD MEDAL IS HEAVY in my hands as I flip the exalted thing back and forth over my palms. The year and city are printed on pink, yellow, and turquoise striped ribbon, which I saw looped around Sulli's neck last night. I nearly smile, remembering.

The greatest in the world.

Damn right, she is.

Something this monumental, this fuckin' rare shouldn't be in oil-stained, scar-lined, rough as hell hands. After a solid minute of staring, I offer the medal to Akara.

He raises his palms. "She gave it to *you* to hold onto."

"And we all know that was a trash idea—"

"You're calling our girlfriend's ideas trash now?" Akara tilts his head, being playful with *me*.

"Nine," I say seriously. "I lose *everything.* I'd lose my damn mind if you two didn't remind me where I put it." I intake a sharp breath. "I'm the last person who should be carrying around her gold medal."

After she won the Mixed Relay with Kingly, Dean, and Frankie, the medal ceremony breezed by and Sulli quickly un-looped the gold from her neck. When she placed the medal in my hand, I figured she wanted me to look at it.

But she said, "Can you hold onto this, Banks? I don't want to keep seeing it and get complacent. This can't be my only gold this year."

She's determined to win an individual event. And she only has one left: the 400m freestyle. Tomorrow night will be her last shot to win a solo gold.

Like it's the Super Bowl of swimming events, news outlets have been hyping the women's 400m free every half hour all day long.

"Can Meadows win a gold without Kingly? Watch tomorrow night at 8 p.m. PST."

If I have to see that tagline one more time, I might flip a fucking table.

Sulli waited for me to accept the job of part-time Medal Holder.

And like a fuckin' fool, I replied, "No problem, mermaid."

Maybe I figured I could pass the gold to Akara, but he's stonewalling me.

Akara pushes back his black hair, then fits on a baseball cap. "She chose you for a reason."

"What reason is that?" I question. "She *wants* the medal to disappear? 'Cause I can Houdini this shit in a second."

His face sobers. "Don't *try* to lose it."

"Lose what?" Jack Highland-Oliveira saunters into the hotel room. Back at this bougie as fuck resort, we're in the *We Are Calloway* production suite. Cameras are already set up facing two emerald plush chairs that Akara and I occupy.

"Sulli gave Banks the gold medal to hold onto," Akara confesses like Jack just perfume-bombed him with truth serum.

I do a double-take.

Jesus Christ, give-no-fucks Akara is more loose-lipped around Jack than he's ever been. I get they're friends, but Akara has practically made Jack sign a *No Sullivan Meadows Talk* contract for the friendship to even exist.

Seems that's been ripped to shreds.

I'm more uncomfortable. Muscles straining, I shift in the chair and straighten up from a casual slouch.

If Akara is more open to spilling his life to Jack, then I'm gonna be the cagey, quiet one. When I thought we'd be smacking deep, personal questions away together like we've done.

Fuck, I remember our first *We Are Calloway* interview with Jack. Akara was more professional than he was laidback. I was more cautious than I was carefree.

Jack wants us to *reveal* ourselves. To reach some inner-core so the world can understand us and our relationship. I talk more than my brother—I'll give myself that. But when I used to meet girls, diving deep was out of my scuba league.

I was stuck on snorkeling. Even when I tried to go deeper.

And then came Sulli, and she was so fucking easy to talk to. I leveled up to pro-diver, but every time I sit in front of cameras, I want to turn in my scuba license.

So far, we haven't sat down for many docuseries interviews, but Akara and I agreed to do them since Sulli wants to discuss our V-triad. We all decided if we ever talked more about our relationship, it'd be through *We Are Calloway*. Not through paparazzi or the media.

And we want to be strong pillars alongside our girlfriend. Not some ghostly figures. Even if that means facing down a camera lens and forty questions.

Jack balances a tray of coffee atop a stack of books. While he sets the tray on the round oak coffee table in front of me and Akara, he casually asks me, "I thought you lose everything?"

For Christ's sake.

I slip Akara an accusatory look.

"Hey, I didn't tell Jack that."

"I know I just mentioned it out loud, but you're the one who's always saying it."

"To *you*." Hurt crosses his face. "Sometimes to your brother, back when we were…" He stops himself from saying *friends*. As though their friendship has fucking died.

I can't see if it's still alive or not.

"Talking," I finish for him.

"Yeah. Back then." Akara bumps his arm with mine. "You know I wouldn't spread that around, Banks." He's worried I still think he'd drag my name through the mud.

I nod, "I know you wouldn't."

I can't picture Akara tanking my reputation. He knows I've *never* wanted the reputation of being fucking careless—I take better care of people than of material things—but somehow this bad rep has followed me to the *We Are Calloway* exec producer.

To Jack, I ask, "All of production thinks I can't locate the ears on my head?"

"No." He appears more ruffled. A hand running across his neck. I just notice a coffee stain on his button-down. "Production thinks you're the lighthearted Moretti brother, honestly. They don't know anything about how you've misplaced things." He tries to smile. "But that happens to the best of us."

I don't need the pity pat.

Akara bows forward, arms on his thighs. "Then how do you know, Jack?"

He rakes both hands through his dark hair, resting them on his head. Yeah, he's tense. Akara and I share a short glance before Jack says, "About that."

Akara groans, "Oscar."

"It's not his fault, Akara," Jack defends.

"He shouldn't be talking that deeply about the *team* to you."

"We're married. We talk about work." Jack's frown deepens. "I didn't think it'd be such an issue." He glances apologetically to me.

I raise a shoulder. "As long as you're not talking to the rest of production—"

"I don't. Anything that's not going in the show, that *always* stays with me."

"And Oscar," Akara notes, leaning back.

Jack lets his hands slide to his neck. Fingers threaded, he sighs out, "Jesus fuck."

I frown.

Akara asks, "You okay, man?"

Jack lets out a bigger breath. "Stressed." He adds quickly, "It's not you guys. Not completely. My brother was almost fired from shooting the Olympics with the crew again. For the *third* time for butting in and not understanding the term *fly on the wall*. It's just…things feel like they're mounting. It's fine." He passes me a late-night coffee.

"Thanks."

Akara gives Jack a softer smile. "Hey, forget about the Oscar stuff. You're right. He's your husband—you should be able to tell him anything."

I nod too. I'm not in the marriage-destroying business, so I'm not about to decree what Jack can and cannot do either.

"I want your trust too, Akara. As a friend and here during interviews, and if you need more from me, I can try to make it happen."

"Jack," Akara says strongly. "It's okay. Really. I might be a tad salty that Oscar knows more about us than we know about the Yale boys at times, but that's not on you. And I'll try not to let that affect these interviews."

Does that mean he's going to dish out his life on a gold platter? I stiffen more.

Whereas Jack eases. He expels an even bigger breath. "Thanks, Akara."

I eye what's under the coffee tray. "What's with the books?"

"That's décor for the shot." He hands Akara a coffee.

Akara scrutinizes the top title and groans again. "Jack."

"What?" He tenses.

Akara reaches for the book quickly and then flings it across the room. I barely have time to glance at the cover, but I'm sure I saw Kingly's face.

Jack smiles into a laugh. "There's not many books to choose from here, you know."

"I have to see that guy every day. I'm not staring at him during this effing interview."

I swig coffee. *Fuck.* It scalds my tongue.

The door opens, and Jesse Highland parades in, carrying three different potted plants. "This is all I could find from the lobby."

Jack walks over to his eighteen-year-old brother. "It'll work. Thanks, Utoy."

Leaning over, I whisper to Akara, "You're positive this isn't a bad idea?"

He massages his palms. "Better now than later. I don't want to rehash this in two months."

"I don't want to rehash this shit at all."

"You said yourself that *talking* is good. Even if it's painful."

That was in relation to my dead brother. "Yeah, and I haven't heard you talk about your dad in a while."

Akara shuts down. His gaze dropping. He goes eerily still. "You got me on that one."

"We got each other."

He lets out a weak laugh. "We're good at that."

Understanding each other.

Yeah.

Comms sound off in my ear. "Thatcher to SFO, I'll be at the hotel for the rest of the night with Jane."

"Copy," Akara responds.

I've been listening for any signs that Sulli is on the move.

Five temps are guarding her tonight, my dad also enlisted his services, and last intel I heard, she's still hanging out with Beckett Cobalt in his room. Trying to relax before tomorrow's big swim.

Safe.

She's safe. Since all the famous families are staying at this resort hotel, security is everywhere. But the attack at the neighboring hotel still unsettles the fuck out of me.

I ran into my dad earlier, and he reminded me, "You and Akara did the right thing. He made the right call to help you. She's okay."

I didn't have much to say.

Just nodded.

All bodyguards are now required to wear covert ballistic vests under our shirts. Indefinitely. But the guys who'll return to just peeling emotional preteens off their clients won't need them after a while.

For Akara and me—this could be our new normal. Sulli might be a high-risk client for the rest of her life.

There is no question about *can we handle it?*

We all know we have to. We chose this together.

And I've known a short-life lived full is better than a long-life lived empty. But I'll try my damndest to make sure we're all living long and full.

Once Jack and Jesse get the equipment squared away, Jesse posts up behind the camera. Jack sinks into a chair next to the tripod like he's a middle-aged dad about to have "the talk" with his teenage sons.

I don't know why I think that.

Sons.

The talk.

I wonder who'll give our kids the sex talk. Sulli if it's a girl. But if it's a boy...

Heat wafts over me. I don't know how any of this works. Me and Akara being dads to the same kid. Me being a dad at all.

Sweat builds underneath my ballistic vest and I miss Jack's first question.

"I'll survive. It's part of the job," Akara says, elbows casually on the armrests. "Sulli didn't get hurt. That's what I care about more."

Jack looks more relaxed. "You have a lot of friends who care about you too."

"I'm flattered, really," Akara says flatly.

I laugh. "He's not used to being Mr. Popular," I tell Jack. "Just Mr. Gets Shit Done."

"What he said." Akara jabs a thumb to me, then takes a big swig from his coffee.

Jack glances between us. "Are you ready to talk about your relationship with Sulli?"

We've already mentioned Sulli in past interviews.

This must be deeper than that.

I ask, "You mean do we want to talk about her being pregnant?" Sulli gave *Oscar* the okay to spill the news to Jack. So I know he knows.

"Wait, Sulli's pregnant?" Jesse stands up straighter, and I can see him more clearly now. His jaw falls open. Eyes wide.

Fuck.

Fuck.

We don't need to worry about Oscar spilling shit—'cause here I am, Banks Roscoe Moretti, doing that all on my goddamn own.

My big fuckin' mouth.

How did I forget Jesse is in the room?

He's been ducked down behind the camera.

Jack runs a tensed hand through his hair. "Yeah, Sulli is pregnant."

No reprimand from Akara—which means he doesn't give a shit that Jesse knows. He just nods to Jesse. "Let's keep this in the secret circle." He motions with his hands, indicating that the circle is *here.*

Jesse's shaggy hair sways as he nods. "Yeah, yeah, of course. Does, uh, Winona know?" He waits for the answer with bated breath. Before we can answer, he's speaking fast. "We're sort of friends—I don't know what you'd call it, actually."

Akara frowns. "Why?"

"She gave me her number this week. But I don't know how much she actually trusts me..." Jesse shrugs. "So she doesn't know? Or she does?"

"She doesn't," Akara says stiffly. "A select few people know, and we'd like to keep it that way during the Olympics. So again, *secret circle.*"

"I won't tell anyone," Jesse promises, eyeing me and Akara back and forth. "Who's the dad?"

Jack lets out a breath. "Jess—"

"Sorry." Jesse raises his hands. "Yeah, I know, not cool. Forget what I said."

"We don't know who the dad is," Akara says candidly. "We don't want to know until the birth."

We're just putting it all out there.

Alright. I try to relax back.

Take the wheel, Kitsuwon.

Jesse bobs his head. "Cool. Cool. You three are like the sickest triad I know."

Jack smiles. "They're the only triad you know."

"Yeah, and all my friends back in Long Beach *love* them. Now you guys are having a baby together. Domestic shit and all that. It's like giving a finger to all the haters. What sweet revenge, right?"

More like, what sweet, sweet *pressure*.

The world will probably be eyeing us keenly. Seeing if we make a misstep as parents. Seeing if we fail. Then they'll say having a family as a triad can't work. *Look at Akara, Banks, and Sulli—they nuked it.*

Gotta be the best dads.

Gotta be the best mom.

Hell, I don't even know how to be a *decent* dad right now.

If I could tear off my ballistic vest, I'd do it—I'd go buck-ass naked right now. A gallon of sweat is pooling underneath the thick fabric.

Jack sees me. "We don't have to talk about the pregnancy."

"Good." I shift again. "Let's just stick to the Olympics."

Akara softens his gaze on me, then nods to Jack. "Just the Olympics."

Throughout the interview, I feel Akara cast glance after glance in my direction. Worried.

I think he's been worried since I admitted I'd be a good uncle but not a good dad.

I'm not going anywhere. That part is true. But how do I eliminate the fear that lives inside me? Being the son of Michael Moretti, I just want a crystal ball that shows me and says, *you'll never be him when you're a dad. You'll be so much better in the end.*

"HOW'D IT GO?" SULLI ASKS, MEETING US RIGHT

outside the interview door. As soon as we got word she'd be here, I couldn't catapult myself out of the interview any fucking faster.

Dressed out of Team USA clothing, Sulli just wears jean shorts, a striped shirt, and jean jacket. *That's my girlfriend.* Seeing her, I yearn like something powerful to just draw her into my chest. But I don't.

Why the fuck am I hesitating?

She's safe.

I realize the weight of the interview is still crushing me. My non-answers. My silence. My dismissal of talking about her pregnancy. I feel cowardly. Like I didn't do right by her.

Her brown hair cascades over her broad swimmer's shoulders. Six feet tall in sneakers, she's still seven inches shorter than me, and I find myself dipping my head a little.

While Akara is chatting with the temp guards, we're all lingering in the hotel hallway, and I nod to Sulli, "Alright."

She watches me stuff my fists in my jeans. "It can be fucking hard for me too."

I hold her gaze.

"Especially at first," she says, "I had such a fucked time trying to get the words out. I kept tripping up."

"At least you tried." I briefly cast a glance down the carpeted hallway (all clear), then return to her. "I might go down as *Worst Interviewee*."

"You can't. That's *my* spot."

I laugh. "I'd give it to you, but I don't know how to get out of it yet."

She curls an arm around my waist, and I immediately unpocket my hands. About to pull Sulli into a warm hug that I've been craving.

But she abruptly disconnects from me. "Oh fuck, fuck, *fuck*." She whirls around, hiding.

Not from me.

Life-or-death alarm isn't pricking my instincts.

She's safe.

In my peripheral, I already see the Cinderella and his wife exiting the elevator. Sulli is cowering away from Thatcher and Jane.

Christ.

How am I supposed to unfuck whatever my twin brother fucked? And Jane—Sulli is running away from *Jane*. Her older cousin.

"Sulli!" Janie calls out brightly.

Sulli looks ashen, and with her back turned, she waves sheepishly in Jane's direction. She never faces Jane. "Uh, Banks, you want to go to the hotel bar? Beckett is down there. I think I might go now." She jabs a thumb in the opposite direction of Jane.

I see right through her. "The elevator is the other way, mermaid."

"Staircase? Kits? We're leaving."

He notices Jane and Thatcher, and the two of them are all too happy to bail and avoid our friends and family. Self-preservation has been the name of the game we've been stuck inside for a while now, and I'm not throwing two people I love into a situation they're not ready to face.

They haven't thrown me in one. Hell, Akara just abridged that interview for *me*.

Honestly, I'm about to accompany Sulli and Akara. My heart is with them, but a few steps forward, Jane shouts, "Banks!"

I stop in place halfway in the hall.

Thatcher is my twin. Janie is his wife, who I sincerely love—and I can't cold-shoulder them so easily. I don't want to.

Akara glances back at me.

I nod to him. "I'll meet you downstairs."

He nods, then hangs an arm over Sulli's shoulders, steering her towards the staircase. Her extra security tags along, and they all disappear into the stairwell.

Spinning around, I see Jane's crestfallen face, her blue eyes on the heavy door that shuts behind the temp guards and her cousin. More noticeably, her five-month baby bump is clear beneath a cheetah-print blouse, some sort of crocheted vest, and a pastel blue skirt. Her frizzy hair is tied into a low pony with velvet ribbon, and my brother has a loving arm around her body.

I don't have to meet them halfway. They already reach me.

Thatcher is grimacing. Pained. "That's my fault."

It hurts me seeing him hurting. "Why do you care if Akara walks away? You act like you don't want to be friends with him anymore."

"I chose you over him—I'm *always* going to choose you over him—and he doesn't deserve a friend like that, Banks." He's cut up over the fallout. That much, I can see.

"Yeah, he doesn't. But there are no sides. From now until I'm in a fucking grave, it's gonna be me and Akara and Sulli. You don't need to keep choosing between us, Thatcher."

I might be the bridge between two sides, but it's not up to me whether Thatcher or Akara crosses. Whether Jane or Sulli crosses. I can't force them to take a step forward.

Jane rests her chin on Thatcher's bicep. Staring up at him, she speaks in a breezy voice, "If Akara is willing to forgive you, then possibly there is hope after all."

Thatcher stares down at her. "I don't know if he should, honey."

"You're *worthy* of forgiveness," she emphasizes.

I think Thatcher wants to believe this. Especially coming from Jane. He swallows hard, his hardened eyes lifting to me. "He has you. He doesn't need me."

I've been hoping I can be *enough* for Akara as a friend—in the terrible case that my brother never comes around—but I know the truth.

So I tell my brother, "I will never be friends with Akara the way you are. You and I—we're not the fucking same, Thatcher. I can't replace you. I never could." I smack his chest. "And I honestly prefer it that way. He's never treated us like we're one in the same—and I love him for that. I know you do too."

Thatcher lets this sink in, staring out at the shut stairwell door. "I thought it'd be easier for both of us to move on."

"How's that working for you?" I ask him.

"Hurts like all hell."

For me too.

I need both my brother and my metamour to stop standing there with their foot on their dicks and *do something* about it.

"Can you tell Sullivan something?" Thatcher asks.

"Yeah?"

He checks down the hallway, then drops his voice another octave. We're also standing away from any hotel rooms so no one can peek through a peephole and recognize us. "I know she's still angry that I told you and Akara she's pregnant, but can you tell her not to take my mistake out on Jane? I fucked it five ways to hell, and I hate that it's ruining the relationship between my wife and your girlfriend."

Mother of God, my brother has this wrong. I clamp a hand over my mouth, groaning inside at the pain I might cause Jane.

Jane reads me well. I'm not hiding this agonized second. "Is she not angry with Thatcher?"

I drop my hand. "I'm not sure it's my place to say what Sulli is feeling right now." I dig in my pocket. Craving a cigarette, but I fit a toothpick between my lips.

Jane arches a brow, hands perched on her hips. "What can you say?"

"I think Sulli did accept Thatcher's apology. She knows you don't feel great about what you did."

"So then why is she avoiding me?" Jane wonders.

"That's between you and her."

"I did something?" Jane asks, looking devastated.

"She's going through a lot, Janie. Just let her process..." Fuck, I'm saying too much. I shut my mouth. Not even *Maximoff* has let this slip to Jane—what's fucking wrong with me today?

Jane thinks quickly. Her eyes suddenly flood. "Merde." She touches her belly. "It's because I'm pregnant and she's..."

Unexpectedly pregnant. Comparing you two.

Yeah.

The realization hangs in the air without me saying a word.

Thatcher squeezes Jane a little more.

She breathes out a controlled breath, trying to push aside the hurt.

I try to sweep this shit under the rug. "How's my niece doing?" I crouch down to her belly-height. "Ready to meet Uncle Banks?"

Jane sucks in a sharp breath. "Thatcher." She catches his arm.

"What's wrong, honey?"

I stand up fully. It's way too early for her to go into labor.

"I think she kicked. She's moving." A smile slowly replaces her hurt.

Thatcher touches the side of her bump. My stoic brother can't restrain the swell of emotion. "I feel her." They lock loving gazes, then share a moving kiss.

How could I not be happy for them?

I'm smiling, and partly, I think I'm happy for me too.

Sulli is pregnant. I'll have this sweet moment with her. And I want a family like my brother has with Jane. I want the *Blue Lagoon* life with Sulli and Akara. Us and our kids. The fantasy element is being on an island. Eliminating all danger and outside criticism. I know I'll never have that.

The world can't just let us fucking live.

"You want to feel, Banks?" Jane asks.

I touch her pregnant belly. Sensing tiny fluttering movement. Toothpick between my teeth, I smile over at my brother. "She's a strong one. Fifty-percent a Cobalt."

"Fifty-percent a Moretti," Jane finishes.

I drop my hand. "I'd say that's the strongest combo of them all, but there might be a Meadows-Kitsuwon on the way."

"Or a Meadows-Moretti," Jane notes.

I lift a shoulder. Am I more afraid of a Meadows-Moretti baby? The other combo means I have the possibility of defaulting to the "fun uncle" instead of the dad—which keeps freaking Akara out. It's freaking *me* out. He wants us in this paternal role together.

I do too.

Easier said than done.

I thread my arms. "You come up with a name?"

"Not yet." Jane adjusts her slipping purse. "My grandmother keeps pushing for Violet or Dahlia."

"I'm guessing those are definite *nos*."

"Affirmative," Thatcher says.

"No flower names. Though we're considering *Rose* as a middle name. Maybe Gloria."

Gloria. "Ma will flip," I say to my brother. "I can already hear her now with a big grin. *You shouldn't have, but you should have.*"

Thatcher smiles into a deep laugh.

Jane beams at his happiness. "We also thought maybe you'd want to use Gloria as a name." She speaks to me. "In case the baby is yours."

Baby names.

We haven't discussed 'em. Haven't even contemplated buying baby stuff. A crib. A nursery. Haven't even told her parents she's pregnant yet.

I stiffen.

Ryke Meadows might kill us. I'm not looking forward to being on his bad side again.

"You should use it," I say. "Our baby could be a boy." *And there's no way in hell we're naming him Michael.*

33

Sullivan Meadows

MAYBE AKARA AND I should've stayed up there with Banks. Not only am I agonizing over what Jane and Thatcher and Banks could be talking about right now, the hotel bar becomes the opposite of a fucking sanctuary.

I slide low onto the buttoned couch. Wanting to disappear into the swanky gold-stitched pillows. The 1920s prohibition decorated bar is small. Only one lounge area and only about five whiskey barrel stools at the sleek bar.

My family and I stamped our names and asses on the lounge furniture. Watching as unwelcome faces claim the unoccupied barstools.

The Rochesters are here.

Beside me, Charlie and Beckett's piercing yellow-green eyes are nailing *fuck you* glares onto the family we all hate. I think...I think my ex-boyfriend is absent.

Quick peek over there and *yep*, I only spot Wyatt, Wesley, and Winnifred. For as long as I dated Will, I never really hung out with his family. They followed me on Instagram, then quickly unfollowed me after the break-up.

Then blocked me after I confronted Will at his family's house.

All I know is that Wyatt is in his thirties, works for Rochester Industries, an entertainment & media conglomerate.

My ex is the next oldest at twenty-eight.

Wesley is twenty-five, also works for their family.

Winnifred is eighteen, and last I saw before the Instagram *block* is that she was accepted to Columbia University.

Eliot has been seated on the armrest of Luna's chair and makes no effort to hide like me. He's staring the Rochesters down. "There are four different bars here, and they're choosing this one."

"I'm not leaving," Tom declares, spreading his arms out over his chair. "They think we're easily intimidated."

"Or they want a fight," Luna says softly. Like me, she avoids eye contact.

Charlie, Beckett, Eliot, and Tom weren't *burned* by the Royal Leaks like me and Luna. The scorch marks still sting, and for as much as I want to confront my ex-boyfriend—to finally tell him how I really fucking feel—he's not here.

And I feel the most betrayed by him. Not by his brothers and sister.

Akara has also left the lounge area. Which doubly fucking sucks. He joins Oscar and the bodyguard wall that silently barricades us from the barstools. Keeping the peace in the feud.

All four Cobalt boys are eye-murdering the Rochesters. Luna busies herself on her phone, and I'm sinking further into the fucking pillows. The most important swim of my life is tomorrow, and my fight-or-flight response is all-in on *flight*.

I cast another fast glance at the bar.

Winnifred exudes the same preppy fashion choices as her Wall Street dressed brothers. She wears a plaid skirt, and a big red bow is tied around her dirty-blonde, pin-straight ponytail.

Carbon copies of each other, the Rochesters could fill the same pages of the same J.Crew magazine. Whereas me, the Cobalts, and Luna look like an eclectic, ragtag family.

Charlie in a wrinkled white button-down.

Beckett in a *Team Sulli* homemade tee and black leather jacket.

Me in jean shorts and a jean jacket.

Eliot in a crisp button-down and black suit vest like he's a hotshot lawyer or Sherlock fucking Holmes.

Tom in skull-and-crossbones athleisure wear.

And Luna in a cropped *Moon Child* shirt with leggings.

We might appear mismatched, but the Cobalts are totally put-together—and Luna and I can hold our fucking own. I might be more nonconfrontational at the moment, but that doesn't make me a wilting flower.

Charlie lets a cigarette burn between his fingers. "If they wanted a fight, they would've provoked Moffy by now."

"Like you always do," I mumble, which I thought would only be audible to *myself*.

Beckett is in the middle of me and his twin brother—the three couch dwellers. And he must hear my statement because he puts a protective arm around my shoulders while Charlie leans over him to confront me.

"Instead of failing at whispering, just say it to my face, Sulli." An insult and a challenge. I'm not interested in the mental-fuckery from Charlie—not before tomorrow's 400m free.

"I'll fucking pass."

"Coward," he says plainly.

I bristle, hating when Charlie thinks he can walk all over me. "I'm not chicken-shit."

Except for the fact that I just fled from Jane, and Charlie *knows this*. He knows I'm pregnant because I figured if Maximoff, Beckett, and Luna know—it'd only be right that Jane and Charlie do too.

To prove that I'm not chicken-shit, I tell him to his face, "And I said *like you always do*. Happy?"

"No." His tone is unbothered. He puts the cigarette to his lips and blows smoke a little carelessly.

Beckett wafts the air, then snatches the cigarette. "She has an event tomorrow." He snuffs the cigarette in an ashtray. My best friend is doing his best to limit my inhalation of secondhand smoke.

Charlie glances to Beckett. "Smoke won't make or break her." But he doesn't light another one.

"Dude, are they laughing?" Tom asks, aghast and pissed.

I peek again.

Wyatt and Wesley have angled their bodies and observe us like we're observing them. Only difference is that they're *smirking*. Ugly fucking self-satisfied grins, and Wesley snickers a little as he sips whiskey on ice. My stomach simultaneously curdles and blazes on fire.

Eliot clenches his squared jaw. He flips open and closed a Zippo lighter. "How should we strike, brothers?"

"In the front," Tom says. "What they didn't do. You want to talk about cowards? Those three are leagues above Sulli in the chicken-shit department."

I put a hand to my face. How did I get dragged into this? Oh yeah, I have no fucking *filter*.

"You're not chicken-shit at all," Beckett whispers.

"Thanks, Beckett."

Eliot bows forward. "Lex talionis."

"Who?" I ask, fucking confused.

"The law of retaliation," Beckett defines.

"An eye for an eye," Tom chimes in, just as Eliot tosses his little brother the Zippo lighter. He's about to stand, but his bodyguard along with Oscar and Akara are sending warning glances.

Eliot's ass stays on Luna's armrest for now. And he continues to eye-murder Wesley. "A foot for a foot."

"They can't be serious," I say more to Luna since these are *her* best friends.

"They're not *not* serious," Luna replies.

Beckett asks Eliot, "Why are we invoking the law of retaliation again?" *Again?* How many times has Eliot said *lex talons* or whatever-the-fuck? Beckett adds, "It's pointless."

"It's justice."

"It's *revenge*," Beckett refutes.

"It's deserved," Tom rebuts.

"It's stupid," Charlie says in finality. "Little brother." He directs his pierced gaze onto Eliot, who turned twenty-one on June 1st. "Are you really prepared to create a Royal Leaks 2.0 and expose the Rochesters' secrets? Because that is a foot for a foot in this instance."

"If I had secrets to spill," Eliot says, then eyes *me*.

Oh fuck.

Beckett slips Charlie a look. "Not helping."

"He won't," Charlie notes like he's ten moves ahead on the chessboard. Like he knows his brothers too fucking well.

Still, Eliot asks me, "What dirt do you have on your ex-boyfriend?"

On Will? "Nothing. He was nice to me and never said a bad thing about anyone…at least not to me."

"What about his siblings?" Eliot interrogates. "Did he ever talk about them?"

I frown, realizing that he almost never did. Just like I rarely brought up my family. "Not really."

"Dude, she's in *Ben's* grade, isn't she?" Tom says to Eliot, and it's clear he's speaking about Winnifred. "They went to Dalton together. Ben has to know something."

Wesley laughs louder while eyeing us.

Beckett is glaring. "He's such a prick." I think only Charlie and I can hear Beckett's quiet words.

Eliot lifts his phone to his lips. "Text Ben: *what do you know about Winnifred Rochester?* Send."

The Cobalt brothers' phones *ping*, and I'm guessing Eliot used a group chat that doesn't include me or Luna.

"You really think he'll respond?" Tom flicks the Zippo lighter, then tosses it back to Eliot. "He chose to stay in Philly over New York with us."

"So did Luna," I point out. "And you three are still fucking close."

At this, Eliot, Luna, and Tom use their thumbs and pointer fingers to create a W, and they each raise the finger-letter to their own foreheads.

The Rochesters suddenly go quiet. Solidifying. Like the resident troublemakers in my family have mocked them and their names.

I'm pretty sure they're just calling themselves weirdos.

Wesley takes a tight sip of whiskey. None of them shout inciting words. Mostly, they just glare.

Eliot checks his phone. "Still no reply."

"Ben wouldn't last a day with us in Hell's Kitchen," Charlie says plainly. "He's smart to stay away."

None of the Cobalt brothers disagree. Ben probably fits in better with my family, the Meadows, than with the Cobalts anyway, and he's my sister's best friend. He just graduated high school, and I'm glad he'll still be in Philly, attending University of Pennsylvania while Nona is a junior at Dalton Academy.

Ping.

Ping.

Ping.

Ping.

A text reaches all four of their phones. Eliot uses audio to hear the message against his ear.

I peek over at Beckett's cell. He shows me the reply.

Winnifred doesn't speak very often. She might be selectively mute. I think she only talks to her older brother Will. – Ben

My frown deepens. I'm not shocked I didn't know this. But if Will is nice to his sister, is this a notch in the *Will's Not a Bad Guy* category? Then *why* would he participate in The Royal Leaks?

Why would he actively try to hurt me?

No one speaks.

Eliot is studying Winnifred Rochester like she's a theatre partner he hasn't quite figured out yet. Like he might need to rehearse ten more scenes, ten more times, to truly understand, and the longer he stares, the more his gaze reddens. Is he conflicted?

Upset?

I wish I fucking knew, but I'm so much closer to Beckett than to Eliot.

Winnifred has kept her back to us this entire time, and with her head down, she writes or draws in a notebook.

Charlie scrutinizes Eliot. "And what do you say, little brother? Are you ready to expose their sister?"

With a head-tilt back to Charlie, Eliot says, "You know I can't."

Beckett smiles.

"Why not?" Charlie presses on. "They hurt Luna—why not hurt their sister?"

"I'm not a monster," Eliot says tightly, tearing his gaze off Winnifred.

"And that will always be the difference between them and all of you," Charlie says pointedly. "You have a heart."

"And you don't?" Eliot challenges. "I see through you, Charlie, and your heart beats just like the rest of ours, dear brother."

"If only that were true."

Beckett's phone suddenly rings. He answers, and as I distinguish the breezy voice on the other end, I freeze. *Jane is calling him.*

"Yeah, we're still in the hotel bar," Beckett says. "Yeah…"

Maybe she's just asking so Banks knows I'm still here.

She's not headed here.

She's not.

I shift up on the couch.

Tom types on his phone. "*Finally.*"

"What is it?" Luna asks.

"Drummer auditions. The label finally scheduled them, so I can *finally* have a permanent drummer before Summer Fest."

"That's what you said for the last ten auditions," Charlie says in a bored tone.

Tom pockets his phone. "This time has to be different. The band can't play at Summer Fest without a drummer."

"Okay…yeah. We'll be here," Beckett says over the phone.

I tense more, then he hangs up.

I'm caging breath. "That was Jane?"

"Yeah." His gaze softens on me. "She's coming down here to hang out with us." Beckett knows I want to flee. He nods to me like, *it's okay. You can go.*

I hug his side.

He hugs me tighter and whispers, "If I don't see you before the event, swim hard tomorrow. You deserve this win."

That gets to me. His undying support, his knowingness of all the dedication and work I've put into this year's Olympics, despite committing to the competition late. I hug longer. "You're the best, Beckett." As we break apart, Eliot and Tom see I'm about to GTFO.

"Are you avoiding our sister?" Eliot suddenly asks.

Blood drains from my face. Nausea roils. "Uh, no…why would you think that?"

Because it's true.

Tom chimes in, "It's sorta strange how you're leaving right when Jane says she's coming here."

"Coincidence," Luna sing-songs, totally covering for me. I fucking love her.

I accidentally make eye-contact with Charlie. He arches a brow, and my face burns at a terrifying thought.

What if Charlie exposes my pregnancy. Right here, right now. With the Rochesters in plain view. He *knows* Eliot and Tom are out of the loop.

He totally could bomb-drop them and others. Just like he exposed Banks and Thatcher's twin switch. He threw them under a bus and backed it up for good measure. Which *hurt* his own sister.

The world can't know I'm pregnant.

Not right now.

I have too much at stake.

Sickness rises and scalds my throat. I swallow it down.

Laughter ignites at the bar. Wesley makes a show of flashing his phone screen in our direction. He has a gossip website popped up, and I can barely distinguish the title of the article he's reading. But I catch two words: *Tentacle Porn.*

It must be about Luna and how The Royal Leaks exposed that she writes erotic sci-fi fics.

Fuck Wesley.

Instantly, Eliot stands from the armrest. Bodyguards surround him, but Eliot says coldly, "The laughter of lily-livered, *spineless* bastards sounds like fish flapping at our feet, so keep laughing."

Wesley lets out a weaker laugh, then eyes Wyatt. Both guys *burst* into laughter.

Eliot stakes them with a murderous glare. Not retreating.

Luna collects her sweatshirt and stands. "See ya later." She makes an abrupt exit, not wanting to entertain the Rochesters.

Tom races after her, so urgently that he forgets his phone. His bodyguard picks it up on their way out. Tom slings an arm over Luna's shoulders as they leave.

Charlie hasn't exposed my pregnancy, and I ease more and more as he stops paying attention to me. I start believing he'll keep my secret. Either because the Rochesters are occupying his interest or because Eliot is right—Charlie does have a heart in there somewhere.

"They won't say anything to us," Beckett tells Charlie. "It could compromise the legal battle."

Which must be why they aren't verbally sparring with Eliot.

Charlie rises from the couch, and after two steps towards the Rochesters, Oscar immediately cuts into his path. "Not today, Charlie."

He looks directly at his bodyguard. They have a silent staring contest, and for a single second, I wonder if Charlie thinks he can get Wesley to admit to The Royal Leaks. But what low, *low* levels will Charlie need to stoop to make Wesley break?

Nausea rises tenfold.

I'm going to be sick. Hurriedly, I jolt to my feet, and Akara is already pushing towards me. "Sul?" he whispers as I catch his wrist.

I'm going to be sick, Kits.

I can't get the words out.

"Just breathe through your nose," he whispers and leads me towards the exit. Whether the Rochesters are watching me morph into a green-cheeked ill emoji, I don't care right now. I just trail behind my boyfriend, fisting the back of Akara's shirt.

Don't let go of him.

Don't puke on him.

I'm so dizzy.

Barely seeing doors swing open, barely seeing bodies slip through, barely hearing Jane question, "Sulli?"

I snap my eyes shut. Nauseous like I'm on a Tilt-a-Whirl at high speeds. I inhale big, *big* breaths through my nostrils.

Don't puke.

Don't puke.

Rough but affectionate hands touch the tops of my hands, then rest on my biceps, and then those same hands lift me. *Banks.* Banks is cradling me, and Akara places a palm to my cheek. And once Kits breaks away and I jostle a little, I open an eye.

They're jogging. Running.

Akara leads the way.

I'm pregnant with their baby.

How much of this sickness is because of the little champ? My hands shift to my belly. No baby bump this early. Besides the missed period and ultrasound, I've had no big physical reminder that I'm carrying a piece of me and Banks or Akara.

Now the signs of pregnancy come crashing like waves against me.

Too real to push aside.

Too real to ignore.

A sheen of sweat gathers on my forehead, and Banks sets me in front of a toilet. Must be a guest bathroom in a hotel lobby—it's all I think as the contents of my stomach fill the porcelain bowl.

"You're alright, Sulli," Banks says gently. "Just let it out. We're not going anywhere."

I let that sentiment carry me through seconds, then minutes.

My boyfriends take care of me for the next half hour—Akara placing damp paper towels on my forehead and Banks holding back my hair. And when the nausea finally recedes a little bit, I land back carefully on Akara's lap and slump into Banks' chest. All of us seated in an intertwined heap in the toilet stall.

Thankfully the floors smell recently cleaned. Lemon and citrus more potent than toilet water and what ascended from my stomach.

Plus, I breathe in Banks' musky scent from his shirt. The familiar smell relaxes me. So do Akara's hands around my waist.

Banks assesses me in another sweep. His eyes move over me like I'm his to take care of beyond fame.

"She looks better," Akara says to Banks.

Hoarsely, I say, "Good enough to ride a dick."

Banks wears one of those shadowy smiles. "Which dick you plan on riding?"

"Yours. His. Both."

Akara makes a teasing face. "You don't look good enough to suck a dick, let alone ride *two*."

"Try me, Kits." I imagine shifting and straddling him but I'm too comfortable on his lap and leaning into Banks' chest. I barely grind my ass into Kits.

"Like I said."

We all laugh a little. I wish the sound stayed longer, but the world is calling us to go. Back to reality. I don't want to leave our sanctuary yet.

They must not either because none of us move.

I thought being *public* with our relationship meant that I'd never want these quiet moments with them. I'd never need them. But I still crave to be alone with Banks and Akara time and time again. Lost in our world where no one can disrupt us or reach us.

"A part of me just wants to live in the toilet stall," I mutter to them.

"And become Moaning Myrtle?" Banks questions.

"You know who Moaning Myrtle is?" I ask, surprised since I didn't think Banks had ever read *Harry Potter*.

Akara interjects, "He protected Xander Hale, the geek of geeks, for how many years?"

"Six," Banks answers. "And he's the coolest geek I know. Not that I knew a lot before him."

Right.

Sometimes it feels like Banks has been my 24/7 bodyguard for years since he floated on my detail so much. I forgot he had more than a half-decade protecting my younger cousin.

"I won't be Moaning Myrtle," I say. "I can be the Lady of the Latrine."

Akara laughs. "Now you're ripping your favorite show?"

I flip him off.

He captures the middle finger in his hands. Holding lovingly, and my heart swells.

"*Big Brother*?" Banks asks.

"Yep," Akara says. "Only in the show, it's the *Lord* of the Latrine." He whispers against my ear, "You want us to be your lords, string bean?"

String bean reminds me of the bean sprout.

"Yeah, I do," I say, then ask just as quietly, "Do you guys think this was morning sickness?"

Banks bobs his head.

Akara glances from Banks, to me. "It's possible, yeah."

"We looked it up," Banks admits.

"While I was puking?"

Akara nudges my arm lightly. "While you were resting your head."

That causes me to relax my cheek more into Banks. I hear his heart *thump, thump, thump* in a hypnotic rhythm. "How can this be morning sickness if it's at night?"

Akara keeps his voice at a whisper, maybe on the chance anyone hears outside the bathroom. Even if extra security is posted there. "Apparently, you can have morning sickness at any time, Sul."

A ball lodges in my raw throat. "I can't…I can't have it *tomorrow*. It has to fucking stop. I need to compete." They know I don't want to lose because I'm pregnant. I don't want the baby to be the reason I fail.

Not now.

Not when I'm *this close* to the finish line.

My last chance at individual gold.

"Just rest tonight, mermaid," Banks says comfortingly. "Don't worry about anything else."

I breathe in.

"Tomorrow is a new day, Lady of the Latrine," Akara teases with a kiss to my cheek. "We'll take it from there."

Celebrity Crush – July 30th

Sullivan Meadows Is Under the Weather the Night Before Women's 400m Freestyle Finals

Our sources have confirmed that Sullivan Meadows was "under the weather" last night at a hotel bar outside the Olympic Village. We heard she might've been hugging a toilet. Was she partying with her family and had a few too many to drink? Allegedly, she's been known to not handle her alcohol well. The apple doesn't fall far from the tree, does it? With her last individual Olympic swim event tonight, everyone is wondering if Sullivan Meadows will be able to win gold without Kingly. She better rid that nasty hangover soon. Looks like the odds aren't in her favor.

Watch tonight to see the results.

Subscribe to *Celebrity Crush* to keep updated on the Hales, Cobalts, and Meadows' whereabouts during the Olympics.

34
Sullivan Meadows

"JANE AND MK WENT Back to Philly?" After dodging Jane all day yesterday, I shouldn't be shocked she left, but I'm guessing this has less to do with a personal rift. And more to do with the four men who tried to attack me at a hotel two days ago.

It's dangerous here.

But I just thought…this shit happens to people like us, right? Jane is so used to paparazzi and the invasiveness of it all. I figured she'd stick it out like normal. I didn't think she'd flee L.A. for the safety of home so soon.

"They just want to be extra safe," Akara tells me.

Banks looks a little peeved at that phrase. He shoots him an annoyed glance.

Akara shakes his head, confused.

While I'm sitting between Akara and Banks, the self-driving shuttle rolls along, and my muscles feel tight. Tense. Taut. I'll need to stretch them out for longer tonight.

The 400m freestyle final is in a few hours, and we're on our way to the stadium.

Being there early means missing some of the bigger crowds. It's always sweet bliss walking through a door without the feeling of being stampeded.

Akara's words keep puncturing my spirit.

They just want to be extra safe.

I get that Jane wants to protect her baby at *all costs*. And I'm guessing Farrow, Maximoff, and Millie Kay all agreed that returning to Philly is best for the safety and health of both Baby Hale and MK.

So what does it say about me that I'm willing to stick around California for a few more days? I'm here for the Olympics. But is my dream really worth risking my child's safety?

My stomach tosses.

Please no morning sickness.

I puked once when I woke up, and I'm fighting my body from producing another wave.

Two deep breaths, and I feel physically better. But maybe not mentally.

Banks whispers something in Akara's ear. I don't hear. I'm too focused on the palm trees outside and the desert hills rising off in the distance. A touch of smog clouds the air, obscuring my view of the horizon. I squint harder, wondering if I'm looking in the right direction of the Hollywood sign.

"Sul," Akara says quickly, almost urgently. "I didn't mean to imply that *you're* not being safe."

I hug my arms around my legs. "But I am taking a big fucking risk staying here. And doesn't that make me a bad mom?" *Mom.* I'm going to be a mom. That word shoots panic in my lungs. "A future mom," I rephrase like it'll slow my pulse.

It doesn't.

I won't be as good of a mom as Jane. Definitely not as good as my mom. *You don't have to be Janie to be a good mom,* Banks told me.

I try to breathe in those words.

I fucking do.

But maybe it's the fact that I know the world will be comparing me and Jane, just like the world compared my mom and her sisters—and that scares the fuck out of me. Or maybe it's knowing if I fail as a mom, that failure will be a reflection of our triad. Or maybe it's my competitive side that's biting my insecurities.

I pride myself on outperforming my competitors, and this just feels like a competition that I'm destined to lose.

"Hey," Akara says, turning more to face me. His arm slides along the headrest of my seat. "Remember what your dad said about us becoming public? Just living your life is going to be a spectacle. So if you run away from *every* risk, you're not going to be able to live at all."

My pulse slows to a steadier rhythm. "But you can't promise it's completely, *totally* fucking safe?"

"It's safe enough." Akara is assured.

Banks lowers his gaze.

"Banks?" I question. "You think it's safe *enough*?"

"It's Akara's call."

"As a dad though—as *parents*, this is your kid too."

He raises his brown eyes to mine. And I want to dive deep, *deep* into the comfort of them. "It'll never be as safe as any of us wish it could be, Sulli. But Akara is right. It is safe enough. And one day, we get to tell the little champ about their champion mother. And how they were with her every fifty-meters gained." He grips my gaze strongly. "What's the story gonna be? Retreat or push forward?"

The story of our lives.

What makes life worth living?

There is no life if we're all dead.

Being cautious or being fearless—things we have to decide as more than just a triad. We're going to be parents.

I glance at my tattoo. "Onward." Fuck caution right now. I can be more careful further along into my pregnancy.

The shuttle lurches to a stop.

Once we climb out to the dry heat, my boyfriends lead me towards the stadium. Sun beats down, and a tiny gust of wind cools my skin. Our steps are brisk. We've learned to rarely *stroll*. Or else too many paparazzi could catch us.

Coming up on the plaza outside the stadium, some attendees snap pictures inside the giant Olympic rings. A fountain spurts pillars of water, and kids squeal, hopping through the spray.

We have to walk around the fountain.

So far, so fucking good.

No one has really recognized me yet.

I'm about to dip my baseball cap more, but I suddenly freeze halfway around the fountain. My eyes grow, and I catch Akara and Banks' elbows.

"Stop."

They already see what I see.

Banks curses under his breath.

The Rochesters are here.

At the end of the mist, Will, Wesley, and Winnifred congregate around a park bench. Wesley smokes a vape, and Will chats with his brother.

They haven't spotted us.

"Let's take the rear," Akara suggests.

"No," I say, surprising myself. "I should talk to Will."

Banks and Akara both whip their heads back to me. Their confusion mounting. Akara touches his earpiece, trying to keep eye contact but he can't. He's watching our surroundings with Banks. "Why now? I thought you let it go, Sul."

"I still regret not speaking up last time, and I have to tell him how I feel. I may not get another chance, Kits."

Missed opportunities are the fucking worst. I'm going back to Philly soon, and the likelihood I'll run into Will again is slim. Especially since I'm prepared to hide out in the penthouse for most of my pregnancy.

I remember how we've all been told to *not engage* with the Rochesters. Bodyguards, most especially. And I don't want to get them in trouble at work. "Can't you guys just tell Wylie and Greer it was my idea? That I fucking *demanded* it?"

"No way in hell," Banks says. "We're not throwing you under the bus, mermaid."

"Kits?"

He's considering.

I cross my arms, then notice how Will laughs to his brother. They're unaware I'm watching, but if I go over there, I'm doing what *Charlie*—

the most confrontational family member—didn't even get to do at the hotel bar.

Speak face-to-face with a Rochester.

Nerves spike my pulse.

"You're scared?" Banks asks, seeing my breath catch.

"Maybe I am," I admit. "But I'd rather confront him, nerves and all, than know that I never used my voice."

Banks is all-in. "I'll have your six."

"*We'll* have your six," Akara amends.

Banks cracks a smile.

Correction, *they're* all-in.

I'm smiling with them.

"I'm right behind you," Banks says.

"I'll be in front." Akara already starts to lead.

"Boob and ass coverage is back," I joke, and even if I can't see, I can feel their smiles widening. With extra confidence at my toes and heels, I walk forward.

My heart pounds in my ears as we close-in on the Rochesters. As soon as they see us approach, they quiet like we're the incoming storm.

The raging fire inside me has sputtered into hot embers. Able to be lit, but I'm not wielding a bat. I'm not coming in swinging.

Six months have passed, and the biggest swim final of my life is tonight. I'm just here to talk now.

Quickly, they realize my bodyguards are not a fortified wall barring me from them. They're letting me pass, and the Rochesters tense like I might *deck* Will.

Lucky for them, I still want to be a lover, not a fighter.

I don't want to use my fists.

"Will," I say fast, before he can utter a fucking thing. "Can we talk?"

Wesley pipes in first, "We have nothing to say to you." He blows out a puff of smoke from his vaping pen. "Sulli the Slut."

Akara is the one who takes a threatening step forward. Banks grabs his arm. They're here as bodyguards, but I'm sure they'd rather punch Wesley's lights out as my boyfriends.

My eyes are on Will.

My ex.

He winces a little, and his face reddens in…embarrassment?

Wesley doesn't notice. He's fixated on Akara and Banks. "One assault charge will tip this legal battle in our favor, so if you want to hit me, do it." He opens his arms wide.

Will walks forward. "We can talk." He drills a disapproving look into his brother. Wesley drops his arms and rolls his eyes. Winnifred ignores them both as she scrolls on her phone.

"This way," Will says.

Akara follows closest to Will, and Banks still tails me. We leave Wesley and Winnifred behind at the park bench, and soon, Will brings me to an abandoned snow cone cart near the stadium's fire exit.

No one is really loitering.

It's pretty private, and I think about how Will was always good at that. Finding private places, knowing I hated being so public with my life.

Hate might be the wrong sentiment.

I didn't hate it as much as I was scared.

I was so fucking terrified of the attention, mayhem, and spotlight that I burn under now, and for the first time in a while, I let myself be proud.

I did what I thought I couldn't do.

I'm still standing.

And for as nice as Will was to me, he's not someone I ever wanted to brave the world with.

Since my final is tonight, I want to be quick. Akara and Banks block me from view. Backs turned a little, knowing I need to do this on my own.

My throat dries, but I manage words this time. "What you did to my family was fucking horrible, Will."

He stares down at his cognac loafers. He says a fuck load of *nothing*.

My heart breaks. "You were my first boyfriend, you remember." I shift my weight.

He barely lifts his gaze.

"My first kiss," I push on with hurt burning my lungs. "I *trusted* you when I barely trusted a soul outside my family. And what's worse is that…you fucking *knew* all of that. You knew I cherished my privacy. And you still did this to me. I can't figure out why."

Why would he hurt me? I thought he was *good*. Even after our break-up, he had been nice. I could look back at that first kiss and not hate it.

He scuffs his shoe on the ground. "I can't…I can't talk about this…"

"Why?" Pain blossoms everywhere. "I just want answers."

He lets out a defeated sigh. "There's a really intense legal battle going on between my family and yours and if I say anything to you—"

"I'm not going to tell anyone *anything*," I interrupt him with this promise. "That's not why I'm here."

When I first confronted my ex, I wanted revenge.

But Beckett is right. Revenge is pointless, and I want to be able to look in the mirror and be okay with who I am. I always knew the steps that I've been taking would change me.

The media will change me in my lifetime.

People will change me.

My love for Banks and Akara will change me.

Having a baby will change me.

But I can't let anything change me for the absolute worse.

Especially not an ex-fucking-boyfriend. So this is different now. I want closure for myself. I want to feel like I wasn't fucking stupid by trusting him.

Maybe I won't get that today, but I have to try.

"You're not going to tell anyone?" Will reiterates.

"I promise," I emphasize. "This is just between us."

Will nods a few times. "My brother…" He winces. "He came up with the idea for The Royal Leaks. Pitched it to our parents like a business proposal. They were all over it."

"Which brother?" I wonder.

He laughs, but it's a sour laugh. "Which do you think?" He avoids casting a glance in the direction of the fountain, but I know it's Wesley.

"I didn't want to do it at first, Sullivan. I tried to stop it. But once it started…" He frowns. "And it felt kind of good, I'm not going to deny that. You can tell me every day you didn't cheat on me. You didn't have a *thing* for your bodyguard when we were together." He briefly looks at Akara's back. "But I saw what I saw. I know something was going on. You're not all innocent in this."

Heat gathers in my heart. "So I deserved to have my private life blasted to the world?"

He lets out a rough breath. "Maybe, yeah. Actions have consequences."

I glare.

He breaks our gaze first, eyes to his loafers. "It may have gone too far." His guilt ripples off him, and I wonder if that's why he's confessing. To absolve himself of some of the blame.

If he is telling the truth, and I do believe he is, then he wasn't the fucking mastermind behind The Royal Leaks. He was just a son of a powerful family and he got swept up in a chess move.

I don't want to play those fucking games. I'd rather be in the water. In the woods. I'd rather be free from the Rochesters and their grasp. So I let it go.

"We should never talk again," I tell him.

Worry catapults his eyes. "You're not going to say anything—"

"I won't. Because, unlike you, I want to be the kind of person people can fucking trust." With that, I turn to my boyfriends. "It's time to swim."

35

Sullivan Meadows

HERE IT IS.

The start to the finish.

Goggles on.

Swim cap on.

Arms stretched, blood running through my loose muscles. Mind awake. Focus on the Olympic pool.

I'm ready.

Bare feet on the block, one in front of the other—I bend my knees and wait to grip the platform. Fingers tingling in anticipation. Pulse thumping to the beat of the cheering crowd. Enthusiasm howls around me and my competitors, and I let the Olympic fervor ignite my spirit.

My fucking hopes.

My determination.

My dream.

I mutter under my breath, "It's you and me, little champ."

To my left, Frankie adjusts her goggles, untiring gaze staring down her lane.

Don't think about her.

This last individual swim isn't about beating Frankie. It's not about Kingly. It's about proving to myself that I still have what it takes to be *the best* swimmer *I* can be. Whether that means I'm the best in the world, I don't know.

But I'm about to see.

Panic tries to surge, but I blow out a controlled breath.

Crowds roar, "MEADOWS!"

"HANSEN!"

"JONES!"

"NONAKA!"

The chants fade in my mind. My eyes land on the pool, and nerves start to wash away. The water already ripples, and I'm five again.

Slipping goggles over my eyes, glancing to the sidelines of the Hale's backyard pool on Fourth of July. "Daddy, look!"

My dad stops the flip of a burger to clap. "Go, Sulli!" His scruffy, broody features lighten with a smile.

I'm six.

"This was you once," my mom says to me, teaching Nona how to swim at the lake house. "When you were just a *wee* itty-bitty little thing."

Hi, squirt.

I'm seven.

Positioning myself on the starting block at the stuffy Philly Aquatic Center. I look to the noisy aluminum bleachers.

"GO, SULLI!" my dad cheers.

I'm eight.

Readying to dive off the dock at the lake house. In a race against Moffy. Glancing to the upper porch deck.

"Go, Sulli!!" my dad cheers.

I'm fourteen.

Fitting on my goggles at World Championships.

"Go, Sulli!"

I'm eighteen.

Gripping the starting block at Olympic qualifiers.

"GO, SULLI!"

I am twenty-two.

And I am here. Now.

I don't need to glance to the stands or sidelines to see him. I don't need his voice to be loud to hear him. I know he's there.

My dad has always been there.

Go, Sulli!!

"Take your mark."

I grab the platform.

Beep.

Diving into the cool water, I glide and kick. Head breaching the surface, I fucking swim like I'm six, eight, twelve, fifteen—every *year* of my life sings inside my body, and I don't stop. *Instinctual.*

Muscle memory overpowers my movements, and I push myself to the brink. The very last edge I can go. Body searing, I do a flip-turn at the wall—kicking off, I'm on lap two.

Eight laps total.

Seven to go.

400 meters.

Lungs on fire, I roll my head and intake a breath, then return my face to the water. I'm gliding. I'm soaring. No one can touch me.

I'm fast and free.

I love how happy this sport makes me.

Exhilaration sings through me, and I pump and kick and sink my arms into the water. Like always, I give *everything* I have. And I leave the gnawing thought—*what if it's not enough*—in my wake.

Frankie is at my heels.

She's at my bicep.

She's closing in.

Four laps to go.

I swim.

I swim.

I swim.

Go, Sulli.

Final turn.

Last lap.

Last fifty-meters, I remember Akara. I remember Banks. I remember our baby. And in the last stretch, I swim to them.

My hand slams into the wall.

I'm gassed, and as I pop up, I heave for air, not wanting to look at the scoreboard. Barely able to breathe. Screams and cheers and hollers erupt around me and in the stands. But I don't know who for.

Pulling off my goggles, I take labored breaths as other swimmers touch the wall. Frankie has been in the lane beside me.

Her goggles already off.

Has she been here the whole time? Before me? My stomach muscles tighten, and she squints up at our final times.

Finally, I spin around and look.

What?

My mouth slowly falls open in shock.

Utter fucking shock.

Tears pinprick my eyes.

Screams and cheers seem louder.

"Sulli!" I hear from behind me.

"SUL!"

My heart leaps, and I quickly pull myself out of the pool.

Overcome.

Over-fucking-whelmed with new feelings. My hands to my mouth, I'm sobbing, and I don't need to run to the voices. They've already run to me.

Banks and Akara pull me into a tight hug.

I won gold.

And I set a new world record.

36

Banks Moretti

STANDS GROW HUSHED as three swimmers take the podiums one by one. The pool scoreboard above them reads: *Victory Ceremony. Women's 400m freestyle.*

Cameras fix on the swimmers—Sulli and Frankie in white Team USA track suits—and a big blue wall with Olympic rings are the photo-worthy backdrop behind them. On television, the ceremonies look like a change in venue. But the Olympic pool looms behind the reporters and lenses.

Akara and I stand somewhat off to the side. Bodyguard perks. We have a close angle of our girlfriend.

My mouth curves up, watching as Sullivan waits behind the tallest platform at the medal ceremony. Watching as she soaks in the triumphant atmosphere.

At twenty-two, my enlistment ended and I wasn't exactly sure where my boots would land. Eight years later, and I thank God I landed here.

The pride I have for Sulli could swell beneath ten-thousand grounded ships and cast fleets upon fleets out to sea. Not many will ever understand how much she overcame to win, but Akara and I do—and the people around us get it too.

Her parents, Ryke and Daisy, and her sister Winona—they've joined us poolside for the medal ceremony. I was almost pitched ass-backwards when the call came over comms.

"Akara and Banks, the Meadows are coming down to you," Price informed us.

They could've stayed in the audience with the families. Could've cheered and snapped photos from that vantage and waited for Sulli to climb up to them.

Akara said they're not here for a close-up picture. Four years ago, they didn't come down and stand with him while he was on-duty.

They're here now because they know what we mean to Sulli, and I imagine, in this single fuckin' second, that I'm not a bodyguard. I'm not attuned to the static in my eardrum.

I'm not strung out on vigilance. Not letting my gaze flit to sudden movements and misplaced noises. Not thinkin' about how to safely guide Sulli out of the stadium after her big win.

I imagine I'm just her boyfriend.

Just a South Philly guy who lucked out and found the kind of love that rarely comes around once in a fucking lifetime.

Standing proudly with Akara, her only other boyfriend, and her wild, adventurous family.

Bronze and silver are awarded, and Frankie stands on the second tallest podium, having won silver. One podium remains vacant. Waiting for the beautiful, radiant smokeshow.

And then, the announcer calls, "Winner of the gold medal… Sullivan Meadows!"

She steps onto the podium and waves to the crowds and to us.

I'm a six-seven, muscled man—but I have trouble keeping my shit together. We all applaud with emotion barreling through. Akara's hands clapping over his head.

Tears stream down Daisy's cheeks and proud smile. She videotapes her daughter on an old camcorder and whistles, two fingers between her lips. Winona howls and hugs onto her mom, jumping up and down with happy tears.

No one claps harder or more vigorously than Ryke Meadows.

I rub my wet eyes with my fist.

Akara blinks a ton before he has to use his shirt to wipe his face. "That's our Sulli!"

I cup my hands over my mouth and shout, "Hot damn!"

Sulli laughs into a bigger, happier, more overwhelmed smile. God, knock me over. That smile is an arrow piercing through my heart.

I'm fucking done for.

My phone buzzes in my pocket a few times.

I ignore.

Not wanting to miss a beat.

The Jumbotron above the champions shows flashes of the audience. Maximoff, Luna, Beckett, and more—SFO, her aunts and uncles—all clapping. Barely a dry eye in the house.

I sniff hard when Sulli bends her head, and an official slips a gold medal around her neck. A woman passes Sulli a small bouquet of orange California poppies.

We clap harder. Daisy lets out another whistle.

Sulli yanks her sleeve, and then lifts the medal to her lips. She bites the gold, a signature pose for all her golds. But clear as fucking day is the tattoo on her wrist, facing every camera.

Forward & Onward.

My chest rises in a deeper breath.

Akara reaches up and holds onto my shoulder. We exchange a determined, strong look, and I *lightly* smack his upperchest. Careful of his stitches.

The three of us aren't just surviving.

We're *thriving*.

How long that'll last—I can't say, but I take these moments as they come, and God, is this is a beautiful fucking one.

When Sulli splays the medal flat to her chest, cheering dies down as the competitors lift their gazes to the flags. The national anthem starts playing. Hands to our hearts, time seems to stop for a second.

Tears crest her reddened eyes.

She pinches them away, trying to see through the emotion. Cameras zoom in on her overcome face, and my heart is beating stronger for her.

You did it, Sulli.

Three flags are hoisted up. Two American flags and then the Japanese flag on the far right.

I see Sulli break through the tears into another big smile. Seeing her radiate the sorta joy I wish I could bottle and shelve and save for later. When the world won't be as kind to the girl I love.

That's tomorrow.

That's another day.

Sulli pulls her eyes off the flags and looks towards me and Akara. She tugs her ear.

We tug ours back.

We love you too, mermaid.

After the ceremony ends, Sulli hops off the podium and bypasses cameras and reporters. She heads straight for us.

Ryke and Daisy wrap their daughter in a hug.

"World fucking record holder," Ryke says, messing Sulli's damp hair as they pull apart.

She smiles. "I heard you, you know, Dad. Cheering me on."

"Yeah?" Ryke wears a rare gentle expression. "What was I doing?"

"Yelling *go, Sulli*."

Daisy brightens. "The accuracy of it all."

Ryke laughs—and just as Sulli turns to us and her sister, Ryke's laugh is choked off with a violent, *bang!*

Shrieking pitches the air. People stir at the sound of a gunshot. Instinct shoves me more than fear.

Protect Sulli.

Protect our girlfriend.

I curve an arm over Sulli, quickly—in the blink of a fucking eye. Pulling her down, and she's already ducking. Akara swoops in, shielding her frontside.

Wylie covers Ryke.

Price covers Daisy, and Greer is on Winona. We're all *seconds* from racing the Meadows out of the stadium. We start to move.

"*Fuckfuck*," Sulli cries in terror. "Dad?"

"I'm alright, sweetie."

And then our comms ring in our ears.

"It's a confetti popper," Farrow says loudly.

Oscar confirms, "A kid shot off a confetti popper. Section three-hundred, around the twelfth row."

Fucking kidding me. Unblinking, I sweep the pool, where reporters crouch and hide behind camera equipment. And the stands where people stampede out of their seats and to the nearest exits.

Akara speaks hushed in his mic. "No threat, no threat. Everyone stay close to your clients."

Even with the *no threat* call, adrenaline is pumping and we guide the Meadows family into a back exit with urgency, leading them down a hall.

Quiet.

We're all fucking deathly quiet, and my gaze is sharp. Narrowed.

I'm frosty.

She's safe.

They're safe.

We enter an emptied locker room. Smells like chlorine and wet socks. But I push out ahead of everyone and do a quick scan.

"All clear," I tell Akara and the Triple Shield bodyguards.

Sulli, Winona, and Daisy sink onto a wooden bench between a row of lockers. I put a comforting hand on Sulli's head while she catches her breath. She keeps muttering, "Fuck," over and over again.

Trained for this shit, I listen closely—probably too closely if I'm being honest with myself. I hear faraway footsteps. I hear the *drip drip* of a leaky showerhead. I hear the creaking of old pipes. Senses are humming—on a fucking live-wire, and I can't shut off.

"Hey, we're here, Sul," Akara consoles, bending down to our girlfriend. "It was just a stupid confetti popper. Kinda sounded like a giant fart." He nudges her arm with a weak smile.

Sulli almost snorts.

Akara stands up, more rigid. He's speaking into comms. Probably the temp frequency because I hear nothing, and his playful side with Sulli shifts from *buddy*guard to *boss*.

I try to fixate on more than the *drip drip* and creaks. Like how Winona holds Sulli's hand.

Ryke crouches near his wife.

"Dais?" he whispers.

She presses a shaky palm to her forehead.

"Akara, can you go get a few waters?" Ryke asks, and I think he's asking his daughter's boyfriend. Not his daughter's bodyguard.

"Yeah, of course." He touches my arm to silently say, *take care of Sul*, before he finds the nearest vending machine.

I nod to him as he shoves off.

"We should've brought Goldi," Winona says softly, mentioning Goldilocks, Daisy's service dog for PTSD.

"I'm okay," Daisy breathes and tries to smile at Nona.

"What about for Sulli?" she questions.

"I'm alright, squirt." She looks queasy as hell. And then she hangs onto my shirt with big eyes that scream, *I'm going to be fucking sick, Banks*.

I only tear her hands off me to grab a nearby janitor's bucket. Putting the blue thing under her mouth, Sulli vomits.

The room tenses.

Winona collects her sister's hair into her hands. I'm bent down to keep the bucket steady for Sulli. Her eyes are squeezed shut.

My body is in knots seeing her sick *again*. I want to do more. Take the fucking pain away. Let me puke so she doesn't have to.

Comms go off in my ear. "I'm coming back inside." *Akara*. Footsteps pad, and Price alerts the family, "It's Akara," before I can.

My metamour rounds the lockers with three PuraFons water bottles. He nearly drops one seeing Sulli puking.

"Shit," he curses.

Even if I had free hands, I wouldn't slug him right now. We're on-duty. Our girlfriend is puking up her guts with a gold medal dangling around her neck. And her family is rattled from a confetti pop that sounded like a fucking gunshot.

Sulli doesn't open her eyes.

Akara passes around the water bottles. His questioning, concerned eyes drill into me.

"She just started," I say quietly to him.

"Sulli," Winona consoles. "It's okay. No one's coming to hurt you. We're all here. You're safe now."

I send Akara a hard look. I don't think that's why she's sick. This isn't from the fear of a bullet.

"Akara and Banks are here." Winona keeps talking. "They love you. They won't let anything bad happen to you. Right?" Her attention zeroes in on us.

I nod strongly. "Cross my heart."

Sulli is too weak to say, *hope to never die.*

"Never anything bad, Nona," Akara smiles at our girlfriend's sister, but his lips falter on Sulli. He's worried about her, and he squats down to my level and whispers to me, "Maybe I should call Farrow."

Sulli shakes her head once.

"Just take some deep fucking breaths, sweetie," Ryke coaches his daughter.

Daisy stands, less shaken, and rubs Sulli's back. "She looks so pale, Ryke."

Akara touches his mic, a second from calling Farrow.

"I'm fine, Mom," Sulli squeaks out. "Really." She swallows. "I think I'm done…barfing…"

Once she straightens up more, I move the bucket away. Setting it aside.

Sulli grips her thighs, and Ryke's intensity on his daughter suctions oxygen from the fucking room. She shrugs up at her dad. "I just…got a little fucking…" She can't lie to him.

But it's clear Sulli isn't ready to reveal the truth.

That she's suffering from morning sickness right now. Not a panic attack. Not PTSD.

"I'm okay, Dad," Sulli breathes. "Really fucking really."

Look, I'm not about to announce her pregnancy without an *okay* from Sulli. Neither is Akara, and if she's not ready, then neither are we.

We have no clue how Ryke will handle the news, especially since it's an *accidental* pregnancy. He's gonna be an accidental grandpa.

And then add in Price, Wylie, and Greer in the locker room. I want that fuckin' headache like I want to trigger an actual migraine.

Ryke tries to ease and nods. "We don't need to rush the fuck out of here. Drink some water."

Sulli relaxes more.

Akara unscrews the cap, and I take a second to peek at my phone. The missed texts.

A bunch.

From family.

I only have enough time to click into two.

SHE DID IT! Give your girlfriend a hug for me, Banksy. Tell her we're all proud. — **Mom**

Did a gunshot go off? They cut the ceremony on TV. Are you okay?? Is she okay?? Is Akara okay?? Please call me when you can. I'm worried if you couldn't tell. — **Mom**

Ma.

I wish I had time to ease her worries. But I don't. Later, I'll call her, but I think about my mom and how many times she must've worried about her sons.

Me and Thatcher—coming home in caskets.

How she must've been so happy when our time as active Marines ended. And then we go and sign-up for private security.

How much she must worry now.

Life as a parent sounds like shoveling mountains of worry out of a ditch. Over and over again.

And still, I'm the dumbass who's going to say, *give me the shovel.* 'Cause deep-down I want to be a parent.

37

Akara Kitsuwon

@eggzelent3: can't believe you all thought it was a GUNSHOT at the #LAOlympics. Sounded nothing like it. Freak out over nothing.

@Vic!WhistlerFan: so security is gonna be extra tight at closing ceremony because of a fucking confetti cannon thing? lol so dumb #LAOlympics

@meadowsbabes20: there've been bomb scares at past Olympics before. Stop acting like it's nothing!! #LAOlympics

@DeviousBulb12_9: sullivan meadows deserves to die, go jump off a building bitch no one would care if you killed yourself #LAOlympics

"FUCK HIM," BANKS GROWLS UNDER HIS BREATH, biting hard on a toothpick. We're huddled together reading the trending Olympic hashtag while Sulli packs up her bathroom toiletries. Our duffels are already zipped closed.

"Might not be a guy." Like Banks, I'm fixated on the worst tweet so far in our endless scroll.

"Fuck *them*," Banks rephrases, and he's about to snatch my phone, but I do the honors and pop up our anonymous fan account.

"At DeviousBulb12_9," I say out loud while I type faster than Banks could. "I care if she dies." I post the tweet.

Banks breathes easier, but he watches me pocket the phone. "You aren't waiting to see if they reply?"

"No." I grip his frosted gaze. "We already know the response will be something like, *so what? She should still go jump off a bridge.*"

He massages the back of his neck, aggravated over the hatred. He lowers his voice. "I hate these nameless, useless shitbags. For the death threats, the rape threats, for thinking she *deserves* to die, for trying to goad her to take her own life. For getting the nerve to type out those fucking words. Who does that, Akara?"

It seems unbelievable.

That anyone would post that crap, but they do. All the *dang* time.

We've seen it since our early days in security. This has always been a part of the Hales, Meadows, and Cobalts' lives.

And now it's a part of ours.

I can't see Banks ever becoming desensitized to this stuff when Sulli is the target and the topics include death, rape, and suicide. And a part of me keeps envying Banks. For not being as jaded as I've become. Because I'll look past it all eventually.

But the bigger part, the more *important* part, knows that his soft heart is an easy place to pierce. And in the end, they're only hurting Banks.

They haven't touched Sulli and they won't.

"…they said it'll be safe during the Closing Ceremony, Beckett." Sulli must be speaking to her cousin on the phone. The bathroom door is cracked. "…you stay safe too. Alright…yeah, I feel better. Less morning sickness for fucking sure…"

I pry my attention off Sulli, just to focus on Banks. I can't let this go yet. "Social media is never changing," I say quietly to him, and he watches me more than Sulli again. "It'll always be like this, Banks."

"I know opening the fuckin' thing is like a gateway to hell that I'm willingly entering."

And I'm letting him.

Shoot, I've *encouraged* it at this point. "We should stop."

"*No.* If I can't deck these fuckheads, then this is the best release." His muscles are flexed.

"Because you look so *very* released right now."

He rubs his tensed jaw. "What happened to giving no fucks?"

"I give a fuck about you."

Banks inhales a stronger breath. "Then what do you suggest I do?"

The bathroom door creaks.

Sulli appears in the doorway in the Team USA track suit. Phone turned off. "I have a suggestion." She turns to him. "Hold me. Fucking kiss me. Remember what's real. *I'm* real, Banks. Whatever stupid shit you're reading online—that's imaginary. It's not what matters, and I know it takes practice to get there—but you have to get there. Or else they'll take some of the best pieces of you."

His eyes redden. "And what's that, mermaid?"

"Your light."

"Your levity," I add.

Banks blinks a few times, and then he leaves my side to trek towards Sulli. Bridging the distance between them, he wraps his muscled arms around her broad shoulders and tucks her against his chest.

He's okay.

She's okay.

And then I decree, "No more social media security checks, Banks. I'll handle it from now on."

I think he'll agree, but his head whips to me. "No—you're not doing that shit alone."

"It won't affect me after a while."

"You say it won't, Akara, but maybe it will." He pulls away from Sulli to come over to me. "The whole point was to be in the trenches together. And I'd rather get to a place where we can both joke about those accounts than to a place where you're suffering alone."

Our hot gazes are latched in tensed silence.

Sulli stands on edge. "Are you two fighting?"

"No," Banks and I say in unison.

He isn't letting me carry the weight or pain alone. It's what I've known how to do. My dad dies and then my mom leaves for New York, and then I'm left gutted and grieving at nineteen *alone*.

So alone.

So very alone.

At some point, you tell yourself, *I'm not suffering anymore.* You tell other people, *I'm fine.* And then you forget to ask yourself if you're okay.

Because you're so convincing that you've convinced yourself you are.

And no one asks if you're doing alright. If you feel okay. If you're sad or happy or angry or hurt or upset—and then you surround yourself with people who care.

And you wonder why they do.

You push them away.

You try to convince them what you've convinced yourself.

But they know you now.

And they're good and selfless and loving.

And they love you.

Let them love you, Nine.

I exhale and nod to Banks. "Then don't suffer without me either. If that crap hurts, *stop reading.* We shut it off. You go kiss Sulli."

"You *both* can kiss me," Sulli emphasizes like she's waving a white flag between us.

I smile at her. *So cute.*

She's been more freaked about trying to maintain "equality" between us than I've been. If Banks or I feel like we need more time with Sulli, we'll communicate with each other and seize it. And if he needs to kiss her to ignore trolls, then I want him to kiss her.

I won't need *exactly* what he needs.

But let's make this clear, I'm *never* rejecting a kiss from my girlfriend. Gladly, I'll take a hundred.

Banks and I exchange a look, grinning, and we both swoop down to Sulli and kiss her cheeks at the same time.

She bites the corner of her lip, smiling. "You guys are too much." She shoves us away, but also hangs onto us.

"Hey, let's take a pic before we leave."

"For security?" Sulli wonders, taking out her phone.

"No. Your parents, aunts, and uncles are on the social media diversion. We don't need to add to it tonight." The Core Six are posting on Instagram about staying in L.A. for another week and doing a road trip up the coast to Malibu. In reality, the private jet leaves late, late *tonight* after Closing Ceremony. Everyone is returning to Philly.

We're hoping for an easy entrance into our hometown.

Less paparazzi.

Less chaos.

Fingers crossed for no tornadic disasters. I can't predict what'll be the hardest part of my job: security tonight at Closing Ceremony or trying to get home.

Sulli passes the phone to Banks. His long arms the best for selfies, and we crouch down closer to her cheeks.

On one side, Banks kisses her cheek, and on the other, I stick my tongue in her ear. Sulli is mid-laugh when Banks snaps the photo.

"We can't post that," Sulli laughs, trying to steal the phone from Banks. "God, I look so stupid."

"You look smoking," he refutes. "Whose Instagram do we post on?"

She blushes a little, still deciding whether she wants it online. "You sure I look okay?"

I take the phone and inspect Sulli. "Dang, Sulli."

"What?" She grins.

"I think you have a booger."

Her smile is punctured, and I laugh. She slugs my arm hard. I wince—yeah, *deserved that*. And she snaps, "I look really fucking beautiful, Kits."

"You do," I agree. "Right behind me."

Sulli snorts.

My smile falters once she focuses on the phone and the photo. Why'd I do that? Why'd I tease her like that? *She likes our kind of flirting.*

It's what we do.

But it's not romantic. It's not panty-melting.

Pulse skidding like I'm running my heart over with a Mac Truck, I rest my hand on her shoulder, my thumb grazing the softness of her neck.

Her green eyes flit to me, a smile in them.

I breathe, feeling like maybe I didn't totally fuck up.

"Let's post on Akara's Instagram," Sulli suggests. "He has less followers than Banks." The two of them were a confirmed couple before we confirmed our triad publicly, and Banks' followers shot through the roof. I still haven't caught up yet.

Banks smiles. "Right on."

None of us mention *after* tonight.

Pregnancy.

Babies.

Paparazzi.

Death threats.

Paternity tests.

So much is teetering at an unrest, but we won't let anything ruin this moment for Sulli. She deserves to celebrate.

THE STADIUM ERUPTS IN CHEERS AS FIREWORKS blast off overhead.

The blaze in the sky lightens the darkened arena. On the stadium floor, I check on Sulli every other second.

She's a little stiff but not flinching at the noises. She's been breathing in the elation. The celebration.

Banks and I smile in the brief seconds we take to see Sulli soak in the moment. Five medals hang around her neck.

Two silvers.

Three golds.

After she won the 400m freestyle, she smashed another record the next day in the women's relay. With her medals from four years ago, she has seven golds. Nine Olympic medals in all.

Sullivan Meadows is now one of the most decorated female swimmers of all time. Only a handful of swimmers outranking her medal count. It's hard to feel anything but pride for her. Of what she accomplished here.

I walk a few steps behind Sulli.

Pausing as she stops to snap selfies with swimmers from Japan.

Closing Ceremony has a different vibe than opening. Competition is over. Nerves are gone for athletes. Even those who only tasted defeat are high-fiving and celebrating.

Countries meld together and casually enter the arena. No one lines up behind the flagbearers. The symbol of unity feels palpable in the air. Like Sulli, athletes snap photos with other athletes from different countries.

For as much as Sulli has stopped for pics, other athletes have stopped her ten times more. Nearly every foot, swimmers from around the world ask for a selfie. It takes a concerted effort to keep my eyes focused on her surrounding, watching threats.

Really, I'd just like to watch my girlfriend.

Each footstep, a dull pain throbs my abdomen where my wound heals. A reminder of what could have been. A reminder of the danger we face every day. It keeps me sharper. I adjust my earpiece, and Banks glances over his shoulder, leading out front.

Sulli tears away from Swiss swimmers, drawing closer between us, and fixes her tangled medals.

"You're letting the silver sit on top of the gold?" I raise my voice over the loud celebratory music. "I thought you'd bury those under a pillow."

"No, these are being displayed front and fucking center in my bedroom."

"So you can do better next time? Motivation." I fling a piece of hair in her face.

She laughs, lightly leaning into me. And even on-duty, I wrap my arm around Sulli. Banks glances down briefly, listening to the conversation as Sulli says, "The silvers mean just as fucking much to me because they're reminders to be humble and to be happy for others."

Banks smiles down at her.

My lips rise more too. "I'm so effing proud of you, string—"

"Meadows!" Dean hollers, cutting me off. But as he approaches, Kingly slings an arm over his shoulder, and suddenly spins Dean towards him.

Into a *kiss*.

Dean is grinning before they deepen the kiss in an arena full of people. He holds Kingly's jaw, and Kingly grips the back of his neck. Their faces are projected on the *Jumbotron*. So the audience sees.

The world sees.

We see.

All the U.S. athletes turn and cheer. Including Sulli, and yeah, even us. I'm clapping for Kingly's *romance*.

Who would have thought?

Me.

Celebrating *Kingly*.

I'm even smiling. I guess I've learned something from the Olympics too. *Be happy for others*. Just no one better expect me to clap for the Rochesters. That's *never* happening.

I tell Banks, "Looks like we're the number one platonic bromance."

"Rightfully."

I laugh, and then our attention sharpens as Sulli is on the move. We follow her, Banks out front and me behind, and maybe five minutes in, Dean catches up to her again.

"Meadows!" he calls again like before.

"Hey, congrats," she says. "I didn't know you two were together."

"Uh...we weren't really—not officially at least." He laughs a little. "He wanted to wait until after the competition to make things official. Keep our heads in the game."

Sulli nods slowly. "Sounds like Kingly."

"What?" Dean can't hear over the fireworks.

"Sounds like Kingly!"

He nods, grinning. "Definitely is! Picture?!" They snap a couple, then he moves in even closer, and I abruptly extend an arm to stop him.

What's in his fist?

Dean looks pissed. "I'm her teammate, man!" Fireworks pop, pop, pop. "Christian Dean...remember me?"

"I know who you are!" I yell back, not admitting that four years ago, I thought maybe he'd end up with Sulli. *Why'd I even push for that?* If they hooked up, I would've smacked my head into a brick wall and called myself an *idiot* on repeat.

"Then what's the problem?!"

"What's in your hand?!"

"Oh..." Flustered, he outstretches his palms. Small bottles of liquor in his fist. "Want one?! I brought lots! Was gonna offer Meadows one too!"

"I'm good." I pat his shoulder and sidestep to let him pass. I already know what Sulli will say to him, but I'm still going to let her make the choice herself.

Banks hawk-eyes Dean as he moves towards Sulli.

Through comms, I hear Banks ask, "What does he have?"

"Minis," I tell him.

Banks nods and turns back to face forward. Like me, he knows what Sulli will do.

"Meadows!" Dean holds out a mini bottle of vodka.

She shakes her head. "I'm good. Thanks."

"You sure?!" Dean asks. "It's a party!"

"I'm fucking sure!"

After an awful night months ago, Sulli made the decision to stay sober. Banks made the decision to give up smoking in solidarity.

And me, I just tried to hold the three of us together. Besides the gunpoint incident, that frat party was one of the worst nights of our summer.

For all of us.

38

Sullivan Meadows

PANIC SURGES THROUGH me as I scream into my phone. "LUNA!" I yell, trying to capture her attention. It's an obvious butt-dial. Loud music blasts from her side and muffled voices pile on top of each other.

But I know what I heard.

Someone said: *You fucking bitch.*

It sounded nasty.

Now everything on her end returns to a jumbled mess of commotion.

Sweat drips off my brow, the barbell in its rack. I straddle the old weight bench in my bedroom and try to catch my breath so I can listen better.

"Fuck…a dick…bitch."

My heart pounds. "LUNA!" I scream again, hoping she can hear me. I just want to make sure everything is okay. Especially since she's at a frat party tonight. She texted to see if I wanted to go. She's one of the few family members who don't mind tempting me with a good time, knowing I'll reject the offer. I appreciated the invite, even if I felt a little fucking badly telling her I had to train.

Akara has been Luna's bodyguard for months now. I could call Kits and ask if everything is okay—but calling Akara involves hanging up on Luna. Something I hesitate to do until I have more answers.

"Suck…it." The deep drawl comes across the phone again.

"LUNA!" I yell.

My bathroom door whooshes open. Banks appears completely buck-naked. I'm too worried to really soak in his confident, unbothered stance that practically says *I'm ready to cross the Wild Wild West for you.* His concern doubles as he sees my panicked expression.

"What in the fucking hell is happening?" He rushes to my side.

"I don't fucking know." I hop up from the weight bench and explain the butt-dial and what I've heard so far.

First thing he grabs is not a pair of pants. He goes for his radio on the dresser. I watch as he quickly switches on comms. Clicks the mic. "Banks to Akara, who's on Luna's detail tonight?"

My stomach lurches.

"Isn't Akara supposed to be on her detail?"

Banks wipes a hand down his mouth. "He had some meeting with my dad…"

Fuck this. I round to my nightstand and grab the keys to the security SUV. I can't stay here while Luna is at some frat party getting hounded by assholes or worse. *Please don't be worse.*

Please fucking please.

Banks frowns deeply, and I suspect he got an answer.

"What?" I ask him.

He shakes his head once. "Akara was short with me. Just gave me a couple names." His eyes flit to mine. "One of them is Frog."

Frog.

Akara's cousin.

The greenest of the green temps! Fucking fuck. "He put Frog on Luna's detail? For a frat party?" My blood runs ice-cold. Eyes bugged wide.

"There's another temp with her," Banks reminds me like it should be okay.

It should be.

But I know what I fucking heard!

"It doesn't sound good, Banks."

"Is the line still connected?" He picks up my phone.

"A lot of it is muffled," I admit, but I know Banks believes me. He puts the speaker to his ear, listening intensely.

"I can't hear Luna."

"She might be too quiet." She's a fucking pro whisperer.

Urgency suddenly narrows his gaze, hardens his face.

"What'd you hear?"

"A guy shouted, *get back here.*" He hands me my phone, just as his cellphone rings on my bed. I see the Caller ID, and Banks sprints to answer the thing. I put my cell to my ear, trying to hear the conversation from the frat.

"Fuuuuuck." A deep groan comes out in a frustrated tone. "Where are you going?"

I don't know what's happening. But after the sound of footsteps, the line goes quiet. I check my phone screen. Call dropped.

Did she hang up?

Did her phone die?

Did she lose fucking service?

"We've got to fucking go, Banks," I say, and then I add something I'm betting Luna would want. I tell him, "Don't alert Moffy. Not yet. Whatever is happening…if it's something innocent, Luna won't want her brother involved unless it's totally necessary."

She would call Moffy if it's an emergency.

As far as I'm aware, Maximoff is still sleeping. And that lessens the fear that squeezes my throat in a vice. *She has to be okay. She hasn't called Moffy. She has to be okay.*

But I want to make sure.

Banks talks to Akara, cell pressed to his ear, and gives me a nod. "Akara's gonna meet us there. Luna's temps aren't rogering up."

They aren't rogering up?

What the fuck…maybe they all did lose signal.

I'm pushed into hyper-drive. "Go, go, fucking go." I'm practically shoving Banks out the door. I head into the hallway while he's still jumping into a pair of joggers. No time for Banks to grab a shirt, he just seizes a blue jacket off the coat rack at the front door.

We're lucky that everyone is asleep in the penthouse. It's easy to leave without passing Moffy, Jane, Thatcher, or Farrow. My hands tremble slightly by the time we reach the car.

"I should've gone with Luna," I mutter to myself. "I should've fucking been there instead of...lifting." Eliot and Tom are in New York, and they couldn't attend the frat party in Philly. I'm not sure she asked anyone else to go with her.

Fuck.

Fuck.

Banks climbs into the security vehicle, the SUV undulating under his weight. "Don't put that on yourself, Sulli," he tells me while I slide into the passenger seat. "She's probably fine."

Probably. Maybe.

I want fucking certainty.

"Can I borrow your phone?" I ask.

He reaches into the cup holder with one hand, the other firm on the steering wheel. Once we're out of the parking deck, paparazzi vans skid out. Tailing us, even in the dark.

I've oddly grown used to the white lights and the bumper-fucking. My heart rate still climbs but not to perilous heights anymore.

Quickly, I scroll through Banks' contacts until I find Donnelly's number.

I add him into my contacts and quickly compose a text message from my phone.

Hey Donnelly, this is Sulli. I got your number from Banks. Have you spoken to Luna tonight?

I hit send before rereading my message.

Banks grips the steering wheel tighter, briefly glancing at my phone, then back at the road. "You going rogue, mermaid?"

"If anyone *might* know what's going on with Luna, it's Donnelly."

Banks winces. "This is that thing again—the *I don't want to know* thing?"

"Yeah. It's that thing." Though, I do know for certain that Luna and Donnelly never hooked up since that one-and-only time.

They're at least still friends, and Luna's biggest friend on security is Farrow, our roommate. Who's asleep right now, so I doubt he has any news to share.

I remember the awkward bit where Donnelly thought Luna asked him on a date to Wawa, but according to Luna, the Wawa invite was *just* a friend thing. She told me she cleared up the miscommunication, but they've still really only seen each other in group settings. I honestly was a little jealous at how well Luna was able to breezily repair that awkward snag.

For me, my friendships feel messy and any small fissure of awkwardness usually breaks open into a giant cavern. Maybe Luna is just really good at not overanalyzing the awkward things in life.

My phone buzzes quickly.

No. Everything ok with her? — Donnelly

Fuck.

I text back: Don't know. She's at a frat party. Can't get ahold of her. I'm about to slip my phone in my pocket, but it buzzes almost immediately after I click send.

Which frat? — Donnelly

I'm not sure if he's asking just to gather more intel or so he can go to the frat himself. Either way, it wouldn't hurt having another bodyguard involved. Right? Fuck, I don't want to mess this up for security.

I ask Banks, "Donnelly wants to know what frat."

Banks says easily, "Just tell him. He's gonna worry otherwise. Any of us would." *Any of us.* He means SFO. The security team. Because they all care about us and our safety.

I text back: Omega Theta Phi.

Thx — Donnelly

THE FRAT HOUSE SMELLS LIKE CHEAP BEER AND weed. Bass thumps the floor, and chatter is indistinguishable over popular remixed hits. Banks clasps my hand tight like he's worried we might be separated.

Girls adorn faces full of makeup, bandaged dresses, and four-inch heels like it's a night out on the town. Not a night in a dingy frat house with a broken disco ball, beer pong tables, and inflatable swords and dolls. Guys wear boat shoes and Polos—putting in *half* the effort of the girls.

I put in *zero* effort.

Looking out of place, Banks and I are still in sweats. He zips up his jacket so he's not bare-chested. I tip the brim of my Eagles baseball cap low over my face.

Hiding as we weave between bodies in the living area. Beer bottles already littering the sticky floorboards.

If people have recognized us, they don't say anything. I scan the crowds quickly and try calling Luna back. Her phone goes to voicemail.

Fuck.

We push towards the oversized kitchen. Half-filled liquor bottles cover the humongous island. Vodka, whiskey, rum, and tequila. Two frat guys man the keg.

"Leggings!" the one with a collared palm tree shirt shouts.

It takes me a second to realize he's talking to *me.*

"Recon?" I ask Banks.

"Couldn't hurt."

Moving towards the keg, Banks rotates his head like he's scanning for threats. Not for Luna. But it's possible he's doing both.

Palm Tree Guy fills up a red Solo cup. "You're both looking dry," he says like it's a sin, then nods to Banks. "Bro...you're *huge.*"

"Six-seven," Banks says before he can ask.

"Shiiiiit."

Banks is eyeing the guys' hands as he fills the cup. I am too. My mom once got roofied at a party, and the story has been drilled into my head as a cautionary tale. Of what not to do and what *to* do.

No fast ones have been pulled.

Palm Tree Guy passes me the Solo cup. I want to blend. Plus, this might calm some of my haywire nerves. Putting the rim to my lips, I swig once, then twice. Letting the beer wash down the back of my throat.

Hoping my pulse stops jumping.

I take a large swig as he begins filling another. "We're looking for someone."

Banks adds, "A girl around 5'5"—brown hair, probably glitter on her face?"

He doesn't come out and ask *have you seen Luna Hale?* because there's no way we know that Luna didn't come here under some cloak of disguise. And it's not smart to alert the whole frat house a famous girl could be here.

Palm Tree Guy laughs. "Man, there's about a million girls in this house that match that description."

"A million?" My brows rise.

He rolls his eyes. "You know what I mean." His head swings back to Banks. He narrows his eyes at him. "You look really familiar, man. Are you on the football team?"

Banks shakes his head. "Thanks for the help." He puts a hand on the small of my back, ushering me away from the kitchen.

"The help?" I look to Banks. "You mean the opposite of fucking help."

"Getting in a fight with frat bros isn't gonna help us find Luna." He seems on edge. Like he thinks this is a fucking possibility. "This isn't my crowd."

"It's not mine either," I mutter, uncomfortable as people push up against me to shift into a hallway. Banks tucks me closer to his back, his hand slipping up to my forearm for a better grip.

"You alright?"

I nod, finishing off my beer. I collect an unopened beer can off a fold-out table and pop the tab. Chugging. Something is in Banks' eyes that I try to ignore.

Concern? I don't fucking know.

You do know.

I don't.

I don't.

We check the living room, the dining room, and the den to no avail. Passing the laundry room, I hear deep grunts and overenthusiastic moans. My face contorts. *No.* That can't be her. Banks adjusts his earpiece and looks faraway before telling me, "Akara will be here in five."

Third beer. I pop the tab.

I drink.

Banks is stressed.

I'm making him stressed.

I reach for a fourth beer before I've even finished the third. The knots in my stomach won't subside and go away. *Go away. Find Luna.*

I drink.

"Where the fuck are Frog and Tovin?" Banks questions huskily, glancing around.

We've returned to the living room. "We must keep passing them." I sip and look. Sip—

"Oh my God that's Banks and Sullivan!"

Oh.

Fuck.

I freeze.

Banks draws me to his chest. I hide. I bury my face into his jacket. My pulse is jumping as girls shriek, "What are you doing here?!"

"Oh my God!"

"Can I have a picture?!"

"Where's Akara?!"

People cram around us. I feel them pushing. Touching. "Banks," I choke out.

"Back up!" Banks yells caustically, shoving. He shoves people back. I roll my face to the left. Peeking. Holy fuck...college students circle us with their phones out, recording and snapping photos. Like we're about to break dance.

Instead, we're stone-cold statues.

And they just keep videotaping us.

Banks has a protective hand on my head. I'm afraid to leave him. To break away. But the music grows louder and the drunken shouting is inarticulate. I piece some apart.

"SULLI!"

"SHE'S MY BESTIE!"

"FUCK ME, BANKS!"

He's mine.

Fuck you.

Hands are on me again. Banks tears them off, and I hear an angered frat bro bark, "Hey, don't touch my girl, man!"

And another guy yells, "Just let us take pictures with Sullivan!"

"Let us fuck her!" Laughter.

Banks is pissing off the frat guys as much as they're pissing off Banks.

"Fuck you!" my boyfriend yells what I want to but struggle to scream.

"We hear she likes multiple dudes! Is that why she's here?!"

A guy reaches for my ass.

Banks catches his wrist, twists, and socks him in the nose.

"Ohhhh!" the crowd reacts and winces.

And then, the frat brothers all seem to swarm us.

"Sulli, go," Banks whispers against my ear. He literally puts my hand into another hand. Who's fucking hand is this? *It doesn't feel like Akara's hand.* It's too small.

I hold tighter, trusting Banks, and when I risk a glance backwards, I see Banks in a full-on fucking *brawl.* With four frat brothers. Smashing into beer pong tables. Into furniture. Throwing punch after punch.

"Kits," I breathe.

Akara has entered the frat house. He's pushing towards Banks, to help him. I'm being pulled, *dragged*, away from my boyfriends.

And when I face forward—that's when I see the long, pin-straight black hair.

She steals a bucket hat off a drunken dude, passed out on the staircase. Without turning, she passes me the hat.

I replace my Eagles cap with the bucket hat, and she swipes an abandoned leather jacket off the banister. After she hands me the jacket, I slip my arms through, spilling some beer, and she reclasps my hand.

"I saw her last this way." She climbs up another flight of stairs. The third-level.

"Ahhh! Ahhhhh! Fuck me, yes, *right there.*"

As we pass that room, I peek through the ajar door. A redhead. Definitely not Luna. I chug the rest of my fourth beer and crumple the can.

Banks and Akara are in a frat fight.

Luna is missing.

My pulse is still haywire.

"Frog," I finally say.

She spins around. Meeting my gaze for the first time tonight. Whenever I see Frog, I'm blown back and think, *wow, Akara has family.* I've never met his mom or any relatives until now. And besides being Thai, Frog *looks* like Akara. They have the same photogenic features that verge on delicate but also strong. Like they could simultaneously laugh and throw a punch.

Wispy cat-eyeliner highlights her brown eyes, and her earpiece is hidden behind her hair. Where'd she put her radio? A spaghetti strap red dress hugs her thin frame, and she's barefoot?

I frown more. "How'd you lose Luna?"

Frog sighs, "She *ran.* I had to ditch my heels. Wait—there they are." She snatches four-inch heels out from under a hallway bench. Less college students are up here, and I avoid their drunken glances as they pass.

I leave Frog to knock on doors. "It's me!" I shout, knowing Luna will recognize my voice.

"Not you too. Slow down," Frog orders.

I don't slow. "It's me! It's me!"

"I think she might be hiding in a bathroom."

Where's the other temp? Before I even think to ask, a familiar face enters the hall from the other side. Ripped jeans, an old Van Halen shirt, chestnut brown hair and tattoos—Paul fucking Donnelly is here. He opens doors, not even giving courtesy knocks like me.

"You see Luna Hale?"

"Luna Hale is here?"

He shuts the door.

Opens another, does the same.

Just as we meet in the middle, Donnelly opens a door, and I peer inside with him.

"Come on, baby. Open up," a drunken dude curses. "I'm sorry, baby. I won't be mad at you anymore. I know it was an accident."

Frog whispers to Donnelly, "That's him. She's in there."

I'm about to bum-rush the fucking room. Grab my cousin—wherever she is, but as soon as I step through the doorway, Frog wraps her arms around me.

Sorry, Frog.

I rip out of her hold.

Stronger.

A lot fucking stronger, and she curses as I barrel ahead. But Donnelly has already reached the six-foot-something brown-haired frat boy. Beer stains his Polo shirt, and his face is reddened in alcohol-induced rage. Or maybe just pure rage.

He's mid-pound on the bathroom door when Donnelly calls out, "Luna, you in there?"

"Donnelly?" Luna sounds hopeful.

"Back off, dude," the guy tries to shove Donnelly, and Donnelly decks him once, twice, and the lights go out. He thumps loudly to the floor.

I rush to the bathroom and jiggle the locked knob. "Luna? It's me!"

"Sulli?!" I hear her race to the door.

"Donnelly knocked the guy out." I barely release the words, and Luna swings open the door. I wrap my arms around my cousin.

She clutches tight, and I clutch tighter. "Are you hurt, Luna?" I ask, tears welling.

"No, he was just...I thought he...he was just really angry over nothing..." She pulls back. Mascara is smudged under her amber eyes. Glitter streaks uneven on her cheeks. Her fishnets are ripped, but maybe on purpose. Frayed jean shorts are wet. Her *Thrashers* sweatshirt hangs oversized on her frame. "We were dancing. I spilt beer on him by accident." Her voice shakes. "...I don't want to talk about it..."

"Oh hey, you don't fucking have to."

She glances to Donnelly. "I don't think frat parties are my thing."

"Nah?" He assesses Luna, up-and-down, then nods to her. "They're not mine either." He pauses. "You okay?"

She shrugs.

"We're getting out of here," Donnelly says. "That alright?"

She nods vigorously.

My hand catches and clasps hers.

Luna asks, "How'd you guys know to come?"

"Sulli texted me," Donnelly says.

"And you butt-dialed me," I proclaim.

She frowns. "My phone died though."

"It must've been before that."

Donnelly speaks into his mic, saying something about finding the space babe, the mermaid, and the frog, then he eyes Luna for a long beat before turning to me. "We need to bail. Akara and Banks are outside."

"They're okay?"

"Yeah." His blue eyes drift to the doorway. "But we might have a problem."

I learn quickly.

The frat guys slashed all of our tires.

We have no way of leaving.

NEVER DID I THINK THIS NIGHT WOULD END WITH me, Frog, Luna, Banks, Akara, and Donnelly in my Uncle Connor's limo. But after Akara had a tow truck take the SUV and its slashed tires back home, he called my uncle.

Apparently, he knew my uncle had a meeting in the area. And Uncle Connor quickly sent his driver to pick us up and take us to the penthouse.

Now we bump along the city streets, and while Luna sprawls upside down, face hidden in her sweatshirt, Donnelly has been sketching on cocktail napkins he found in the limo. Reading glasses perched on his nose.

I'm smushed between Banks and Akara, and I scoop ice from the ice bucket into a baggie. The bottle of champagne catches my eye. But I focus on filling the baggie, then pressing the ice to Banks' head. A goose egg already forming.

"You wore heels?" Akara says to Frog. "While you were *on-duty?*"

"You said if I went to a party, I needed to blend *in*. This is what I wear to parties, Nine."

"No one's going to look at your feet, Frog." He throws up his hands, heated and exasperated, and his eye is already reddened from being punched or elbowed or whatever-the-fuck. Akara keeps checking on me in quick glances, to ensure I'm fine.

He checks on Banks, to ensure he's fine.

He checks on Frog.

On Luna. On Donnelly.

"Here, Kits. For your eye." I gather more ice into another little baggie, used I think for trash in the limo. I hand him the ice bag.

He's distracted on us. "I'm fine."

"*Kits.*"

He reluctantly takes the ice, then presses it to his eye and uses the other to glare at his cousin. "No more heels."

"I seriously think that's the least of the screw-ups tonight but go on."

"You're right. Tovin should've never left you. He's fired."

Frog eases a little. I already heard that Tovin, the other temp guard, ditched Frog an hour into the party. His friends called him to go hang at a local bar, and he thought that sounded more exciting, I guess. The pay must've not been incentive enough.

"You need to take another course in using comms," Akara says with the shake of his head.

"They're not easy," Frog defends. "Like, there has to be a simpler system. Text messaging was invented for a reason."

"It's not fast enough."

"Hello, there's a thing called *emojis*."

Banks laughs.

Akara tries not to smile, and he shakes his head at Banks. Why is my pulse still skidding? Why am I still panicking?

The champagne catches my eye again.

I'll just drink enough to let tonight go away.

To drift off into the ether.

Maybe it'll help me sleep. I reach forward and capture the champagne bottle out of the sloshy water. Donnelly and Frog watch me from the other side of the limo.

And I can feel Akara and Banks tense beside me.

"Anyone want champagne?"

Frog shrugs.

"No drinking on-duty," Akara reminds her.

"I'm *almost* off-duty. Doesn't that count?"

"No, and you're eighteen."

She groans, "You're such a dad."

"I'm not," he snaps.

"You are," she snaps back.

Banks is paying more attention to me as I unspool the foil of the champagne neck. I pop the cork, and I press the bottle to my lips.

Gulping and gulping—and then he tears the bottle out of my hands.

"Sulli."

I wipe my mouth with the back of my hand. "You want some?"

"I want you to stop." Banks looks pained.

"It's nothing." I grab the bottle.

He won't let go.

We're in a tug of war. "*Banks.*"

"Stop."

"You're overreacting!" I yell. Why am I yelling?

His eyes redden more. "You don't need this."

"I want it. Just like I bet you want a cigarette."

It's a low blow. His face twists. "I'll quit smoking. I'll quit with you."

I don't respond.

I want the champagne tonight.

I need it.

I need it.

"Give it to me," I say.

Akara cuts in, "Sulli, let go."

Pain shoots into my chest. Not Kits too. "No—I don't have a problem. I can prove it." I tear the bottle out of Banks' hands. Champagne sloshes on us, but my head spins from all the beer tonight. And I don't care.

I don't care.

I want to care even less. So I drink.

And I drink.

I hate myself.

I hate how I empty the contents of the bottle down my throat with total ease. I hate how Akara is staring at me. Like I'm someone he hardly recognizes. Like I've morphed into a stranger. Like he wants to shake me and wake me and he can't see how.

I hate how Banks breathes steady, sharp breaths. Like I've staked dagger after dagger into his chest. I hate how he gently pries the empty bottle from my hand and rests a hand on my wet, sticky leg.

How much did I spill?

I hate that I don't know.

I hate who I am.

I need air.

I need air.

I want out.

Fumbling with buttons, I find the one that opens a portion of the roof. They call my name, but I don't look or listen. Wobbling, I stand up through the roof—feeling hot, I breathe in the big gusts of air. Night sky and city lights of Philadelphia all around me. We zip fast, and if paparazzi sees me—I don't care.

I can't care.

That's what I wanted right?

Tears squeeze out of my eyes. Drip down my cheeks. The wind takes them, and for a second, I wish the wind would take me.

And then, Akara and Banks are outside. They fit through the sky roof with me. Their arms are around me, and I'm crying on their shoulders. How do I deserve this love tonight? How do I deserve them?

I'm shaking my head as I stare between them, "I don't want to drink anymore." My voice breaks. But I repeat the sentiment over and over into their chests. Their arms. Shoulders. Into Philly as the wind whips against us.

I promise them, the city, and myself—*I don't want to drink anymore. I won't drink.*

I'm going to be sober. For good.

39
Banks Moretti

IN THE COVER OF DARKNESS, we leave Los Angeles.

Redeye on the private jet is a fucking blessing. I don't care much about the bougie amenities. Only the luxury seats with the extra space to stretch my long-ass legs. Flying commercial, I feel like a praying mantis squeezed into a thimble. On the private plane, it's easier to sleep. And sleep comes easy for most bodyguards. Seeing as how we might be confronting money shot-thirsty paparazzi when we land, it's better to rack out now. *What kind of hellfire awaits us? What kind of hellfire awaits Sulli?*

That depends on whether anyone leaked our arrival into Philly.

So when I wake up, I first look to Akara.

He'd know if we're headed for a shit storm.

And he's already on his phone. Typical Kitsuwon.

"Any issues?" I ask quietly while Sulli is still asleep between us. She's drooling on Akara's arm, and he's careful not to disturb her.

"None." He smacks his phone to his palm, his brows cinched. "Press still thinks the families are in L.A."

"Then why do you look like you dropped your phone in the toilet?"

He shakes his head, a smile inching up his lips. "Dang, Banks. Taking shots at my phone already." After a quick glance to Sulli, he keeps his voice to a whisper. "It just feels too good to be true."

"Too easy?"

"Yeah."

"I'm gonna take the easy when it comes." I stretch out my stiff legs. "It might not be coming around again."

Akara nods, looks out the plane window as sunshine streams onto our row. With the time change—it must be closer to the afternoon in Philly than the early morning. I can tell Akara is trying to relax, but he'll only do a good job of that when Sulli wakes up.

She'd actually *prefer* to be up while we're up, so I stretch my right leg over into her space. Knocking calves and ankles.

Sulli stirs. "Wah…" She squints at the sunlight.

Akara instantly smiles.

God, I rock. I lean further back, hands behind my head in a deeper stretch.

"Hey, drool monster," Akara says.

Sulli flushes. "Oh…" She touches her slick lips, then rubs the wet spot on Akara's sleeve. "Fuck, sorry, Kits."

I stretch my arm over her shoulder. "He's never washing that shirt."

Akara smiles, "Yep, it's going in a display box over the bed."

"No it's fucking *not*." She knocks her knees into our knees. "It's going in the wash."

Akara tilts his head to me. "Should we get an engraved plaque? *Sulli's Twentieth Drool.*"

Sulli's jaw drops. "I haven't drooled *twenty* times on you, Kits." She slugs his arm.

We're all laughing and joking and smiling when the plane does finally land. And here I am, thinking good things. Happy things. That maybe the biggest threats were left back in L.A. With the Olympics behind us, the worst of my fears are left in our wake.

No paparazzi are on the tarmac.

We've landed at Emerald Aviation, a fixed-base operator that serves the private jets here in Philly. It's away from the hustle and bustle of the Philadelphia International Airport.

Airplane hangars fill up the area more than people.

No one to spot us. No videos and pics will end up online.

Still, we're ahead of the media.

I'm feeling good.

But as we descend the short stairs to the tarmac, Akara receives a phone call. His face turns serious. Grave. "This is Akara Kitsuwon. Yeah…okay?" is all I hear him say.

I busy myself with our luggage.

Tossing Sulli's suitcase and Akara's duffel into the backseat of a security SUV. When I go to grab mine, Akara rounds the trunk to whisper, "It's security from the apartment building."

"Of the penthouse?"

He nods stiffly, still on the phone.

And then Akara forces a smile on Loren Hale, who peeks over at us. I give him a cordial wave. He's been talking with Sulli near the mound of suitcases.

Lo is considered the pettiest person among the families, and I reasoned that's why he was an arctic blast towards us and Sulli when he heard we were all together. *That* and he's going to side with his brother Ryke on just about everything.

So when Ryke was feeling on edge around us, Lo was feeling more protective of him.

I have a brother. I get it.

But Lo means something to me. I've protected his youngest son for *years*. And I always thought he liked me and Thatcher.

Lo nods back to me with a less sharp-edged smile.

It'll take it.

Hell, since Ryke is more accepting of our triad, Lo has been too—and I'm not gonna toss aside these small moments like they mean nothing. However brief and fleeting, they count for me. I never expect too much out of people. Especially men who I want to look up to.

My dad taught me that.

"Can you send me the footage?" Akara rounds to the hood of the SUV now for privacy and to be out of eyeshot of the families.

Footage?

Apartment security at the penthouse?

I rake a coarse hand through my hair. *Fuck*. My mind travels to the Cinderella ad fiasco and the bare-naked perv that I caught about to jack off on Janie's bed in the townhouse.

Let the good times roll in my fucked-up head.

Did someone break into the penthouse?

Muscles flex more. I'm feeling like tonight won't be about decompressing. Taking a fuckin' load off. It's been a long two weeks, but Akara and I were more prepared for war than a vacation after the Olympics. And strangely, I think we'd prefer it this way.

We're both cracked.

I hope Sulli knows that.

As she comes over to me, she smiles this soft, faraway smile.

"Must've been some conversation," I say to Sulli as I sit on the opened trunk. The SUV sinks with my weight.

Sulli is more eyelevel. "It was. My uncle, he gave me this…" She digs in her jean's pocket. "He said he never used them, but he thought it's something I'd like since I keep chasing after medals." She produces a green coin, a little bigger than a quarter. "For being two months sober." Sulli passes me the coin.

My thumb runs over the *2 Months Recovery* engraving, but mostly I can't take my gaze off her. "You know how proud I am of you?"

Tears crest the greenest eyes I've ever seen. "I'm proud of you too, Banks."

In my head, cigarettes seem easier to kick than alcohol, but I'm not gonna downplay anything. Sulli won't allow me to.

So I stand up and weave my arms around her athletic frame. "I love you a whole damn lot."

She buries herself into my body. "I love you a whole fucking ton more."

I kiss her head, and when we part, she's digging in another pocket. I wonder if this is another gift from her sober sponsor. She has two of them.

Her dad and her uncle. But she went to Lo first after the frat party. She was afraid of disappointing her dad. She didn't.

Admitting that she needed help—she made Ryke just as proud too.

"Oh I forgot." She reveals two blank envelopes. "Uncle Lo said these are for you and Kits."

I frown. "You sure it's for me?" I'm thinking it has to be a check for security. Maybe the parents felt like Kitsuwon Securities extended their services to them.

"Yeah, he said, *your boyfriends, Akara and Banks.*" Her cheeks redden, embarrassed about something. "And he also fucking teased me about 'putting rings on it'…and I stupidly asked, like proposals? And he said, no, I want you to go to Mordor and destroy the Ring." She touches her forehead, flustered. "And I don't know.…that's stupid, right?"

"Mordor or proposals?"

"Proposals. We can never really get married?"

I stiffen and sweep her head to toe. Marriage. Haven't contemplated it for too long. Christ, I used to always take less. But now I just want to take more than anyone says I can be given. Two people to love.

A union.

A commitment of forever.

Why the hell not? Why can't that be for us?

"I think," I say as I'm thinking, "this is something we should talk about with Akara."

"Where is Kits?"

Before I can answer, her mom shouts, "Caw-caw!"

Sulli whips her head and returns a, "Caw-caw!" Quickly, Sulli says to me, "I'm going to tell my mom goodbye. Then I'll be back."

I nod, and as Sulli leaves, I skirt around to the front of the SUV.

Akara is leaning on the hood and pinching the bridge of his nose. Phone still to his ear.

Mother of Christ, this is bad.

Crossing my arms over my chest, I start packing on armor.

"Yes, that's my email…correct. I'll be in touch," Akara says, tensed. "Thanks." He hangs up.

"Nine, talk to me."

He pockets his phone and lets out a frustrated, distraught noise. Closing his eyes, he says, "The Jeep was stolen."

Stolen.

Stolen.

Pressure wells in the back of my head. Thumping like a panic-induced migraine.

I couldn't have heard him right.

"Say again."

"That fudging Jeep is gone. Stolen. Robbed. How many synonyms do you want?"

"*Fuck*," I curse hotly, gaze narrowing on her family. They're blissfully unaware of their most prized possession *gone*. Booger…that Jeep—*fuck*.

Akara crouches at the tire, face in his hands. He's a heartbeat from screaming, and I squat down to him, tucking my hair behind my ears. Trying to cool the fuck down for him. He's going to take the brunt of this disaster on his shoulder.

I wanna pry some off.

"Maybe there's a good explanation," I start out.

Akara drops his hands, eyes bloodshot. "We know *why* they took the Jeep. It's the most famous, recognizable vehicle."

"But how the hell could a thief get through apartment security? That parking garage is like Fort Knox." On the chance they entered, they'd have to find the right level and then break through a passcode-protected metal gate that stores everyone's vehicles from the penthouse.

"I have no idea," Akara sighs heavily. "I told Sulli it'd be safe there… and it wasn't." He runs a stressed hand through his hair. And when I put a hand to his shoulder and stand up, he rises with me, saying, "The building's security is sending me footage of the parking garage's cameras. Someone broke in. They're hoping we can identify the thief."

My brows furrow. "How do we know this isn't an inside job?" It seems more reasonable that someone who had *access* to the parking garage would take the Jeep.

"It could be." Akara massages his knuckles. "Maybe staff or another resident. We won't know until we look at that footage."

"Footage of what?" Sulli peeks around the hood.

Akara and I both go quiet, just as Price's SUV passes our vehicle. Passenger window rolls down, and Ryke waves a hand outside. "See you guys soon. Pack for warm weather."

We've been invited on a Meadows family trip. As Sulli's boyfriends first. Bodyguards second.

Where we're going—hell if I know.

Ryke and Daisy decided they'd surprise all of us, and Sulli and Winona's guesses have ranged from Alaska to Chile to Costa Rica. I don't care where we go, as long as we're together.

And packing isn't even on my list of things to do when we haven't even unpacked from this trip yet and some shitbag has Booger.

"Will do," Akara waves a hand.

I nod curtly.

Ryke gives me a weird look, but he loses time to respond as the SUV drives on by. Leaving the tarmac with other cars. The only ones left are Luna, Maximoff, Farrow, and Baby Ripley. Looks like Farrow is snapping Ripley into his car seat.

Sulli spins back on us. "What's going on? What footage? And why do you look like you stole a cookie from the cookie jar?" Her eyes are on me.

I look that fuckin' guilty? I explain, "We have intel that we're trying to keep discreet."

"Am I in the need-to-know category and I don't need to know?"

"You need to know," Akara and I say together.

She sighs heavily and rubs her eyes wearily. "It's bad news, isn't it?"

Fuck, I hate laying this on her. We're getting pounded with shit storm after shit storm, and even if I like being on my toes, I wouldn't choose *this* disaster in a million fucking years. Give me a normal overly excited fan to tell, *stay back*. Give me an annoying cameraman who's slightly pushy.

Hell, give me twenty questions about me and Akara fucking (even though we're not fucking)—anything but *this*.

I want Sulli to bask in the high of her Olympic wins, but we can't keep this secret from her. Not for a day or an hour or even a minute.

She'd hate us for it.

I'd fucking hate me.

Akara opens his mouth and his phone chimes. Sounds of planes taking off the runway rumbles the ground. Sulli focuses on me for answers as Akara checks his cell.

"There's no good way to say this, Sulli." I gear her up for bad news. "Booger was stolen."

She doesn't say anything. Has no expression. She's in clear shock. "What?"

"Stolen," I tell her. "The Jeep. Booger. She's gone. But we're gonna get her back."

She fights tears. "She's the only thing I have of his."

Adam Sully. Her dad's best friend. A rock climber who died on a mountain in front of her dad. The guy she's named after. That Jeep is sentimental in ways I understand. I was willing to miss my brother's wedding for Booger when she broke down on the road trip out west.

I did miss most of his wedding.

That Jeep means too much to the people I care about, and I would do almost anything to get her back. I know Sulli and Akara would too.

I remember how Akara said Booger is *famous*. So famous, some fan even made an Instagram account to document sightings of the Jeep in public. "Maybe the fan page has spotted her."

Hope lightens her green eyes. "Maybe."

"Crap. Effing *garbage*," Akara snaps. He looks up at us. "They just sent the footage. The file is too big to download. I need a computer."

"Mount up," I tell them both. "We're headed home."

Only when we're all in the car, and I go to grab the wheel, do I realize I'm still holding the envelopes. The ones Lo gave to Sulli to give to us.

"What's that?" Akara sees.

I realize they have tiny letters on the back. I pass him the one with an *A*. "From Lo."

We rip open the envelopes, and Sulli sticks her head between the two front seats, peering at the contents.

Not a check for security.

Not security related at all.

It's a short, concise letter.

> *Welcome to the family.*
>
> *It's messy. But you already knew that and wanted in anyway. Either you're nuts or you must really love my niece. Either way, you'll fit in.*
>
> *Treat her well or there'll be hell to pay.*
>
> *Hugs, kisses, love & light & all that shit.*
>
>
> *Sulli's favorite uncle,*
>
> *Loren Hale*
>
>
> *P.S. Banks, thanks for looking out for my son all those years. I don't think I said that enough.*

Surprise chokes me up.

I didn't expect more from Lo. He didn't have to do this.

A man who rises above expectations is a man that I've rarely met. And I'm stunned quiet for a second.

Glancing over at Akara, I see Lo wrote the same letter with a different ending.

> *P.S. Akara, don't work yourself to death. The people you love will remind you of that more than I can. Lily always does for me.*

His lips rise. "Lo's handwriting is literal chicken scratch."

"Janie's is worse," I say.

"For fucking sure," Sulli breathes, and we're all quiet, rereading the letters one last time. I feel my mouth curve up, and Sulli is smiling softly too, one that wanes fast. But I thank the Lord for the short distraction. Maybe this good feeling can carry us home.

40
Sullivan Meadows

MY DUSTY OLD LAPTOP rests on my bed's turquoise quilt, and I'm standing hunched over the keyboard. I rewatch the security footage on max-zoom to inspect the thief's face. He's wearing a fucking ski mask. A ski mask! It's so comical that I almost laugh, but then I remember what he stole. All humor fades away to be replaced by something hollow.

Something cold.

I hug my arms around my body and back away from the laptop. "She's just gone," I whisper sadly. "Just like that?"

All these years, I vowed to protect that Jeep. Keep her safe. For my dad.

Failure roots me down, and this failure isn't like losing Olympic gold. This failure is far more eviscerating.

"We're going to get the Jeep back, Sul," Akara assures me without glancing up from his cellphone. He's composing an email to the rest of SFO and attaching the footage. All of Omega will be on the case of the Missing Jeep.

She's just a car.

I try to convince myself.

But it's not working. Because I know, deep down, the Jeep is not *just* a car.

Banks rewinds the surveillance footage, examining the perp closely. "Definitely a man. Maybe five-nine to six-foot." He looks to Akara. "This is really the only footage they've got?"

"Yep." Akara breathes out a tensed breath. He turns to me. "Do you want us to tell your dad, Sul?"

My stomach tosses. *I failed him.* "The family trip is in a week…" And I've declined most trip invites while I've been training. With the Olympics over, I was looking forward to an adventurous getaway. "If my parents pick Costa Rica, I'll be ruining one of my favorite places on Earth with tears and stress…and I really fucking wanted you guys to see the treehouse."

The Costa Rican treehouse. Off the beaten path. Secluded among tropical foliage and wildlife.

No bodyguard has ever been. We leave them behind in the nearest city, and outside my immediate family, only Moffy has ever stayed there.

I keep thinking *maybe* my parents will want Akara and Banks to see the treehouse. To really be a part of the family, but I can't tarnish something so pure with something so awful. Now I'm wishing upon every fucking star we're not headed there.

Before they can speak, I add fast, "We can't tell them the Jeep is missing if we go to Costa Rica. But if it's some other place, maybe…" I blink back tears, picturing my dad's gutted reaction. "I don't know if I can survive this trip with my dad knowing I lost the Jeep."

Banks softens his gaze. "You didn't *lose* it. It was stolen."

"Same fucking difference," I mutter.

"Hey," Akara says strongly. "It's not just on you. And if anyone knows the definition of *losing* something, it's Banksy."

"Exactly," Banks nods heartily.

I love that they're trying to uplift my spirits. Even if it's not working. "We need to find it." I try to replace sorrow with determination. "*Before* the family trip. Let's scour Philly. Hit the streets and start combing backroads."

Banks and Akara share a look like it's a failing prospect.

"You two don't have to come with me. Put a temp on my detail. I'm fine to drive around the city without you."

"Whoa," Akara holds up a hand.

Banks nods to me. "Don't go ditching me so quickly, mermaid."

I smile a little.

Akara stalks closer, just to hug me and fling my hair at my face.

I shove him, smiling more.

He smiles back, "I also don't remember volunteering to stay home, Lady Meadows."

I hold onto his forearm, my heart aching with love and grief. "That look though…" I thought they didn't want to help me.

"We're just worried we won't find it," Akara explains. "Not that we won't go. We'll be beside you."

"Every time." Banks already has the SUV keys.

They're agreeing to my plan. The plan with 5% chance of success. But it's better than sitting here and twiddling our thumbs.

Banks drives. Akara sits in the passenger seat. I'm in the backseat, focused. I tune everything out, even Banks and Akara's chatter from the front.

Please.

Please.

The car bumps along the road, and I spot a woman crossing the street with a stroller. Tears begin to rise. In my heart, I really wanted my kid to know that Jeep. To smell the leather seats and spill Cheerios in the backseat. To one day grip the steering wheel as they learned to drive. I dreamed of the day Banks would have to toil over the engine and replace parts to make Booger safer. Better.

She would be the family Jeep.

Now she's somewhere else. Unloved. Uncared for. Strangers touch her.

I fight more tears. A horrible thought crosses my mind: If I'd never been in a poly relationship—if I'd never invoked this impossible, unwieldly, uncompromisable kind of fame, would I still have the Jeep?

What ifs plague me. Even into the dark of the night, they stay with me.

Headlights on, searching for the Jeep that's probably stripped of parts or on a shipping freighter being sent overseas. It's useless.

"Guys," I call up to them.

Coffees in both their hands, they look back. Banks can't take his eyes off the road for too long. They haven't asked me if I was done looking. Not once. For that, I'll always be grateful.

"Maybe we should call it a night. Search tomorrow?" I ask them.

Akara and Banks share a look before Banks says, "One more pocket of the city, Sulli. Then we can go back."

I almost breakdown. But I keep it together. "You sure?"

"Positive," he tells me.

Akara passes me his coffee. Mine already empty and gone hours ago. "Drink up, string bean."

41

Akara Kitsuwon

WORST WAYS TO START *Off a Meadows Family Trip* by Akara Kitsuwon is the title of my memoir. I'm copyrighting it, so no one can infringe on my reality.

If we thought this through, maybe we would've picked a better time to dump so much news on Sulli's parents. Then again, a different time would mean postponing, and pushing this all off sounds like the most brutal call.

Anyway, we're not in Costa Rica.

Once we boarded the flight, we figured out fast we weren't going international. Which means our agreement to bad-news-dump on her parents is a go.

I've wanted to see the Costa Rican treehouse since I became Sulli's bodyguard, but I'd much rather be there without unloading the missing Jeep saga.

Still missing.

One week of no progress.

The large twelve-seater van bumps along Utah roads. Red rock passes by and paddleboards clap together on the roof. Price grips the steering wheel and checks the GPS on his phone.

We're in beautiful Moab.

Home to Arches National Park. Half hour from Canyonlands.

Red dirt underfoot and eagles cutting through clear blue sky. It's definitely not my first time here with the Meadows.

But it is my first time here as a boyfriend to their daughter.

In the bench-style seat behind Price, Ryke and Daisy are chatting *happily*. (We're about to pop that happy bubble.)

Winona got car sick after snapping photos, so she's sprawled down on the middle seat. Not in view. But I hear faint music playing from her earbuds.

Banks, Sulli, and I squish together voluntarily in the backseat, shoulders pressed together. "Who's going to say it?" I ask in a whisper, leaning closer to Sulli so Banks hears me. He's caved forward to avoid banging his head on the car roof.

"It should be me," Sulli says.

"You're not in this alone," Banks tells her.

The van hits a pothole.

Unbuckled, I take air and career forward slightly. My healing abdomen hits the middle seat uncomfortably. I wince.

"Sorry about that!" Price calls out.

I stifle a remark. I doubt he's being malicious. Just a *crap* driver. And his presence in this van is making everything more difficult. He'll hear our news at the same time as Sulli's parents. There's no avoiding that.

We all agreed that before we're on the Colorado River, we need to be free of secrets.

Sulli holds my hand and his hand. "I'll tell them about the fucking cinnamon roll. You two can spill the beans about Booger."

"Deal."

"Right on," Banks says calmly.

We all put out our hands, hooking pinkies three ways, and then Sulli clears her throat loudly, "Mom…Dad…"

I push my hair back over and over, and I remind myself, the worst thing that can happen: Ryke catapulting over his sixteen-year-old daughter to throw a punch at either me or Banks in the backseat.

I just don't see that happening.

Ryke and Daisy rotate in their seat. Facing us as best they can.

"You rang?" Daisy wags her brows.

Sulli smiles nervously. "Uh, yeah, so we have some news to share. Before you start guessing what the fuck it could be—not all of it is *good* news."

Daisy frowns. "Okay…?" She peeks at Ryke.

His brows harden, and he immediately drills an intense, questioning look onto Banks, then me. I stop pushing my hair back, letting the strands fall. I'm guessing he thinks we didn't protect Sulli fully.

We didn't.

We accidentally got her pregnant. And don't get me started on the Jeep…I'll carry that loss forever. I've only ever wanted to protect the Meadows family, and one of the most beloved pieces of them is gone. And I wish I could turn back time. To tell myself to do *something* else. Something better.

I could've done better.

"Is any of it good news?" Ryke asks his daughter.

"Yeah, I think so." She bites her lip, then puts a hand to her chest. "*I* think it's good news at least."

"It's good news," Banks reaffirms.

"Really good news," I chime in.

Daisy swivels more, unbuckling. "Good news first. The sun before the clouds is totally better."

Sulli tucks her legs to her chest. "I'd rather be a sunrise slut than Sulli the Slut anyway."

"You're not a slut at all," Ryke defends roughly. "Fuck them."

Sulli tries to smile.

Ryke searches her uneasy expression. "I agree with your mom. Fuck the bad. Let's hear the good."

Sulli squeezes our hands. "I don't know what you're going to think of me, Dad. Honestly, I don't know if you'll be mad or happy—but just don't take this out on Banks or Akara. I'm *just* as much a part of this. It takes two to tango—or in this case, *three*."

Ryke freezes. "Sulli, just fucking tell me—"

"I'm pregnant," she interjects.

Daisy's hands fly to her mouth, overwhelmed tears building. "Really?" It's a hopeful *really*, and not the reaction I expected at all.

Sulli almost starts crying. "Fucking really."

Immediately, Daisy crawls over her seat into the middle one.

"Whoa, *Mom*," Winona whines as she sits up quickly and pops out an earbud. Her annoyance dissolves into confusion when she sees her mom crying. "What's going on?"

"Your sister is pregnant," Daisy says. And then swiftly wraps her arms around Sulli's shoulder into a loving hug. Sulli leans forward to return the hug. Her tears spill on her mom's shoulder.

I hear Daisy whisper to Sulli, "I'm so very glad it was easy for you, my peanut butter cupcake."

I see now.

Why Daisy is so happy for her.

I start smiling.

All the struggle Daisy had to face just to have Sulli—it's not something Sulli will have to worry about. *Easy.* I wonder if that's the goal all parents seek and wish for their children. An easy, uncomplicated journey through the world.

No, Nine.

My dad...I can't push him out of my head. I just can't. I never really could. And I remember that for the seventeen years I had him on this earth, he never said anything like that to me. He never wished *easy* for my life.

He wished for success—whatever that word meant to me. And he wished for happiness. And my life—how I turned out—is the messiest of messes.

And I've loved every messy moment, every complex second of this journey with him and her—and if I went towards easy, where the heck would I even be?

Alone.

Miserable.

I would've never known how much love and how much *life* I'd be missing. Sometimes, the messiest roads are the best ones taken, and I know when our kid is here, I'll be telling them that.

Winona is crying. "You're pregnant? *Sulli.* You're having a baby."

"Yeah, squirt." Sulli messes her hair. "I'm having a baby. And you're going to be the coolest aunt around." They laugh and hug, tears slipping down their cheeks.

Banks is choked up, and my eyes are burning from emotion, watching Daisy and her daughters hug and cry over the pregnancy news.

Ryke's gaze is bloodshot. Price is keeping a focused gaze on the road. I'm not able to see his reaction, and I'm digging harder to understand Ryke's.

I swallow the ball in my throat and nod to her dad. "Ryke," I call out to him.

He opens his mouth but only a choked noise comes out. He glares at the van's roof and smears a hand over his tear-filled eyes.

Daisy breaks from her hug with Sulli and gives her husband a soft smile. "It's *great* news," she tells him.

He nods repeatedly. "It really fucking is, Dais."

That slams me back.

Banks begins to smile.

Ryke Meadows watched Daisy's pain. Stood by her through the trauma, the sadness. I doubt he ever wished that on his daughter either.

He takes a controlled breath and focuses on Sulli. "I love you, Sul. With my whole fucking heart." He pauses to gather his breath, to say the next words—but his voice comes out shaky and tearful, "I'm going to love your baby just as much."

"Thanks, Dad." Sulli is close to another sob. She rubs at her face.

Ryke rubs at his, then he nods to me and Banks. "Which one of you is the father?"

Expected *that.* The question doesn't provoke bitterness or anger. I'll answer that truthfully with pride every time. *Both of us are the fathers.*

But Banks beats me and says, "It wasn't planned, Ryke."

He lifts his hardened brows. "I fucking figured that after the last time." He spares us another lecture like he gave *last time.* "So you don't know who the dad is?"

Banks is shaking his head as I say, "We both are." I shoot my metamour a look.

"He's talking about the *biological* dad, Nine."

"I don't care. I need to make this 100% clear, Banks." To them, I say, "Regardless of who's the bio father, we're both going to be parents to the child. We'll both be raising them with Sulli."

I fear if the child is biologically mine, people will push Banks aside. He'll let them.

I won't let anyone tell me I'm not a parent to Banks' biological child. I'm forceful. I can be pushy. I will butt in.

Ryke is processing. "So you'll both be dads?"

"Right." I add, "DNA doesn't matter. At the end of the day, who raises you is a bigger indication of a father or mother than the cells in your body. Our child can have two fathers and one mother."

Banks curves his arm behind our headrests, his hand settling near my shoulder. "Anyone who says otherwise," he tells her parents, "we'll be employing a Meadows' motto."

Sulli smiles, "Fuck them."

I smile more.

Ryke nods, his lips rising. "Fuck them," he agrees.

Winona rests her chin on the backseat, facing us. She seems nervous. "The world might take bets on which one of you is the bio dad."

Banks lifts a shoulder.

"We're expecting a lot of crap, Nona," I tell her. "You don't need to worry about us versus the world."

"That's a life-long battle we signed up for," Banks pipes in, "and Akara and I like a good fight."

I tease, "Sulli is the lover."

She makes a face. "Hardy fucking har."

Ryke is quieter, digesting everything. Until he asks, "Are either of you nervous about being the father or *not* being the father?"

"No," Banks and I say together.

Of course I have my fears, but I prefer just sharing with Banks and Sulli. To everyone else, I just hope to appear solidly confident. Like nothing can take us down.

Ryke finally says, "Whatever you need from me, whether it's support or just to be a grandparent—I'm fucking there. For her. For both of you. For all fucking three of you."

"Four," Winona corrects, adding our baby.

"Four," Ryke says strongly.

Pride fills Daisy's eyes for Ryke.

"Thank you," Banks says deeply.

I'm too choked for words. I just nod. It's taken us a long time to get to this point, and Ryke's support is rarely freely given unless you're family.

Family.

That word punctures me. After my dad died and my mom moved away, I lost sense of family. I know I've been trying to recreate it all these years. First with my gym. Then with security. Surrounding myself with people who care. My men. My client. I want family so badly that I've been clinging desperately to any piece that fills that void.

Banks reaches over and squeezes my shoulder. I lock eyes with him. I'd never choose anyone else to do this with. To be a third of my heart.

Ryke braces a hand on the seat as the van hits another bump. "Your kid is going to be strong as fuck," he tells Sulli, Banks, and me. "They'll have to be."

They will be.

And if they aren't, we'll be strong enough to fight for them.

Daisy glances to us. "You'll need to be ready for all the attention with the media while Sulli's pregnant. That can be hard."

"About that," Sulli says. "I'm actually not going to tell the public. I'm thinking of holing up in the penthouse. It's the best thing for the baby. Zero risk. Just…hide out until the birth."

Daisy's face drops. She looks to her husband.

Ryke's brows furrow in equal confusion and concern.

And then the van comes to a screeching halt. Price turns off the ignition. "We're here."

42

Banks Moretti

THROUGH ALL THE TEARS and hugs, we failed to mention the other news. The *bad* news. The Meadows family, Akara, Price, and I unmount from the van. It takes an ungodly amount of time to pull each long paddleboard off the roof. Even with my six-seven giant ass, these things were tied down tight.

The van is parked in a small alcove off the road, right beside the Colorado River. Humongous red cliffs border either side. Triple Shield's security vehicle sits behind us, Price speaking covertly and quietly with Wylie and Greer. Thank God I'm out of earshot of *that* conversation.

Price must be updating them on the big news. Hell, by tomorrow, all of Triple Shield will know that Sulli is pregnant.

I lift the last paddleboard off the van and carry it closer to the river. Dropping the board, it *thumps* to the soft dirt. Akara has already finished unloading the life vests near the water, and he starts rubbing sunscreen on Sulli's back. Winona is fitting a waterproof bag over her camera—she likes snapping nature photos. Animal photos.

Whenever she posts on Instagram, it's usually of the scenic shots she's captured, so it's not surprising to see her camera joining this adventure.

Daisy is bringing the oars near the river. And closer to where the river meets the sandy bank, Ryke straps dry bags to each paddleboard.

His wife smiles over at him, "Hubba hubba, you're one handsome stud. I don't think we've met before."

Ryke's smile seems brighter in the sun. "Is that so, Calloway?"

She mock gasps. "And he knows my name!"

He reaches forward to the river and splashes water at his wife.

She splashes back, laughing.

He wipes water out of his face, watching his wife stand back up and go help Winona rub sunscreen on her shoulder blades. Daisy makes a crude gesture to Ryke with her tongue, and I pretend not to notice.

Ryke mutters something lovingly about Daisy being trouble.

He's still smiling.

God, I wish I could bury this news in the dirt. Never let it out. Ryke doesn't just *appear* happy. He *is* happy, and no part of my soul wants to snuff out that light.

But I've got to.

I bend down to help him with the dry bags. "Before we get on the water," I say, "Akara and I wanted to tell you the bad news."

"Fucking forgot about that," he grumbles and nods towards a canteen. "Can you—?"

I grab the canteen and pass it over. He says a quick *thanks*.

"What bad news?" Winona asks, tying off a messy braid.

Before I can take one for the team, Akara chucks some sunscreen in a dry bag and announces, "The Jeep was stolen from the parking garage at the penthouse."

"While we were in L.A.," I clarify, just in case they think we didn't do our jobs. Akara isn't responsible for this fuck-up.

Ryke rakes an aggressive hand through his hair. His face coiling in a look I know well. It's the look of someone battling an onslaught of grief. "It's fucking gone?" He shakes his head, darkened confusion rolling over his hardened features. "How? When?"

Akara explains the details.

Break-in at the parking garage.

One week ago.

One guy.

He hotwired the Jeep. Sped off. Instagram has no clues as to where he went. Paparazzi didn't catch him. Press wasn't staking out the parking garage. We were at the Olympics.

The thief *knew* that. The whole world did.

Ryke sits back on the bank of the river. In shock, I think.

Akara and I exchange hesitance. Not sure if Ryke needs space or reassurance. Daisy meets him on the sand and sticks her toes into the water. They're quiet together, and Winona also takes a moment to herself. She wanders into the river with her paddleboard.

Sulli is pacing behind us.

I mouth, *it's alright.*

Wide-eyed, she motions to the backs of her parents.

I'm still tying this motherfucking dry bag, and Akara goes to Sulli, whispering, "They're not mad at you, Sul."

She replies to him against his ear, then she mouths to me, *they should be.* Her eyes redden, trying to restrain tears, and Akara wraps an arm around her shoulders while she hides her face.

A pang clenches my heart. I hate seeing Sulli cry. My instinct is to go hold her, but Sulli suddenly drops her hands. "Dad?" Her voice cracks. "I'm...*so* fucking sorry."

"No," Ryke says firmly and fast, swerving around and picking himself off the bank. He brushes sand off his hands while approaching his daughter. "This isn't your fault, Sul. You hear me?"

Akara lets them have a moment and comes over to me, his nose flaring and Adam's apple bobbing. So as soon as he sits beside me, I tell him quietly, "It's not yours either."

He's disbelieving.

Just like Sulli, who says to Ryke, "It is, though. You trusted me—"

"You have a bullseye on you the size of fucking Mars." He places his hands on her shoulders. "It's not your fucking fault."

Sulli hangs her head.

I pry my gaze off Sulli as Akara whispers to me, "Her safety and belongings are my responsibility."

"They're mine too."

"You're my responsibility."

He's always throwing down the hierarchy card like an ace of spades. Hushed, I say, "I might be beneath you in security, but I'm beside you in our lives—and one of these days, you're gonna let me unburden you."

Akara searches my gaze. "You want more responsibility?"

Is that what I'm saying?

I think it is.

I've always been dependable. Someone to count on. You need me, I'm there. But I've never sought after more responsibilities.

I think that I know the kind of man I want to be. The one who expects more out of himself. Who people can come to expect more from, and not less.

Not just with my job, but in life. What Akara said in the van—about being parents together—I know despite my fears of being a shit dad, I *want* what he's advertising. Sign me up.

But to *say* that I can handle the responsibility of being a parent on the level of Akara fuckin' Kitsuwon is one thing. To actually be tested is another.

"Yeah," I nod once, accepting the challenge. "I want more."

Akara grips my shoulder with a love we can't justly explain. Respect, pride, and something deeper wrapped into an eternal light. Like a torch unable to burn out in the darkest spaces of time.

He starts to smile.

We hear Ryke tell Sulli, "Your life is different now, and shitty things are going to happen. Shitty things that I can't prevent. That security can't prevent."

Tension stretches along the bank of the river. Everyone watching Ryke and Sulli. Clearly, shitty things have been happening. Building up like bricks mortaring a house.

"I know," Sulli breathes. "I'm ready for the unpreventable things. I told you, I would be willing to take all the fucking risks for my relationship. But the Jeep—"

"Is just a fucking Jeep." Ryke tries to hold her gaze, but something raw surfaces in his eyes. A pain that causes him to look away for a beat.

"You know that's not true," Sulli whispers.

Ryke shifts his hands to her hands. Eyes on his daughter. "You're more important than that Jeep. Adam Sully would have agreed with me, if he were here now. Fuck, he'd tell me *it's just a stupid Jeep, man.* He'd be fucking shocked it's still running." He puts a hand on his daughter's shoulder. "My friend isn't *just* in that car. He's in the mountains. He's in the sky. Every time you climb. Every time I climb. Every time you reach a summit. He can feel that."

Sulli wipes away her tears. "I still want to keep looking, Dad. I'm not giving up."

"Then we won't fucking give up." Ryke gives her a hug.

"Price!" Daisy jogs over to her bodyguard, probably to inform him of the news.

I'm not excited about Triple Shield trying to rub our faces in this loss. When there's *nothing* we could've done.

I feel the disdain in my grimace. And when Ryke returns to the dry bags, he's eyeing the mother-loving hell out of me.

"Two teams are better than one on this," he says roughly. "Unless you have a fucking problem with Triple Shield helping look for the Jeep?"

"We don't," Akara says quickly, trying to keep the peace. Bringing Ryke and Daisy into our issues with Price, Greer, and Wylie is plain unprofessional. And I won't ruin Akara's reputation as the CEO of Kitsuwon Securities over my beef with Price's men.

I shut my mouth.

When the gear is safely in the dry bags and clipped to the paddleboards, we all head down to the river. It's idle here but up ahead, rapids swell and roll the water.

Price puts an inflatable kayak into the river. He'll be kayaking beside us, while Greer and Wylie meet us at the end of the river with the vans.

I don't have an earpiece in.

No radio.

I'm here as Sulli's boyfriend. Same as Akara.

But I still find myself scanning the area. Vigilance sharpens my senses. Alert. No humans in sight. We shook off paparazzi somewhere around Salt Lake City, and they shouldn't know our destination.

Less people and no paparazzi are some of the few saving graces of traveling to more remote locations.

Nature practically hums in the air. Didn't think I'd like the outdoors as much as I've come to love them. But really, I think it's because of the company I share when I'm here.

Shielding the beating sun with my hand, I see Daisy, Ryke, and Winona easily stand up on their paddleboards. My muscles tense, watching them glide around the water with clear agility and balance.

Fact: my ass has never been on a paddleboard before.

"It's easy," Akara says beside me as he fixes the straps of my life vest. He tightens them like he's choking the last bit of oxygen from me.

"You trying to kill me, man?"

He laughs. "It's supposed to be tight."

"I'm about to take my last breath," I refute.

Sulli pushes her board into the water. "Don't say that."

"Yeah, don't say that," Akara snaps like I invoked death into our relationship.

"You know what we are?" I tell him.

"Hot," he answers with a self-satisfied smile.

"I was gonna say a bunch of superstitious freaks."

Akara laughs.

I cock my head. "But yeah, we're fuckin' hot too."

"And she knows it," Akara states while we watch Sulli bite her lip and check us out. We're in swimming trunks. Sun beats on my olive-skin, and Akara's stab wound is visible from his waistband. The healed cut puffing in the heat.

Sulli's life vest covers her sporty bikini top, and unlike Winona's water-resistant cargo shorts, Sulli just wears bikini bottoms. I sweep her long, *long* legs like she continues to take us in, like we're something unreal. Something she's dreamed up from the motel on the road trip to now.

From bodyguards to boyfriends to soul mates.

My mouth curves up more.

"Is she drooling?" Akara tells me while we stare at our girlfriend.

"I think she's blushing."

Sulli blushes more, then kicks the reddish sand at Akara's ankles. "If I'm drooling, it's over *Banks*."

I laugh.

Akara laughs at first too, but as soon as she spins around, his smile slowly vanishes.

"She's kidding," I remind him.

He pushes a hand through his hair. "Yeah, I know…"

Does he?

Sulli only notices Akara is second-guessing that interaction when she's already on her paddleboard. Momentum glides her further out into the water. "Kits? Fuck. What's wrong?"

"Nothing!" Akara shouts as she drifts away.

I call out, "He doesn't think you drool over him!"

Akara shoves my arm like I pants-ed him in front of our girlfriend. "*Banks*."

"What? It's *true*."

"Semi-true."

"True enough."

Sulli paddles closer to the shore, digging her oar in the water. "I was wrong, Kits."

He grimaces. "No, I'm being sensitive."

"You can be fucking sensitive," she says. "There's nothing wrong with that."

He winces more. Like this whole exchange is a shot to his ego.

I try not to laugh.

Akara notices, and he smiles, "Shut up, Banks."

I can't kill my laughter.

Sulli suddenly declares, "I wasn't drooling over anyone. Not you, not Banks. No fucking one. Because I, Sullivan Minnie Meadows, don't fucking drool."

"Mic drop," I say.

Akara is smiling more.

"Okay? We're okay?" Sulli asks for confirmation.

"Of course we are," Akara says strongly.

I think he should talk to her about his insecurities. But he'd rather not cast doubt in our triad. Like if he surfaces that shit, it'll detonate the three of us, and all he wants is the three of us standing at the end together.

Maybe he's thinking he'll get over it on his own.

I'm not even a relationship expert, and I know pretending everything is okay isn't better than hashing out the things that eat at you.

"Banks?" Sulli asks.

"I'm good, mermaid."

She's smiling, then paddles towards the center of the river.

Akara continues fiddling with my life vest.

I'm staring through him.

He's tense. "Don't look at me like that."

"Like what?"

"Like I screwed up."

"If you're jealous of me—"

43

Banks Moretti

"I'M NOT JEALOUS," he whispers tightly, running another hand through his hair. "It's my crap to sort through."

"And you can't sort it through with her because…?"

"I'm sorting through it with you." He slaps my arm lightly.

I withhold a smile. "Like I said before, I'm not the one you need to fucking talk to about this. It's your relationship with *her* that you're second-guessing."

He winces at that word. "I'm not second-guessing me and Sulli. Not even a fraction of a fraction, Banks. And that's why I don't think I should bring this up. You know how many different ways I could screw the wordage? It's not a simple thing. It's a *feeling*. Not jealousy. I just feel…" He shakes his head, unable to articulate the grinding emotion. "And then she'll be afraid I might leave or I'm questioning what we have—when that's *not it*."

"Then tell her that."

He exhales a strained noise and watches Sulli paddle in circles. Waiting for us. "I know I have to…I'll talk to her…I will."

"Now."

"Later," he decrees. "I'll do it later."

"Nine—"

"I just want to enjoy today. This."

Alright.

I get that. So I stop pushing.

He finishes with my life vest.

"You try to mess with my balance, you're going in the water," I warn him. "I have a longer wingspan, and I'll tank your ass in seconds."

"I won't mess with you." He's smiling. "You next."

Me next?

I check the unsteady river, then the solid ground. Then look to Akara. "You scared I'll stay on the shore?" *I'm thinking about it.*

"No." He holds my gaze. "I just don't want to leave you behind."

That gets to me for a solid second, and I take my emotions with me to the board. Ankle deep in the cool water, I hoist myself onto my knees, grab an oar, and paddle into the river. *Alright, Banks Roscoe Moretti, stand your tall ass up.*

I pretend like I'm on solid land, and I climb to my feet.

Oh shit.

Unstable. Rocking.

I careen over, face first into the water. Not cold, but not too warm. When I hike myself back on the board, Ryke uses his oar to steady the board for me. "Try again," he coaches. "Crouch lower. Hold a squat if you can, and then when you feel steady, you can stand up fully."

Water dripping off my temples, I try to stand up again. Doing as instructed. This time, it's easier. My feet wobble like I'm on a teeter-totter, but I don't fall into the river.

"Good job," Ryke says. "It's going to be harder for you, since you're so fucking tall. Lower center of gravity helps with balance."

I nod stiffly, trying to focus on my balance but my mind travels someplace else. Ryke coaching me like I'm his kid. I imagine it's in his nature. He'd do it for just about anyone that needed help—even his brother—but it feels different today.

Maybe because he knows I'm going to be a dad to his grandkid.

Maybe because he's a better father figure to look up to than my old man.

I hold that thought as he plunges his oar in the water. "Just keep doing that and you won't fall in," he tells me. "But it doesn't really fucking matter if you do. Dais and Nona try to fall off—"

A splash catches both of our attention. Sure enough, his youngest daughter is in the river, while Daisy attempts a handstand on the board. Seconds later, she tumbles into the water.

Ryke smiles as he paddles over to his wife and daughter.

Akara and Sulli paddle next to me, on either side. Wedging me in the middle. I do my best to stay upright. "I didn't order a sandwich."

Sulli grins. "But you're the peanut butter to our bread."

"We'd be bland without you," Akara jokes.

I crack a smile. "You're full of shit."

He laughs, then asks Sulli, "Is Banks crunchy or creamy?"

"Crunchy," Sulli says like it's not even a contest.

He nods to me. "She wants your nuts."

"Kits!" Sulli splashes him with her paddle.

He splashes back. As the middle of their sandwich, I'm being doused with the most water. It's amusing, but not as amusing as me leaning over and pushing Akara in the water.

He goes down with a louder *splash*.

Sulli gasps with a smile. "You didn't."

"I warned him."

I also see Kitsuwon swimming near our girlfriend. She doesn't notice. Not until he catches her ankle and yanks her in the river. Waves buck my paddleboard, and I slip off in seconds.

Daisy, Winona, Ryke, and Price drift further away where the river bends, and they disappear out of sight. For a moment, it's just the three of us wading in deep water. Laughing. Splashing.

Sun glistening on the water, sparkling against her eyes and his eyes. Red rocks jutting up to the bright blue sky around us—and for as open and wide as the world is, for as endless as the Colorado River flows, this place feels like ours. Secluded in nature and time, and I could spend eternity here with them.

We hang onto the paddleboards like floats. Letting the current carry us downstream as we face one another. Her legs brush up against my legs. His arm skims my arm, and I wipe water out of my eyes as the sun shines brighter.

In the calmness of this moment together, Sulli asks, "You ever think about marriage, Kits?"

He skims her, then me, "Why aren't you asking Banks this too?"

She winces. "Fuck, I kind of mentioned it to him. But he said we should wait to talk."

Realization washes over Akara.

She adds fast, "It wasn't a long conversation. I don't even really know how Banks feels."

"That's true," I tell him.

"Hey, it's okay. You guys can talk about stuff without me. But I appreciate being included in this one." Now's a good time to bring up *his* insecurities, but maybe he'd rather do it alone. Without me here as a crutch. "What about marriage?"

"Did you guys ever see yourselves getting married? Before me? Before our triad?"

"I mean," Akara starts with a sigh, his wet hair pushed out of his face. "I'd be lying if I said *no*." He looks more intensely on Sulli. "If things were different, we'd be married by now."

Her eyes grow. "Really? Already?" She looks infatuated with him.

"Yeah. I would've pulled a move when it felt right, and you'd be shocked and maybe you'd say yes—I'd hope you'd say *yes*, or you'd freak out and say, *it's too soon, Kits*. And I'd be like, *I'll save this for later then, Sul. Don't forget about me.*" He nods a few times, imagining that lost possibility.

My brows knot, hating that I'm the one who screwed this picture. "You two can still have that," I say, willing to give them that. 'Cause I love them, but damn me to hell if I can't have a romantic commitment too.

"Not without you," Akara says to me. "It doesn't work without you, Banks."

"But legally you two could—"

"Fuck legally," Sulli interjects. "What does it matter? It's a piece of paper. It's nothing. And it'll always leave someone out and we're *not* doing it by the books."

Water rushes around us. Pushing our boards and us closer. Our feet knock. Legs intertwine. A bird soars low over the horizon, and everything about this moment and her passion and our triad and our love makes me appreciate *life*. That I'm still living and breathing and able to experience *more* with the people I love the most in this god-forsaken world.

I nod, "I can get behind that, mermaid."

Akara is smiling. "Have you ever thought about marriage, Banks?"

"Not really. Before you two, I figured I'd be a good uncle. Maybe a bachelor for life."

"And now?" Sulli asks.

"Now a future is all I'm thinking about. And like Akara here, I'd pull the move when it feels right." I lift a shoulder. "Come what may."

Sulli tries to restrain an overcome smile. "Spiritually, we can do the whole marriage thing? It's not out of the question for us?"

"Is that something you'd want?" I ask her now.

"Yeah…yeah, I want to have a binding commitment. Something that joins the three of us for life. Maybe a ceremony that's just one-hundred percent Kitsulletti."

We're all grinning at the sound of our ship name that Sulli speaks into the air.

Her smile fades at a thought. "But…I don't want to rush anything just because of the cinna-bun. Your proposals—if you fucking propose—could be years from now. Maybe it should be."

Akara and I exchange a quick look. We can wait.

He tells her, "You'll forget about it and be surprised when it does come."

Sulli is all smiles, and I'd say this is turning out to be one of my favorite trips. Once we've drifted long enough, she climbs back on the board. Akara starts teasing her again.

They laugh.

Splash.

He tips her board over.

She crashes into the water. Popping up laughing, and I'm thankfully on *my* board without flopping over like a dead seal.

Oorah.

I stand up.

Sulli and Akara are done fuckin' around, back on their boards. Sulli kneels, wringing out her wet hair. Akara sobers for a second. He stands up tensely.

Something's wrong.

She eyes him with a heavy frown.

"Nine?" I call out. "What's wrong?"

"Kits?" Sulli stands, oar in her hand as the current keeps drawing us downstream.

Akara paddles, but not hard enough that I can't keep up. "I probably shouldn't have done that. *Shit.*" We're out of reach to slug him.

Sulli paddles to the other side of Akara, so he's the middle of the sandwich. "What do you mean?"

His eyes fall to her belly. Even if she wasn't wearing a life vest, she's too early along to be showing.

"You didn't hurt the cinnamon roll," Sulli tells him. "I'm fucking fine."

Akara wipes more water off his face.

"She's fine, Nine," I reiterate.

"Still," he breathes. "I can't be as rough with you. I have to remember that."

Sulli stares at the water, contemplating. "I guess things will change once I'm further along."

I'm planning on staying with her in the penthouse during her pregnancy. Even if we don't ever go out for the next eight months, I'm going to remain by her side. I know Akara will too, though he has other responsibilities with Studio 9 and the security team that will pull him away.

We paddle harder and catch up with her family. Rapids approaching, I concentrate on standing upright and not flipping.

Alright, I'm getting the hang of this.

One rapid through.

A few more are incoming, and I get tossed in the water a couple more times. But so does Ryke.

"That was the last rapid!" Daisy yells back, three meters ahead.

Thank the Lord.

I hoist my ass back on the board, the current floating me along as I kneel. Water drips off my hair and glides down my bare chest.

Sulli and Akara wait a couple meters ahead for me, already finished with the rapids. She's fully unzipped her life jacket and pulls the thing off, like her sister and mom. Letting the sun soak her skin.

I'm about to stand up on the board again when movement catches my eye on the bank.

A man.

Not an animal.

And he's pointing a telephoto lens towards us. Towards *Sulli*.

44

Banks Moretti

FUCK.

Fuck.

I grind my teeth, protective of her, and I paddle closer and I keep thinking, *here?*

In Moab?

I shouldn't be surprised paparazzi got wind of our location, but I didn't realize they'd drag their asses all the way to the Colorado River for the Meadows family. I'm not saying they never have, but they're just more likely to follow Lily and Lo.

The Hales.

Not the Meadows.

Without a radio to call this into Akara, I paddle faster to him.

He must've made a joke because Sulli's laughing so hard she's snorting. He raises his brows at her before swinging his head to me. "I told her..." His voice fades as he sees the look on my face. "Banks?"

"Six o'clock."

He looks over my shoulder, and his lips form a line. Nose flared.

Sulli frowns. "What is it?"

"Paparazzi," I tell her.

She gapes. "What the fuck? They came all the way out here?" She tries to spot them. "Moffy isn't even here..." She explains to me, "They like money-shots of Moffy when he's around my dad to perpetuate the whole paternity rumors."

I nod, knowing that "fun fact" already.

We float further away from the camera. Quiet. Akara and I keep an eye on the man, until he's out of sight. Desert bushes hide the road beside the river. But I'm guessing he's in a car now.

Sulli is deep in thought until she says, "We're always going to be as famous as my Aunt Lily and Uncle Lo." It's a tender realization.

Something that had weight months ago, but the knowledge floats on the river with us. All we can do is ride the rough currents. We knew from the beginning we couldn't fight it.

"Yeah," Akara breathes into a whisper, wind stirring around us. "This is how it's going to be."

I nod a few times. "We'll protect you," I tell our girlfriend. "And we're gonna protect our cinnamon roll."

She tries to smile hearing me say the code name. "Yeah…I know."

We share each other's company. Paddling in silence. The air is still light. Even if my head is on a swivel now. The water seems to go on and on forever, but we choose a spot to hop off.

Headed to the bank, I'm in shallow water and pull the board further up the dirt. Ryke, Daisy, Sulli, and Winona are way ahead of me, unclipping their dry bags and taking big gulps from canteens.

Akara sips from his own and then his attention swings to the Triple Shield boss. "Hey, Price," Akara calls out. "We have some intel."

Price lets out a heavy sigh as he drags his kayak up the bank. "If this is about the paparazzi, I already have Greer and Wylie on it." His eyes ping from Akara to me. "You two are here as boyfriends, right?"

I grind my teeth. *Don't interject. Keep your mouth shut, Banks.*

Akara caps his canteen, seriousness drawing his brows together. "If I see a threat, I'm still going to report it. No matter if I left my radio in the van or not."

Price has stricter features. "It's hard to tell what you are, Kitsuwon. The lines have blurred *considerably*."

Alright, fuck him for talking to Nine like that.

"Respectfully—" I start.

A hand clamps on my shoulder. I barely glance back to see it's Ryke. Fuck, I did not expect her dad to jump into security shit.

I shut up again.

His eyes aren't on me though. He's staring hard at Price. I suddenly realize our conversation was loud enough for Ryke, Daisy, Sulli, and Winona to hear.

"Price," Ryke breathes. "We've been through a lot together over the years."

Price nods. "Yeah, we have." Something passes between them. Decades. I don't know what it's like to be a bodyguard that long, but it must forge something unbreakable between them.

"So I don't fucking say this lightly," Ryke says. "But you need to start looking at Akara and Banks differently. They're Sulli's bodyguards, but they're also my sons."

His sons.

Akara and I share a look that nearly bowls me over.

Didn't think we'd get here.

But damn it feels good.

Price's mouth draws down before he lets out a long breath. "You're right…" He nods over and over. "I know you're right."

"Change is fucking hard," Ryke tells him. "But we're all going through it. I just don't want tension between your firm and Akara's. Otherwise, I'm going to have to make a decision that I shouldn't have to fucking make." It's not a threat. Not even a warning. Just the truth.

If Ryke is forced to pick a side between Triple Shield and Kitsuwon Securities, he's going to choose family. He's going to choose Akara.

I feel my lips begin to lift.

Yippee-ki-yay motherfucker.

I'm not gonna shove a win in someone's face, as much as I'm internally gloating. Usually I'm around some ego-boosting, pie-shoving asshole that I'd call a friend—and usually that's a Yale boy, and fuck, do I miss the rest of SFO.

They would've loved this moment.

Color is already draining from Price's cheeks. Can't imagine this is easy for Ryke or for him. I don't envy their positions, and it's why I'm happy I don't call the shots.

"Did taking two dicks hurt though?" Winona's whisper becomes awkwardly audible as the wind dies down.

Ryke goes motionless like someone just threw a grenade at his feet. I scratch the back of my head, doing the thing I shouldn't do—and I'm making eye contact with her dad.

He's glaring like he's partially in shock but mostly protective, and I read his expression as, *you hurt my daughter, you're fucking dead.*

I did not hurt your daughter with my cock, sir—that is what I don't fucking say. Mostly because Akara is shooting me daggers to shut the fuck up.

Winona and Sulli stop chatting by their paddleboards. Sulli turns beet-red. "Oh fuck, fuck, *fuck.*" She's cringing.

Winona looks more protective of Sulli. "It's not a big deal, Dad. It's her sex life—she can do what she wants, and if she wants to take two—"

"Nona," Akara cuts in like she's signing our death warrants. "Please stop talking."

"I'm Team Kitsulletti, Akara," she reminds him passionately. "Dad should be too, and so I don't see what's wrong if Sulli likes having you and Banks—"

"He's supportive, squirt," Sulli jumps in now, and I'm trying not to laugh. God, I love how strange my life is.

Winona is uncertain.

"Like *totally* fucking supportive," Sulli emphasizes. "He just doesn't need the details."

Ryke rubs his eyes with a nod. "I heard nothing." He's walking off in a hurry towards the street like maybe he can outrun the past conversation.

"*Mom,*" Sulli whisper-hisses.

Daisy waves at her. "He's already wiping it from his memory." She quickly follows his pace to go talk to him, and Sulli turns to us.

She mouths, *Sorry.*

I'm still laughing.

Akara sees and begins to laugh too.

Winona leans into Sulli and whispers again, "But did it hurt? Was it good?"

Was it good?

Our first time inside Sulli together. That's a night none of us will forget, not anytime soon.

45

Sullivan Meadows

"SULLIVAN, LOOK HERE!"

"SULLI, OVER HERE!"

"SULLIVAN!"

"SULLIVAN! YOU LOOK GREAT!"

"SULLI, RIGHT HERE!"

Paparazzi wail and bellow a version of the same taunting thing. Trying to capture my petrified gaze into their bright flashes and big lenses. They swarm like bees, buzzing around. Flapping their invisible wings and wielding their cameras like stingers. Fuck, I shield my eyes with my hand, keep my head low, just so I can concentrate on my feet.

One foot in front of the other.

One foot in front of the fucking other.

Aunt Lily told me to just keep moving. Don't pause for too long. And being my mother's daughter—*moving* and *speed* are familiar friends of mine.

Akara leads. Banks' hands clasp my waist behind me. Then extra security shields me from every other direction. I'm cocooned in a secure bubble—at least I pretend I am.

For a second.

On my way to the Jeep, I leave the Aquatic Center behind. Hair still wet, and chlorine is like perfume imprinted on my skin. Spirits are high after tonight's swim.

I beat my record in the 200m IM.

Nothing can bring me down. Not even the constant fucking shouts. The encroaching bodies. It's all background to the pride bubbling up in me.

Beating my time instills more *hope*. Hope that I'll do well this year at the Olympics. As we come up to the SUV, my feet stop cold.

No, *no*.

Fuck no.

Someone *defiled* Booger.

Across the passenger door, someone painted the words *SLUT* in red.

My stomach overturns. She's not a slut. And I'm not a fucking slut! I want to scream, but they're waiting for an epic meltdown.

Banks' back presses up against mine, his mouth dips to my ear. "Sulli, keep moving." My body reanimates.

"SULLIVAN! How do you feel about your car?!"

"ARE YOU ANGRY?!"

"LOOK HERE!"

I can't hide my ire and hurt. I'm giving the press *exactly* what they want. Enter-fucking-tainment. More photos to flame the gossip and news.

"BACK UP!" Akara shouts, pushing cameramen away who try to provoke a bigger reaction.

"BANKS, AKARA!" they shout. "HOW DO YOU FEEL KNOWING YOUR GIRLFRIEND IS BEING CALLED A SLUT?!"

Heat radiates off Akara.

Banks is a solid brick behind me. I can't see either of their expressions, but their body language screams, *fuck off* and *fuck you*.

I'm curved more inward, and I'd flip paparazzi the bird—but I'm enjoying my safe fucking bubble too much to reach an arm out.

But fuck, how I *hate* after three long months, my relationship is still so newsworthy.

I knew this would happen.

Yeah, but I didn't think Booger would pay the price. I don't think Adam Sully imagined his Jeep would end up here like this.

I suck in a breath and when I'm near the car, I climb into the backseat. Akara drives. Banks takes the passenger.

I let them concentrate on leaving the parking lot through the flashes, the bodies, the screaming. The arduous, panic-inducing process takes a good fifteen minutes. By the time we're on the road, Banks finally rotates to look at me. "Sulli—"

"I'm fine," I say sharply. "I won't let them fuck up a good night." Media has taken a lot from me these past few months. They won't take this fucking feeling, too.

"You sure you're okay?" Akara asks, glancing through the rearview at me. "That was effing hectic."

"No more hectic than it's been, Kits." I take out a water bottle from my gym bag.

"The Jeep…" Akara starts.

I shrug, words stuck in my throat.

"I'll repaint Booger," Banks tells me. "She'll be good as new."

"Thanks," I say softly, lost in thought for a second. "It's fucking weird, right?"

"What is?" Banks asks while Akara pulls into the parking deck to the apartment complex.

"I think I might be getting used to this. The…madness of it all." I take a small sip of water and recap the bottle.

Banks nods slowly. "Our new normal."

"In this new normal," Akara says, "we should probably not leave Booger in random parking lots anymore."

I want to tell him that the Aquatic Center isn't "random" but I get his point. She's going to be cooped up in the parking garage more now than ever. Sadness washes over me because I think Adam Sully would rather have his Jeep defiled with the word "Slut" than gathering dust in a garage.

But I can't lose this Jeep, and if that means keeping her safe for a little while, I'll do it.

ON THE ELEVATOR UP TO THE PENTHOUSE, WE'VE
been joking about the paparazzi.

"They have a hard-on for us," Banks says, his arm around me as we ascend.

"Obsessed," Akara agrees.

"And we're blue-balling them," I grin.

Akara smiles. "I'm a whore for blue-balling paparazzi."

"You have a half-chub then?" I nudge his arm.

They laugh, and Akara says, "I'm only fully erect for one babe." Akara is undressing me with his eyes, and I feel exposed in the best, most tempting fucking way. What's sad is that this is about to end. They'll say goodbye to me and head three-floors below to wash off today and prepare for tomorrow.

I'm not ready.

Between my boyfriends, I face Akara, "You're a whore for me then?"

He stares down at me. "The biggest whore." He drops his lips to my ear, but I feel him staring at Banks with a grin—and I strangely *love* that. How the three of us always connected, Banks' arm still around me, Akara still engaged with him as he whispers to me, "For your pussy. For your heart." He lifts my chin with two fingers. "For your lips."

Please fucking kiss me, Kits.

He tilts his head, bending closer. He whispers against my mouth, "For your tits." He squeezes my boob, and I pulse between my legs.

I understand how Akara is a sex god to women. He's the playful, dominant fuck that toys with tender places and alights craving pieces.

And he's teasing. Pulling away with a greater smile.

"You're fucking evil," I rasp.

He grins. "You'll thank me for the foreplay later."

"Later?" I glance between them.

Banks is checking me out in a way that tingles my toes and veins. Like I'm unquestionably *hot*. Like he wants to bone me, and I would love for them to do just that.

Bone me. Fuck me.

Make sweet love to me.

"So you guys are…you're staying over?" I wonder.

Akara starts to frown. "You want us too, right?"

"Yeah, fuck *yeah*." I tuck my hair behind my ear. Hot all of a sudden. "You can use my shower too."

Banks' mouth curves up, and we're all sexy, horny things until we enter the penthouse. Until we skid to a stop in the living room.

No one is around, but one of my roommates left the television on—a late-night entertainment news show like TMZ plays footage of *me*.

And Akara.

And Banks.

They're in bodyguard-mode and pressing up against me as we leave the Aquatic Center. This footage is from *tonight*. Holy fuck, paparazzi work fast.

"…they won't speak to press about their relationship," the reporter says, "but there's been speculation on which one of her boyfriends will break up with Sullivan Meadows first. The pressure is intense, and there's just no feasible way Akara, Banks, and Sullivan will all stay together for that long."

I freeze, anger puncturing me again. Only this time, it's different. I'm *pissed* at the world. Not just at the paparazzi. "They can go eat shit," I curse hotly.

Banks is stewing too.

Akara tries to stay calm, but his impassioned eyes are flaming. Especially as the reporter says to the other awful journalist, "My money is on Sullivan breaking up with Banks. She has a clear relationship with Akara. They've probably been dating long before Banks even came around."

"Allegedly," the reporter notes.

I turn to Banks. "I'm *not* breaking up with you."

"I know that." He's scraping a hand across his hardened jaw. Superglued to the TV.

"We're blue-balling them, remember," Akara says to us. "They don't know what we're about—and even if they did, they'd still promote this division. It's more salacious than saying we're all *happy*."

The reporter seems to grow louder. "I give them till the end of the year. Whatever they're doing—it'll never work. They're probably fighting over Sullivan Meadows right now."

They're not.

"Joke's on them," Banks says coldly.

I can't listen to these fucking idiotic reporters slander us anymore. Akara grabs the remote before I can. He shuts off the TV.

I've never wanted to be wrapped between Akara and Banks more. Like a middle finger to the world, I take *both* of their hands in mine, and they end up leading me. Walking ahead of me.

I follow, but as soon as we're inside my dimly lit bedroom—the door closed—I spin around and touch Akara's belt more playfully, a little fucking desperately. I've just never wanted *them* so carnally, so emotionally, and I ache to feel their caring hands, the weight of their protection, their desirous eyes, their hot words of lust and love, of enduring and persevering—every fucking bit of them, on me and in me.

I tug at Akara's belt. "What a fucking strange contraption, Kits."

He takes my wrists in his hand. "Lady Meadows," he eyes me with a smile. "Surely you know what a belt is." He tilts his head. "Or at least what we could do with it."

I swallow hard.

Fuck yes.

Banks stands behind him, arms crossed, watching me. "Turn around, mermaid."

Turn around?

I suddenly concentrate on my surroundings and not just them. I sniff the sweet scent of the air, like I'm in a Krispy Kreme factory. "Is that...donuts?" I whirl around. Candles...about twenty scented *candles* line my dresser and weight bench. Light flickers romantically around my bedroom. Casting shadows on the turquoise quilt of my iron-framed bed.

Akara's fingers slip off my wrists, letting me leave his side.

I go to my dresser, finding a vase of wildflowers and a box of chocolate protein donuts. The candles are all *sprinkled donut* scented.

My heart clenches.

Reporters think I'd break up with one of them—that we're just here *fighting*. Tears nearly prick my eyes. I know some days take work, but that's how *all* relationships go, even monogamous ones.

"You both did this?" I ask, swept up in the gesture.

"Technically, Akara," Banks says. "Since I've been on your detail all day."

"It was both our plan," Akara states. "He called me when you beat your time."

They're celebrating my time. My achievement today.

I wipe at my watery eyes. "This is seriously the sweetest fucking thing." I take in their confident postures. Both tall, unyielding, and mine. Both look at me as if to say *I'll protect you until the end.* But Banks wears his pain on his body, and Akara wears his in his eyes.

"You deserve it," Banks tells me strongly.

I pick at the tape on the donut box. Doubt is a nasty fucking beast. "Even if I'm putting you two through hell?"

Banks shakes his head vigorously. "I'm not in hell."

"We chose this," Akara says with fire. "We *chose* you; we chose the world trying to pit us against each other—and they're putting us through nothing. Screw the reporters. Screw it all."

Banks has a shadow of a smile seeing my smile appear.

"Screw me too, Kits?" I ask, voice raspy again.

"Screw you with love," he breathes. "With our hands. With our hearts." He draws closer, so does Banks, and I watch with rapt attention as Akara comes up behind me. As Banks comes up in front of me.

I'm wedged between their tall, muscular builds, and as their eyes stroke, as their hands travel with careful, slow affectionate need over my body, we're no longer just sexy, horny things.

We're uncompromising, vulnerable, burning things.

Heat crawls over my skin, their large palms blazing a fervor in my blood. Banks kisses me—yearning, gripping, blistering kisses exchange between our stinging lips. And Akara melds into my back, his hands driving down my breasts, down to my pussy. His hardness grows against me.

Clothes.

We're still dressed. "I haven't showered yet," I rasp as their hands continue to move, as Akara's lips trail breathy, hot lines across the nape of my neck.

I shudder. *Fuuck yes.* "I smell...like chlorine."

Very huskily, Banks says, "I like that smell. It reminds me of you." He pulls the band out of my hair, wet strands cascading over my shoulders.

"Same," Akara breathes, closing his lips over a tender spot.

They like that stuffy chemical smell because of me. "Well...fuck," I almost moan.

They're both smiling. Akara's fingers brush along the line of my broad shoulders, pushing aside the thin strap of my tank top. The fabric slips.

I clutch Banks' waistband as they push in closer, my knuckles brushing his radio. While Banks unties my sweatpants, I relax my head on Akara's shoulder. Akara kisses me from that angle, and I'm basking in his sensual tongue, in the way they both clutch me. Grip me. Love me.

My body hums for more.

They undress me, and I intake this moment. Welded between Akara and Banks—two men I once doubted were even attracted to me, and now they pull off my shirt, snap off my bra, pull down my sweatpants. Their gazes and hands setting me on fire.

"Step," Akara breathes.

I step out of them. Cold barely nips my skin. Sweat has already built. No bra, my nipples visibly harden and my breath shallows.

Their hunger isn't just primal hunger for any flesh. They're longing for *me*, Sullivan Minnie Meadows—and I'm giving all of myself to them. To do whatever they fucking please. Because I know, really, our desires are intertwined into a tether of unbearable tension. One that's begging for an explosion, a euphoric fucking release.

Consumed with each other, Banks slides his hand up my neck, to my jaw and gathers a fistful of damp hair while Akara tracks his hands down my ass beneath my panties. He shifts his hands forward, fingertips brushing my clit.

"Fuck," I cry.

They kiss my body. Arousal, desire, and something deeper overwhelms me.

Akara moves his hands to my breasts but leaves my nipples aching. Untouched.

"Kits," I plead.

Banks lets go of my hair, cupping his full, large hand against my heat. Sky-blue panties still on, I just feel the pressure, and I quiver and pulse.

"Banks," I cry out.

"The mermaid must want more," Banks says in that deep, rough voice. He's speaking to Kits.

Akara leans over and takes a long, *hot* look at my tits. "She wants me to suck her nipples." That lights me up too.

"Yes," I pant. "Fuck." I squirm as Banks rubs my panties.

Oh my fuck.

Electricity sparks in my skin, shooting energy through my body.

My nipples still ache for touch.

Akara thumbs one. He leans further over my shoulder and flicks his tongue over my sensitive, perked nipple. A shockwave ripples through me, and I tremble.

Oh fuck.

Standing and melting between them, I'm almost naked in their clutch. Should I be undressing them? I lose sight of where to move my hands, their shirts—their bodies, but they seem more entrapped with me. And I'm more entrapped with what they're doing *to* me. With how they handle me. With care, with fucking *passion*.

Their movements speed like they're reaching a breaking point with the toying and teasing. Kisses are hotter, rougher. They, too, need fucking more.

Banks scoops up my hair again and starts to tie off the strands in a high messy bun. They seem coordinated. In sync.

Like they both know how this night is going to go, and I'm left at the mercy of their plans.

It stimulates me to the core, and I squeeze my thighs together, wetness building between my legs. Panties still on, I'm grateful for them—Akara grips the cotton and yanks it to the floor.

Fuck. Breath catches in my lungs.

"Step," Banks tells me this time.

I step out of the last piece of clothing on me.

Just as I do, Banks' fingers slip up my thighs. "Jesus, Sulli," he whispers into a groan. He looks to Akara. "She's soaked."

"Please put them inside me," I beg. I want his touch. Their touch. I want my tits to be gripped hard and the feeling of being rocked against.

I want the thread between us wound so intricately, so strongly that no one—and nothing—can unravel what we've fucking tied.

Banks presses his forehead to mine, our lips achingly close as he whispers, "Not yet."

Not yet.

"Put her on the bed," Akara breathes, his voice utterly fucking sexy. I'm consumed by those words and the way Banks lifts me up over his shoulder like a sack of naked potatoes.

"I'm going to get your fingers," I tell Banks.

"You're gonna get more than my fingers, Sulli," he says huskily.

Holy fucking fuck. I want to sink into this moment and never come out. By the time Banks tosses me onto the soft, velvet turquoise quilt, I'm a pile of trembling mush.

I spread my legs open for them.

Their muscles flex, chests rising and falling in aroused breath. I knock my knees together, then swing them back open.

They both seem to force themselves away from the bed. Like I'm a siren calling them into the water to their demise.

"Are we going to…?" I trail off, watching Banks pry off his gun, his radio. Akara does the same, working carefully as they store their weapons.

Next to come off are their clothes.

Banks yanks his tee over his head. Akara sheds his pants. I eat up their bodies that come into clearer view. Akara's inked shoulder and upper-chest, and the lines of his sculpted abs. Banks' muscular build, the hair that tracks down to his bulging package, molded against navy boxer-briefs. And Akara's V-line that points towards his hardened cock, hidden behind black boxer-briefs.

"Are we going to what?" Akara asks, sliding his boxer-briefs down. He's totally naked, his erection standing at attention. I imagine him filling me.

I breathe, "Are we going to bone?"

He smiles. "You want his boner?"

"And yours." I eye them, breathing heavier. "I really want to feel close. I want you back on me. I want you up against me. I want you inside me. I never want you to leave me."

"I'm not going anywhere," Banks promises.

"I'm here," Akara whispers. Like he can see that's not enough, he repeats, "I'm here, *I'm here. I'm here.*" His words breathe into my spirit. Lifting me.

Banks removes his last piece of clothing. He's so hard, and I'm so fucking wet. What a great fucking combo. *Let's go.* Condoms are out. Condoms are on. They exchange looks to each other. They actually whisper to each other.

Planning something.

I writhe into the quilt, hips bucking, and my hand travels down my belly, nearing my clit.

"Get her," Akara tells him.

Banks scoops me in his arms, and instinctually, my legs wrap around his waist, his lips are on mine, and we're kissing with forceful need again. Until I feel him climb further onto the bed with my ass in his hands, and I break for breath and see where I'm going.

He's on his knees, and he tucks me to his chest. Swiftly, he's on his back, lying flat against the mattress, and I'm straddling him, lowering closer to his muscular build.

Banks' hand encases my cheek, our foreheads close. "You ready to take us both, mermaid?"

Shock lies beneath utter desire. I practically *moan* thinking about Akara and Banks being inside me together. With candlelight flickering, with this string of vulnerability twisting around our hearts and souls, and I nod quickly. "I'm fucking..."

Ready. The word is lost as I look up into the mirror, the one that lies above the short, iron headboard. Akara has climbed onto the bed. A bottle of lube is in his hand.

He's staring straight into my melting gaze with the same emotional look Banks is giving me. The look that says, *I love you, Sulli. We're going to take care of you and make you feel good, Sulli. Breathe, Sulli.*

"You're fucking what?" Akara asks.

"Ready," I breathe, watching him through the mirror as he lubes his erection with two strokes. Oh my *fuck.* They've never done double penetration before, but they seem confident. I doubt they'd even try if they weren't.

I grind a little against Banks. Wanting friction and fullness and closeness and *them.*

He sits up some and stares down at me. He has my ass in his hands. I cling to his gaze. To Akara's gaze through the mirror. Watching as Banks lifts me up and *carefully* sinks me onto his hardness.

I gasp, another noise catching. "*BanksBanksBanks.*" I careen forward into him. Forehead on his shoulder, I shudder.

"Sulli?" he pauses, breathing heavier. "Talk to me."

"Holy fuck." *It's a lot.* The instant pressure tenses my body.

"Sulli." He's about to pull me off, but I dig my fingers into his bicep and moan, "Keep fucking going." My eyes roll at the building sensitivity. I try to add friction, to take more of him inside me.

"She's okay," Akara breathes, massaging the small of my back.

I clench around Banks, and he curses into a low grunt. And he tells Akara, "She's fuckin' swollen around my cock."

Akara smiles, his gaze meeting mine in the mirror as he says, "She's about to feel swollen around two cocks."

I pulsate.

Banks stifles another groan.

"Please, thrust. Fucking thrust." I want mind-blistering orgasms to ripple through me. I want their bodies closer than close.

Banks doesn't move though.

I whimper.

He kisses my cheek. "We're going to thrust. Just hold on."

We're.

I'm glued to that word.

Banks lowers his elbows to the mattress. I'm practically attached to his chest. Following the movement, and he draws my hips further down onto him.

I take more of Banks between my legs. My breath hitching, I watch him disappear into me. Instead of thrusting or rocking against me, he reaches between our bodies and circles my clit with his thumb. I quake and cry into his chest.

"*Fuckfuck.*" I'm lit up and waiting for Akara.

I feel his waist pressed up against my ass. He now holds my hips instead of Banks. Candlelight casts more shadows on us, and the dizzying smell of donuts mixes with their musk and something feminine.

Akara bends forward, just to kiss me. Tongue slipping into my mouth, hands carving lines down my body. When he breaks away, he says, "Take a breath for me."

I inhale and watch him through the mirror.

He's knelt behind my ass. He glances to Banks, they speak through these brief glances, then Kits breathes, "Relax, Sul."

"I'm trying," I rasp, the anticipation swelling up inside me. Banks is literally *in* me. It takes everything not to grind against Banks. Not to dig deeper.

I watch Akara run a hand along my ass. I feel the cool sensation of lube on my skin.

His deep brown eyes lock with mine, and it feels like I'm lost in those beautiful orbs. His black hair falls a little in his eyelashes. "If anything hurts at any time," he says, "what do you say?"

"Octopus," I say my safe word that I've been using since Akara started tying me up more often. "Or *That really fucking hurts.*"

"Good." Akara runs a hand down my leg. "Now breathe."

I let out a soft breath. Inhale. Exhale.

Banks stops touching my clit when Akara slowly slides into me. I'm suddenly aware he's bigger than the toy I've used as practice. The fullness is too much for a moment, and my eyes cinch tight. After a second, I let out a breath and try to relax. New sensations build up through me. I moan a little into Banks' neck, and he strokes hair out of my face as Akara flexes into me.

"Sul?" Akara asks, seeing me twitch, maybe.

"Fuck," I curse, shaking. This feeling…is unlike anything. We're all soaking in the way we're together, and their necks strain like they're doing *everything* not to take me hard and deeper. What we're all craving, but I'm betting it'd be too much—because this is *a ton.*

Akara takes a risk and rocks in and out a little more.

I see him fuck me through the mirror, and Banks thrusts up into me. I breathe like I'm climbing Everest, the peak of all peaks. "I… *fuck*," I cry.

Akara drinks me in. "*Sulli.*" He rests his hands on the bed, pounding a little deeper. And that movement brings me further onto Banks.

"*Fuck*," he curses. "Akara."

"I'm okay," I choke out. "Don't stop."

Banks holds my head while I lie against him. And Akara melds into my back, into my body, and I love this feeling. I cling onto them, not wanting to reach the summit.

Not wanting to see the end.

Love and lust churns through my body in a hypnotic chorus with their groans and grunts. And soon, they're breathing out, *I love yous*, and *harder* and *deeper* and even though they can't deepen the movement without hurting me—we do go deeper. We're the deepest we've ever been. My spirit and my soul—the two of them are coiled and fused around everything I am.

"*Kits*," I cry. "*Banks*." My back arches. Toes curl, tears squeeze out of my eyes. I come as soon as they choke out my name.

Carefully, they both pull out. I'm in a daze. Dizzy. Lightheaded.

"You alright?" Banks ask, sweat caked on his body. "You hurt anywhere?"

I shake my head. We're heaps on the bed, our legs tangled, and I roll partially onto his chest, not wanting to leave. Akara splays an arm over my ass. He's checking out my whole body. Assessing.

"Am I intact, Kits?"

"I think your pussy and ass will survive," he teases.

I smile, having little energy to kick him. Though, sadness overtakes me. Sad that this has ended. And I ask, "You think..." I redden. *You got this far, Sulli*. Might as well ask now. But they seem a lot older all of a sudden, and replaying what we just did—them inside me—heats me up again. "Can one of you be inside me when we go to sleep?" I see their confusion, and I talk fucking fast, "I just want to feel as close to you...is that wrong?"

I avoid hiding under the quilt and sheets, but fuck, I want to hide.

46

Banks Moretti

WE ASSURED SULLI HER idea was okay, but I've never been inside a girl in the middle of the night. Neither has Akara, apparently, but the idea fisted my cock. Akara even got hard as we talked it over. After we showered and ended up back in bed with Sulli. We did the mature fucking thing to see who'd be inside our girlfriend while we sleep.

We played rock-paper-scissors.

I lost.

Fuckin' predictable. But I almost like this better. All of us on our sides, she usually sleeps facing me, but tonight, Sulli's back is curved against my chest. And while I hold her, her leg is hiked over Akara's waist, and she hugs onto him like a koala to a tree.

He gives me a brief glance like, *this is going to be hard*. He's probably half-erect, at least.

I start to smile. He asked for the struggle.

Akara rolls his eyes, but we're both watching Sulli nestle between us, comfortable. Safe. I've never felt closer to her or him.

Our love tonight is a big *fuck you* to anyone who says we're a disaster. The only thing we are is *enduring*. We're the things that'll crawl through the tragedies—the things that'll come up for air in the end.

I fall asleep.

Not sure for how long. A couple hours. Three or four, and then I feel movement.

Sulli shifts her hips a little. I hear her soft breaths. The bed creaks. And slowly, I open my eyes. They're awake. I lift up the quilt and see Sulli pushing into him, then backing her ass into me.

I harden.

Akara whispers, "Sul." He's trying to still her grinding, but she's clawing towards him, and then his eyes meet mine with an apologetic look as he fucks our girlfriend against me.

Go right on ahead.

I'm not trying to fuckin' sleep or anything.

Joking. Not sure if the humor lands inside my head this time, but I'm the only audience member. So fuck it.

While the bed rocks and he pushes her against me with each thrust forward, I slip Akara a look, not sorry about this. Hell, I wouldn't have lasted as long as him—and I expected a round two, but the reality is a boiling inferno compared to whatever I cooked in my brain.

I prop my elbow on the pillow and hold her hip with my other hand. She moans into his neck.

His nose flares, and I feel their heat build under the sheets. I'm hard as a rock, but I'm content letting this one go down on its own. Sulli reaches back for me—she must feel me hardening—but I splay her hand on him and whisper against her ear, "Finish what you two started, mermaid."

"Banks—"

"I'll get mine later." Another fucking time. Not everything *has* to be perfectly equal in the moment. I don't need to go again, and this is more than enough.

I just want to hold her.

She curls more against me, and Akara pumps in a rhythm that feels like we're on a boat. Swaying together, and I honest-to-fucking-God fall asleep to the calming tempo of their love.

Celebrity Crush – August 12ᵗʰ

Exclusive Photos: Sullivan Meadows Caught with a Baby Bump?!

Wow, does *Celebrity Crush* have news for you! We've obtained *exclusive photos* of Olympic gold medalist, Sullivan Meadows, in Canyonlands and Moab with her family. The clearest photos come from a sunny, sweaty paddleboarding sesh with her boyfriends. And Sullivan appears a little...well, shall we say bloated? Her stomach is 100% more swollen than usual. Is a baby on board? And if so, who's the father? Akara Kitsuwon or Banks Moretti? As expected, fans of the families are already criticizing the theories to these photos. But we smell a coverup. What are they hiding? Since her bump is relatively small, some fans think this could be the case of a hearty morning meal. Sullivan is out of training now that she's won her gold, after all.

What do you think? Preggers or not? Check out the photos below to make your own decision!

47

Akara Kitsuwon

NOW

@cobaltempire4ever: This is so dumb. Her stomach is barely big. Y'all need to grow up. #MeadowsBaby

@ravenhowl: Like this is the definition of bodyshaming. Leave Sulli alone! #MeadowsBaby

@Lilosupremacy: She's not pregnant. Period. Drop it. Stop fueling the media's gross obsession with this. #MeadowsBaby

@CoKeisCool: Def food baby. #MeadowsBaby

@raisinsrule21: I dunno. Sullivan Meadows could be pregs. #MeadowsBaby

I scroll through the tweets on my phone. Brows drawn together. I should feel ten-feet high that fans are actually defending Sul, especially since she really *wasn't* showing in Moab. But I'm pissed that the paparazzi took photos of her.

Pissed they're dissecting her body.

Pissed that her being pregnant is now in conversation, making it harder to keep the truth from spilling.

Sulli munches on a bag of chocolate-coated, powdered-sugar-dusted cereal and reads over my shoulder. Her lips downturn. "Maybe I'm going to have to hole up in the penthouse earlier than we fucking expected."

I don't want that for her. To become a recluse because of our baby, but I can't promise this won't blow over. She's almost eight-weeks pregnant now—the baby the size of a blueberry (Sulli Googled it on the car ride here). And the intensity of the press, the media, the world will explode when she does start showing.

Right now, Sulli and I are sitting in the third row of an old but beloved theatre in New York. Popular rock bands frequently play here, and today, The Carraways are auditioning drummers on stage.

Potential drummers stand in a long line that streams through the aisle and out the double doors. Most are cradling drumsticks and nerves as they anxiously await their turn.

The Carraways aren't a small punk band anymore. Their label houses big named alt-rock bands that fill arenas and sell-out international tours. And they're currently promoting the crap out of Tom and company. I saw *four* posters of Tom's skull-and-crossbones half-painted face on bus stops while driving here.

I keep an eye on the drummers. Once they're vetted by security, they're allowed to take a seat in the back of the theatre.

Banks had to help his Uncle Joe fix some old Mustang, so I'm alone on Sulli's detail.

And I'm aware she's here, now, to watch her cousin's band auditions so she can spend time with Luna before she does have to "hole up" at the penthouse.

"Upside," I tell her and reach into the bag of chocolate cereal. "You won't have to hear the rise and fall of The Carraways at Summer Fest."

As soon as I say the words, a horrible *clash* comes from the stage.

A white guy with a shaved head steadies the cymbal. "Oops. Sorry, fuck. I can try again?"

Tom Cobalt sits in the front row, two ahead of us. He seems more nervous than the drummers. "That's okay, dude. I think I've seen enough." He anxiously scans the line, hoping someone meets his impossible standards.

"Really? But—" He stops talking as Tom's bodyguard, Ian Wreath, walks over to escort him off the stage.

Sulli winces, then leans into my shoulder. "It's been an hour already, right? Fuck. Why are they all so bad?"

"Because they're trying out just to see Tom Cobalt." I pop the overly sweet cereal in my mouth. "They're all probably beginners or worse."

"It fucking sucks," Sulli grumbles.

I toss a piece of cereal at her nose. As it bounces off, powdered sugar remains. I laugh, and she elbows my ribs.

"Be fucking careful, Kits. You start a food fight with me, you start a war." She sticks her hand into the bag.

"Are you Sulli or is this Sulli's alter ego?"

She makes a confused face.

I smile more, tossing cereal in my mouth. "Pullivan the Powdered Sugar-Nosed Princess—" I grunt, then gasp as she slugs me *hard*. "Pullivan."

"The name is *Sullivan*." She's a close second from tearing the cereal box out of *my* hands and pouring the contents on my head. And I wouldn't mind that—but I just picture my dad sweeping my mom off her feet with an impromptu slow-dance and sweet, unexpected gestures like poetry and neck kisses.

And I'm tossing cereal into my girlfriend's face and calling her a powdered sugar princess.

I almost groan at myself.

What am I doing?

Ex-girlfriends—I never *teased* the way that I tease Sulli. Not to this extent. But I also never really *loved* any exes like I love Sulli. And it's not like I'm overly playful with every *friend* the way I am with Sulli either.

Flirting.

I'm flirting with her. How the heck did I never see that from the beginning?!

Denial.

Well, I'm not in denial anymore. I know what the hell I'm doing and *why* I'm doing it, but does she?

I chew cereal more slowly and sink back into the theatre seat.

"Kits?" Sulli touches my bicep where she punched. "Fuck, did I hurt you?"

"No." I try to force a smile, and I hate that too. I'm not okay—and she doesn't need me to try to be. Banks is right; I just need to be more open with Sulli. "This is hard for me," I breathe softly.

She frowns. "What is?"

I scan the theatre as a lanky drummer with a giddy, fanboy smile takes the stage. He's clearly infatuated with Tom.

Back to Sulli, I try to express what I know, "You think I'm better at relationships than Banks, but I'm not. Not really. And I feel like a *fudging* fraud every time I recognize how badly I actually suck." I shake the cereal box a little.

Sulli turns more towards me. "I mean, aren't you better than Banks? You've been in more relationships than him and me."

I shake my head a few times and try to keep my gaze on hers. "For every girlfriend I had, I don't think I ever let myself be that vulnerable. I understand how to make women feel good in bed. I knew sex, but I don't think I ever knew love." I extend my arm over her seat as she leans closer to me. "Until you. And I loved you before we ever slept together."

Sulli nods me on when I grow quiet.

"In past relationships, if something bugged me, I'd convince myself it's not a big deal and I'd just move on. Never make anything too personal. Everything's A-okay." I keep my voice quiet, even as the drummer bangs harshly. "I thought that made me the *ace* at relationships. There were never any big issues. But there was never anything under the surface either."

"That's the past, right?" Sulli tries to whisper. "That's not how you are with me, Akara." It's strange hearing her say *Akara* and not *Kits*.

Don't panic.

She's fine.

We're fine.

I take a breath. "You were my friend before my girlfriend, Sul, and I've always had an easy time talking to you about my dad. My life. But the crappier the media, the more hellish your surroundings, I find myself defaulting to bubble-wrapping you and keeping you out of *my* crap. And I'm scared I'm turning *us* into one of those surface things that you don't deserve."

"And things…things aren't okay between us?" Sulli questions.

Seeing her concern is what I hate, but I'm starting to realize these conversations are part of being in a relationship that runs deep.

That lasts.

"Things are okay," I reassure quickly, "but I can be insecure." I have to look away every few seconds when I wish I could just duct-tape myself to her green eyes.

Sulli chews her lip. "About my fucking love for you?"

"No," I say even faster. "No, I *know* you love me, Sul. You do a great job showing me you love me, and Banks does an effing *stellar* job showing his love for you. He runs circles around me, and I'm over here throwing your hair in your face, chucking cereal at you, pushing you off paddleboards—"

"I love all that," she interjects with certainty. "I've fucking *loved* that since I was sixteen."

My chest concaves, and our hands find each other. "We've talked about this before," I add quickly, almost *nervously*. Like I'm one of the panicked drummers lining up for the audition of a lifetime. Only, I've already auditioned for the role of Sulli's Boyfriend, and I'm *here*—so why am I freaking out? "On the sleigh ride, my birthday—you told me I don't need to be romantic any other way than I am."

"That's still true," she says strongly. "That hasn't fucking changed." She frowns. "But…something has changed with you?"

I push my black hair back. "I guess I just need you to know that whenever I tease you mercilessly—it's because I really *effing* love you.

Not as a friend or like some Kindergarten crush—I *love* you like a man loves a woman, like something eternally deep. And it might not feel that way when I call you string bean or steal your gummy worms, so if you want me to stop—"

"Never fucking stop, Kits," she interjects, eyes glassing. "I know your love is deep. It's never been some shallow thing to me." She brushes tears away. "Fuck, I don't know why I'm crying." She sniffs hard.

I breathe fuller breaths and find a napkin in my backpack for her to blow her nose into.

"Thanks," she mumbles. Blowing hard.

We laugh softly.

And she says, "You don't always need to be our rock, you know. You let Banks be there for you, and I want to be there for you too. And no matter how bad things get in the fucking world, I hope you feel like you can always talk to me."

I relax into that and nod. "I'll try to be better about it. I want to be."

She squeezes my hand. "Cut the bubble-wrap, Kits. Set me free."

I smile and lean in, cupping her cheek. "What if I just bubble-wrap the three of us together?"

"Sounds like love to me."

I press my lips to hers, deepening the kiss for a second. Her body bends closer, and no one records us or snaps photos. Anyone auditioning had to sign an NDA.

When we pull back, we stay close and listen to offkey music, and Sulli looks around.

I read her expression and eat a handful of cereal. "Banks isn't on his way yet."

She slumps. "I feel fucking guilty."

"For kissing me?"

"Yeah, and for spending the whole day alone with you. Like I need to make up this time so you two are okay—"

"We are okay, Sul." I curve my arm over her shoulders. "You don't need to stress about equal time between us or kissing us when one of us isn't here."

"I do fucking stress," she admits. "I don't want to cause ill-will or bad fucking feelings."

"It won't always be equal, and it doesn't need to be." Banks and I have already talked about it and come to this realization.

She's confused. "Are you sure?"

"Yeah, don't be paranoid about who kissed who and how many hours we spent alone with you. If it's bothering us, Banks and I will do something about it," I whisper. "We're two different people. We need different things at different times, and as long as all three of our needs are met, we're happy."

She eases more, smiling. "Thanks, Kits."

We're both feeling better.

I lean in to plant another soft kiss on her lips, just as another offkey drumbeat echoes throughout the room. Cringing, I pull away.

"Hey Hi Heidi Ho," Luna whispers as she slides into our aisle. Gabe, who has floated onto her detail today, slips into the aisle behind us.

Luna carries a tray of iced coffees. "I brought refreshments. Decaf for Sulli."

"You're the fucking best." Sulli takes a coffee.

I tell Luna, "I'll pass, but thanks."

Sulli nudges my shoulder with hers. "He had like five coffees this morning."

"Three," I counter.

"I'll give yours to Frog then," Luna says in a shrug. "She loves iced coffee. She kinda got me into it."

Speaking of my cousin, Frog sits at a long table near the front door, another temp guard beside her. Today, she's in charge of the NDAs. I specifically shifted Frog here so I could keep an eye on her. To gauge how she's doing on-duty.

About three months as a temp guard, and really, she's still too green to have this job, but the frat party mistakes were on me. She was *way* too new to be put in that situation alone. I didn't think the other temp would bail on her, but I should've quadrupled security on Luna.

"I can give the coffee to Frog," I say, then look from Luna to Sulli. "Can you two stick together for a sec?"

Luna nods. "Uh-huh."

"My butt is planted," Sulli promises.

I stand, fixing my earpiece, and look to Gabe. "Stay with them."

"Not moving, boss man."

Boss man.

Sulli snorts.

"Hey, you're dating this boss man," I whisper to her as I slide out of the row. I'd say *screwing* instead of *dating* but Luna is around.

Sulli's smile grows bigger. Seeing her happy right now, especially after our heart-to-heart, also feels good. I didn't implode our relationship.

After Luna hands me the iced coffee, I descend the aisle and approach the long table. Frog currently slides an electronic tablet to a short, doe-eyed blonde girl. I do a quick mental sweep.

Uneven bangs, longer strands hide her darker brows. Her soft-cheeked face screams *young*, and her ears seem unnaturally big for her round face and smaller frame. She's paler than a sheet of paper and dressed in a black Metallica T-shirt, plus plaid green pants. I can't tell if she *is* grunge or just putting on the clothes for show. To look the part of emo-punk.

She has to be underage.

Tom made it clear that no one younger than eighteen can audition.

I keep scrutinizing this girl, even as I pass Frog the iced coffee. "This is for you. From Luna."

Frog smiles. "She's my favorite."

I give her a look.

"Not that I have a favorite." She glances warily to the blonde girl, who is overhearing *everything*. "We're not supposed to have favorites." She sticks the straw into her mouth quickly, like she's trying to stop herself from speaking.

My muscles tense, and I ignore my cousin to speak to the girl. "How old are you?"

"Oh, I already took her ID," Frog says swiftly. "She's cleared." My cousin stands to grab the tablet back from the blonde.

"Hold on." I outstretch a hand to the tablet.

Frog passes it over, but my senses are shooting off a million-and-one signals, blaring out the words SOMETHING IS WRONG.

48

Akara Kitsuwon

THE BLONDE SHIFTS her weight, arms crossing in defiance. She's sucking on something. Candy? And what I mistook for big blue doe-eyes aren't soft or innocent.

She peruses me in an up-down sweep like I'm a roadblock she needs to shove and hurdle. What's worse: Frog and this girl share a cagey glance.

Why is Frog in cahoots with a stranger?

I read the signature at the bottom. It's messy as hell. Illegible. "Harry…"

"Harriet," the girl says sharply and crunches on what I think might be a Jolly Rancher. "But you can call me Harry if you want."

"Last name?" I ask her.

"Fisher." She lifts her chin to appear older and taller.

Yeah, that's not working at all.

She's short.

Like head-at-my-chest short.

"Fisher without a *C*," Frog adds. "Like a fish."

"Do you two know each other?" I ask them.

"No," Harriet says plainly. "We just met."

Frog nods, and I stare at my cousin for an extra beat. I believe her, but something is still up.

"Can I see your ID?" I ask Harriet.

Frog hooks her arm through mine and whisks me away from the table. "Excuse us," she says, and I let her guide me out of earshot but still in the middle of the long wide aisle.

"What the heck is going on?" I ask.

Frog lets out a heavy breath. "Look, Harriet told me her whole story. She's *seventeen*, but she's *really* good at drum—"

"You don't know that."

Frog glares. "I can sense it. You know, your mom told me I'm highly intuitive."

I tilt my head back, trying not to groan. I've been driven off feelings plenty of times. I've made decisions from the heart. Gut instinct is important in security too, but the rational pieces of me are combatting everything.

She talked to Harriet for two seconds. What happens if a fan manipulates Frog with some fake sob story and she lets them near a client?

"Regardless of what you feel," I whisper, "Tom doesn't want an underage drummer."

"She'll be eighteen eventually," Frog whispers back.

"Tom is a client."

"To Triple Shield."

"No," I snap at Frog. "He's still a part of the family, and we're not enemies with Triple Shield. We work together."

"So that's why Omega keeps a tally of wins and losses between the two firms?"

I stare at Frog for a long moment.

She's not wrong, and she smiles, knowing she got me.

Yeah, yeah.

Before I can reply, Frog adds like it's important intel, "She said she's sort of the black sheep of her family. She needs this."

I don't just feel protective of Tom and our clients. I feel protective of Frog. She's green, for one. She's my responsibility, for another, and despite how she can annoy the living crap out of me, I want her to do *really* well in security.

I want her to stay.

The realization overwhelms me for a second.

I snap my finger to my palm. "There's no way to fact-check her right now, Frog. You don't know if she's lying to get you to cut corners for her."

"I'm int—"

"Intuitive, yeah, I got that." I run a hand through my black hair.

Frog lowers her voice. "You can't trust people, which, *fine*. I understand to a degree. But I do trust her. And can't you just…trust *me*? What was the point of giving me this job, if you're going to treat me like I'm a kid?"

You are a kid.

This was for my mom.

If my mom were here, she'd side with Frog. I know that.

I stay quiet, mulling over my words. Every reply that runs through my head won't bring me and Frog closer, and I'm surprised that I don't want to push her away.

It'd be easier. Have Frog quit.

I don't want her to quit. I want her to succeed in Philly.

In my silence, Frog's face breaks. "What do I know, right? I'm just the fuck-up from Buffalo. You're the golden boy who started his own gym and security company."

What?

Is that how the family sees me? A golden boy?

"You're wrong," I tell Frog.

She frowns.

"I'm not some golden boy that got a silver platter handed to him. My dad died. My mom left. And I *fought* for what I have. Every day, it still feels like I'm fighting, Frog."

She's about to reply, but I take her hand and rush back to Harriet who's loitering alone. Her eyes wander around the theatre, and she's pulled drumsticks out of her back pocket.

"Everything set?" Harriet asks us.

"Did you fill out the audition application online?" I check her information on the tablet.

"Yeah." She bites down on the Jolly Rancher. "It should be in there."

I have access to the list. I search her name. Eyeing all her credentials.

Harriet glances between us. "So you two are brother and sister?"

"Cousins," I answer. "Our dads were brothers."

"*Are* brothers," Frog corrects, and to me, she says, "That doesn't change just because your dad is gone."

I've never really considered that. And I don't argue with Frog. Because even though I'm an only child, I realize how much I admire the bond of siblings. I'd like to think Banks and Thatcher will *always* be twins, no matter who outlasts who.

They better be old men when that time comes.

Because I can't lose Banks, and Thatcher and I might be on awkward terms—but I can't lose him either.

Focusing on Harriet's application, I realize she left her age and address *blank*. "What's your address?"

Harriet shifts. "125…" Her gaze drifts to the theatre chairs. "Red Robin Lane. It's outside of New York." She seems more nervous.

Frog touches my arm, and I follow my cousin's gaze to a college-aged guy in a chair. He's wearing a Batman & Robin shirt. Harriet just made up the address.

She knows we know. "Please, just let me audition. You can tell Tom whatever he wants afterwards. Just give me the chance."

I could tell her to get out.

But maybe Frog is right. Maybe I have grown a little too jaded. Not everyone has some sinister plot. Some people are trying to get by. Just like I was.

"Okay," I tell Harriet. "We'll leave it up to Tom after you audition."

She lets out a breath of relief, and before she takes a seat to wait her turn, I do one better. After the drummer on stage is dismissed, I suggest to Tom that Harriet should play next. She cuts the line, and practically hop-skips towards the stage.

Frog smiles at me.

I smile back at her. "Hey, I can be nice."

"I know, your mom said as much."

That softens me. I'm eager to know what else my mom might've told her, and Frog must see.

"She said you work too hard, and you'll work even harder to protect me. Sometimes that means you might be fiery-tempered, but
underneath everything, your heart is caring and sweet."

I miss my mom.

I try to push back emotion, but I've missed her since she left. As
Harriet begins to play one of The Carraways' most popular emo-punk
songs, I decide to shoot my mom a quick text. I'm in NYC today with
Sulli. You doing anything later today? We can head to Queens
and stop by, maybe for dinner or coffee? I press send and hear
melodic drumbeats.

I look up.

Harriet is completely in the zone, her drumsticks flying with total
rhythm. I bounce my head to the beat. Halfway through, I realize Frog
is also nodding her head and tapping her fingers to her thigh. Exactly
like I am.

We share the same quirk, and instead of being freaked out like I
might've been a few months ago, I smile.

Harriet is in the beat as her sticks move quickly from snare to tom
drum. A longing crashes into me—to remember the feeling of those
sticks in my hands and the *thump* rolling through my body. I stopped
drumming after my dad died.

My life changed direction, but I'm back *here*.

Why am I back here, staring at the path I left behind?

I inhale strongly.

Harriet not only plays well—she plays with desperation.

Tom leans forward, eager and excited. When she finishes, he asks
me, "Do you have her application?" since I'm holding the tablet.

I come over to him. He'll find out soon enough.

Tom skims her credentials. "Harriet, right?"

"Yeah." She comes to the edge of the stage. "I, um, left some stuff
blank, but I'm good. Better than anyone else here."

Drummers cough in the back rows, pissed at Harriet.

She's nervous again. "So what do you say?"

"How old are you?"

"Seventeen."

Tom scrapes a hand over his face. He slumps down and mutters something like, "Of course this happens." To Harriet, he says, "It's not just up to me. The label doesn't want the legal liability of hiring a minor right now. Sorry—there's nothing I can do."

I didn't know that.

She glares at her feet, stuffs her drumsticks in her back pocket, and rushes out the door as other drummers *boo* her.

"Who's booing?" Tom stands up, turning to the audience. "Dude, you—you did that? Out. Get him out." He's talking to his bodyguard.

Ian Wreath goes and starts escorting assholes out of the theatre through a fire exit.

Excited squeals come from the double-doored entrance towards the back of the theatre. Quinn squeezes his way through. Girls pull at his jacket like a rock god just appeared.

"He's hot but…whoa, they're all over him." Frog sips her coffee like she's watching a movie.

He shuts the door, closing them out, then descends the aisle towards the stage.

Towards me.

I notice the piece of paper in Quinn's hand, grin blinding as he approaches. "Akara." He's so excited, I can easily guess what happened.

"Farrow cleared you?" I ask.

"150%." He hands me the sheet of paper.

Frog eyes him like she's trying to solve a riddle. "What are you like extra good in bed or something?"

He flushes, caught off guard.

I make a face like I sucked on a lemon. "*Frog.*"

"What?" She frowns. "It was an honest question. I'm a virgin, if you want to know."

"I do *not* want to know." Eff my life.

Quinn tells her, "That's cool."

No.

It's not cool.

"He has a girlfriend," I tell my cousin.

Frog gives me a look like *I'm* being weird. Right, I don't need my cousin (who is also a temp that is around the main roster *way* too much) to be involved with one of them. Not that there are many single guys left.

Quinn (taken).

Gabe (single).

Donnelly...*don't think about it.*

I don't want to know what Donnelly is up to.

Don't need to know.

Yes, you do, Nine.

I realize if this has *anything* to do with why Donnelly has been tattooing more—I should know. I haven't pried too hard, but if he's in trouble...?

I want to protect him.

He should be a bigger priority. He's SFO. He's one of my men. He's a *friend*. He's been there for *me* as backup while Sulli is being hounded. I need to be there for him.

I focus back on Quinn and smile. "Welcome back, Quinn."

He's grinning. "Where am I going?"

That...

"I still have to figure out transfers. I'll work it out tomorrow." I pat his arm, and then Tom goes and talks with Luna and Sulli (they're safe). He's speaking fast, and they're gesturing over to me.

I frown as Tom approaches. "Akara?"

"Yeah?"

Frog slurps on her coffee.

"There is a *high* probability I might not find a drummer today, but Luna and Sulli said you can play."

"I'm a bodyguard—"

"Just for Summer Fest," Tom interjects fast. "Dude, please. It's the biggest music festival in Philly."

I haven't played in years.

Shoot, there's no way *I'd* even reach his standards.

But Tom says, "I trust you—you're dating my cousin, and that's already a leg up on everyone else. So what do you say?" He's wincing like preparing for an impact. If Eliot were here, I'm sure he'd be hanging onto his brother's arm with added dramatics.

I eye the drumkit. My dad would've never wanted me to let something I love go, but grief wouldn't let me return. And I think I'm finally ready to embrace what I lost again.

I nod. "Let me audition first."

He does.

And when I'm behind the snare, when I touch the kickstand, the beat pumps through me, and rhythm is engrained in me. I play with a smile. I bang each drum like the music never left. Like it's always been there, waiting.

"That'll work," Tom says with a deep exhale when I jump off the stage.

Sulli is smiling, and I'm about to playfully sneak up around her, just to lick her cheek—when my phone buzzes.

I dig out my phone and check the message.

Don't worry about coming to Queens. We can chat later on the phone. I think I'd prefer that. Tell Sulli that I said hi. I love you, Nine. — Mom

She doesn't want me to see her.

I'm not surprised. The entire reason she left Philly was to be away, so I don't have to worry. Me visiting more often isn't what she's desired, and I'm going to respect that. But I feel better knowing I tried.

49

Banks Moretti

"COME JOIN THE PARTY," I urge my mopey, stressed-out metamour. Akara scribbles a bunch of lines across a sheet of paper, crumpled up balls already strewn across the room.

When we officially moved into Sulli's room after the Olympics, Sulli and I bought this white oak desk and pushed it up underneath the window. That way when Akara works he can at least have the best view in the room.

He shakes his head and balls up another sheet of paper.

"If I'd known you would glue your ass to this desk, Sulli and I would have never bought it for you."

"Just give me ten minutes."

"That's what you said *twenty* minutes ago, man," I refute and wave a hand towards the papers. "All this shit will work itself out in the morning."

He laughs dryly. "It won't. Now that Quinn is ready to come back, I have to figure out transitions on the team. *And* I have to find a new manager to handle an overcrowded gym. *And* the baby still needs a *fudging* bodyguard."

Yeah.

I heard that conversation during the last security meeting.

Went something like this:

Akara: Baby still needs a bodyguard.

Oscar: Babies. Redford is having another one.

Farrow: Okay, but Maximoff and I aren't the only fuckers here having kids, and yet, we're being pressured like hell.

Thatcher: I'm putting temps on my baby, and I'm guessing Akara and Banks will do the same.

Me: *nodding*

Akara: Yep. You're the only one who's refusing temp guards, Farrow.

Farrow: You all feel comfortable with temps on your kids and that's great. But I don't want a stranger breathing down my neck while I'm trying to protect Ripley. They always get in the way, and I'm not babysitting security. So it's either I'm the bodyguard to my kids or someone from SFO. That's it.

"It's a lot," I agree to Akara. "And that's why you need to step away."

He lets out a breath. "Where's Sulli?"

"Pretending to be obsessed with Orion and Arkham so she can hide from Jane."

Akara grimaces. "Crap."

"Yeah, you're not the only one swimming through shit tonight. *I'm* here to pull you both out." I grab his elbow. "So let's go."

He follows my movements, thankfully. Many a times, Akara has been the one to keep the ship from sinking. It feels good being the one holding him and her above the water.

"What do you think I should do?" Akara asks me as he steps over the crumpled paper.

"Fuck if I know," I tell him. "You're the one that makes the decisions."

He rubs the back of his neck, tensed.

Shit. What would Thatcher do? He'd be brainstorming with Akara— coming up with a Master Plan. I think fast and smack his chest. "Put Quinn on Baby Ripley's detail. He's good with kids. It's what you *were* gonna do before he broke his leg anyway."

"Then who goes to Luna? I can't keep temps on her forever."

I reach in my pocket for a cigarette like second nature, but I pull out a toothpick instead. No cigarettes on me. *No smoking.* Still haven't fucked that up since I quit after the frat party. "Are any temps good enough yet?"

He shakes his head.

"Gabe?"

"Then there's no floater."

"Do we need one?"

"Yeah, the roster is too small," Akara says. "You were the best floater we had."

My stomach roils. "Alright, then send me back."

He glares. "I won't. I can't."

It'll make his life easier if I'm punted off Sulli's detail. Returned to the position I excel in. Floating around. Lending help wherever I can. But it'll mean seeing her less. Seeing him less.

I don't argue with Akara because deep-down, I don't want it. I want her. And fuck, I'm not falling on my sword for the team.

Aware of the complete fucked situation he's in, I place a hand on his shoulder. "Beer."

He locks eyes with me. "Beer," he agrees.

Leaving the bedroom, we run into Sulli outside the door, and it takes less convincing to get her to join the party. We all stroll out into the living room.

And then we skid to a sudden stop.

The TV is broadcasting an episode of *Suddenly Famous*, the limited docuseries about Jack & Oscar. We missed the premiere while we were in L.A., so Omega wanted to throw a small watch-party at the penthouse. On screen, Jack speaks to the camera with a megawatt smile, but I can't hear what he's saying over the argument blasting off in the middle of the room.

Oscar and Farrow stand opposite Donnelly.

Beanbags, spilt popcorn, cat toys and baby toys scatter the floor. Among the furniture and chaos are Jack, Maximoff, Baby Ripley, Jane, Thatcher, Gabe, and Quinn—a full house. And everyone but the Yale boys are quiet as hell.

"I'm figuring it out," Donnelly says strongly. "You're both making this into something it's not."

"Bro, you can't keep doing what you're doing," Oscar replies just as forcefully. "It's not sustainable."

"I'm sustaining fine."

"You're not," Farrow says with heat. "You look like a ghost, man. How much weight have you lost?"

Donnelly rakes a hand back and forth over his head. "I'm *fine*. You have nuthin' to worry about."

How are they not yelling? House I grew up in—you ask someone for a beer and the decibel shoots to blown-eardrum levels. An actual fight? We sound like hyenas.

The Yale boys are relatively *calm* but intense.

"See, I have *everything* to worry about," Farrow says. "You can't lay down on railroad tracks and expect me not to pull you off."

Akara mutters under his breath, "What the heck did we miss?"

"A fuck ton, apparently," I whisper.

Sulli has her fingers to her lips, wide-eyed.

"I'm going to pull myself off," Donnelly assures him. "Just give me some time, man."

"We've given you *months*," Farrow says, eyes growing and reddening. "Just take what I'm offering."

Donnelly grimaces. "I'm not takin' your money, Farrow."

He needs money. We've known he's been tattooing on the side. Not the biggest fuckin' revelation for me or Akara.

"Take my money," Oscar offers.

"I'm not taking yours either, *Jesus*." Donnelly paces, about to turn his back to them, but he swings forward to say, "You two married into money—you know how happy that makes me? And not because I want a *thing* from you. So stop offerin' shit to me."

"You're in this situation because of me." Farrow points at his chest. "Let me get you out, Donnelly."

"I chose this, man. I knew what I was doing, and not so you could bail me out in the end."

I lean a shoulder into Akara's. "We just walked into some deep shit."

"Yep." Akara lets out a breath.

Me or him, one of us, spoke too loudly and heads whip in our direction. Including Farrow, Donnelly, and Oscar's.

"You want to do this in front of the boss?" Donnelly asks his friends.

Neither have time to react. Akara is already speaking. "Hey, you can tell me what's going on. I can help you."

Oscar says, "He doesn't want anyone's help, Kitsuwon."

"That's the problem," Farrow chimes in.

Donnelly slips a cigarette behind his ear and comes clean like it really is nothing. "I'm giving my paycheck to Scottie."

What?

"Your whole paycheck?" Akara is stunned.

Donnelly just nods.

Sulli's jaw slowly unhinges.

Shit, I didn't think it was that bad, and we were Donnelly's roommates.

By the lack of shock in the room, I'm guessing the three of us are the last to find out. Except Gabe—Gabe Montgomery is confused as fuck.

"Who's Scottie?" Gabe asks.

Jane answers, "Ripley's biological father and Donnelly's uncle."

"Is Scottie a threat?" Akara asks.

"Nah," Donnelly says.

I cut in, "What if you stop paying him?"

Farrow is glaring at Donnelly, and Donnelly shrugs, "Alright, maybe he becomes a problem, but that's *my* problem."

Akara outstretches his arms. "Why do you even need to give Scottie your paycheck."

"'Cause I made a deal with him a while back. He'd terminate his parental rights and Farrow and Maximoff could adopt Ripley, *only* if I give him my paycheck—he knows how much I make."

Farrow tries again, "Let me and Maximoff pay him—"

Donnelly backs away. "*No.*"

The room tenses—someone muted the television. Oscar is frozen on-screen and playfully tipping Jack's baseball cap down over his eyes. In the flesh, he's a whole lot more serious right now.

"You can't live off nothing," Farrow says more calmly.

"I'll up your pay," Akara says like it's that easy.

I slip him a look. With what fuckin' money? He's not making a profit through security right now, and he's maxing out credit cards. One saving grace, he's let Sulli pay for security again. Mostly because he feels like she's paying for extra temp guards, not for him.

Donnelly looks uncomfortable. "Nah." He touches his ear piercing. "Just leave me alone." Those last words come out exhausted.

Farrow takes a breath, face broken.

Donnelly sees. "I don't want to drag you or Maximoff into it—that's not how this was gonna go. And if I'm the problem, I can leave." He starts for the door, catapulting over the couch like he's hopping a fence.

"Wait!" Oscar shouts.

"Donnelly!" Farrow yells, worry almost choking his words.

It's the first shouting of the whole fight. They follow their friend, but the closest person to the hallway that leads to the front door is Luna.

She pops up from her beanbag and spreads her arms up and legs out like she's making a giant X with her body. Barley barricading the wide hall.

Donnelly tries to side-step and she bounces in front of him. Still in X formation.

He goes to the left. She bounces to the left.

Donnelly comes to a halt in front of Luna.

They're both staring at one another for a long beat.

"Hale," he says.

"Donnelly," she replies.

"I'll up *everyone's* pay," Akara suddenly says. "All of SFO is getting a raise. It's not debatable."

I hang my head, trying to conceal how big of a *bad idea* I think this might be for Akara. But the reaction from Donnelly—that's worth everything. And I know he's made the right call.

Donnelly breathes in like it's his first breath in months. "Akara—"

"Pay Scottie the same amount. Save the difference."

"We're all taking the money, bro," Oscar tells his friend.

Donnelly says to Akara, "You don't have to."

"I do," Akara says strongly. "You're SFO. You're my family."

I'm smiling. Hell, after a second, all of SFO is smiling. And Sulli, Jane, Luna, Maximoff, and Jack are quick to share the good feeling with us.

Donnelly nods a few times. "Alright." He breathes in again. "Thanks, boss."

Farrow nods to Akara in gratitude.

The air is calmer, until Akara says, "Maybe don't thank me yet." He swings his arms, snaps his finger to his palm, then motions to Luna and Donnelly. "Are you two dating?"

50

Banks Moretti

I'LL BE FUCKING DAMNED—Akara is going there.

I thought I'd be the first to accidentally ask, and he's saved me from that foot-in-mouth syndrome.

All heads turn to Luna and Donnelly. They still stand close.

Luna eyes Donnelly, and Donnelly is shaking his head to Akara. "Nah, man. It's not like that."

"You're sleeping together?" Akara questions.

"Not really," Donnelly says casually, but he's avoiding Akara and me. Fuck, we really are the two in the dark here.

"Not really?" Akara repeats like that makes no sense. He looks to me.

I shrug.

Like fuck if I know. Maybe she just gave him a blowie.

Luna is searching for a scapegoat. "Moffy?" Her brother stands up.

Donnelly coughs into his fist and walks away, going towards Farrow and Oscar.

"Alright, party is over," Oscar suddenly says, holding hands with Jack as they step over tubs of popcorn. "As sad as I am to miss *this*, I have an early morning with a Cobalt."

Oscar passes Akara. "Loved the question. Popped it just right." He pats his shoulder.

As he leaves the penthouse, Akara tells me, "That doesn't feel great coming from a Yale boy."

"I'm shocked I didn't nuke it first."

Sulli catches our arms, "Hey, I can probably fill in the fucking blanks." And for once, she's leading us away.

RETIRING TO THE LIBRARY, THE DOOR LOCKED, SULLI

places a bucket of popcorn on the desk and explains the missing pieces.

I stand, arms crossed, and Akara sinks into the nearest chair. Head in hands as Sulli recounts what happened.

Donnelly went down on Luna two years ago. One time. That's it.

It obviously didn't end badly if they're still friends.

"Akara," Sulli breathes. "She doesn't want this to be a big deal."

He doesn't say anything. Sulli looks to me for help.

"Nine, it was just head."

He shoots me an annoyed look. "He gave a client head when she was *eighteen*."

"She asked him to," Sulli snaps. "And they're still friends."

"Exactly." I lift my shoulders. "I'm with Sulli on this one. Forward and onward. No looking back."

"How am I supposed to make decisions for the team without looking back?" Akara asks me. "I have to figure out who should be her full-time bodyguard, and this complicates crap."

"Why?" I ask. "Were you planning to put Donnelly on her detail?"

"No, but I don't know if she won't ask her next young bodyguard for head—"

"She's *not* like that Akara," Sulli snaps angrily. "I can't believe you'd even say that."

"What am I supposed to think?!" he yells. "I don't know what to do here!" Stress has been building up in him and he just breaks. Face shattering as he buries his anguish into his hands. Split open. He's trying to restrain tears.

"Nine." I come to his side. Pain wells up in my chest seeing him ripped apart.

Sulli comes to his other side. We both bend down and wrap our arms around him.

"It's alright," I breathe.

He's tensed. Sulli holds tighter. He doesn't shove us away, and he drops his hands, his eyes wet and face twisted. "Price was right to think I'm building a firm with a bunch of broken toys," he says roughly. "I can't make this work. The numbers don't effing work."

He's trying to hold everything together for security, but it's more than just the transfers. He's now bleeding cash from every end, and on the other side of the library door, they have no clue about the sinking hole Akara is standing in—if they did, they never would've taken the raise.

Adding to his most recent expenses: all the extremely expensive stab proof vests he just bought for the company. The lightweight vests will protect from punctures and blades like glass from broken bottles, and depending on the threat, we'll be required to wear them instead of the bulletproof vests. And hell, I understand it was a necessary cost, seeing as it might have saved Akara that day at the hotel.

I can't fix the financial problem. What I have to give is pennies compared to what he needs.

"I can pay off your credit cards," Sulli suddenly offers.

"No, Sul—"

"Just once your credit is good again and we go over your books— then we can talk about you paying me back, if you fucking have to. I want to help you—let me help you."

Akara breathes in those last words. "I'll pay you back."

"I know you'll fucking want to," she nods. "Just don't do it too soon."

He exhales, then nods. "Thank you." He bows his head, thinking. "The transfers."

I can help solve the transfer puzzle.

Then it hits me.

"Put Frog on Luna's detail," I tell him.

"What?" Akara frowns. "She's barely good enough to be a temp."

Sulli meets my eyes. "No, Banks is right, Kits. You said yourself that Frog *loves* being on Luna's detail. Luna likes Frog. They're buddyguard compatible."

I squeeze his shoulder. "Add a temp with Frog if it'll make it better. Keep Gabe as the floater. Quinn goes to Baby Ripley."

Akara stares at the ground, rubbing his swollen eyes. "It could work. But it still leaves my gym without a manager."

We all grow quiet. Unsaid truths swinging in the air. Studio 9 has been more of a thorn in Akara's side than any bodyguard transfer decision. He won't sell, and Sulli and I won't tell him to abandon the legacy of his family.

Sulli nudges Akara's shoulder. "Maybe the Oliveiras have a friend who'd be interested in the job?"

Akara stares faraway. "I'll figure this one out." He glances between Sulli and me. "Thanks for the rest. I needed it."

I say, "That's what we're here for."

Sulli gives him a tight hug.

Among these stately bookcases—like I'm back in Warwick University's massive library—the three of us find ourselves on the ground. Not ready to leave that quickly.

Sitting in a circle, we pass the bucket of popcorn around.

"Nemo," Akara says.

I almost choke on a kernel. "Like *Finding Nemo*?"

"Yeah." He fits a baseball cap on backwards, his face dried of tears. "I used to love that movie when I was a kid."

I bite onto a toothpick. "You get dropped on your head as a baby?"

"You know I'd ask the same of you, Banksy."

"We're not naming our kid after a fuckin' goldfish."

Sulli elbows me with a smile. "He was a clown fish."

"Even worse," I say. "Poor little guy will get teased mercilessly."

Akara throws a popcorn kernel at me. "You're the one that wants to name her Ariel after *The Little Mermaid*."

"She's a Disney *princess*," I refute. "Not a clownfish."

"Is it bad luck to pick out a name so early?" Sulli asks as Akara passes her the tub.

"I don't know," I say. "Never had a kid before."

"Same." Akara stretches out his legs on the floor. We both see Sulli's worry building. "We can put a pin on the names, Sul."

She relaxes.

Truth: picking out names is the least stressful thing for me. Thinking about the other shit that comes with parenthood skyrockets my nerves.

The hard choices.

Guiding them to do the right thing.

The quick decisions.

I pray I have that in me.

Sulli takes a fistful of popcorn. "Do you guys ever think about *when* I got pregnant? We know how far along I am, but which time was *the time* of conception?"

I grind my teeth back and forth on the toothpick, thinking. "It'd be sometime around Training Camp, I'm guessing."

"Yep," Akara nods, "based on the timeline." He leans back on his hands. "I didn't notice the condom breaking so it must've been some epic sex."

Sulli smiles, "Top fucking tier."

"Gold status," Akara adds.

I pipe in, "Sounds like every time we fuck."

Sulli grins more, one that falters too fast. She's deep in thought. "You know, I made a mental list of all the times it could've happened."

"Let's hear it," I tell her.

She lists off her fingers. "I think there were a few times we banged in the bathtub. Or it could've been one of the many times on the bed. Or the less likely options. The night, here, in the library."

Akara and I glance at the library table we fucked Sulli on. Great fuckin' night.

"Or the locker room," Sulli continues, "ooooor, maybe the time we fucked on the bedroom floor." She flushes a deeper red. "I had to throw that rug out."

"It was an ugly rug," Akara says.

"Kits" she gapes. "It was shaped like a cupcake."

"Exactly."

She chucks a handful of popcorn at his face.

He laughs, letting the kernels rain down on him.

I hang an arm around her shoulders. "The list is long."

Sulli leans into my body. "What do you say, Hardy Boys? Can you solve this mystery?"

"I'd bet us on the bed," I say.

"The library," Akara guesses. "But we have no way of verifying."

She sighs. "It's bugging me that I'll probably never know."

I hug her closer. "Some things are just meant to be that way, mermaid." History we don't know. Preserved in time somewhere we can't reach.

51

Akara Kitsuwon

TONIGHT IS THE LAST night before Training Camp in Hawaii, and Sulli won't leave the pool.

"Come on, string bean." I bend down and hold out a hand.

She kicks away from the wall. "One more lap."

Banks chews on a toothpick, watching beside me. "Don't you want to catch some sleep before traveling tomorrow?"

"I can sleep on the plane." She flips over on her back to practice the backstroke.

Banks and I share concern. The gun incident happened five days ago, and she's been shaken since. She cried herself to sleep last night because a thunderstorm kept jolting her awake. And *today*—today, *Celebrity Crush* posted a fudging article about the "incident" with vague, speculative details.

We're not letting anything reach press.

Just when Sulli has started growing used to parts of the chaos, *this* happens, and I feel helpless. Like I can't cheer her up for long enough. I can't rid her fear or Banks' hypervigilance.

Swimming is a big distraction from the outside. She already changed out of her regulation swimsuit and just wears a turquoise bikini.

She meant to go home earlier, then changed her mind at the last second.

Back in the water.

All over again.

Lately, one lap usually turns into another. Then another. Then two hours later, she'll finally be ready to pull her exhausted self out of this pool. Any other night—I might entertain the devotion, but a couple hours won't make or break her chances.

Besides, that's what Training Camp is for.

To train.

"Let's pull her out," I tell him.

"You sure?" Banks asks.

"Yeah."

"Right on."

Sulli finishes her lap. "One mo—" She cuts herself off, watching as Banks and I shed down to our underwear. Like Sulli and Banks, a waterproof bandage is secured tightly around my wrist, protecting the new tattoo.

Quickly, on my phone, I disable the Aquatic Center's security cameras for a couple hours. I have access. Swim ropes section off the Olympic-sized pool into ten lanes, and Sulli hangs onto a platform while seeing us kick our clothes aside.

Her smile rises. "Are you guys…?"

"There room for two more?" Banks asks huskily.

"Fuck, yeah…catch me if you hot-shots can." She kicks herself backwards away from the swim platforms.

We keep our boxer-briefs on, and then we jump in. Banks is ungraceful. I'm not any better, but I am faster, swimming beneath the ropes to Sul first.

When I pop out of the water, I'm in front of our girlfriend, treading water and pushing my hair away from my face. "Hey," I say.

"Hey," she breathes.

Banks comes up behind her. "Mermaid."

She treads with us, the pool nine-feet deep.

"We've come to collect you," I tell her.

Her eyes fall to my lips, and mine fall to hers. A little swollen from the amount of times she's chewed on them since the incident. Her lips bled badly last night, and I rub my thumb across her bottom one.

She winces.

"That still hurts?"

"A little…"

Sul.

Her eyes redden. "You can still kiss me. Unless you're afraid." She challenges me and Banks.

He encases a hand over her jaw, kissing her with urgency and swiftness—I barely blink, and they're pulled together. She clings onto him, then claws for me.

I clutch the back of her head. She turns her lips onto mine. I kiss her savagely and her body bows closer, then pulls back. I break apart to her panting breath and my aching cock.

I skim her up and down, how her collarbones peek out of the water. Her strong, squared jaw and determined eyes. Sulli is a babe.

Gorgeous.

Ours.

The stillness of the empty Aquatic Center ratchets up the heat. Banks wipes water out of his face, and Sulli watches him swim around her.

"One more lap?" she breathes.

"No," I tell her. "No more laps."

Her face flushes in arousal. I swim closer, my chest up against hers. Banks wraps an arm around her waist from behind. Lifting ropes and pushing them aside, I guide them to the corner of the pool. The far left lane. Banks braces his body with one shoulder on the ledge.

I press her between us by planting my arms on either side of the cement.

Instinctually, her legs wrap around my waist.

I start massaging between her thighs over her bikini bottoms. She lets out a low heady moan against my neck. "Kits…" Her head lolls back.

Banks bends down to silence her with a kiss.

Fuck.

I harden watching them deepen the kiss. His tongue slips into her mouth. I've watched that tongue slip into her pussy. I pull the fabric at the crotch of her swimsuit to give me access to her heat. She breaks from his lips when my fingers enter her beneath the water.

"Fuckfuckfuck…" Her thighs tighten around my waist. Her hands grip harder to Banks' forearms.

Banks watches her writhe between us and he clasps the back of her swimsuit, slipping the straps off her arms, exposing her breasts.

He kneads her tits, and she whimpers.

I harden more, just hearing her.

"Please…I want…your cocks…"

I'd love to take Sulli in the pool, but the condoms are in the gym bag.

I lean forward and kiss her deeply. She reciprocates like I'm delivering her oxygen, fingers clasped against the back of my neck.

When I break, I pull my fingers out.

"Wait, no," she breathes.

Climbing out of the pool, water drips off me. I step towards my gym bag at the side, and by the time I have the condoms, Banks and Sulli have also hopped out.

Shades cover the windows this late at night. It's private, but Banks keeps checking in that direction, like a cameraman will barge through and smash the glass.

They won't. Not unless they want trespassing charges, and most aren't that idiotic.

Sulli leaves her wet bikini top on the wet tiles. Tits still out. Nipples perked. Confidence blazing in every step she takes. "I don't want to leave yet." Her breath shallows, and she bites the corner of her reddened lip. "Let's do the fucking deed. With two capital Ds. One V."

Banks wipes a hand over his smile.

I'm near there.

"You two do want to fuck, right?"

Banks and I exchange a glance.

He tips his head like, *I can stay for a long while.*

I nod, agreeing.

Gazes back on Sulli, Banks says deeply, "I want to make love to you, mermaid."

Her eyes melt.

"Long," I chime in. "Hard." I pass her a condom. "Put this on Banks."

She's panting more. "Me?" She takes the foil.

I mockingly spin around the pool room. "Any other string beans here?"

She smiles. "Hardy fucking har." Seeing her smile tonight is everything to me.

Banks sheds his sopping boxer-briefs, fully nude and his erection is about as hard as mine. Sulli drops to her knees and rips the packet open. He cups the back of her head. And slowly, she glides the condom over his length. I engrain the image in my head.

When she's done, she pops up to her feet, and lightly punches our arms. "I'm so good, you think I could take your jobs away from you?"

"You can wrap my dick anytime you like," Banks tells her.

"I'm not as giving," I tease.

She sticks her tongue out at me.

I laugh.

She slugs me again. "And I don't believe that for a second, Kits. You'd give me your whole body, if you could."

"I've given you more than that," I whisper.

I've given her my entire spirit. The brightest pieces of me are lights that Sulli sparks on fire.

Banks has given her his entire soul. The deepest parts of him are wells that Sulli overfills.

She smiles a softer smile.

I run my hand over her smooth arm. She shaves daily to reduce drag for swimming—and as cute as Sulli is cursing out her razors in the shower—I miss the hair on her arms and pussy and legs.

"Sul," I say her name into a smile, "let's play a game."

"What game?" Her grin expands. I know—she loves the competitive games.

I step closer and loop my fingers in the band of her bikini bottoms. Slowly, I pull her bathing suit down her thighs, down her legs—until the fabric pools at her ankles. As naked as Banks now. I track my eyes over her soft, bare skin. Blood pumping hotter through my veins.

"The floor is lava," I tell her. "But you're the only one not immune." I look to my metamour. "Banks."

He hoists her up in one effortless motion, her legs wrapping around his waist. The two of them naked, pieces of her wet hair cling to her squared jaw. She breathes heavily. His dick presses against her belly.

"Ready?" Banks asks her, his hands cupped under her ass.

She nods.

"Words," I tell her, coming closer behind Sulli. I brush wet hair off her cheek and neck.

"Yes. Fuck yes."

He lifts Sulli a little higher and then guides our girlfriend down onto his full length. She's been taking more and more of Banks ever since the first DP night. I press a kiss to her neck, and I palm myself, watching Sulli sink onto him. Watching her lips part, breath hitched. Watching how he disappears inside her, and my muscles tighten in blistering need. I kiss the line of her shoulder.

She lets out a breathy, high-pitched noise. Her fingers dig into his biceps. Hanging on.

A husky sound escapes Banks. He moves her up-down on his shaft. Shit, I need her. I want her.

"*Fuckfuck*," Sulli cries.

Banks whispers, "You enjoy me inside you, mermaid?"

She nods into another pleasured noise. I kiss her neck again, and she shivers. Against her ear, I whisper, "How about me inside you?"

"Fuckyes," she gasps.

"What do you say, Banks?" I ask. "Should we both fuck her?"

Sulli drinks in the way we communicate with each other. How Banks lifts a shoulder to me. He's trying to be subtle, keeping Sulli on the edge of her seat. Or literally, on his cock.

I motion with my head towards the locker rooms. He nods back. In less than a minute, red aluminum lockers in about seven rows surround us. Wooden benches in each row, along with forgotten water bottles and goggles.

Banks pushes Sulli up against the first locker he can find, and he bucks up in her. She claws at his back, crying out his name, and then he moves her to the bench. Their wild eagerness, their desperation to be *closer* and deeper is a hand around my cock—begging to join those feelings I know and share with them.

While Banks lies her down on the bench, their heavy, pleasured noises echo in the locker room. The sounds race my pulse, and I'm entranced as I rip open a condom packet. I never would've imagined how much I *love* seeing Banks make love with Sulli.

But knowing I'm about to join is the ultimate peak. Nothing else compares to this intimacy we share. The three of us all together. Whether he's in her, I'm in her, we're both in her—it doesn't matter. Just being here with them ignites a passion and embraces a greater peace and solace.

Once I'm out of my boxer-briefs, Sulli sees my need. "Oh fuck. *Fuck.*"

After Banks pumps two more times into Sulli, he pulls out, still rock-hard.

My turn.

I slide on the condom and don't give Sulli time to process. Entering her feels like coming home, and I keep the same wild, frenzied pace as Banks. Rocking in her so hard that Banks has to hold her waist down on the bench so she doesn't slide off. They kiss, upside-down.

Heat bathes the locker room. Emotions pooling between us. She grips me, him—our eyes traveling to each other with powerful intensity, as though we're all promising the same thing. To stay, to never leave, to be *here* together. Forever. Her high-pitched cries and breathy moans grow louder, only to be silenced when I pull out. Banks takes my spot. Back inside.

I kneel where he'd been. Holding her waist as she gets pounded by him.

"Fuckfuckfuck," she cries, her eyes rolling.

My lips touch the base of her neck and she bucks up into Banks, her toes curling.

"Switch," Banks says.

I stand up. Take his place.

He takes mine.

We go like that for what feels like forever. I could live in this moment. Inside her. Out of her. Holding her. Watching them. Feeling us.

It's a cataclysmic moment fueled by the fact that tomorrow we're leaving Philly. Tomorrow is the beginning of everything. The road to her dream. The threats that lie ahead.

Tonight, we fall into a familiar rhythm of love and sex.

We're all sticky with sweat and the smell of chlorine has infused with our skin. Banks continues to thrust as I kneel beside the bench and rub Sulli's sensitive clit. "I can't. *I can't.*"

"That doesn't sound like a winner," I breathe.

"I can't," she cries a phrase she often says when she's about to come. And she's already come once during this.

"You can take him," I whisper against her ear.

She moans.

It's killing me.

"You better come," I whisper.

"Not...yet, notyet," she pants. "Keep going. Don't fucking... stop."

Banks and I switch, and as soon as I'm inside Sulli, she clenches around me, "*Shit,*" I grit into a groan, coming as I thrust forward. Black spots dance in my vision.

She pulsates around my cock, almost hitting a peak. But she's resisting. I milk the climax with two more pumps, then pull out. While

I discard my used condom, Banks is inside Sulli again. His movements grow harder, deeper. She shivers. Trembles.

Arousal snakes through my body, and I grow hard again. His grunts, her moans, they fill the air, and as Sulli writhes, Banks turns to look at me, a question in his eyes.

I give him a nod.

He lifts Sulli up, keeping himself inside her, and I tear open another condom. Grab some lube, and while Banks is standing with Sulli in his grasp, I come up behind our girlfriend.

"Kits," she pants, seeing us in front and behind her—she lets out a tiny, wanting whimper.

"Fuck," Banks groans and his aroused gaze hits me like, *you better hurry up, man.*

I slip my hand along her waist. "Breathe, Sul."

She inhales.

I tease around her ass, and she leans forward, more into Banks' chest. But she cranes her neck to watch me, and I gently slide into her—the sensation wraps around me in a vice, and my breath catches. "*Sulli,*" I groan, flexing forward.

She trembles. "Fuck, *fuck.*"

"You alright?" Banks asks.

She nods, "Yeah, holy fuck. *Holyfuck.*"

We're both inside our girlfriend, and Banks grips her legs harder, tighter. While I hold her waist, I push further in, and Banks thrusts carefully into her pussy. In slow movements, we find a hypnotic rhythm together—what feels like pure ecstasy and bliss—and we watch Sulli lose her shit.

Her eyes roll, limbs tremble, and we're saying her name with heavy breath, deep groans.

"BanksKitsfuck…" Sulli's words taper off into a primal sound of need and want as she closes in on a peak.

From behind, I cup her breast and squeeze, thumb flicking her nipple.

She leans back against my shoulder in a cry while Banks thrusts deeper. His movement pushes me inside her more.

She can barely keep her eyes open. "I can't...I can't..."

I'm on the precipice of losing *my* shit, and Banks is only a few pounds away from reaching his.

"Come for him," I whisper to her.

She erupts and arches into a scorching orgasm.

"*Fuck. Sulli*," Banks grunts, staying inside while she cries out. While he comes too.

I hear them. I feel them.

It sends me.

I release with the same mind-numbing body high. More heavy breathing and soft whimpers of pleasure puncture the air. Slowly, Banks and I pull out. He carefully shifts Sulli so he's cradling her in his arms, and after coming down and checking on our girlfriend, we all find ourselves collapsed onto the locker room floor.

Wiped. Emotionally spent.

Our chests rise and fall heavily.

Sulli lies face-down on top of both of us. Left arm spread over Banks' chest. Right arm spread over mine. I cup the back of her head tenderly. Banks places his palm on her ass, and then he touches the top of my head in the same tender affection that I'm touching Sulli.

"That was...fucking wow," she breathes.

"Fucking wow," Banks says in agreement.

"Effing wow," I add.

They both laugh.

We're all quiet. Peace lies inside our sanctuary. Where it's just us three. I want to remember this moment and feeling. Like a snapshot in time. Where we're all in harmony and whole before the world tries to rip us apart again and again. And again.

Love inside the chaos.

As we lie here, as my mind wanders, my lips slowly rise.

There is no doubt, no indecision on my part, no wavering, no questioning, no backtracking or leaving. I believe in the strength of us.

52

Sullivan Meadows

WE LEAVE THE LIBRARY, and I feel a little drained from
dodging Jane all night, so I'm extra thankful when my mom calls. It's a
nice cherry on top of a slightly burnt cupcake.

"Hi, Mom." I curl up on the rooftop bucket swing. A new addition
thanks to Luna. She likes to write here, and I can't deny it's the comfiest
thing on the patio.

Akara and Banks followed me up here, but they currently jump into
the pool for a late-night dip. I pull my eyes off my boyfriends to focus
on FaceTime.

Potted ferns surround my mom while she's tucked on the window
nook. Goldilocks sleeps on her lap. "How's the party? Any food fights
yet?" She has a wicked smile like she's the one up to no good. No
matter how old I get, my mom never seems to age. Youthfulness is so
a part of her soul that I imagine she'll live forever. Even if I know it's
not true.

"Fucking sadly there were no food fights. And the watch-party
ended early."

"Oh bummer." Her eyes soften.

I shrug. "I'm kind of still avoiding Jane so…"

"You were also avoiding the party," she realizes. "That's not like
you."

"I know," I say quietly. "I don't really want to talk about Jane."
I've already confided in my mom about my feelings, and she's been understanding, especially as the youngest with three older sisters—she's dealt with comparison before.

My mom switches subjects for me. "Was there any cake tonight?"

"I wish."

"Tacos?"

"Nope."

"Salsa?"

I shake my head.

She smiles. "Your Uncle Lo and I would not call that a party then. Therefore, thy beautiful peanut butter cupcake did *not* avoid a party. Just a plain ole get-together."

I laugh. "That's my favorite kind of logic."

She mimes a high-five at the phone.

I air-five my mom back on-screen.

I really fucking love my mom. Spirits a little higher, but I watch her tuck a strand of blonde hair behind her ear. And I feel like something is up.

"Everything okay there?" I wonder.

"Everything's groovy." She smiles again, one that softens on me. "So I have this theory…"

I listen closely.

"…that the greatest, most unexpected moments in life are often the ones where risks are taken."

I think about choosing both Banks and Akara. The three of us choosing each other—the hardest, most dangerous, *risky* path we could've taken—and how much fuller life *feels* being with them.

"I like that one," I mutter.

"Then are you sure you *really* want to hide out at the penthouse for your pregnancy?"

My body tenses. "No…I…Mom, I'd *love* to go out, but this isn't just about me anymore. It could put the baby at risk."

"That's why you have security, Sulli. So you don't have to worry as much and you can take those risks. So you can *live* your life and not be a prisoner to it."

I blink back tears, eyes burning. "I have to make sacrifices, though. Right?" I'm not so sure I'm even making sense. I backtrack to what I know. "You and Dad, you both sacrificed *so* much to keep me and Nona out of the public eye." My throat swells, emotion building. My mom's green eyes are a comfort that I don't want to meet. "I realize…I fucked that up, didn't I? I just tossed all your hard work in the garbage."

I'm unable to step out of the spotlight.

My privacy has been obliterated with the snap of a finger.

"Oh cupcake," Mom says with sweetness but also worry. "Your dad and I, we wanted you to have a choice. To choose whether you could be public or private. I'll *always* be happy that I gave you that choice, and we were so lucky we could let you choose. My sister knew her kids would be in the public eye, no matter what she did."

"Aunt Lily?" I sniff hard, holding back tears. "Maximoff and Luna."

"Xander, Kinney," my mom finishes. "Lily and Lo raised some great kids, Sulli. Don't you think?"

I nod, my nose running before my tears leak. I wipe my face.

I love my cousins. Moffy is my big brother, and Luna has become one of my closest friends. But I know their struggles were different than mine. Sometimes harder.

My mom tucks her legs to her chest. Just like I tuck my legs to mine. "There are different ways to raise a kid in the public eye," she tells me. "Your Aunt Lily and Aunt Rose—they did it different from me. Not better. Not worse. Just different."

But I've always looked up to my mom.

I've wanted to be like *her*. If I had a baby, I always imagined I'd raise my kid the way she raised me and my sister.

Motherhood for me can't be that, can it? I won't be able to take my kids on daring adventures in the wilderness without the fear. Without legions of bodyguards.

I'm painfully stuck in the spotlight.

I chose this.

And I can't hide.

I shouldn't.

I'm quiet with this knowledge.

And I remember, *Maximoff was never afraid.* He was never afraid of the cameras that followed us to ski resorts and backpacking trips. Because he grew up to understand them more than I did. His parents helped him normalize the attention.

But Xander…

Xander's not the same as his older brother.

My mom sees my indecision. "Staying indoors forever will chip away at you. You're a Meadows. You're not meant to be caged."

A tear spills down my cheek. I brush it away. "I don't want to put the baby at risk just for me. It's selfish. I can wait seven more months indoors." Confidence peels away from those words.

"Then what?" she asks. "You return to the land of the living? You'll say the same thing when the baby is born. *It's safer to stay inside.* Sullivan Minnie Meadows, you need to choose to live. I know it's hard, but…"

"The hardest things are usually the right things," I breathe my dad's words.

Choose to live.

Life.

Death.

I feel as if my family has always teetered between the two. Loss. Almost loss. It hangs around us like a cloud. Depression has clung to my mom before, and maybe she's worried for me. Worried that my spirit will be snuffed. I want to pacify her worries. Tell her I'll be *fine.* I won't suffer inside.

But I can't.

Her love for me wraps tightly in this moment.

I nod. Okay. *Okay.*

"You always have Lily," she says softly. "My sister will *always* understand what you're facing. Her fame was about as soul-crushing as yours right now. She had Moffy, then Luna."

"Xander," I finally mutter, the weight of his name hanging in the air. "He's getting better. It gets better."

My eyes hit hers. She gives me a soft smile. "I love you."

That hits me. "I just wanted to be like you," I say, choked on the words.

Tears well up in her eyes. "I love my sister to the moon and back. It gives me *extraordinary* joy to know you'll raise your kids like her. She is my fairy, you know. Magical creatures like fairies need belief to exist. I believe in her every single day I'm breathing, and I'll always believe in you. My strong, daring mer-daughter who lives in the sea."

I laugh a little, rubbing my wet cheeks. Realizing this is her blessing. To move forward. Onward. No hiding.

I love you too, Mom.

We say a few more words before I hang up. Taking a deep breath, the night air swirls around me. Akara and Banks watch from the pool. I kick off my shoes and race to them.

I jump in.

The water bathes all of me.

Home again.

53

Akara Kitsuwon

SUMMER MUSIC FEST in Philly. Five stages have been erected in the city's park, and I've attended one of these packed outdoor festivals before. Way back when.

I've been a sweaty sixteen-year-old letting the sun roast me as I wait shoulder-to-shoulder with sweaty, boozed twenty-somethings for a popular band to take the stage. For *someone* to spray me with a water bottle. Hoping the sky would part and rain would shower us all.

Hating the third day of the fest when rain would actually come, and my friends and I would be sloshing through mud and piss. Shivering our asses off as music pounded the beer-littered ground. Yet, we stayed outside. Never missed a second.

Never let the experience pass us by. And even though I'm on the other side of the stage, I feel that same effervescent energy course through me, the need to encapsulate the experience—and how happy I am that Sulli chose to be here.

With us.

I smile at my girlfriend. We're backstage, but "backstage" is really the side-stage where VIP and the band wait for their set, and we can easily peek out and see Summer Fest crew setting up The Carraways' equipment.

Drums, guitar, bass.

Crowds have amassed for Tom's band. Packing tight under the hot August sun, some are already exhausted, others drunk, considering it's now evening. The sun finally beginning to lower.

The Carraways are the lead-in band for Nothing Personal, a main headliner. When I called us the "opener"—Tom nearly had a stroke. He actually grabbed onto Eliot and said, "Water."

Apparently, Nothing Personal shares the same label as The Carraways and their drummer once auditioned for Tom's band.

Tom turned him down.

Now he's experiencing more success than Tom, and it's a thing. A thing that I can't weed-whack through. I'm not trying to make Tom Cobalt faint.

His fans would come for my head.

I hear crew tuning the guitar and doing mic tests. And the crowd gathers bursts of energy to chant, "CARRAWAYS! CARRAWAYS!"

Drumsticks sweat in my palm, and Sulli hands me a water bottle while Banks surveys the VIP side-stage area. Most of the Hales, Meadows, and Cobalts are here, and while I'm off-duty, Banks is completely *on*. I have less stage-fright and more apprehension about not being able to lead my men today. I'm handing the wheel over to Thatcher.

And this is a *big* event for the families and security. Big for Sulli, too. I keep smiling at her, seeing her smile rise again and again.

Sulli can't restrain a happy one. "I might cum watching you on the drums."

"Me too," Banks jokes into a crooked smile.

Sulli's brows rise. "I'm being serious."

"We know," Banks and I say at the same time.

She elbows us.

We all laugh.

A pyrotechnic goes off with a *blast*. Sulli flinches, her laugh dying immediately. "Fuck. Sorry."

I wince a little. Crap, I wish I could be here as her bodyguard. I want to shield her from the anxiety that's been pummeling her every so often.

"Don't be sorry, Sulli," Banks hugs her close to his tall frame.

She glances over at the stage. We see smoke roll over the ground as they test a fog machine. "I shouldn't be this shaken. The Olympics didn't bother me this bad."

"It did at first," I remind her. "And eventually you had something to focus on."

She's back home now. No goals to train for. It's easier to remember the gun incident.

"In that case," Sulli says, "I choose to focus on *you* and your hot-as-fuck drumming skills."

I playfully avoid her eyes and look to Banks. "Watch this one. She's going to be soaked during the show."

Sulli gapes. "Kits!"

I place my hand on my chest. "That's what you told me, Sul."

Her cheeks heat. "Fuck, I did...didn't I?" Her eyes dart to the left. To her aunt. Black high heels, black dress, and black sunglasses, Rose walks hand-in-hand with Connor Cobalt. He's dressed for a Fortune 500 business meeting, not an emo-punk concert, but they carry themselves with importance, like everyone else are the ones who don't belong.

And they're here to watch their son.

They come over to say good luck to me, and we chat for a few minutes. Sulli avoids their eyes since she's avoiding their daughter. And before they can question her, Luna calls Sulli to the side balcony that overlooks the stage. Farrow and Maximoff are with Luna, and Banks is about to follow our girlfriend.

I grab his arm, then radio Thatcher. "Akara to Thatcher, swap onto Sulli for a second."

He's here as a floater. Jane had bad morning sickness. She planned to come cheer on her brother, sick and all, but she threw up in the elevator. And that was enough to sit out this year's Summer Fest.

She's back at the penthouse, watching the show from a livestream.

"Copy," Thatcher responds.

Banks frowns, and I say goodbye to Rose and Connor as they go stand with Ryke and Daisy.

"What's going on?" Banks asks, checking over his shoulder. Ensuring his brother is climbing the balcony to Sulli.

Yep.

She's okay.

Is he? "Can you please rely on Thatcher tonight?" I ask him. "I understand the *need* to protect her during high-stress situations like this, but this is also sensory overload." Crew is testing drums now. Banging. Chatter is morphed into a strange, muffled noise that grows loud, then soft. Music plays off in the distance from another stage, and soon, The Carraways will overpower his ability to hear *anything*.

He grimaces. "Is that an order?"

"Partially, yeah."

"What's the other part?"

"Me caring about my metamour. I love you, Banks, but you don't always take care of your health."

Banks sighs out a rough breath, knowing I'm right. "Alright."

"How's your head?"

"Screwed on."

We laugh, and he begins to smile. He listens to the crowd chant the band name again. His gaze is faraway, and I don't have to ask. He's telling me, "Skylar always wanted to go to one of these. Dad wouldn't let him, but I swear he snuck out once." He drops his gaze, something gnawing at Banks.

And I reach up a bit and hold his shoulder for a second. Remembering a while ago, how Banks mentioned Skylar telling him something before he died. Whatever Skylar said, Banks has been cradling the weight of his words for years. Dragging him down.

He looks at me.

He sees that I'm here, and I feel him grappling with the words. I nod to him, "You can tell me, Banks. What he said."

Banks swallows hard, then lets out quietly, "He said, *Banksy, I hate it here. I'd rather go jump off a bridge than listen to Dad one more day.* That was a day before he died."

"You were twelve," I remind him just as softly. "You couldn't have known what would happen, and maybe he was just exaggerating, Banks."

"Or he could've been serious. He was asking me for help—"

"Banks—"

"I could've done more, Akara, and I *didn't*. I didn't save him, and I've never blamed myself the way that Thatcher blames himself. The way my parents do. I always just blamed Sky. For leaving me with this *fucking* mess of feelings." He glares up at the top of the stage, then down at the ground. "For making me feel like I had a chance to help him, and I didn't."

"What could you've done?" I say to him like I'm reaching for the alternate path, the alternate history that *can't* exist.

He shakes his head repeatedly, breathing heavily. "Something."

"Listen to me"—I grip his other shoulder, bringing him closer— "it's okay."

Banks nearly breaks down.

I hug him.

He hugs me, and I repeat, "It's okay. Skylar wouldn't want you to carry his pain, man. It's okay."

Banks breathes and breathes.

We hug for a moment longer, and his body feels lighter. And lighter.

For every nightmare I've ever had where Sulli and Banks are suffering, the second we're together—we've been unconfined. Unencumbered. Unfettered. Freed. I think the three of us were always meant to find each other. So we could finally be weightless.

54

Sullivan Meadows

FEAR CONFUSES ME.

How the essence of *fear* flickers in and out like a flame. How in one second, I can be all smiles. All jokes and good times and pleasant fucking thoughts. In the next, my skin feels too thin. My heart too frail. My body all sticks and fragile bones.

I didn't expect the concert to slam me backwards to the incident. I stand uncomfortably fucking still while I watch Akara perform with The Carraways. Flames blast off around Tom as he strums the guitar and sings a punk rock anthem with life-or-death passion. He rouses the crazed audience with the way he sings, each word leaving his lips in feverish glory. Like he *feels* every melody and lyric.

From my vantage on the side-stage balcony, crowds bounce up and down, a mosh pit forming near the front of the stage. The sun is nearly gone. Fire explodes again.

Fuck.

I blink a few times. Every explosive *bang* and *pop* feels like a gun to the face. I swallow a rising lump, sweat built on my neck and not from the heat of the fire.

Banks holds my wrist tight.

I think he might be taking my pulse.

His lips dip to my ear, and he whispers loudly, "Let's get some air."

I shake my head. "I want to watch him."

He follows my gaze to the stage.

Tom lets the guitar hang around his neck and claps to the beat of the drums. The bassist keeps playing, but I'm watching my boyfriend. Sweat drips down Akara as he bangs the small drums, the big one, the kick stand thing. I don't know what they are, but I'm fucking amazed he memorized The Carraways' set list so fast and plays without falter.

That's my Kits.

A total fucking boss.

Hair sticks to the sweat built up on his forehead. He chose to go shirtless, abs in panty-dropping view, and his snake tattoo is fucking *hot*. I imagine a lot of the cheers are for him.

My dreamboat.

I'm really fucking proud of him for playing. I can tell he missed picking up the sticks.

Banks places a comforting hand on my shoulder. Another pyrotechnic blasts off and my breath hitches.

I hug onto Banks. The further through the set, the darker the night, the faster my heart races. If I asked Tom beforehand, I'm sure he would've cancelled the pyrotechnics for the night. But I'd never fucking ask him to change his performance. If I can't handle this, then I should just go home.

The next pyrotechnics come out in a wave of three.

I barely breathe through the blasts. I barely blink anymore.

"Sulli?" Banks asks how I'm doing every few minutes.

"I'm okay," I repeat.

I'm okay.

I'm okay.

The rest of the concert is a blur, but I stand my ground. I don't run away or hide. I'm here, riding this out. Before the final song, I turn to Banks. "Maybe I should head to the car early? Beat the crowds?" I speak as loud as I can.

I'm scared of over-the-top pyrotechnics for the finale. If this is a fucking strategy, it can't be considered running away, right?

Except something in me says, *stay.*

Don't leave this early.

Stay for Akara.

Stay for yourself.

He was on the sidelines cheering me on every *second* at the Olympics. I want to be there for him, but I'm warring with going and staying. Tugged in two directions, and before Banks speaks, I speak into his ear, hands cupped so he can hear, "You think Akara will mind if I go early?!"

"Not at all," Banks says against my ear. "He just wants you to feel safe like I do. Some air will do you good." Fog machines have been rolling, and it's stuffier back here. I ease a little bit, knowing we're about to go. Instead of radioing Thatcher, he simply turns to his left and smacks his brother's chest. I squeeze in close to hear.

"We're gonna head out," Banks tells him.

Thatcher speaks loudly as Banks backs up a little bit. "Banks! You wait for Akara! I'll take Sulli to the car!"

"I'm not leaving Sulli!" Even yelling, I can barely hear them over the booming speakers. "You can come with us!"

They suddenly have a staring contest. I look from Banks to Thatcher, back to Banks. "What's going on?!"

Banks dips his head to reach my ear, "He wants to take you to the car himself. You'll be alright with just my brother? I'll meet up with you in five."

"Why just him?" I ask Banks.

He lifts his shoulders, but the way he glances at his brother, I realize Thatcher wants to tell me something. I've been avoiding Jane, and I can't avoid him if he's my car escort.

Normally, I'd be like *fuck no*, but his stern, no-nonsense demeanor seems softer tonight. Apologetic. He awkwardly clears his throat, then nods to me like, *please, give me a chance.*

I feel like I owe Thatcher and Jane more of an apology.

Maybe this is *my* chance too.

"Will you be alright?" Banks asks again. He's hawk-eyeing the balcony and our exits, and I think he might need air too. Even if his supreme vigilance calms me, Akara said it's not always a good thing for Banks to be this on-guard.

"You'll join us in five?" I ask again.

"You won't even notice I'm gone."

"Okay." I inhale deeply. "I think Thatcher is right!" I try to speak louder. "One of us should stay for the end! For Kits!"

Banks nods, then cocks his head to his brother. Seeing me about to leave, Banks looks more uncertain. Not wanting to stay here while I go.

"Gabe is coming with us," Thatcher calls it into his mic. "We'll be fine, Banks." He gives his brother a look that I'd bet only Banks can interpret.

Banks cracks a quarter-smile. "You're such a fucking gabbadost'."

"Always will be." Thatcher pats his shoulder, then puts a hand to my back, leading down the metal balcony.

Muscular, wide Gabe Montgomery walks ahead.

Once we leave the stage entirely, I inhale a bigger breath. Sandals hit squishy grass the further we trek away from the stage through a back VIP exit. Basically how rock stars leave without being swarmed by fans.

Comparing yourself to a fucking rock star. Good one.

I feel my confidence draining. Pulse still jumping up and down. Especially without Banks or Akara, but Thatcher keeps a hand on my back. Like he knows that touch calms me.

I breathe.

Stars twinkle overhead, and the smell of funnel cake grease and weed mix in the air. Rows and rows of big trucks have ruined the grass and kicked up dirt. Back here in the VIP, I see all the innerworkings. Where the equipment is housed. The tour buses for the bands.

Crew shuffle around hurriedly, some more leisurely.

As we continue walking along the grass, I work up the nerve to speak to Thatcher. An explanation of why I'm dodging Jane. An olive branch...? "I—"

"I'm sorry." Thatcher gets it out first.

I stare up at him, our pace starting to slow.

His strict eyes carry a lot more emotion than I think I've seen. Maybe because Thatcher is fucking intimidating and staring into his gaze sometimes feels like staring into the sun. So I tend to look away.

I'm not right now, and he keeps talking. "Banks instantly treated Jane with warmth and love, and I didn't give you the same grace—and I'm sorry."

I didn't expect that kind of apology, and in my shocked silence, he adds more, "Skylar used to joke that Banks is love and I'm war, and we were twelve back then. Some things are hard to grow out of, harder to change, but…" He takes a beat. "I know I'm not just built for war anymore, and you deserve that love and warmth from me."

I'm speechless, emotion balled up in my throat. "Thatcher…" I swallow, unable to say the fucking words I want to say.

"You're my family, Sulli." Thatcher picks up my string of silence, which shocks me again since *he's* usually so quiet with me. "The moment my brother fell in love with you—you became my family, and I should've told you that. I should've told you that I'm rooting for you, Akara, and Banks. I should've told you that I'm here if you need me. I should've told you that I hope I can raise my daughter alongside your daughter or son—I should've told you that I love you. And I'm fucking sorry I never did until now." His voice cracks.

I'm seeing Thatcher Moretti for the first time. He's letting me see him, and I think I finally understand how Jane fell in love with this man.

Why Gloria also calls him her "good son"—and I suddenly really want to be closer than further away from Jane and Thatcher.

I'm not good with words, but if he said all of that to me, then I can say more to him. "Thatcher—" A sudden, violent push thrusts me off my feet—so powerfully, so severely that I'm on the ground in a split-second with breath trapped in my chest. Did Thatcher just push—?

Pop!

I jolt.

POP!

The second pop rings my ears. Screaming. Shrieking. Fearful noises pierce the air—wind is still knocked out of me. Confusion, spiked adrenaline all disorient me in a dizzying mess. My palms are on soggy grass.

I barely see Gabe running away from me. Sprinting with all his might towards something, and before I can glance behind me, Thatcher grips the back of my shirt, tugging me up to a stance. His arm swoops around my shoulders.

My feet move before my head.

He pulls me behind a tour bus.

We sink to the ground to hide from the amassing people who stampede. Mostly crew.

"Stay down," Thatcher tells me.

My ears are still ringing, pulse hammering in my temple, my throat— *what happened?* What just fucking happened? *Please be more confetti poppers.*

That didn't sound like a confetti popper. That sounded like a fucking gun. I can't catch my breath, panicked, and my eyes dart every which way, until I feel Thatcher's arm go slack on my shoulders.

I turn.

Leaned up against the tour bus, he's lost color in his face, but he's still surveying our surroundings. Ensuring no one is nearing us.

Something feels really fucking wrong.

"Thatcher?" My eyes flash over his body.

He's bearing his forearm to his abdomen, a gun in his hand. His black button-down seems wet. His security badge and lanyard are stained red...

Blood—he's bleeding. No, no, no, *no.* "Those pops were bullets?" My voice sounds distant in my ears. In my head.

"His, then mine," he says in a shallow breath.

The second *pop* seemed louder because Thatcher had pulled the trigger. And before the guy even fired, Thatcher shoved me to the ground.

To save me from being shot.

He took the bullet. "You're wearing a bulletproof vest?"

He shakes his head, wincing and breathing strangely.

Stab proof vest, I remember. Some of SFO switched to stab proof vests, which don't stop bullets. *No, no, no, fuck, fuck.* "Thatcher," I choke. "*Thatcher.*"

His hand goes limp on the gun. "Take this." He passes me the Glock, his arm weak against his abdomen now, weak against the gunshot wound. *He's bleeding. He's fucking bleeding.*

Holding the gun, I use my other hand to apply pressure against his wound.

He swallows hard, nose flaring. "Sulli…" He's taking short breaths. *Stop the bleeding. Stop the bleeding.*

"Fuckfuckfuck." Is all that comes out of my mouth.

His eyes flutter. He's about to leave.

Don't.

Don't go.

"No, *please*," I beg, tears and snot coming out. "Please don't go. Please. He needs you. He can't lose you. *Please.* Jane—Jane can't lose you…I can't lose you." I sob and then I rip the earpiece out of his ear. Maybe he already called this in—but I move fast in case he didn't.

I find the mic button, the one I've seen Banks and Akara press a thousand times. Choking on my words, I say, "Sulli to SFO, Thatcher has been shot. He's been shot. We're behind a tour bus."

Muffled voices come out next, but I abandon the mic to keep applying pressure to the wound. Thatcher puts his blood-stained hand over my hand, and he chokes out, "Call Jane." He's fighting consciousness.

There's so much fucking blood.

I'm shaking as I drop the gun and frantically dig in my pockets for my phone. *Call Jane. Call Jane.* I struggle to dial the number, blood smearing on the screen. And I keep one hand on Thatcher's wound, not letting him bleed out.

"Call Jane," he repeats weakly, desperately, like he knows he's losing time. Like this is it. "I want to hear her voice…" He chokes down a strange, pained noise.

Jane…Jane.

My beautiful, lively cousin. Thatcher's wife. The love of his life.

She can't survive this.

Banks can't survive this.

Please.

The Morettis can't lose another son.

I finally hit the *call* Jane. And I have no signal. I have no *fucking* signal. "Thatcher," I'm bawling. "Just stay with me. Stay strong. Hold on."

"SULLI!" Farrow yells.

Thank God.

"Help is coming," I say through tears.

Farrow skids down to the ground, trauma bag in hand. "Can you talk to me, Thatcher?" He checks his pulse with his gloved hand, and to me, Farrow says, "Don't move, Sulli."

I nod frantically, over and over. I'm not moving. I'm not moving.

"Check Sulli," Thatcher chokes out, "I had to push her…"

Farrow briefly glances to my belly.

I'm pregnant.

"I'm fine," I almost snap frantically. "Pay attention to him. Don't worry about me." I would shove Farrow towards Thatcher, but he's already working fast, assessing Thatcher under his clothes while also grabbing supplies from the bag—I barely make sense of what he's doing with the readiness and intense pace at which he moves.

"No exit wound, Thatcher," Farrow says with calmness, but there is palpable urgency in his eyes that scares me. "I'm going to lie you on your back." He pulls Thatcher away from the tour bus, so he's supine. "You did great, Sulli. I have this now."

I can't move.

Someone touches my shoulder, and when I glance over, I realize it's Moffy. My cousin. My big brother. "Sul." His tough green eyes soften on me. "You can let go. It's okay."

I exhale a staggered breath and scuttle backwards on my butt to give Thatcher room. Hands stained red. I can't tear my eyes fully off Thatcher. Like if I blink, he'll disappear.

Maximoff kneels beside me, and I'm gripping the life out of his hand.

Farrow has already taken over, putting pressure on Thatcher's abdomen with some sort of special dressing and bandage.

I stay beside Thatcher. "Hang in there," I speak through an avalanche of tears and sharp breath. "You're doing fucking great." I'm using the words Farrow said to me. I don't know what else to do. He's losing a fuck ton of blood.

Thatcher is barely responsive. He blinks slowly, staring up at the night sky, then at Farrow.

"EMTs are on their way," Farrow says, applying a lot of pressure to the wound. "You have a chance here, so stop looking at me like you're saying goodbye. You're the hall monitor. Write me up later about all your little rules I broke."

Thatcher's chest rises in a strained laugh. I swear I hear him say the word, *friend*, to Farrow.

Farrow has pain in his eyes.

And then Thatcher stares up again and chokes out, "Banks."

I turn, and I let go of Moffy. Standing up, I see Banks and Akara *running* towards us at full speed. "He's coming—Banks is coming."

"THATCHER!" Banks screams.

And when I glance back at Thatcher, I stagger like I've been kicked in the gut. His eyes are shut—he's no longer awake. Farrow looks as destroyed as I feel, but he's checking his pulse. His airway.

Banks lurches backwards, as though he's being shot. He sees his twin brother unconscious on the bloody grass, and Banks can't even reach the tour bus where Thatcher lies. His legs buckle, and he drops to his knees. Wrenched in anguish, and Akara is holding onto Banks.

My heart is being shredded. I manage to find balance on my feet. I float towards them and then collapse to my knees beside the men I love.

Akara's arms are wrapped around Banks as he cries into Akara's chest. Guttural sobs from somewhere deeper than here. I press my forehead to Banks' back, wanting to take the agony from him. To soak the pain up inside me.

Akara keeps whispering to him. Keeps talking.

"Just breathe….breathe."

Tears spill down my cheeks. A darkness burrows through me, hollowing the light out.

Thatcher Moretti took a bullet for me.

He's going to die protecting *me*.

All because I had to leave the concert early. Because I was *scared* of fucking fireworks.

Because I'm a coward.

I want to rewind time. Take it away. Tear it from history. *Please.* Fucking please.

55

Banks Moretti

I HATE HOSPITALS.

I hate that I'm back here, worrying about my brother. Last time, his dumbass ran into a burning building for Tony Ramella. This time, he took a bullet for the love of my life.

My eyes are bloodshot. Raw. Everything feels raw. Hell, if someone touches me, I just might crumble and turn to ash. How do I explain being an identical twin? Loving someone for all your life. How pieces of you are a part of them, and if they die, you die.

The waiting room is crowded while Thatcher fights for his life in surgery.

Every chair is filled; every space to stand is jam-packed. With SFO, the guys from Triple Shield, and Morettis, Piscitellis, Ramellas, and Cobalts. Some Hales and Meadows—all would've come but hospital staff said we were already past capacity for visitors, so they agreed to go back and watch Jane and Thatcher's cats.

Sitting on either side of me, Akara and Sulli are quiet comforts that I'm grateful to have. Just feeling Sulli's hand on my leg, feeling Akara's arm on my shoulders—I remember to breathe.

I can't do a thing for my mom. Even if I was fully-functioning.

She grips her knees and speaks to my grandma, Uncle Joe, and Nicola, "He'll be fine. He'll pull through. He always does." She's pushed away my aunts who try to console her. "I'm fine, Carmela." Her pained eyes meet mine across the waiting room. "He'll be fine, Banksy."

Her denial is killing me fuckin' slowly.

Janie.

She keeps pacing back and forth, hand on her belly. Hair frizzed and wild and cheeks tear-streaked. I want to tell her it's going to be okay, but I don't have the fucking words. I don't feel like it is.

Of what I've seen, Jane only says more than a few words to Maximoff. The rest of her family, she just nods like she's somewhere else. Gone into the operating room with her husband. Rose will walk over to her daughter and squeeze her hand every so often.

Jane seems to respond to that.

Sulli keeps flipping her new 3-month sobriety coin over in her palm. She's muttering *I'm sorry. I'm so sorry* under her breath. I put a hand on her head to try to comfort her, but she winces. Like she's underserving of the solace. And I get that pain. It lances me everywhere, but neither of us shift away.

Sulli is safe. The only relief I have is knowing she is safe and healthy. Baby's fine. A nurse did an ultrasound.

"Banks."

I swing my head to the doorway.

Other heads swing to the doorway.

My dad—he stands there. Stoic. Unblinking.

He's about to lose another son, is all I think. But he lost us years ago. So why does he care?

He gestures his head towards the hallway. Like, *let's talk for a sec, you and me.* I feel like a ghost already. Drifting. I rise. Follow him out into the empty hallway. Further. To the vending machines. He punches a button for a coffee.

Some nurses pass by and he waits until they're gone to speak again.

"Are you okay?" he asks me.

My throat swells closed. I've been asked that about a thousand times tonight. Truth: I think I should be sedated. I don't feel right in the head. I just want to be under during this part. Wake me up if he's alive. Kill me if he's dead.

My eyes cloud and I stare hard at the floor, trying to get them to stop.

He tries to touch my shoulder. I jerk away, arms staying crossed, and I breathe hard through my nose. Jaw clenching.

"Okay," he says, looking me up, down. "I talked to Akara. He said the police report has been filed. Everything has been taken care of."

"My brother has one foot in the fuckin' grave—everything's not taken care of."

He stands more stoically. "I meant the threat is neutralized. Thatcher did exactly what he's called to do. The target was aiming for Sulli—"

"I know," I snap back. "You don't think I fuckin' know this?" Anger overrides whatever fucked emotions have been eviscerating me. "You don't think I keep replaying what I heard? Some demented, obsessive guy *wrote* that he wanted to 'eliminate' Sulli from this fuckin' earth."

My dad stands so still.

It enrages me more. "You hear about that from police? He hopped the fence to VIP without anyone noticing. He managed to find her." I grow hotter, hotter. "You hear what Thatcher said on comms tonight? How he saw this motherfucking *shitbag's* gun already pointed at my girlfriend." My eyes sear. "Thatcher drew his gun and shot to kill. He killed the target, but not before taking a *fucking* bullet to his body, and that should've been me." Tears spill through my rage. Rage that bleeds into visceral pain.

I point at my chest. "That should've been me! I should've been with her—I should be the one on the fuckin' operating table. I should be the one who's dead—not him. It should've been me. It should've *always* been me." Voice broken, I'm so far gone—I can barely see.

He grabs onto me. Pulls me into his body. I don't remember ever being hugged by my dad like this. But he's hugging me. "You're wrong."

I shudder into a ragged breath.

"It shouldn't have been you," he breathes into my hair. My head bowed to his shoulder. "It should have *never* been you. You hear me?"

I clutch onto him, dying inside.

"You are meant to be here, okay?" Emotion cracks his voice. He holds tighter, like I'm twelve again. Like we're back to the worst night of our lives. And it's the other brother we're grieving. "You're going to pull through this, Banks—we're all going to pull through this. I know it hurts, son…I know it hurts."

I try to breathe. I take big, exhausted breaths.

"I love you," he chokes. "I know it hurts."

I shut my eyes. Hatred leaving me as I grip onto my dad, his words so different now than from back then. I would've given anything to hear him say I'm worth the air I breathe. I'm worth this earth under my feet. I should be alive.

Not dead.

It shouldn't have been me.

It should have *never* been me.

He's saying them now. That means something to me. Can't process how long we stay like that, but as we pull back, his hand is on my shoulder, and he asks me, "What do you need?"

"A sedative," I say the only thing that makes sense.

He turns around and waves down a nurse.

56
Sullivan Meadows

BANKS SLEEPS ON THE waiting room chair at Philly General, head on Akara's shoulder. I keep staring at the coin that I pass between my palms.

It calms me.

Settles me.

But I know what I have to do.

Pocketing the coin, I rise to my feet. Akara reaches for my wrist, his concern drilling into me.

"I'm okay," I whisper to him.

He doesn't say anything.

I glance to Banks. "Stay with him."

He nods and then drops my wrist.

Each step is pain. But I take each one. I should have done this a long time ago—and I hate that it's taken me until now, until this fucking moment. I come to a stop in front of my blue-eyed, splotchy-cheeked cousin.

Jane.

Six months pregnant, her belly swells in a pastel-blue tulle skirt. Her T-shirt says *Caturday*—something I know Thatcher bought her out of the blue.

She stands by a poster of a foaming teal sea. I think it's here to calm people, but she's gripping onto a cup of coffee with enough anxiety to put half-moon dents into the Styrofoam. Her five brothers and little sister stare up at us from chairs, like we've taken the center stage of a play.

Even the Morettis watch us.

Jane and I—we're in relationships with brothers. And all this time I wasted running from Jane, I could've become closer to her. We could've shared in the fucking fact that we're with the Moretti brothers. Joked about how low they need to duck on airplanes. Talked fondly about their love of pizzelles and whiskey and porters. Confided in how good they are—how sweet, how much we really fucking love them.

And it's too late.

Even if I start now, I'm too late, aren't I?

I open my mouth to speak, but words don't form.

Your husband might die because of me. Guilt is a parasite that has infected every cell in my body.

Jane reaches for my hand. I let her take it. She gives her coffee to Audrey. And to my surprise, Jane silently leads me out of the waiting room. I think she means for us to go to the hallway, but she keeps walking.

I barely notice how Oscar and Donnelly have followed like shadows behind us. Here to protect us. Like Thatcher protected me.

We continue onward. Until we stop in a long, random hallway. Art decorates the walls. Each painting is a scene from a classic fairytale. Little Red Riding Hood. Sleeping Beauty. *Cinderella.*

Only these aren't highbrow works of art. Watercolors and crayons are smeared and smudged and poorly drawn like a child's doing. I glance over my shoulder. Oscar and Donnelly stand far off by a vending machine, pretending to give us privacy.

"Farrow showed me this last time," Jane says softly.

Last time. "After the townhouse fire?"

She nods. "Children from a local school paint them every year, and then they're auctioned during a charity event for the hospital. According to Farrow, it's all for show because the winners of the auction just donate the paintings to the hospital anyway."

With our hands clasped together, Jane and I view the children's artwork. I focus in on the messy drawing of *The Little Mermaid.* The eyes are off center. Her hair is purple. I love it. "They're beautiful," I breathe.

"Insider tip," Jane says. "This is the most private hallway in the hospital."

I glance at her, and we share a soft, fading smile. Even though she seized my hand first, I hold onto Jane's stronger to comfort my cousin. "Jane, I'm…I'm so, so sorry. That…I didn't know…I tried calling…I…" Tears build in both our eyes. "I wish it would've been me."

Jane takes my hand in both of hers. "He would have rather it been him." We're both crying. I put my other hand on our hands. Face-to-face with Jane, our tears fall to our knuckles and fingers. Then slip, making wet droplets on the ground.

She breathes out, "Banks would have done the same for me. Don't carry this with you, Sulli."

"This is different. I've been fucking awful to you." My voice cracks. "I've avoided you—and Thatcher knew I was icing you out. And all the kind things he said to me…and all that I didn't get to say to him…"

"He *knew* you weren't awful to me," Jane cries, neither of us letting go of each other, not even to wipe our cheeks. "I knew you weren't being awful. You just needed time…and it hurt a little." Her breezy voice fractures.

God. I cry harder.

She cries more. "I just envisioned us being closer."

"I know," I cry. "I'm sorry. I'm so fucking sorry. You've always been so maternal and sweet, and you're going to be the *best* mom around, Jane. The absolute fucking best, and I just see the world constantly telling me I'm the *worst* in comparison. Bottom fucking tier, and looking at you, being with you, I was just confronting that stupid insecurity—"

"It's not stupid," she cuts in, shaking her head vigorously. "I'm *terrified* of motherhood too. You know who *I'm* going to be compared to? My mom. The most *brilliant* mother who kicked ass raising seven children in stilettos *while* owning her own world-renowned fashion company. I'm not her."

I didn't realize Jane would share the same insecurity. Silent tears keep cascading. "It fucking sucks."

"It really does," Jane says in a broken voice. "Raising cats hasn't prepared me at all. I'm not a good disciplinarian. I love being a sibling to my siblings because I don't have to be strict like my parents. I'm too soft—" She starts bawling again. "And I thought…I imagined Thatcher would level us out as a team, as parents. He'd be tough but loving in all the ways I'm not."

I let go of her hands and wrap my arms around her. She hugs me as though her legs are about to buckle. But I use all my strength and keep her on her feet. I keep her upright. I keep her against me.

Jane cries into my shoulder.

I touch the back of her frizzy hair. "He's not gone, Jane. He's a fighter. I know he is because he's best friends with Akara and Banks—the three of them are fighters, and they don't go down that easily. They just don't. He's coming back to you and your daughter. And you'll both raise her together, and she'll grow up alongside my daughter or son."

Just like Thatcher wanted.

Just like I want.

Just like I can tell Jane wants. Her tears slow with deep breaths. After several minutes, she's able to stand more on her own. We gently pull apart, wiping our cheeks. I rub my nose with my forearm.

I've never fully felt a part of the Moffy-Jane friendship. They share such a deep fucking bond. Charlie has always been closer to them, since they all went to high school together. Beckett and I were the fourth and fifth wheels, the home-schoolers. The goal-seekers.

But I can't be afraid of stepping into a bigger friendship with Moffy and Jane. I can't be afraid of the possibility of growing apart from Beckett. Change is hard. And I just want to sink into it. Not fight it anymore.

I rub my wet cheek. "I love you," I tell Jane, "and we will be close. No more hiding from you, I promise."

"You don't know how happy that makes me," Jane says tearfully, like she wishes she could be happier in this moment.

Oh Jane. My heart is breaking.

We're about to hug again.

"Jane!" Farrow is running down the hallway. We both turn, my blood goes cold. Is it good or bad news? I can't fucking tell. Farrow passes Donnelly and Oscar without a glance. He's wearing medical scrubs and he takes Jane's hand. "Come with me."

57

Akara Kitsuwon

IF I KNOW ANYTHING about Thatcher Moretti—it's that he's made to last. Ever since I've met him, he's loved *The Iliad*, and every now and then, I'll hear him and Banks speaking about Greek mythology. Athena and frigging Aphrodite—but mostly, Thatcher talks of warriors and the lessons behind myths, and nights like tonight, I see someone who's withstood the hardships of time, just like the ancient stories he reads.

I lean an arm on the doorway of a hospital room in Philly General.

Thatcher lies on a bed, clicking a TV remote and scrolling through channels on mute. An IV line pumps him with pain meds and fluids.

My scuffed Vans squeak on the hospital tile.

He's staring at the TV. "Took you long enough."

Thatcher sees me in his peripheral. I begin to smile, knowing he'd spot me, but I just think, *he's the same Thatcher I've always known.*

He's alive.

A few hours have passed since Thatcher could have visitors. The last of the Cobalts and Morettis left about ten minutes ago. Now just a single person from each family remains.

Jane sleeps on a tufted chaise in the corner. Banks is passed out on a double-wide cushioned chair, his legs propped up on an ottoman. His dad found him a sedative, but I woke him up once visitors could see Thatcher. Banks and Jane were the first to see him.

Right next to Banks, Sulli is curled up and snoozing against his chest.

I come forward towards him, quiet enough not to wake the others. "I wanted to give your family a chance to visit."

His brows furrow, his gaze on mine. "You are my family, Akara."

His words push through me, and the tension behind losing his friendship just unravels. Like a twisted, gnarled knot that finally unspools and loosens. Something easy rests between us. Knowing he wants me here. Knowing that we're not so far gone, him and me. Me and him.

Knowing there's a way back.

There always has been, Nine.

I smile a little more and grip the handlebar to his hospital bed. "Family perks from being in a triad with your brother."

He tries to lift himself up higher on the bed. "You had family perks before you got with Banks and Sulli." He looks to me again. "You've always had them. I'm just a fucking asshole—"

"Hey, I'm the asshole between the two of us. Stop trying to take that from me, man."

Thatcher almost laughs, a deep, breathy sound leaving without his lips parting. Then he nods to me. "Whether you like it or not, you're the good cop. I'm the bad cop." He nods over to Banks. "And our cowboy is sleeping."

"I like it," I tell him. "I miss it." *Our friendship.*

"Me too." He clutches my gaze with familiar intensity. "You might have no siblings on paper—but you're my brother, Akara, and whatever quicksand we're in together, we'll get out of eventually. That's just what brothers do."

My eyes burn as I take a sharp, raw breath. *Brothers.* Brotherhood. I never want to let it go. He's saying I can't.

Good.

I nod and clasp his hand in a strong grip. He squeezes stronger. And I tell him, "What you did for Sulli—"

"You would've done for Jane. Any one of us would've done for any of them."

"But you're *the one* who did it. You can't undercut that shit." I say with emphasis, from my core, "*Thank you.*"

He nods back to me, his chest rising in a deeper breath.

I exhale with him. "Hey," I say, letting go of his hand. "Do me a solid?"

"Of course."

"Don't tell Banks I cursed."

Thatcher laughs, the full movement inflating his lungs, elevating his body—he winces.

"Take it easy," I tell him. "You're missing a whole organ."

He adjusts himself again, half-wincing, half-smiling. "I feel lighter already." Bullet struck his spleen, which ruptured. That, plus major blood loss, had Thatcher knocking on death's door. Surgeons successfully removed the bullet and spleen and gave him a blood transfusion. He was hanging on a thread, though.

They said his heart stopped for a minute.

To see him awake, responsive, and on the road to recovery is still a shock to everyone. "Some-pounds lighter and a miracle," I tell him.

"Not a miracle," he says, still adjusting. "I'm just down to seven of my nine lives."

"Jane would marry a cat."

He laughs but tries not to laugh too hard this time. I've noticed how Thatcher takes loving glimpses of his wife every so often, and his lips rise each time.

Once the laughter fades, he's back to adjusting himself up the bed. "God, my ass keeps falling asleep." Right as he says the words, Sulli shifts off Banks as she wakes up.

Our attention veers over to my girlfriend.

She's okay. I can't replay the series of events that led us here. Honestly, it's painful to revisit, and I'm looking forward these nights and days.

"Hey." Sulli tries to whisper and slips off the chair. When she stands, her fist is closed, and I'm pretty positive she's gripping onto her sobriety coin. "Thatcher..." She comes closer. "I've been meaning to talk to you without Jane...or once she fell asleep." Her eyes redden.

I'm about to step out, to give them a second together.

"Kits, you can stay."

So I stay.

Thatcher takes a deep breath, coughing a little, and I go grab his water off the tray. He gives me an appreciative look as I hand him the cup.

Sulli tries her best to hold his gaze. To not look away. "What you said before...when we were walking, I want that too. I want our kids to be friends and to be close, and I don't want to be your least favorite person to be around—"

"You were never my least favorite, Sulli."

"Really?" She frowns. "Who's your least favorite?"

Thatcher thinks, then glances to me. Together, we say, "Charlie." He's burned all of us the most, but we're still smiling saying his name. It's hard for us on security to really hate Charlie. Not only because SFO protects him, but because most of us still don't understand him fully.

And though it's easy to hate what you don't understand, we see the world doing that to our clients—to the people we love—all the dang time.

The world has even been doing that to me, Banks, and Sulli. And so we all try our best not to do it too.

Sulli grows red-faced. "If we're being fucking frank here, my least favorite to be around was you. I hate that it was you."

"It's okay," Thatcher says. "I didn't make it easy on you. I don't make it easy on a lot of people."

She rubs at her wet eyes. "What you did...you...got shot protecting me and..." Her eyes begin to cloud with tears. "Thank you is a stupid fucking word because it barely covers what I feel."

I put an arm around her shoulder. She sinks into my side for a minute, and I say, "That's basically what I told him."

Thatcher gives us a strict look. "I've heard enough *thank yous* between the three of you. I'm topped off. Just...do me a favor, you two."

"Anything," Sulli says.

"Love him forever. No matter what."

"That's not even a fucking question," Sulli declares. "Banks already has my heart."

I say, "And mine too."

58
Sullivan Meadows

1 MONTH BEFORE THE OLYMPICS

JUNE

NEW PAINT JOB, BOOGER is looking more beautiful than ever. Summer breeze fills the car while I stick my head out of the window. Wild and free on an empty backroad. Though, we're still in Philly. So one tablespoon of *wild*, five big cups of *free*.

This might be the last chance I have to ride in her before the Olympics, and she's already been cooped up in the parking garage. Adam Sully would want this. I'm sure of it.

"We're about to pass some of the fish markets," Banks warns me from the passenger seat. "Gonna want to roll those up."

I draw my head back inside. Akara takes a hand off the steering wheel to roll up the windows.

"Maybe I like the smell of fish," I say.

"That's because you are a fish," Akara teases.

"She's a mermaid," Banks counters.

"Again, no such thing."

I scoff. "One of these days, you will believe in the mystical beings."

Akara looks to me from the rearview. "In your daydreams, Sul."

Banks cuts in, "Can you pull off right here, Nine? I have to take a piss."

Akara brings the car to a stop at a hole-in-the-wall pub, the lights flickering out. He parallel parks, only a few other cars parked on the street. We spent a few hours just trying to ditch paparazzi, so I'm not too surprised no one followed us. Our efforts weren't for nothing.

Banks hops out of the car, and I follow suit, just to get some fresh air. I've been spending so much time at the Aquatic Center that my nostrils feel permanently infused with chlorine and muggy humidity. Banks heads into the pub.

Risking a bit of attention, I walk over to the driver-side window. "Hey there, hot stuff," I say.

Akara gives me a look. Up-down. Like he's sizing me up. "D."

I frown. "D? Like dick?"

He laughs. "No. That's what I grade your flirting."

My jaw drops. "F," I say. "For *fuck you.*"

"Ooh, but you already have." He teases and shuts off the Jeep. He takes the keys from the ignition and hops out onto the curb with me. I notice the dangling keychain. An otter. I reach for it in fondness and Akara willingly gives me the keys.

I start to explain. "My sister gave me this—"

The keys are ripped from my grasp. It happens in a blur. A flash. A passerby steals them and rushes away, and I feel Akara shielding me from the stranger instead of trying to grab the keys. My feet react before my brain can catch up.

I untangle from my boyfriend.

And I run.

"SULLI!" Akara's screams are nothing compared to my pace. I can feel him trying to keep up with me.

"SULLI!!" Banks' voice echoes in the air. I can feel Banks trying to catch up to me.

They can't.

I'm faster.

I've always been faster than my boyfriends. Faster than security. Faster than everyone, even Moffy. Even my dad.

I run.

And run.

Adam Sully.

The Jeep.

Those keys.

I don't see where I'm going. I just make sure to keep the thief in sight. A dark navy sweatshirt and an Eagle's baseball cap. *Don't lose him.*
Don't lose him.

My shoes slosh in puddles, and I side-sweep an old dumpster. It takes minutes before I close the distance in a dead-end alleyway. I have him now. *I have him.* I grab a fistful of his sweatshirt, only for the fabric to be yanked from my grasp as he whirls around on me.

He points a gun.

The barrel is dark and endless.

I go cold.

Flashes of my family fill my head like a slideshow on warp speed.

My mom. Blonde hair whipping in the wind. Her smile pulling at her scar. Her green eyes lighting the world.

My dad. Running beside me. His stride strong. His hugs.

My sister. Twirling together on the tire swing.

Them.

Akara and Banks.

Laughing with me.

Holding me.

Together in the frost-covered woods, beneath a globed, glowing moon—smiling with me, breathing with me, *living with me.*

I'm going to die here.

Click.

I choke on air. *No bullet in the gun.*

The thief laughs like it's a joke. The baseball cap shields his face, and he presses the trigger again. My whole body seizes in fear. Wetness seeps between my legs.

Click.

Click.

Click.

Each time he presses it. I feel like I'm dying inside.

And then Banks slams into him, knocks him down into the ground. *Bang!*

That next shot goes off into the garbage can, and I sink to my knees. *It wasn't empty.* The gun wasn't empty. I'm shaking. I…I pissed myself.

I try to breathe.

Trembling—I can't stop shaking. Akara wraps his arms around me while Banks slams the butt of his gun into the thief's temple. Lights out.

"Breathe," Akara whispers in my ear. "Just breathe."

Why did I run after him? Instinct. I let my love of that Jeep fog my brain. But I couldn't let myself do *nothing*. Banks missed his brother's wedding for that fucking Jeep. I wasn't about to let a thief…

"Shhh…" Akara whispers.

I'm sobbing.

When did I start crying?

He holds me. Banks watches, keeping a knee pinned to the thief. Police sirens go off in the distance. Akara says something to Banks, but his voice is faraway in my ear.

"She's already in your hands. Take her home, Nine," Banks says. "I'll deal with the police. We can keep this out of the media."

Those words are the last thing I hear before I'm lifted. Cradled. Carried.

Rewind. Go back.

Go back to where I'm joking with Kits. Rewind to the car where I'm wild and free. Rewind and pause and play and *don't let me run.* Don't let me run.

Never let me run again.

That thought steals more breath, like a knife into my gut, and I think, *Don't rewind.* Fast-forward. Go onward. Press play.

Will I ever be okay again?

Will I ever be okay?

59

Sullivan Meadows

"SULLIVAN! LOOK HERE!"

"How do you feel after the shooting?!"

"Will you ever attend another concert?!"

"Smile for me!"

"SULLIVAN!"

"BANKS!"

"AKARA! LOOK HERE!"

None of us respond—a lot has changed, but giving silence and a middle finger to paparazzi has stayed the fucking same. While I'm sandwiched between Banks and Akara, I flip off the cameras, and flashes ignite, shouting escalates.

Even as my pulse pitches, I breathe in and I remember, *forward. Just move.* I know I stand out wearing Akara's candy-apple red windbreaker. I intentionally put the jacket on this morning—not to draw cameras towards me—but because I've realized, more than anything, I want Banks and Akara to find me.

If we're split apart. If I'm dragged backwards.

I want to know they'll see me.

They'll catch me.

Akara speaks into his mic. Suddenly, more bodyguards surround us, pushing aside the packed media we try to elbow and shove our way to the marina on an early Saturday morning. Really, my security is doing the shoving. I'm just trying to stay upright and not stumble.

Sun has barely risen. Light blues of the early morning shade us, the air cool, and in front of me, Akara has reached back, and I cling tightly onto his hand. Behind me, I lean into the feeling of Banks' strong, protective clutch on my waist.

Familiar. Safe.

They have me. Fucking forever, they have me.

"SULLIVAN!" The shouting never stops.

Most of my family have already reached the entrance of the private marina. Paparazzi can't go inside or touch the docks. Forget my fucking luggage—I'm just concentrated on surviving this madness and I have no assistants to help carry my bags. But Akara ordered extra security to grab our stuff.

Thanks, Kits.

I only worry about reaching the superyacht.

And I realize we're one of the last left fighting inch-by-inch to reach the doors. My dad stuck around for as long as he could. Ultimately, he relinquished the task to my boyfriends—and I'm so fucking happy he trusts that they'll take care of me.

Besides my triad, only one couple remains in the aggressive pits of paparazzi.

"LILY! LO!"

I glance to my right, and through the commotion and pushing and camera flashes—my gangly, green-eyed aunt is looking to me. Aunt Lily's expression swells up inside me like the tides of time. She's nodding to me like, *you can do this, Sulli. You can do anything.*

Uncle Lo has his arm around her frame.

And as they barrel ahead, less media teeming around them, I sense my aunt passing a torch to me. A torch I know she wishes would burn out, but like any fucking Olympian, I grab the torch and keep going.

After the music festival, I could have become a recluse. Locked myself in the penthouse. Never saw the light of day until the baby was born. Maybe longer. Maybe forever, I'd be a hermit.

Except I remember the overwhelming feeling after Thatcher was shot. The shame of cowering. The shame of retreating from the pyrotechnics. I know it's okay to retreat when I'm terrified, but so badly, I just want to be brave.

I want to challenge myself to move forward, even when it's the scariest thing on Earth. And so when Aunt Rose and Uncle Connor announced a spontaneous yacht trip, I didn't hesitate to say, *I'm fucking going.*

I'm here today. I'm joining my family.

I'm *never* hiding.

The world will always try to break us, but my mom is right—I'll lose a part of myself if I stay cooped up, and I'll never have the chance to heal.

And this trip is healing for everyone—not just me. It's a four-day vacation to escape the press, who've been hounding the ever-loving fuck out of everyone about the shooting. Banks said reporters are even bothering his mom and uncles.

Not even two weeks have passed, and Thatcher is still recovering—but he suggested a trip to his in-laws in the first place. He was thinking the lake house, but weather turned out to be surprisingly perfect for the yacht in September. So teenagers took off high school and everyone who needed to cancel work, cancelled.

Even Beckett is missing some ballet performances.

While Thatcher is recuperating, he's not allowed to do any heavy lifting on the yacht. Just sitting, relaxing, being with Jane and his family—because his big Italian-American family are all invited too.

And I smile, knowing the Morettis are already Akara's family—but they might be my family someday far into the future too, once we get hitched. Or maybe they'll just seamlessly be mine like they became Akara's in time. Just like I know my family is already theirs.

And me, Banks, and Akara—the three of us—we're our own family too. In seven months, our baby will be with us. My smile never leaves, even as we keep pushing forward. Even as the cameras flash. Even as they shout our names.

SECOND DAY ON BOARD, WE CRUISE AROUND THE
Baja Peninsula, and night has fallen, twinkle lights strung above the main yacht deck where everyone has been mingling, dancing, and eating dessert.

I've pulled away from the big clusters of people. Now on the bow of the ship, I overlook the sparkling ocean as the full moon casts a glow across the water. Lounge pads surround a low-ground hot tub here, and I stick my feet into the warm water and eat a chocolate sprinkled cupcake.

Whoever chose tonight's dessert menu gets a gold medal from me. Fruit parfaits with tangerines and Oreo crumble, plus chocolate cupcakes and churros.

Utter fucking perfection.

I'm not alone on the bow.

Jane and Millie Kay Miller bask under the moonlight with me, their feet in the fizzing hot tub. "Have you had any bizarre cravings?" I ask them, since I haven't experienced that yet. I'm still superglued to my normal obsessions like chocolate and donuts.

"Cereal," Jane says, dunking a spoon in a parfait. "I can't go a morning without any type of sugary sweet cereal. Lucky Charms. Coco Puffs."

I lick icing off my finger. "Is that why there were like seven boxes of Fruit Loops in the pantry?"

Her smile brightens her eyes. "Thatcher went a little overboard. He's terribly cute that way." Remnants of heartache from nearly losing her husband lie inside her gaze, and I reach out and touch her hand in comfort. She clasps her fingers around mine, then asks Millie Kay, "You haven't craved anything sweet yet, have you?"

"Me?" Millie Kay still seems surprised to be called on.

Jane tips her head with a Cobalt roguish smile. "Yes, you. Who else?"

"Sorry, Jane—it's just…" She eyes me like I'm bigger-than-life Sullivan the Olympian and not just Sulli, then glances to Jane. "There are so many group dynamics between all of you, and I don't know how I fit in sometimes."

"That's my fucking fault," I say with a wince and pick my feet out of the hot tub. I cross my ankles and hold them loosely. "This is probably the first time the three of us are talking alone together."

They both nod, but Jane's smile grows on me. "A long time coming."

I smile back.

I'm not showing at two-months pregnant, but with the Olympics finished, I'm more interested and concentrated on the road ahead, the things they've begun experiencing. And I hate that I haven't really asked them questions until now. But I'm firmly in the camp of better *now* than *never*.

MK has been over the penthouse tons, but this trip is really the first time I've gotten to know her. Like how before the pregnancy, she'd been working at Lucky's Diner as a cook.

"I wish I had a cereal craving," she says, swishing her feet in the water. "All I want is *meat*. Specifically *messy*, spicy chicken wings. And I used to hate chicken wings before this one." She stares down at her big belly, visible through a sheer coverup and red bikini.

Five-months pregnant, a month behind Jane—Millie Kay said she swelled around her ankles, and her cheeks are puffier than when we first met. With wispy blonde hair, blue eyes, and a heart-shaped face, she looks exactly like a heroine leaving the farm for a big city to fall in love.

So I was shocked to hear she's *actually* originally from a small town in Iowa.

"Modeling agencies first ate up the whole farm girl backstory," she told me. "But I barely got booked. They said I was 'basic beautiful' which is just another way of saying I look like every Instagram Influencer. Unmemorable."

Fuck, I didn't even know that her family are fourth-generation farmers and grow corn. Not until I asked her, but only after she dropped her breakfast burrito this morning and exclaimed, *cheese and mice!*

I've never seen someone turn so red. She could hardly look at my parents or aunts and uncles, like they'd judge her for fumbling a fucking burrito.

No one cared, but I realize to Millie Kay, they're the famous "Core Six" and not just Ryke, Daisy, Lily, Lo, Connor, and Rose.

I glance at their pregnant bellies. "The carnivore and the cereal-vore."

They'll be best fucking friends.

Just like Moffy and Jane. And hopefully my baby will grow up strong beside them.

"Oh, for cute," MK laughs into a smile. "I joked to Maximoff and Farrow that their little girl will come out eating chicken bones like Pebbles Flintstone."

I wonder how different this experience must be for MK, being the surrogate carrying the Hale Baby (Farrow's sperm and Jane's egg).

"How'd you decide to be a surrogate?" I add quickly, "Sorry if you've been asked this a fuck ton."

Jane is smiling at me. Maybe she's happy that I'm finally getting to know MK.

"I kind of expect all the questions," MK replies. "I was actually born via a surrogate. My mom had fertility issues after my brother was born, so she did the whole IVF thing to have me. Didn't work out, so her and my dad decided to go the surrogacy route, and here I am." She waves. "I pretty much had in my head that I'd pay it forward one day. Give the gift of life to another couple—or triad…or whatever, I'm not against polyamory." Her face is bright red like this morning.

I really fucking like MK already. "I'm really the last person you need to be worried about saying the wrong thing in front of. I mess up my words *all* the fucking time." I pause. "At least it feels that way." Sometimes I wonder if it's all in my head. If I'm just overanalyzing my social flaws and failures more than those around me.

She relaxes. "I've been single for a while, so I just bit the bullet and figured, why not now? I *never* thought the surrogacy agency would match me with Maximoff and Farrow."

"You knew who they were?"

"I mean…" She blushes again. "Yeah." Her gaze drifts around the yacht. "I still can't believe I'm here, honestly. They've been so nice…" Her smile fades, then she glances warily at Jane.

"What's wrong?" Jane asks while brushing Oreo crumble off her baby bump.

"I really like Farrow and Maximoff. I didn't expect them to make me feel like I have more friends in Philly…and this is their baby girl. Once she's born, I'm not the mom—I do *not* want to be the mom at all." She takes a breath. "And I guess the more I love their friendship, the harder it's going to be when I have to leave."

I frown. "Why can't you stay?"

She swishes her feet in the water again. "The surrogate who gave birth to me never stuck around. She wasn't a part of my life. I don't want to complicate anything for Maximoff and Farrow. So I'm going to go—I have to go."

Aunt Rose gave birth to my little sister via surrogacy, but she's still a part of our lives—and she's never treated Winona as anything other than a niece. Respecting my mom as *the mom*. And I think Aunt Rose was trying to be fair to me too, not wanting to play favorites between me and Nona.

I could say this to MK, but I struggle to share private facts about my sister. MK isn't a fucking stranger—just to be on this yacht as a guest, you've earned a lot of trust—but she's not someone I know 100%. And with how starstruck she'd been around my parents, I'm just cautious.

Before I find a good response in my head, Gabe Montgomery strolls over to the hot tub. "Room for another?"

Is he purposefully flexing?

I blurt out, "Are you flexing your pecks?"

"Am I?" He watches his left tit jump, then his right.

Millie Kay blushes more, fingers to her forehead.

Jane muses, "How does one isolate their pecks?"

"Montgomery!" Oscar shouts from the main deck.

"See ya, ladies and babies." He moon-walks backwards to SFO and Frog, who are drinking and eating around the pool.

After Summer Fest, I heard the whole details of that night. How Thatcher *did* use comms after he fired his gun, and he ordered Gabe to check on the "target"—Banks' words. So that's why Gabe ran away. He was actually running towards the shooter, and it's good to see the whole ordeal didn't shake him too fucking badly.

Akara worried Gabe might quit—too stressful, too dangerous of a job—but he didn't, and he's still living at the apartment with Quinn and Donnelly.

Moffy approaches with a tray of desserts for us.

"How'd you fucking know?" I already finished my cupcake and definitely wanted another.

"Didn't you hear? My mind reading superpowers are *finally* kicking in."

"Oh fuck, I hope not."

They all laugh.

"Is that a bucket of pop?" Millie Kay stands up, eyeing the cooler. "I'm going to get a Fizz Life."

"I can get it for you," Moffy offers, but she's already making a quick exit. He scrunches his face. "Do I stink?" Glancing back at MK, he frowns in deep, deep thought.

"She loves you, old chap," Jane assures.

"And what's not to fucking love?" I chime in.

He wears a softer smile, then sinks down beside me. "I tried to pay for the second yacht. After five-minutes of me saying, *take it,* they wouldn't accept the money."

He means our parents. Jane, Moffy, and I all planned to chip in and pay for Yacht #2—the one cruising alongside us and where we'll hop on to sleep. Our families' own both yachts, but there are costs to chartering them. (Fuel, paying the crew, food, etc.) And with the amount of people onboard, we had to charter two vessels.

We also wanted *all* of Omega to stay on our boat and not on a smaller vessel like security usually does. So Yacht #2 houses almost everyone thirty-five and under. But the teenagers have to stay with our parents on the Senior Citizen Voyager—their nickname, not mine.

Though it's a fucking funny one.

"We have money," I defend. "And we're adults—they have to let us pay for stuff."

"Oui," Jane agrees. "Let's try again. We can make a better rebuttal together."

"I found out it's already been taken care of," Moffy says. "Ryke and Daisy covered it."

"My parents?" I'm a little surprised they'd cover a whole yacht and not involve Aunt Lily and Uncle Lo, but Moffy nods.

Maybe they owed them or something.

Music grows louder, and Maximoff and I share a big grin. Every time a familiar Spanish song plays, we belt out the words together. From Héroes del Silencio to Enrique Iglesias, and the music pulls us towards the main deck under the sparkling lights. Right around the pool, we sing in Spanish with Ben and Winona, dancing together.

Banks and Akara are watching with the rest of SFO, and I bite my lip, remembering earlier tonight, before dessert, how they danced with me. Up against me. Front and back.

I watch Banks tip a water bottle to his lips. Like he needs to cool off from the memory too.

Akara whispers in Banks' ear while his eyes are still on me, checking me out, and I love these fucking moments. Where we're happy. Where their desire pools around me like water I'm sinking deep, *deep* into. Where we'll eventually come together, and I'll feel their utter fucking love in their hands and lips.

I could dance over to them, but I see Beckett alone.

Normally, we're attached on trips, but we've barely hung out during this one. And he seems sad. So I let my boyfriends hang out with SFO, and I go to my friend.

I'm sweaty as I plop onto one of the white couches beside Beckett.

He smiles softly. "Thought you forgot about me."

"Never," I say seriously. "Impossible."

His lips slowly fall, and he stares out at the deck. "Some people drift apart. Maybe that's just life." I see him watching Donnelly, who used to be his bodyguard and friend.

"I know things will change," I say, coming to accept this fact, "but you still have me. I'm going to make a fucking effort to call you when you're free, and I hope you'll pick up—"

"I will," Beckett interjects. "You know I will."

We lean closer, as though to say, *we're here. We're friends.* And maybe our friendship isn't exactly how it was when we were little, but we're not little anymore.

"I thought about asking Akara if I could hire a bodyguard from his firm," Beckett suddenly says.

"You want Donnelly back?"

"I've *wanted* him back, but I know it's not a good idea." Beckett rests his yellow-green eyes on me. "Xander *loves* him, Sul. I can't do that to Xander just because I miss Donnelly." He shakes his head in thought. "O'Malley is fine. Akara doesn't have enough 24/7 bodyguards in order to hire a new client anyway."

O'Malley is a Triple Shield bodyguard.

"Maybe Kits will hire someone new eventually."

"Eventually," Beckett nods, and in the next few minutes, we find ourselves on my phone. Scrolling through social media together.

He has no social media at the moment. So he'll often ask to see what I've posted.

I play about ten different workout videos where I'm messing around with Banks and Akara.

"Get on my shoulders. I'm going to squat you." I'm talking to Banks at Studio 9.

He gestures to me. *"I'm not breaking your fuckin' back."*

Beckett laughs, then plays the video where I'm racing Akara in pull-ups (he won, un-fucking-fortunately), then the one where Banks lets me sit on his back for his push-ups.

"We work out a lot together and started filming stuff," I tell Beckett. "The comment section loves it."

"Really?" I try not to look at public opinion, in case I roll up on something nasty.

Beckett reads, "*I'd workout with Kitsulletti every day of the week. Do sit-ups next.*"

"*Really?*" I say again, more in shock. I read the comments with him, my jaw slowly falling at how many people are asking for more videos. Workout tutorials.

And then Beckett suddenly says, "They're making me reactivate my Instagram."

"Who?"

"The company."

The ballet company. "For marketing, I'm guessing?"

"Yeah. It's good promotion." He's not excited.

"Maybe you can get someone to run it for you."

"Like who?" He seems tired. "I don't trust anyone."

"What about Joana Oliveira? She still lives down the hall from you."

Beckett makes a *what the fuck* face. "Joana? The girl who hates me?"

"Didn't she knock on your door asking for extra toilet paper?"

"And then she proceeded to say that I have no life."

"Because you told her she has no life."

Beckett tries not to smile, but he's fucking smiling. "I told her that she could've used her phone and Insta-carted the toilet paper, unless she suddenly forgot how to work a phone." He pauses. "Was I an ass?" He lets out a sound. "I was mean. But she's *mean.*"

"Beckett." I poke his side. "You have a crush."

"If a crush is lust, then maybe." He'd rather go breaking hearts than get his heartbroken, I think.

Winona, Kinney, Vada, and Audrey suddenly cannonball into the pool together. Water splashes on the deck near our feet, and I nudge Beckett's arm with an idea. "What about Audrey? Your little sis would be fucking *great* at social media."

Beckett begins to smile. "I'll ask her."

Once he goes over to Audrey, we say *see you laters* and split apart. I find myself weaving through my parents, aunts, uncles, and the

Morettis under the twinkle lights. And I spot Aunt Lily eating a churro in a corner. Once Aunt Rose leaves her side, I approach.

"Hi, Aunt Lily."

"Sulli." She hugs me, a warm, tight hug. She's shorter than me, but her hugs seem bigger, taller, fuller—and I breathe into the loving embrace.

"Churro?" she asks as we pull back. She already rips me off a piece.

I bite into the fried dough, cinnamon explosion on my tongue. "I know it doesn't get easier," I say, "the fame and raising kids in the spotlight—"

"It does, some days," she interjects. "It's not always hard. Some days are really happy—and you forget the cameras are even there and that the world is watching." She glances at the cinnamon dust on her fingers. "Those days, I love—because your biggest worry will be the baby vomit on your shirt and whether the frozen nuggets are too freezer-burnt to cook."

Tears gather as I picture myself, Akara, and Banks dealing with normal baby problems like stinky diapers and soothing the little champ through the night. And not just paparazzi problems, like how to use a stroller with hoards of cameramen invading our space. I've been focused on things that I lose rather than things I still have to look forward to.

"Yeah?" I wipe at a tear that escapes.

"You can do anything. Just take every day as it comes," Lily reminds me. "One day at a time, one step at a time."

Uncle Lo told me the same thing, when I confided in him about wanting to be sober. *One day at a time. One step at a time.* To Aunt Lily, I say strongly, "I think I can do that."

"But you can also look far into the future too," she adds fast. "Because good things are ahead." She nods resolutely. "And it's important not to lose sight of those good things."

I think of Akara and Banks. "I won't lose fucking sight of the good things to come, I promise." I eat the last of my churro bite. "Sometimes, I am scared though. That I might screw it all up. The parenting thing."

"That fear is pretty normal." She breaks off another piece for me, thinking. "I was always afraid of our kids being damaged like us, but I never imagined any of you would be infamous like us."

But here I am.

I replay her words in my head. "You don't think I'm damaged?"

"Nonono," she slurs fast. "Lo and I—we were damaged before the world knew who we were. Fame didn't really damage us. I don't think it'll hurt you either. You're resilient. One of the *most* resilient." She nods again, like it's just fact.

I love my aunt so fucking much. "Aunt Lily, if I have any baby questions…?"

"I'm your girl." Lily points a thumb to her chest.

"Good, because I'm going to raise my kids just like you." I say this proudly, fucking happily.

"Like me?" My aunt breaks down with emotional tears because she's rarely first draft pick or considered a role model to the world— but she's become mine. She drops her churro.

I nod, wiping my wet cheeks. "Just like you."

We hug again, people watch us, and Aunt Rose shoos them away with an icy glare. I rub my runny nose when we pull apart.

I spot my mom, and she mimes a lasso. Catching me around the waist and tugging. I smile into a laugh and act like she's pulling me willingly.

I bounce to my mom and throw my arms over her shoulders. She has lassoed me into a hug. Her eyes glassy, her smile bright which pulls at her old scar along her cheek. I trace my finger over her scar, like I used to do when I was little. "You're the most beautiful mermaid in the whole wide sea."

Her tears well. "That's you, Sul." She laughs into a bigger, more heartfelt smile. "I am *so proud* of the woman you've become."

I'm fucking sobbing. I cover my face, and Winona is the only thing that causes me to snort. She literally pops up between me and Mom and says, "Why are we crying? Tissues. Tissues." She unpockets tissues from fucking nowhere and dabs our cheeks.

I can't stop laughing.

"Is this thing fucking on?" My dad taps a microphone, the speakers squeaking.

"Jesus," Uncle Lo winces.

Uncle Connor wears a burgeoning grin. "It's on. The entire yacht can hear you." They reside near a cluster of white couches on the left side of the pool.

"Fuck," he curses into the mic.

I laugh again, my smile hurting my face.

"My daughter, Sullivan Minnie Meadows," my dad calls out, my laughter fading as he says my name. "Come take your mark."

60

Sullivan Meadows

"TAKE MY MARK?" I catch my dad's gaze.

He gestures to the top of the pool. Where Banks Moretti towers with a confident, relaxed gait in just jeans and a white tee. My beefcake.

Beside him, Akara Kitsuwon wears a red button-down and a rising playful, sexy smile. One that I know pretty fucking well. My dreamboat is challenging me to a competition.

Maybe they're both challenging me.

Through the speakers, my dad says, "Your boyfriends want to race you."

"In the pool?" I ask as I practically glide towards them. People part like the Red Sea, and I love how easily I can go towards them. How no one is pushing or shoving or tearing me in half, how their support feels open and loving, and I just freely walk into Banks and Akara's arms. "You seriously want to race me in the pool?"

"Yep," Akara says. "Let's go, Lady Meadows. We don't have all day."

"Oh it's on." I swing my arms. "You're both going to get fucking murdered."

Banks dips his head to me. He has those soft, shadowy smiles that melt my heart. "I've already died a thousand deaths just loving you. What's one more?"

Whoa.

His affection bursts inside me, nearly surfacing tears. "Fuck, if this is a distraction tactic—it's not working." *It's totally fucking working.* I can't stop staring at them.

"Hey, line up," Akara tells me, positioning his hands on my shoulders and guiding me to the edge. I'm in the middle of them, my bare feet on the lip of the pool.

"This is for real?" I ask again, doubting, since I realize they're not in swimsuits. Neither am I—just jean shorts and a striped tee—but who cares, right? I'd go in fully clothed. I think they would too.

Akara whips my dark-brown hair in my face. "What do you think?"

I laugh as the strands stick on my eyelashes. "I think you're going down, Kits."

"Swim your hardest, Sul."

"You know I will." My heart is soaring out of my body, and I ready myself, prepared to dive. Our audience of family and friends start cheering.

Banks and Akara ready themselves too, and I glance from Banks, to Akara, back to Banks. "You're sealing your fate, you know." They have to know this'll be a fucking blowout.

"We know, mermaid."

Okay.

My victory awaits. I'm in the fucking zone. Eyes on the pool.

"Swimmers take your mark," my dad calls. More hearty applause resounds, and I'm grinning. Instead of my dad saying, *beep*—two different hands suddenly clasp my hands.

Banks takes my left one. Akara takes my right, and I stand up straighter with widened eyes, "What...?" On either side of me, they begin to *kneel*. On one knee.

They're fucking kneeling with my hands in theirs, and everyone watching—every fucking person here—is cheering. Like the race is over and a gold medal has been won.

"Kits, Banks..." My voice shakes, tears glassing my vision until I blink. Is this happening right now? Tonight? I thought they'd take years...?

I inhale.

"Sul," Akara begins, "my conscience, my heart, my beautiful foul-mouthed babe." I smile with Kits, and his face wields pure affection as he says, "I've loved you for so long that every time I thought I'd lose you felt like a mortal wound. I can't be without you. I never could. And I never want to be." His gaze reddens, chest rises. "I hope I never have to be. That way, someday, you'll finally make me believe in mermaids."

I laugh through tears, and I hear laughter and sniffles around us.

"It might take forever," Akara says.

"It won't take that fucking long."

He smiles, "Is that a bet or a promise?"

"A promise."

He hooks his pinky finger to mine. "I still want to spend forever with you."

I choke out, "Me too, Kits."

He reclasps my hand, his gaze drifting to Banks, and I'm turning even before Banks says, "Sulli."

I stare down at those comforting brown eyes. "Banks." More tears build. *Fuck.* I have no hands to wipe my cheeks, so they cascade down my face.

He reaches up with his free hand to rub the wet tracks off my cheeks for me.

I swear there are audible *swoons* and *awes*.

Akara is smiling.

Once Banks has dried some of my tears, he squeezes my hand, then says, "You're the most beautiful woman my heart did ever see and hold and love, and if I'm going to walk this earth for short or long, I want to walk alongside you. I'll carry you or crawl with you and stumble with you and fight for you—and when it's my time, I'll be waiting for you in the sky."

I'm fucking bawling.

Banks almost whispers, "For what it's worth, I love you more than the air we're breathing."

"It's worth a whole lot, Banks. It's worth every fucking thing."

And then Akara reaches into his pocket. He pulls out a wooden box. "Sullivan Meadows."

Banks—Banks is pulling out a wooden box too.

Oh fuck.

This is happening.

This is really fucking happening.

And Akara smiles as he says, "Will you marry us?"

"Yes, fuck yes."

Around me, more cheering escalates, and I see my mom smiling and hugging her sisters. To hear everyone *happy* for us makes me cry harder.

They pop the boxes, but I don't see what's inside. They're both standing, and they tie thick braided thread onto my ring fingers.

"Nona made them," Akara explains, knotting the turquoise thread.

My sister made my rings. "It's fucking perfect."

"I *fudging* love you, Sul."

"I fucking love you, Kits."

He kisses me, and I feel his smile before he deepens the kiss.

"Bow chicka wow wow!" I hear my mom.

I laugh as we part, then I turn to Banks. He knots the other ring onto my finger. Our eyes latch and his soft smile curves his mouth. "Looks beautiful on you, mermaid. But everything does."

My heart swells. "I love you, Banks."

He cups my cheek and kisses me, filling my lungs with things greater than the air we're breathing. When we break, Akara and Banks share more than a smile. Love is in their eyes, a kind that not many will ever understand, but their bond is the foundation of what we all are together—what keeps us standing, and it'll never crumble.

It's as durable and steady as the love they've given me, and the love I know I'll always give them.

I glance at my braided rings. I want all the details. Whether the proposal was planned. Who knew? *My sister had to know.* But right now, I push those thoughts aside. And I take in the moment. Blissful and unencumbered with the two men I love most in this mad world.

I DON'T THINK I'VE CRIED THIS MANY HAPPY TEARS
in one night. Not even at the Olympics.

By the time we hop on the smaller boat that carts us to Yacht #2 where we're residing, it's late. It's even later when my fiancés and all our penthouse roommates find ourselves on the bow of the vessel.

Spread out over lounge pads, we stare quietly at the moonlit ocean and the sparkling lights of Cabo in the distance.

Thatcher and Jane.

Maximoff and Farrow, plus a sleeping Baby Ripley in Farrow's arms.

And Luna. She's the only one flat on her back. Stargazing.

We're all here, taking in the last bits of the good night. It's peaceful.

"So only all the parents and my sister knew?" I say after Banks and Akara explain the logistics of the proposal.

"And I knew." Thatcher raises his hand. "It's why we wanted my mom and dad there."

Akara explains, "The three of us planned the trip for the proposal." He motions to Banks and Thatcher.

Their friendship really is back in action. Love to fucking see it—I could high-five them, but I just elbow Banks and Akara beside me. So fucking happy. They wrap their arms more around my frame.

Farrow's brows rise. "Damn."

"I had no clue," Moffy chimes in, his arm over Farrow's shoulders.

"Neither did I," Jane says, then gives a sly smile to her husband. "I'm impressed."

Thatcher whispers in her ear. Seeing as how I've peeked at their type of text messages—I'm guessing it's NC-17 rated. Jane does flush, too.

"We didn't want to wait years to propose," Banks tells me.

"I'm *really* glad you didn't." I lean into Banks' shoulder, my hand on Akara's thigh.

Jane says, "If you need a wedding planner, my services are always available."

I smile. "Thanks, Jane."

I'm not sure how big the ceremony will be, though. Technically we could just say we're married right now, and we'd be married. But I think we want something more intimate to bind us together.

We're quiet again, and unsurprisingly, Akara's phone rings. "Dang it," he mutters as he unpockets his cell. "This can wait for tomorrow..." he trails off, seeing the caller ID.

"Who is it?" Banks asks.

"My Uncle Prin." He stands up on the lounge pad, answering the phone as he hops to the teak flooring. "This is Akara...yeah, I am."

He stops dead in his tracks. Not even reaching a foot further.

Kits?

Something's wrong.

His back is turned to us, but he's frozen solid. "You're just now telling me?" His voice is tight. "That's what she wanted...okay...okay... bye." He hangs up, and when he spins around, his eyes are bloodshot. Face broken.

"Kits?"

Banks and I are already going to him as he says, "My mom died last night."

61

Akara Kitsuwon

MY MOM SAID A LOT, apparently. She'd been in the hospital for a few days. Another brain aneurysm, and she must've known she was reaching an actual end. She said that she didn't want to ruin my trip.

She said to wait until I was home to tell me any bad news.

Uncle Prin thought I was home because when he called, the first thing he said was, "Are you home?" I lied and said, "Yeah, I am."

I felt like I was home with Banks and Sulli.

But of course, he meant *physically* home in Philly.

She said to give me a letter.

I have it in my hand.

She said she wanted a small funeral. Nothing extravagant like my dad's funeral.

So after her cremation, we celebrate her life with a meal among her friends and family in New York. Numbness clings to me. The only people here that I really know or care about are Sulli, Banks, and Frog.

Everyone else feels like a character from a book my mom read to me at bedtime. Not real. Not home. I drift.

I'm still drifting.

Back in Philly at some odd hour like three a.m., Banks and Sulli are seated on the other side of a red vinyl booth. Frog is next to me. Banks called earlier to buy out Lucky's Diner for the rest of the night—but I doubt that many people were here in the first place.

But we're going to be doing that a lot—buying out restaurants and bars and other places, to avoid fans rushing inside and crowding.

I don't mind that much.

I'm thankful for the privacy. We've chosen the furthest booth from the glass windows. Paparazzi try to peer through, cameras still flashing, but a big potted fern and other booths block us from view.

The letter rests on the table. Stuffed in a plain white envelope. Staring at me.

I push my hair back a million times. Smelling bacon and pie from the kitchen. Pots clanking together. Coffee steams from four cups, and Sulli gazes at a plate of sugared donuts.

No one has touched the donuts in the three minutes they've been sitting there.

"You can eat," I tell her.

Sulli doesn't move, but her gaze pins to me in concern. "Kits...I think that was the first thing you've said in hours."

Was it?

It's okay, Nine.

It's not.

She's gone—and she didn't tell me. And I'm *mad*.

Mad that I didn't get to say goodbye. Mad that she wouldn't let me.

I tense more. "I don't know what I'm supposed to say." My words sound hollowed and bitter, and I wince. "No, I know what I *want* to say, and it's not going to be great—so I should just keep my mouth shut."

Banks chews on a toothpick. "That's the last fuckin' thing you should do. It feels better once it's out." I remember the concert, how he told me about Skylar, and how *weightless* he seemed—and that seems so unattainable for me right now.

I'm fixed in anger.

Shit, I don't want to be *mad*. Especially not at her.

She's gone.

I remember the phone call again. I hadn't braced myself for the impact, and the sheer blindside feels almost like...betrayal. I fight back hot tears. "She could have called. Could have told me that she was getting worse. Then maybe..."

What?

She didn't want me to visit her. *I tried.* She knew I would've dropped everything for her. I would have missed the Olympics for her. I would have missed the proposal for her. I would have dropped my life to be with her.

She knew that, Nine. I let my dad's voice in again, comforting me.

"She knew that," I whisper out loud. "She knew I'd leave my life behind to be with her. That's why she didn't want me to see her. I would've known she was getting worse." I glare at the ceiling. "The least she could have done is let me say *goodbye.*"

Sulli reaches out for my hand. I let her take it, feeling her thumb glide softly over my knuckles. "Maybe it was too hard for her. Or maybe she knew it would be too hard for you."

Frog nods in agreement. "Auntie Mint was like that. She was always looking out for everyone else. Even…me." Her face falls. She runs a finger around the rim of her coffee cup. "She was a kickass woman. Literally. She kicked my ass multiple times during training."

Something aches in my chest. It feels like grief, but I don't want to let it in. "Yeah?"

She nods. "*Frog, your teep kick is so weak.*" She mimics my mom perfectly, with some New York bluntness.

Memories flood that I try to shut. "She used to tell me the same thing."

"I know," Frog says. "She'd talk about you a lot. How she trained you too. How proud she was of everything you accomplished. She kept saying how lucky I was to have you as a mentor." She nods over and over. Eyes glassing as she drills her gaze into her coffee.

My own eyes feel raw even without tears in them. With my free hand, I rub at them. My other hand, I keep tight in Sulli's. "Can we talk about anything else?" I ask under my breath.

Banks nods to Frog. "I've been meaning to ask about your nickname."

Frog removes her gaze off her coffee, and I'm glad to see her smile. At the funeral, I wasn't the only one looking lost and alone. I realize quickly she wasn't friendly with anyone there other than her parents and us. In fact, our cousins kept staring at her like she had a scarlet letter on her dress.

"My dad loves the old traditional Thai superstitions," she tells him. "A lot like Akara's dad." She tips her head to me with a soft smile. "Anyway, there's an old folktale that evil spirits are always on the prowl for newborns, so unconventional nicknames are used to trick them. No evil spirits want a *frog*. Even cute little green ones." She rips open a sugar packet. "My mom isn't Thai, but she loves the nickname the most." She smiles, thinking about her mom who I know she misses, then she winces at me. "Sorry, is that insensitive?"

"What? Talking about your mom because I just lost mine." I put a hand to my chest. "I'm not that sensitive, Frog."

She sees that it's fine. "Okay, good." She exhales. "I mean, you can be sensitive. Cry if you need to."

"Tears aren't coming." I sound like an ass. I grimace. "They're just dried up." If I could cry, I would, but I'm wrestling with so many feelings.

Frog rests her temple on her fist, turned towards me. "You know my dad always gave your dad shit about your nickname."

I frown. "What?"

"Yeah." She smiles like she stole something. "They nicknamed you *Nine* because you were born at nine-oh-nine, and my dad didn't think that was good enough to confuse an evil spirit. They must've really loved the name Nine. My dad said you were doomed."

I laugh, then nod. "Maybe he was right."

"Kits," Sulli says. "You're not fucking *doomed*. If you are, then we all are."

"Amen," Banks agrees.

If I was fated for something bad, I shouldn't want to drag them with me—but I'm at a place where I know we're all going down together if we ever go.

"My dad was wrong," Frog says to me. "You own a security firm that protects *famous people* and you own a gym—and you're about to marry Sullivan Meadows."

Sulli smiles.

It's hard not to smile back. And I look to Banks; he nods to me—and to say I'm glad he's here is the biggest understatement of the century.

Their love guides me, and I reach for the letter on the table. Not thinking, just feeling, and I swear they all cage breath as I rip open the envelope.

It's just a simple white sheet of paper, folded into threes. I unfurl the letter, my mom's beautiful handwriting staring back at me.

Still without thinking, I read the letter out loud. *"Dear Nine,"* I say, my throat already swelling. *"I'm sorry that we couldn't say a proper goodbye, but I thought this would be easier…I've never wanted to be a burden on you…"*

Shit. I pinch the bridge of my nose, eyes shut. Trying not to lose it.

I can't speak.

So silently, I read the rest. The letter clenched between my fingers.

You're my strong, unbreakable son. And your dad always said your future was brighter than the stars in the sky. I knew it too. You are our greatest gift to this Earth, Nine. Before I left, there was something I needed you to have.

I know how much family you've lost. From growing up in Philly. From your father's death. And inevitably mine. But she needs you as much as you need her. Hold on to Frog.

Hold on to each other. And know that you may have lost me, but you're not alone. You both have memories to share and stories to tell. You'll keep the ones you love alive.

And just like your father, I will love you forever. Even after I'm gone.

Love, Mom

Now I'm crying, and I put the letter into Frog's hand while I tell Banks and Sulli, "She wanted me and Frog to have each other. That's why she really sent her here."

Sulli starts crying, and Banks curses in shock.

The minute Frog stops reading, she hugs me. I feel her tears soak my chest. My mom knew Frog grew up without family. Like I did.

"She's a legend," Frog manages to say.

Without a doubt.

My anger starts dissipating off my body. My grief will come and go, I'm sure, just like with my dad. But I think it'll be different too. She made sure that my memories of her were limited, maybe to shelter me from the pain.

It's a gift she tried to give me.

I'll always remember that.

62

Banks Moretti

LIFE IS SHORT.

I've known that since my brother died, but hell, it keeps slamming into all of us. Over and over. "I'm sick of losing people," I tell them.

Early morning, the three of us are naked in Sulli's large soup-bowl bathtub. Where Sulli lost her virginity. Bubbles pile high above the warm water, the cedar and pine scent soaking our bare skin, and Sulli lies back against my chest. Her legs opened around Akara.

"Me too," Akara says.

"Me three." Sulli draws a finger through the bubbles, creating swirls.

Akara pushes his hair back with a wet hand. "But it doesn't really end. People die. People leave. It's the story of life, man." A couple days have passed since the funeral, and he's been doing better. Talking more. The letter from his mom helped, giving Akara enough closure to stop bottling that kind of anger. The kind I've been letting go too.

With my arms extended over the lip of tub, I crack a crooked smile, biting a toothpick. "This must be the emo-punk side of you coming out now that you've joined The Carraways."

He gives me a pointed look. "That was a one-time thing."

Sulli snorts. "You loved it."

"He did," I agree.

He blows bubbles in Sulli's face. "I love being your bodyguard more, Sul."

She swats the bubbles away. "Kits."

I drop my arms around her frame and palm her breasts under the water.

"*Banks.*" My name comes out with a moan.

Akara smiles more. "Hey, I'm not trying to bring us down. We're the Life Brigade, remember?"

"I remember," I say into a smile. There's no one I'd rather live *life* with than them. So I say, "When we die, then we can become the Death Brigade, kickin' it in heaven."

They laugh, and Sulli sinks back into my chest. I clutch her tighter while she reaches over and grabs her phone. My mind travels to the beginning of the yacht trip. How my grandma couldn't stop grinning, like she was transported to another land.

"This is like Hollywood," she beamed, sipping her little goblet of brandy with rosy cheeks. Dancing the night away with my mom and Nicola. And after Akara and I proposed, she pinched Sulli's cheek.

"You aren't proposing to each other?" my mom had asked me *and* Akara before we even boarded the yacht.

"No," we said together.

"I'm straight, ma," I told her.

"*We're* straight," Akara clarified.

I prepared for her disappointment, but she just smiled and said, "You're still family, Akara. We all love you here. You know that, huh?"

That got to both of us, and he nodded, "I do." They hugged, and though Akara and I aren't really marrying each other in the same sense that we're marrying Sulli—our bond is greater than any tangible thing. Hell, no word encapsulates what he rightly means to me, except maybe the one that used to be unfamiliar and strange. Metamour.

We were all so fuckin' happy. Still are, even among the highs and lows—we've become used to the undulation. The sinking and rising waves of life, and we're just the buoys knotted together, unable to break apart.

"Have you seen the comments on our workout videos?" Sulli asks, showing me the responses. All the positive feedback. Akara wipes his hand on a washcloth and takes her phone when she passes the cell to him.

I bite onto the toothpick again. "They love *something* we're doing? Get God on the line, Akara. It's a fuckin' miracle."

He mimes picking up the phone, with a real fucking phone in his other hand. "Hello, God. Oh You mean You're too busy for Banks' thousandth phone call in three days. But he's Your biggest fan."

We're all laughing, then we start talking about how fans have loved other shit we've posted before. This really isn't the first time, but the response of *we want more workout videos* is strong.

"We could do this for real," Akara suddenly says.

Sulli smiles. "Like as a job?"

"Yeah, why not?" he wonders, deep in thought for a second. His business brain is spinning, and hell, I'm along for any journey, but there's one point to be made.

"Because you're already swamped with security work and the gym," I remind him.

He shrugs. "This will be different. Fun."

He's too excited to argue with, and the idea of continuing these videos with Sulli and Akara has me more than hyped.

Pack me up and ship me out. I'm going with them. Always, forever.

"Kicking It with Kitsulletti," Akara brainstorms. "Or some other name—we post workout videos, maybe become app-based. People can work out with us."

Sulli is grinning. "I'm totally game—" She's cut off as Akara's phone buzzes on the countertop. We all fall silent. We all stare at his cell for a long moment. He hesitates.

"It could be Frog," Sulli theorizes.

Akara is quicker to move into action. He climbs buck-ass naked out of the tub. Water drips on the tile as he answers, phone to his ear. "Akara Kitsuwon." His brows furrow, shock parting his lips. "You're sure?" Elation, joy, surprise begin to fill his eyes as he turns to me and Sulli. "Yes, yes. I'll be there as soon as possible. Please don't leave."

He hangs up.

Has to be good news.

His smile overtakes his face, and God, I feel the joy before he even says the words.

"They found the Jeep."

WE MEET THE PRIVATE INVESTIGATOR IN THE

Poconos, about a couple miles from Camp Calloway. Not the smartest place a thief could drop the Jeep. But the shitbag probably didn't realize Daisy Calloway's camp was this close.

Booger is covered in dirt, twigs, branches—almost unrecognizable and parked perilously close to a cliff. Overlooking green trees and a bubbling creek below.

Derrick, an older man with a goatee and deep brown leather jacket, greets Akara. The three of us agreed to hire him after the Moab trip, seeing as how our own Scooby Doo searches were coming up empty.

He hikes with us to the cliff. "I almost didn't think it was the same Jeep. Plates have been changed. But I'm glad I stopped to check anyway."

"We're glad too," Akara says.

Sulli follows me to the hood, and I pop it on instinct.

"Mother of Christ," I mumble, narrowed gaze on the innerworkings. They stripped her of parts. Engine gone.

Sulli's face falls. "Fuck."

"It's alright." I shake off my anger. "I can put in a new engine. I'll fix her." I rest a hand on Sulli's shoulder. "Let's check inside." I'm more worried about the interior.

When I wrench open the door—thankfully still on its hinges—I let out a tensed breath. They took the seats. The Jeep…she's a husk of what she was. A container.

My molars grind down, jaw locking.

Sulli steps back in horror, bumping into Akara's chest. He hooks his fingers in her belt loops.

"Booger…" Sulli breathes out.

"Hey, they didn't take the tires," Akara says more positively.

I glance at the wheels. Sure enough, tires are on. Perfect condition. I laugh. "What kind of fucking stunads are we dealing with?"

We all turn to Derrick. He's busy searching for something on his phone. "I was able to get face recognition from the cameras coming down this road."

Camp Calloway is incredibly popular, and on drop-off day, a line snakes miles outside the entrance. The road gets congested, and someone, one year, opted for some better streetlights. Cameras.

Any competent soul who pays attention in Kitsuwon Securities or Triple Shield security training knows this fact. 'Cause there are still clients who regularly frequent Camp Calloway.

"It's up to all of you, if you'd like me to file the police report," Derrick says. "Looks like the guy is already in the system. Name is... Colin Donnelly."

He might as well have sucked the oxygen out of the mountain. The air stills.

"Say again," I mutter.

"Colin Donnelly." Derrick frowns, eyes pinging between the three of us. "You know him?"

"Not personally," Akara says in an exhausted breath. He might be a cousin of Paul Donnelly's. Not 100% sure of the relation.

I clench and unclench my fist, anger surging through me. "The fucking Donnellys."

"Paul can't know about it, right?" Sulli holds her elbows.

I shake my head. "No way in hell."

"Yeah, he's not in on this if that's what you're asking, Sul," Akara says tensely. We both know Donnelly would sell out his family before hurting the Hales, Meadows, or Cobalts. Everyone on Omega knows that.

Akara expels a rougher breath, his hand aggressively pushing back his black hair.

I nod to him. "What are you thinking?"

"This is going to kill him," Akara whispers, mostly to me.

Yeah.

"Maybe we don't tell him?" I ask.

Sulli hears and says, "Yeah, we shouldn't fucking involve him more."

Akara nods stiffly, then pulls Derrick aside. "Can we talk for a sec, Derrick."

"Sure thing." Twigs crunch under their boots as they walk further away and chat quietly. Sorting out the logistics, while Sulli and I inspect the forest-green muddy Jeep a little closer.

I yank off branches, and Sulli checks the inside again. The windshield wipers are missing. *Easy fix.* She'll be good to go soon enough. Just need to find all the right parts.

Coming back out, Sulli skims her fingers over the dirty window, leaving streaks. "I know I should be fucking devastated that she's just a bunch of metal, but I'm so fucking relieved."

I slip her a smile. "We'll bring her back better than ever."

"Risen up from the dead," Sulli smiles at that thought. "Like a fucking phoenix." I stare at her for a long moment, watching Sulli clean the twigs off the tires. I'm stunned by her resilience—her strength of pursuit and ability to keep on going.

She's been dragged down a lot just this year, but she's always had some sort of grit.

My chest rises, lungs filling with the same loving feeling that draws my lips upward. Once we're done clearing the car of tree branches, we lean against the shut hood, our eyes on the creek below the cliff.

We listen to the world around us. The sounds of rushing water and a hawk squawking in the distance. Our easy breaths that drift into the September air.

I peek over at Sulli. "You remember the day we first met?" I lift a shoulder. "Guess it'd be more like the first day we met when I was off-duty, alone. We'd probably run into each other before then, but never really talked much."

"The day you were off-duty…" She thinks, then bites her lip, starting to smile. "Fuck, that day—you were in the townhouse garage."

She remembers.

I can't take my eyes off her, shocked she remembers. Didn't think she would. "Yeah, I was in the garage."

Sulli stares out at the open sky, smiling more at the memory. "You know, when I moved into the townhouse with Moffy, Jane, and Luna—I hadn't really thought too hard about how I'd be living next door to our bodyguards. Not until *that* day—it hit me."

"That's why you remember?"

"Yeah." She tries to hold my gaze but glances away shyly. "Fuck, you were under Jane's blue Beetle when I walked into the garage. All I saw were your legs, and I kept glancing from your legs to my parked Jeep, to your legs, to my Jeep." She pats the hood next to her. "But I didn't want to open the car door and scare you. So I called out your name. You didn't hear me."

"And then you kicked my ankle."

"I kicked your ankle," she laughs, nodding. "You rolled out from under the Beetle. AirPods were in your ears, and I shouted way too fucking loudly, 'I'm Sulli! I'm about to go! I didn't want to fucking scare you!' And you…" She stares faraway. "You had this shadow of a smile just looking at me—the kind you always have that just utterly fucking melts me." Her eyes flit to me, back to the sky. "You were really hot, scorching levels—and like instantly, I knew I was in trouble, but I just figured you probably wouldn't be attracted to me."

I laugh.

"What?" She's smiling. "Banks, I literally shouted at you like a fucking dummy, then I tried to shake your hand, which was covered in oil. So I *elbowed* you." She winces with a face-palm. "And then Kits came inside, and you two were so buddy-buddy. Teasing me, and I realized how much your friendship attracted me to you guys. But I was so fucking *ugh*." She cringes. "I've replayed my awkwardness like a fucking million times."

"You weren't awkward."

"Really?"

"You know that smile that I gave you?"

"Yeah?"

"That was an *I'm into this smokeshow* smile."

"*Really?*" Her lips part. "Seriously?"

I nod repeatedly. "I still had my AirPods in, but I could hear you shouting over the music." I smile a faraway, loving smile, remembering then and now. Emotion pricking my eyes, and I take out my AirPods from my pocket. I fit one into her ear, one into my ear. And I find the song on my phone. "This is what was playing that day."

She listens.

And her head whips to me as soon as the music starts. He green, green eyes welling and diving deep into my gaze. "Banks."

"Swim to me," I breathe. "Oh my heart."

Song to the Siren by Tim Buckley. What I sang poorly to Sulli at the Olympics.

"I…" Words catch in her throat.

I nod, seeing how much this means to her, and I wrap an arm around Sulli. I tuck her to my side, and she leans her weight into me.

We listen to the song, and she whispers, "I really fucking love you, Banks."

"I love you too, mermaid."

When we hear the crunch of twigs and the sound of a car peeling away, Akara walks over and pauses. "Am I interrupting—?"

"Come here." I stand up and put the AirPod in his ear. "Remember that time I was working on the Beetle and you came down into the garage? I was listening to this song." I nod towards Sulli. "And apparently, she had the hots for us and our friendship."

Sulli raises her hands. "Fucking guilty." She points to me. "But Banks had the hots for me."

"Yeah, I know," Akara says like it was obvious. 'Cause it was.

Sulli blows back. "What?"

"Akara was into you too," I remind her. "He was just in denial and resisting."

"And you were resisting because you were a good friend and I was an ass," Akara declares.

"A lovable cock-blocking ass." I bob my head, arms loosely crossed, and Akara listens to the music with a growing smile. We're all smiling at each other—loving how our path weaved and connected.

The three of us together.

Once the song finishes, we all end up in a huddle on the cliffside, and I pocket the AirPods. "Everything squared away?"

Akara nods. "He's not going to file the police report. A tow truck is headed here." A stillness swims around us, but it's broken sharply by the sound of a car.

"Who's here?" Sulli asks.

I have no clue, but by the lack of confusion coming from Akara, I'd say he knows.

63

Akara Kitsuwon

I TEXTED PRICE ON our way to the Poconos.

I decided to involve him like Ryke wanted, but I didn't think he'd come out here. Not until he called and said he was a few minutes away. And that he wanted to talk.

Sure.

Okay.

Whatever that means.

Now Price has parked his SUV and examines the Jeep quickly, hands stuffed in a light jacket. "Good work," he tells me.

Banks stands rigid next to me, ready to launch a verbal assault at Price the first chance Price slingshots one at us. Sulli's parents aren't here this time, and it'd be easy to go toe-to-toe with the Alpha lead.

"You wanted to talk," I remind him.

He nods, and glances cautiously from Banks to Sulli. He's a fortress ready to fight for me. She's a champion ready to challenge him for me. She wears my red windbreaker, her hair blowing in the breeze.

The loves of my life.

Both of them.

I rub my palms, my knuckles. "You can talk in front of them."

Price threads his arm, clears his throat a little. "This is about your business."

I frown. "My gym?"

"Your security firm," Price corrects. He stares at his feet. "I...I should have helped you start it up. We're not competitors. We're colleagues."

"It's running fine," I say sharply. Defensive, sure.

I try to cool down.

"Akara." He opens his arms. "You don't know how much I charge the parents." He specifies, "Lily, Lo, Rose, Connor, Daisy, and Ryke. You've never known how much they pay my firm."

I go cold, confused. "Clients on Security Force Alpha are charged the same amount as any other client."

"No, Alpha *bodyguards* are paid the same as any other bodyguard, except for leads. I've always charged the parents a lot more to cover the expenses of running the firm. If you haven't charged Maximoff and the rest of your clients more than what they were paying through Triple Shield, I'd be fucking floored if you're not in the red at this point."

What...

My eyes burn. In frozen shock. Unblinking.

Sulli asks Price, "Do you actually know what Akara is charging us?"

"Xander Hale is one of Kitsuwon Securities' clients," Price says. "He's still a minor. I asked Lily if he's still being charged the same as before, she said *yes*. She said that you must be charging Maximoff, Jane, Charlie, Luna, and Sulli more." He looks to me. "You aren't, are you?"

No...I'm not.

I push my hair back, finally taking a breath. "Why are you telling me this now?"

Price squints out at the sun that slices through canopies of trees. "Ryke told me to look at you like you're his kid. This is the kind of advice I'd give to his kid. So I'm giving it to you." His gaze is back on me. "I'm not sure we'd have a chance to talk alone again, so I took this opportunity." He nods to me. "But the advice—it's going to extend beyond today. You need help with your books or anything security-related, let me know. If Kitsuwon Securities sinks, so does Triple Shield."

I'm not used to kindness like this from him. Not since I was a lead on Triple Shield. And I've dreamed of my firm dominating. I'm sure he's dreamt the same thing. So for him to come here and extend this olive branch…I'm at a loss for words.

"Price…" I breathe out. "I don't…I don't know what to say."

"Don't say anything. Just start charging them more. They'll pay because that's what their safety is worth, and they want you to succeed as much as you want to, Akara."

"What he said," Sulli grins.

I smile seeing her smile.

Price puts on a pair of aviators. "I have to go pick up some documents from the camp. You three stay safe." He pats my shoulder and leaves for his car.

Banks smacks my chest. "Have I not been saying the same thing?"

"Charging the clients more? Yeah. But I didn't want to nickel and dime them."

"But you will now, right?" Sulli asks hopefully. "Now that you know our parents are paying the same fee."

"Yeah." I breathe. "I will."

I'll ask Price the *exact* amount he's making his clients pay. I'll do the same thing. I'll pay Sulli back for all the mountain of credit card debt she unburied me from. And maybe it seems like an easy decision, but I've never wanted to be the guy that'd overcharge. That'd make Sulli and her family pay more for my mistakes fumbling through a new business.

Now I know that Price wouldn't have kept Triple Shield afloat with the same boat I'm trying to sail. And I want the tools to succeed. Not to fail.

A weight leaves me. Suddenly. Epically, and I smile at Banks and Sulli, "I'm shutting down Studio 9."

"What?" Sulli looks pummeled. "Why? No, Kits."

"Yes, Sul." I'm smiling. "It'll still exist, just privately. For security only and for us."

Banks frowns. "How can you afford to keep it open if it's not generating any income?"

"It will generate income." I snap my finger to my palm. "It'll be our workout studio. For the workout programs." We brainstormed more names on the car ride here but couldn't land on anything. "What if we just call the app Studio 9 Fitness by Akara, Banks, & Sullivan? I won't need a manager for Studio 9 anymore, and the cost of running the place is minimal now."

"That's fucking perfect," Sulli smiles. "With a tagline, *Kicking It with Kitsulletti*."

"Right on." Banks is grinning.

That's set then. We agree that we might need to take some exercise science courses at a Philly college. Just to better train our audience. And while Sulli is pregnant, we can record safe prenatal exercises.

Banks is smiling up at the sky.

I feel his brightness flood my lungs. And I breathe in the woods. The air. Her and him.

"What a great fucking day," Sulli says. She howls upwards like an animal. Banks joins her. Eff it. I'm screaming too. Lit up with these feelings of success. Happiness. All the things my parents wanted for me. Wished for me. Hoped for me. I feel them here with me.

Heavy breaths, we're all laughing and trying to catch oxygen.

"Fucking marry me," Sulli blurts out, looking between us both.

"We already proposed, string bean." I flip a strand of her hair at her face. "Too slow."

She slugs my arm. "I mean *now*. Marry me tonight."

Banks looks to her, affection in a single glance. "Straight to the heart."

She flushes and says, "Feel the fucking moment."

"Come what fucking may," Banks adds.

They both look to me. Love cascading around us like a tidal wave. And then I say, "Forward and onward."

64

Akara Kitsuwon

IN THE DEAD OF NIGHT, we hop aboard a private plane, survive the layover, and after handfuls of hours brimming with anticipation— we finally reach the South Pacific. We tell no one. It's just the three of us.

On a private island in Fiji.

Morning—the night still strong—moonlight shines overhead, and the ocean laps the coral sand and slips over our bare feet. Only one house on the island, the roof is made of straw and palm leaves—but Banks, Sulli, and I aren't looking backwards.

We take each other in. This moment, this place. We had enough time to grab a few things and forget a thousand more. Rent the island. Hop on the plane.

Take a boat here.

We're coming off a long effing travel. Yet, I doubt anyone would be able to tell.

We're in total knockout love.

Infatuated with each other and today.

Sulli—Sulli is *gorgeous* in a white billowy dress that catches in the sticky wind. Seashells nestle in her loose braid.

I haven't told her, but she does look like a mermaid.

Her arms reach up to the darkened sky, then stretch wide and brush our shoulders. I'm enamored with her. With him, as he soaks in Sulli, his white button-down blowing against his chest. Mine does the same, and Banks takes me in, smiling, then nods my way. "We made it."

"I knew we would," I say deeply.

Sulli smiles between us. Our combined confidence feels *mightier* than the ocean beckoning us forward, and with short, playful glances, we know where we're going.

We sprint into the water. Splashing, clasping each other's hands, and laughing. Banks almost goes down, but I catch him around the waist from behind. He seizes Sulli before she trips over him, and soon, we're breathless, and we find ourselves further in the ocean.

Calm.

We form a circle, wading in the water together. She's on her tiptoes, but Banks can stand easily. We hold onto her while she fiddles with two wooden boxes. "Kits." Her eyes lift to mine.

I breathe in. Memories flashing through me, of all the strange hours we woke up together. So I could run with her. So I could chase after her through the woods and deserts and suburban streets. As her bodyguard. But today is solidifying more.

Today, I become her husband.

"Banks." Her green eyes rest against his, and she tucks a piece of his hair behind his ear. He cups her cheek, their heads bowing closer, and then she glances to me, to him. "My spirit and my soul. I promise to always love you, no matter what fucking madness is ahead. It's the three of us."

"The three of us," I say resolutely.

"The three of us," Banks nods.

We promise to protect Sulli. To always love her. To never leave.

And she pops open the boxes. Two more braided rings with our favorite colors woven together. I suspect Winona made them too. Sulli struggles to knot mine, and Banks helps. We share a smile, and Sulli tries to knot his ring, the threads wet in the water, but I also help. How it was meant to be.

We kiss Sulli's cheeks.

We're smiling, laughing, kissing her lips one after the other, and screwing around, splashing water. I dunk Banks at one point. We'd all say that time stands still when we're together. Even on September 7th, the day Sullivan Meadows became our wife.

Nothing crushes our spirits, not the helicopter buzzing above us—yeah, that's been there since our feet hit the sand. Nothing brings us down. Not the paparazzi in the chopper capturing photos of our wedding. Not even the boat in the distance or the telephoto lens.

This is our life. Our fame is fueled by our existence. Our love.

Nothing stops us.

Not even *time*.

The sun rises. Blues, oranges, and yellows in the horizon. And we're still kissing, still joking about *Blue Lagoon*, our island, still breathing and laughing and loving.

Celebrity Crush – December 15th
Sullivan Meadows Confirms Pregnancy & Spiritual Marriage! Who's The Baby Daddy?

What a bomb-drop! After weeks of speculation, Sullivan Meadows *finally* confirms that she's preggers through an Instagram post. And the biggest shocker—she revealed that she was pregnant *during* the Olympics. Which means she won the three golds and two silvers in Los Angeles this summer with a baby on board. Totally nuts!

We also learned that Sullivan did in fact marry her boyfriends in a spiritual ceremony. Remember all those photos from their romantic Fiji island getaway? We predicted a marriage after spotting those braided rings on her boyfriends back in September, and turns out, we were right! What else could we be right about? *Celebrity Crush* has theorized Sulli's due date. We're guessing March. Though, she hasn't confirmed how far along she truly is. She also left the baby's paternity up to the good old-fashioned guessing game. Is the dad either hunky Marine, Banks Moretti, or sexy Muay Thai fighter, Akara Kitsuwon?

And where is Sullivan now? Our sources say she left Philadelphia before posting the baby news. Is she fleeing for peace & quiet while we're all salivating for answers? Not fair, Sullivan! Tell us more!

Subscribe to *Celebrity Crush* for all the updates as we track the scandalous life of Sullivan Meadows and her two ravishing husbands.

65

Banks Moretti

THE WAY THE STORY GOES, an old friend of Ryke's passed away some years ago. In his will, Eddie left Ryke a secluded house nestled high among trees in the Costa Rican rainforest. Eddie said the only person to love it as much as him was Ryke Meadows.

Since I got married, this hasn't been my first trip here.

But it's my first time without the whole Meadows brood. Just me, Akara, and a sleepy, pregnant mermaid.

"I'm not fucking tired," Sulli refutes, fighting sleep and a yawn. We're all naked under a canopy bed, the mosquito net around us. She's barely slept.

The funny thing is, we could all talk for hours, say nothing for hours, mess around and make love for hours, and still it's never enough. She's still battling sleep.

My dumbass is still gladly staying awake.

One more minute becomes one more hour. Becomes a whole fuckin' night and day.

"There is a liar in our bed," Akara says to me.

I crack a crooked smile. "Should we kick her out?"

Sulli snorts, like that'd never happen, but Akara scoops her up.

"Kits!"

He drops her—*gently.*

Breath ejects from her lips, "Whoa."

I laugh, and I have a hand on her belly. Six months along, the baby moves every so often, and I smile over at Akara who pretends not to look at his phone. He's been checking on our Fitness app, which launched after Thanksgiving late last month.

Reception over the workout programs has been mostly positive. Haters gonna fuckin' hate—but I don't give a shit. Akara said they can go suck a lemon as their daily activity.

And according to him, we've surpassed the projected number of subscribers and we're looking at a million-dollar business. Maybe more. Feels good to do something with my wife and metamour, even if we're still full-time bodyguards to the mermaid.

We're also still filming segments of *We Are Calloway* together. It took Jack an ungodly amount of patience waiting for me to spit out my words—but I did. I talked about *us*. The triad. How much I love Sulli and Akara. Our life together. Our future.

That feels good too.

What can I say? I'm fuckin' proud of myself. For doing the things I didn't think I could do.

Sulli pats the phone in Akara's hands, trying to grab the cell. "Didn't you decree the rule, *no phones in bed?*"

Originally this place didn't have electricity or running water, but Ryke outfitted the house years ago with essentials. Just in case of an emergency. We have spotty service from a satellite dish.

But not spotty enough, or else Akara would've ditched the cell.

"I'm throwing out the rule," Akara says.

She gapes. "You can't do that."

"I'm the boss," he says with a teasing smile. "I can make rules and take them away."

Sulli turns to me. "Banks, tell Kits he can't make the fucking rules and then eliminate them whenever he likes."

Akara is sending me a *stay on my side, man* glare.

Sulli is sending me *stay on my side* doe-eyes.

Doe-eyes are fucking me to heaven and hell, but I scratch the back of my head. "You know what, a migraine is setting in—"

"Fuck, really?" Sulli tries to sit herself up, and I catch her elbow, her breath hitches at the sudden embrace. Her gaze gliding down my chest, and I can't help but engrain her body in my head, breasts fuller and belly swollen.

Akara thumbs her nipple, and she squirms at his touch, her eyes pinging from him to me, as we turn towards her. God, I could take her again.

And again.

But I breathe out, "No migraine. Not even a headache, Sulli." My affliction is the thing that hammers at your heart and floods your lungs.

She smiles, then eyes my lips. I kiss her gently, sweetly, and then I whisper, "We have something for you." Might as well give it to her now. She's not going to sleep anytime soon.

"Follow me," Akara says, first one off the bed. We could go outside naked, but even the notion that someone might've followed us on our trek gives us pause and caution. He steps into boxer-briefs.

I pull on mine too.

Sulli ties a loose, white silk robe around her body. She follows our footsteps to the floor-length windows. The sliding glass door already wide open. Morning breeze blows through—the house among the trees is cocooned beneath palm fronds.

Birds chirp endlessly, rainforest noises alive, and floorboards squeak underneath our bare feet as we reach the wraparound porch.

Dew coats the railing, and Sulli reaches out, hanging onto a rope tethered to a tree. She's been bummed she can't swing on the rope, not risking that while she's this pregnant, but she always says, *one day, when the baby is here. We'll come back.*

We retreated to Costa Rica before confirming the pregnancy, and like the lake house, it's peace away from the world and its constant hysteria.

Akara and I left the gift under a blanket outside. While he goes to retrieve the expertly wrapped thing, I grip the rope above her hand.

She stares at my ring finger.

The braided thread is gone. Fallen off—and unfortunately, I did lose my wedding ring for a second there. Akara found the thing stuck in the sink.

His was fraying. So we took ours off, and instead, opted for something a little more permanent. She's eyeing the *ink* on my finger.

Something I can never lose. Three lines are tattooed around my finger—the lines waved like water.

"You ready to get a tattoo?" I ask Sulli. We've kept our braided rings safe as a keepsake, and she's planning to do the same. But until the *very* last minute.

Her two rings are dirty and well-worn. Thread unspooled, and Akara has reknotted them practically every fuckin' day.

"They're still surviving," Sulli says. "It's not fucking time yet."

I look her over with a smile that draws her closer. I tuck her to my chest, kissing her cheek. "Whenever you're ready, Sulli."

Akara hears the tattoo talk as he comes over. He hands me the present, then reknots the ring on her left hand. She flashes him a rising smile, and he whispers something in her ear. She shoves him but reddens, and I go inside, giving them a second and I grab a bite to eat for Sulli.

Coming back, I hand her a chocolate chip muffin first.

"You read my mind," Sulli practically moans. She takes a big chunk out with her teeth, then holds up the half-bitten muffin to me. "Want to eat my muffin?"

"Now you read *my* mind." I take a huge bite of muffin from her hand. I chew and swallow. "One between your legs tastes better."

We're both smiling, and I brush crumbs off her lips and chin.

She brushes crumbs off my unshaven jaw.

Akara is laughing at us. "Always feeding each other, from here until eternity."

"And let death *never* tear us all apart," Sulli decrees, before I pass her the square present. She goes quiet, reveling in the wrapping paper.

It's professional work. Akara wrapped the gift in Sports Magazine covers with perfect creases. The ones where she's biting a gold medal. Where we're hoisting Sulli up on our shoulders after her last gold medal win this summer. Where she has her iconic concentration face: fingers to her lips while she checks out the scoreboard.

Sulli wears a soft smile, then carefully tears the paper. "It's a picture frame?" She's opened the back part first.

I nod to our wife. "We were thinking we could hang it in the nursery." We're dividing our bedroom into the baby's space, just while the baby is small. Eventually, the three of us are looking to buy an apartment a floor beneath the penthouse.

But right now, we're settled where we are.

Akara smiles over at me now and mouths, *she's going to cry.*

I shake my head, doubting.

He mouths, *watch.*

She pries the picture frame out of the paper. Then flips it over in her hands. Her mouth slowly falls, eyes suddenly well. "Wait...Banks." Overwhelmed tears drip down her cheeks. "You kept it?" Her voice cracks.

"Told you," Akara smiles at me, then her.

"All this fucking time?" Sulli asks me, then looks to Akara. "Or did he give it to you to hold onto?"

"No." Akara looks into me. "That was all Banks Moretti Meadows."

We both took Sulli's last name after Fiji, so we'd all have the same last name as our kid. But Akara and I kept Moretti and Kitsuwon as middle names. Can't lie—it's strange being a Meadows. Seems fuckin' surreal, but I'm sure, in time, I'll grow into the name and it'll feel more like my own.

I do like sharing this with Sulli and Akara.

A name.

Didn't think that it'd matter. But I feel more bound to them.

Sulli rubs at the wet creases of her eyes. "I shouldn't be surprised you kept it."

"It's alright," I say. "I surprised myself."

I hope I can keep doing that. Surprising myself. Challenging myself. To be a greater man than yesterday. Expecting more out of myself. Being a man who steps up to the plate of responsibilities and swings a grand slam.

She stares longer at the framed letter. One written with turquoise gel pen. It reads:

DEAR BANKS. DEAR KITS.

I'M PREGNANT. AND I'M KEEPING THIS LITTLE CHAMP.

I never lost the letter. From the Olympics till now.

"Nine picked out the wooden frame and wrapped it," I tell her.

"Thank you." She tucks the framed letter to her chest. "I love it so fucking much." Once she says the words, a flock of birds starts singing. Flying up out of the palm fronds. We turn and watch. It's a quiet, still moment.

I extend an arm over her broad shoulders, and Akara wraps one around her waist. She leans into us. I soak in the moment with the two people I love most on this earth. I could be anywhere right now.

A thousand miles off the coast, floating through life. But I'm grounded here with them.

Happy and home.

I begin to smile, and I look up at the palm fronds and the peeking sky. I look down at her and at him, and I whisper, "Lord have mercy on my soul."

EPILOGUE

Sullivan Meadows

SWEAT BEADS UP ON my forehead, sticking pieces of my dark brown hair to my squared jaw. Akara pries the pieces off with one of his hands—the other, I'm squeezing to fucking death and refuse to relinquish.

Sorry, Kits.

Banks has my left hand in his comforting grip. He hates hospitals, but when my water broke in the Jeep and we were stuck in paparazzi-induced traffic for *three* hours—I seriously thought he would bumper-car our way here. He ran about five red lights.

Booger is in one piece.

But for a minute there, I was afraid I'd be pushing out a baby in the Jeep. Adam Sully would've loved that, I think. My husbands—not so fucking much.

Akara wheeled me into the hospital, and Banks was shoving every non-automatic door open like it was a fucking cameraman.

I'm here now. Safe and in excruciating pain. I try to take controlled breaths, oxygen filling my lungs. *I can do this. I can do anything.*

I'm too far dilated for an epidural, apparently. "Are you fucking sure?" came out of my mouth, Banks' mouth, Akara's mouth about a hundred times.

"Positive," Dr. Wescott said, a short woman with icy eyes. Besides the height, she kinda reminds me of my Aunt Rose. I could've had

Farrow deliver the baby, but I just see him way more as Moffy's husband and a really close friend. And I didn't want him to see my vagina.

He totally understood.

"Hey, you're doing great, Sul." Akara wipes more sweaty hair off my forehead. I catch a glimpse of the tattoo on his bicep. An inked mermaid with turquoise scales and seashells in her brown hair. He tickles my foot in the stirrup, my legs spread open.

I laugh a little into a groan. *Fuck, it hurts.*

"You've got this, mermaid." Banks kisses my white-knuckles—oh fuck, I'm white-knuckle gripping his hand, but he doesn't care. I see his lips press to the tattoo on my ring finger. Three black lines, inked like waves. Just like their forever ring. Permanent.

Ever-fucking-lasting.

That's us. That's been us.

Focused back on my goal, I inhale three more giant breaths. God, childbirth *sucks.* But I know the best part is coming, and so I keep pushing when the doctor says to push.

I grit down and scream through my teeth. Squeezing my husbands' hands in my hands.

"One more big push, Sulli," Dr. Wescott says. "You're almost there."

We're almost there.

We're almost fucking there.

With everything in me, all the grit and determination and fortitude I've ever felt, I summon now. And I push and push—and I scream, not breathing. Not coming up for air until my baby takes a breath—and I hear Kits and Banks, encouraging me, comforting me, here for me. They've always been here.

And then a baby's cry pitches the air. The best sound in the fucking world. Relief surges, and I see our newborn in the doctor's hands.

Akara has tears in his smiling eyes. Banks squeezes my shoulder, his chest rising in a deep, overcome breath, and I collapse back, sweaty. Overwhelmed tears leaking. I don't let go of my husbands yet.

"The baby's alright?" I rasp, not able to see as they clean off our newborn.

Dr. Wescott gently places the crying baby on my chest. "He's perfectly healthy. Congratulations on your baby boy." She speaks to all of us.

Akara and Banks exchange a loving look.

I cry harder as our baby stretches his little fingers and tries to cling to my sweaty chest. I hold him against me. "He already has your hair," I cry-laugh to Banks. Brown tufts of hair on his little delicate head that matches Banks' hue. His skin is so soft.

"He's smaller than I thought he'd be," Banks tries to joke, but tears slip out of his eyes. He rubs the creases, as Akara says, "We'd have serious problems if he came out six-seven."

We all laugh through waterworks. Banks touches his little hand, and our son tries to clasp his finger. He is falling instantly in love with him. So is Akara, as he combs the little tufts of his hair, and our baby calms, his cries softening—little breaths puffing out of little lips.

My whole heart belongs to so many boys.

Akara wipes his own wet cheeks. "He's perfect, Sul."

"He really fucking is, Kits," I breathe, looking up at Akara.

He bends closer to me and clasps my jaw with a determined, powerful hand. I sink into the kiss like a little girl sinks into a pillow. Letting a dream consume her.

When I turn to Banks, his hand is strong and callused, encasing my cheek, and he dips his head to meet my lips. My heart swells with each second under the weight of his love.

Our gazes stay latched, even as our lips break apart, and I ask, "Who wants to hold him first?"

"Let Banks," Akara says.

Banks nods, and I'm already handing him our baby. He cradles him with ease, already having tons of practice. Akara smiles, "He looks just like you."

Banks shakes his head, swaying a little with our son. "He has his mom's beauty."

When I'm sweaty and gross and exhausted, Banks manages to make me feel like a fucking goddess. I ease back into the love and the way

Akara keeps brushing my sweaty hair out of my face. The stroke and rhythm relaxing every bit of me, and Banks passes the baby to Akara.

Kits can't stop smiling—a smile that reaches and glitters his eyes tenfold.

The doctor and nurses have left to give us more alone-time with our newborn. But I glance over at the closed door. "Can someone go get him?"

Just as I say the words, I hear loudly outside the room, "Grammie Daisy, Grampie Rykie—can I see Mommy now?"

Banks calls out, "You can let him in!"

The door cracks open, and a little boy with black hair and a big smile that reaches and *glitters* his eyes suddenly races one-hundred-and-fifty miles per hour, no brakes, into the hospital room. "Daddy!"

He bounds straight for Banks.

We're all smiling as our son playfully hides behind Banks' legs. Banks scratches his head. "Anyone seen a little champ anywhere?"

He's giggling.

Akara is in cahoots with our son. He puts his finger to his lips, "Shhh."

"Shhh," our son mimics back. "Dad, I'm quiet like a mouse." He is a lot quieter now, and then Banks spins around. He squeals into full-bodied kid laughter.

Banks lifts him up onto his shoulders.

Born on April 7th, five years ago, Seven Kitsuwon Meadows *loves* being up high just as much as he loves his two dads. There was never a moment, never a day, where Banks wasn't so much a part of his life and so influential in who he's become. Banks says he surprised himself again—how well he took to fatherhood.

Akara wasn't surprised at all.

Neither was I.

And though I never knew Akara's dad, I know he'd be proud to see Akara thrive as a father. Teaching Seven how to snowboard and play little kid drums and pick himself up after a fall. The kind of father that creates new legacies and keeps old ones alive.

And me, I love being a mom. More than I ever thought I would. Sometimes the public might think I'm not the best mom in the world, but to Seven, I'm the greatest mom that ever lived.

"Mommy, why do you look so tired?" Seven asks me in concern. "Dad? Daddy?" He's scared, and I pick myself up more against the bed.

Akara tells him, "She just brought your baby brother into the world."

"She's alright, champ," Banks says.

"You want to see him?" I ask.

He nods, then grows much quieter seeing the baby in Akara's hands. He places our newborn back on my chest. Banks lets our five-year-old down.

Seven crawls onto the bed beside me, and I watch Akara go to the windows. He peeks out of the blinds, and he slips Banks a cautious glance. Guns are holstered on their waistband, right next to radios. A mic cord runs behind their necks, earpieces in.

Paparazzi must be swarming the hospital. I let them worry about how the fuck we're leaving.

"Gentle," I breathe to our five-year-old. "He's *very* fragile. He just took his first breath not too fucking long ago, okay?"

Seven hugs onto me first. "You're not hurt, are you, Mommy?"

My fucking heart. "I'm okay." I kiss the top of his head.

Seven has my eye color. Those pools of green look a little more tentative, which is strange for him. He has the Meadows' thrill-seeking, fearless gene.

Inquisitively, he eyes the newborn who stretches out his hand and yawns.

"This is Blue Meadows," I tell him, "your baby brother."

Seven has tears in his eyes. "He's so small."

"What'd I say?" Banks smacks Akara's chest, and we all laugh.

This wasn't an accidental pregnancy. Blue Moretti Meadows was planned. We got pregnant not too long after I came home from the Summer Games in Athens last year.

My third time at the Olympics.

Banks and Akara return to the bed. They rest their palms on my shoulder, my hands, and we watch as Seven edges closer to our newborn.

He holds Blue's little hand, and he whispers very quietly, "I'm your big brother, Blue. I'll always take care of you." He talks on about showing Blue his toy cars and playing with his cousins, and how much fun they'll have together—and there isn't a dry eye between the three of us.

We're all crying.

Brotherhood—it's a powerful thing. They know that well. Banks and Akara understand the love of brothers, some formed by time and duty, some formed by blood.

I wipe my face, and Banks and Akara kiss my wet cheeks. While we watch our sons meet, I smile more and more through the deep tidal wave of emotion that swells underneath us. That carries us forward. Onward.

Forever.

And very strongly, I breathe, "My Meadows boys."

GBANewYork.com – May 3rd

Sullivan Meadows & Husbands Welcome Second Child

Sullivan Meadows, the twenty-seven-year-old Olympic swimmer, gave birth earlier today to a healthy baby boy, Blue Moretti Meadows. Her husbands Akara Meadows & Banks Meadows were lovingly at her side. They're expected to bring their newborn home to their residence in Philadelphia soon. Blue is the triad's second child, as Sullivan Meadows notoriously gave birth to a son five-years ago in a highly publicized pregnancy.

Blue's birth comes a year after Sullivan Meadows dominated the Summer Olympics in Athens. She took home six gold medals in women's swimming. With three Olympics under her belt, Meadows has a total of thirteen golds, two silvers—fifteen medals overall. She is currently the most decorated female swimmer in history. After being asked whether she'll be back for the next Summer Games, Meadows replied to GBA News, "If I can swim, I'll fucking swim. I'm not stopping until I have to."

Sullivan Meadows is universally regarded as one of the greatest swimmers of all time.

ACKNOWLEDGEMENTS

If you're reading this, that means you've completed Book 10 in the Like Us series. Ten books, you've spent with the Hales, Meadows, Cobalts, and their bodyguards—ten books, you've spent with us. Thank you. Thank you for spending your days and weeks and minutes and hours with these families and this world. Most days, we look around and can hardly believe there are readers picking up what we've written—most days, we feel like we're twelve again, writing feverishly and wondering if someone out there will enjoy our stories.

To know there are other people who've loved the Like Us series— that these books have brought you happiness like they've brought us— that is our dream. A dream we're grateful every day to be living. Thank you for coming back to the next one and the next one. Long series are a commitment, and we cherish yours in every universe. You're why we can keep going, and like Sullivan Meadows, we have no quit in us.

If you're reading this, it also means you've seen how Sulli, Banks, and Akara's journey ties up five years into the future. We hope their love has made you as happy as they've made us. Thank you for taking a chance on them and for being there through the waves of their lives.

Thank you to our beautiful mom, you Rose Calloway goddess—this entire series, this whole world of characters, would be nothing without you. Thank you for always being there under our intense deadlines. If we could dole out gold medals, we'd give them all to you. We love you a waffle lot.

Thank you to our agent Kimberly Brower—you are our champion. We're so grateful to have you in our corner. Thank you for always rooting for our books and these characters.

Thank you to Lanie, Jenn, and Shea, our friends & the Fizzle Force admins—your love & support has meant the world to us every single year. You've kept the Fizzle Force thriving, and it goes without saying, but you're the powerful and rare kind.

Thank you to Haley, Andressa, and Margot, our friends—the gorgeous works of art you've all created based on the Like Us series is something that will always bring tears to our eyes. You've inspired us. You've given us bursts of happiness on our bluest days, and we're so happy to call you three our friends.

Thank you to the Fizzle Force, our readership—thank you for picking up this novel. Thank you so very much for taking a chance on our work. Your support means everything to us.

And thank you endlessly to our patrons on our Patreon—our writing is fuller, brighter, and stronger because of all of you. Thank you for the inspiration, the support, and love. You always make us fall in love with writing again.

Though this is Book 10, it's not the end. Misfits Like Us is next, where you'll finally see the out-of-this-world romance between Luna Hale & Paul Donnelly. The epilogue of Infamous Like Us might've been a time-jump, but Misfits Like Us begins around the time of Kitsulletti's island ceremony.

You won't miss a beat ;)

xoxo Krista & Becca

CPSIA information can be obtained
at www.ICGtesting.com
Printed in the USA
LVHW090804190122
708609LV00035B/224

9 781950 165346